T0198585

THE TRUTH WILL
SET YOU UP

OTHER TITLES BY HANES SEGLER

THE TRUTH WILL SET YOU UP

A NOVEL

HANES SEGLER

THE TRUTH WILL SET YOU UP
A NOVEL

iUniverse books may be ordered through booksellers or by contacting:

iUniverse
1663 Liberty Drive
Bloomington, IN 47403
www.iuniverse.com
1-800-Authors (1-800-288-4677)

ISBN: 978-1-5320-9997-7 (sc)
ISBN: 978-1-5320-9998-4 (e)

Print information available on the last page.

iUniverse rev. date: 05/04/2020

"And ye shall know the truth and the truth shall make you free."

Christian Standard Bible, Book of John, Chapter 8, Verse 32. Jesus admonishing a crowd of professed believers, telling them they must follow His words of truth in order to cease being a servant of sin and thus become free, circa 29 A.D.

"You want the truth? Whatcha' want the truth for? You're better off not knowing nothing. The truth'll just get you set up."

Last words, unknown American gangster, circa 1929 A.D.

This one is for my friends Joyce and Henry Bynum, who have supported my writing endeavors through the years.

I needed a special character near the end of this tale, and I couldn't imagine a better model than Henry Bynum. So I've borrowed Henry and changed his name without altering one of the real characters I've met in my life. I hope y'all like him and the story!

PART I

Coahuila, Mexico, Federal Highway 2, outside the town of Guerrero:

The two men in the box truck looked enough alike to be brothers, as indeed they were. Nicolas Castro drove at a steady eighty kilometers an hour—about fifty mph—while the younger one, Isidro, sat by the passenger window idly watching the passing countryside in the afternoon sunshine. The two looked relaxed, almost serene, as though they were taking a casual drive through this rural area south of Piedras Negras, Mexico.

The men traveled with the windows down and the radio blaring native folk music from a station in Nuevo Laredo, across the border from Laredo, Texas. Windows down because the truck did not have a working air conditioner, and the outside temperature on this warm day in late November was almost twenty-seven degrees Celsius, about eighty degrees Fahrenheit. The folk music constituted the sole entertainment the Castro brothers would enjoy this warm afternoon; that is, unless one thought of loading and unloading the truck for a two hundred and sixty-kilometer—about one hundred and sixty miles—round trip as fun and games. This afternoon's trip was the second of the day, the first having begun before dawn. The pair would make two of the round trips today and almost every day, so long as the cargo was ready for transport. The cargo was heavy and its transport was dangerous, so the road time offered a welcome change from the labor portion of the job, if no relief from worry.

The men's look of relaxation was a far cry from reality. Their standing instructions were to drive steadily, same speed, no stops whatsoever. This part of the trip was being made with the cargo they had loaded at the horse farm some twenty minutes before. In another one and one-quarter hours or so, they would be approaching the warehouse near Nuevo Laredo where it would be unloaded quickly under careful scrutiny before heading back to the farm. There was no down time at the warehouse, no chatter or camaraderie with the warehouse workers, so the drive back to the farm—empty— would have to suffice as break time from both work and the dread of discovery.

Because now, anywhere along this leg of the journey, they might be stopped by the federal police or military units assigned to patrol the highways of Coahuila, Tamaulipas, and Nuevo Leon, three adjoining states in Northern Mexico. If the truck were searched thoroughly, the brothers would be arrested and jailed when the cargo was determined to be, in addition to bag upon bag of livestock feed, eight bricks of cocaine—strategically placed inside some of the *mass of feed bags, of course. The sheer volume of livestock feed and its obvious weight and bulk were the only deterrents to a thorough search by ambitious enforcement officers.*

Transport trucks like the one being driven by Castro had been stopped before and, upon being searched with more enthusiasm than usual, were sometimes found to be carrying contraband. Such events were invariably the result of a tip given by a competitor in the same illegal business. What better way to reduce competition and buoy market prices than taking product off the market, along with its temporary caretakers? Government officials knew of this cat-and-mouse game among the narcotraficantes and accepted the information gladly in order to proclaim success in the war on drugs. Without a few victories along the way, the money from government agencies of Los Estados Unidos would cease, along with the opportunity to split the money…

Nonetheless, the truck and cargo would be seized, the operators jailed without a chance of bail and little chance of competent legal representation. Before their trials, they would be questioned at length about the source and destination of their illegal cargo. But neither Castro brother would divulge any information regarding any facet of the operation, and with good reason—their families would be killed by their employer's enforcers. Informers were not tolerated by the cartel's overseers, so they would give the authorities nothing but silence. Consequently, the men would be subject to the harshest of sentences: up to life in prison. It was for this risk of arrest and imprisonment that the Castro brothers were paid, though not very well.

CHAPTER 1

Well, I guess you enjoyed being on holiday. You look a lot better, so it must have done you some good."

Carlton Westerfield sat down gingerly in the straight-backed chair in front of the desk, carefully positioning his right leg for optimum support. Looking at the speaker, he smiled briefly and nodded his acknowledgement of the remark while trying to detect any sarcasm. Notwithstanding Faustino Perez' use of the European term for vacation—*holiday?*—he saw nothing to indicate anything beyond a polite greeting, genuine pleasure at a friend's improved health. Not that he expected to discern anything telling on Tino's flat, impassive face. The man was an expert at keeping his countenance devoid of emotions or intentions—a valuable skill for someone in his line of work, Carlton reminded himself. Except for the occasional sly grin, Tino was the most inscrutable man he'd ever known.

He decided to elaborate with a little verbiage. "Yeah, Tino, it was fine, nice and relaxing. Must have been just what I needed, because I feel a lot better now.

"While I was in rehab, my knee responded well to heat, so I was glad to oblige it with a few days in the sun," he added, failing to mention that the increased temperature came not only from the Mexico sunshine, but from his "holiday" companion, and that his knee wasn't the sole recipient of the recuperative powers of warmth.

Speaking of the damaged joint prompted him to lean forward in the uncomfortable chair and massage his tender knee, the victim of a gunshot wound a few months earlier in an underground parking garage on the north side of San Antonio. The injury had occurred while carrying out a drugs-for-hostage exchange with Tino's arch rival, Brujido Ramos, in a

1

meeting that went bad and erupted in gunfire. It had cost Carlton two surgeries and several days confined to a bed, followed by weeks of painful rehab. It had cost Brujido Ramos and six other people their lives. In all, a far too-exciting event for someone supposedly employed by Kingpin Perez solely in an advisory capacity.

The afore *un*mentioned (and delightfully warm) companion, DEA Agent Heather Colson, had been in the gun battle with Ramos and his men, intent on making the collar of her career without it becoming a "bust" in the worst connotation of the word. She too, had taken a round, a fairly serious wound to her side. In the end, the bust had been a good one for the DEA, the shooting ruled justified, and the hostage released safely, thanks to a bit of trickery on Carlton's part and not a small dose of luck.

During his time in the hospital, Carlton had plenty of time to review his career path, past and present—and contemplate his future. At the time of the gun battle, he was working for the South Texas crime boss, advising him on ways to maintain the upper hand in a battle among the players. That Tino's line of work included importing illicit drugs from Mexico didn't bother Carlton, since he'd spent years working for a mobster named Big Mo (now deceased), executing certain people for money. His work had been flawless and his penchant for meticulous planning and maintaining a low-key existence was so effective, he'd never even been questioned by law enforcement. Alas, Big Mo departed this life the same way he'd lived—violently—and Carlton saw his chance—and need—for a change.

Following Big Mo's death, a series of events enabled Carlton to retire from the gun work—or so he thought. After all, the work for Perez was merely advisory in nature, wasn't it? He wasn't expected to do any actual drug hauling. That was handled by a crew of eight or ten guys called "movers" led by Jaime Arredondo and Willie Bardus, or so Carlton had heard. He'd only seen the guys once or twice and had never laid eyes on the actual smuggling operation. Physically moving or distributing the contraband product was not in his purview, and it remained apart from Carlton, almost an abstract concept.

So *exactly* what a man chose to do for a living was none of his concern. All business operated on basic principles of planning, logistics, finance, communications, and inventory management…right? And Faustino Perez had occasionally consulted Carlton about a number of things in the past months, mostly concerning planning and logistics of transporting illegal goods without being caught.

However, during the brouhaha with Ramos, his employment status changed from "consultant" to "combatant," a transition he hadn't wanted and didn't welcome. Even though Ramos had expired during the gunfight and was no longer in competition with Perez, Carlton wondered when he would again be called into the violent end of the business. It was not a pleasant thought for a man almost old enough to receive maximum Social Security benefits.

When the bloody kidnapping exchange was over, Perez and his friend Reynaldo Gomez had, as promised, paid him very well for the work. They worried and hovered over him like mother hens during his hospital stay and thanked him repeatedly for solving several pressing problems: ridding Perez of his violent, insane competitor; saving his distribution business; and freeing Gomez' young daughter—all done while engaging the help of the DEA to accomplish the feats, a detail that Tino and Reynaldo found hilarious. They agreed that government-funded assistance in eliminating competition was a good business tactic.

And the boss wasn't alone in applauding his performance. Throughout Perez' small empire on the south side of the city, Carlton Westerfield was now something of a celebrity, respected by the area's largely Hispanic community for his loyalty to the one they saw as their *patron,* the guy who employed hundreds, either directly or indirectly in his many business enterprises. Reserved, low-key, almost shy by nature, Carlton was embarrassed by the attention; still, it was a good end to an unpleasant episode.

But the real payoff was the Mexico trip, which had stretched from before Christmas through New Year's Day. Agent Colson, whose assistance he'd employed in taking down Ramos, joined him at the *Acapulco* Princess Hotel the day after his arrival. A short romance of sorts had emerged, with Carlton wondering why the younger woman had singled him out for a ten-day fling. He figured she was wondering the same thing.

In any event, both found the affair to be a pleasant diversion from memories of their recent harrowing experience, with hours of talking, eating, and drinking, punctuated with periods of soothing silence, save the Pacific Ocean breeze. As to why she had agreed to meet him in Mexico might remain a mystery…however, he wasn't going to over-research the reason for his good fortune, since no previous relationship with a woman had gone as well as those ten blissful days in Mexico…not even close.

After a couple of tumultuous on-and-off years with Perez' half-sister, the tryst with Heather had been a welcome change. Compared to Paula Hendricks, Heather Colson was the girl next door, someone the *Lovin' Spoonful* sang songs about…whereas Paula might be the subject of an *AC/DC* tune. Besides, Carlton reminded himself, there was no commitment to Paula, nothing that officially tied him to her, nor her to him. But he wasn't sure how—or if—he should broach the subject with Tino, hence the abridged description of his recent trip. He decided to keep it to himself for the time being.

Tino's next words made the past several minutes' charade seem ludicrous. "Did your DEA friend enjoy her stay at the Princess Hotel?" The question was delivered with a sly grin, one suitable for starting a boys' locker room discussion.

Carlton couldn't help himself. He burst out laughing and shook his head in true wonderment. "I didn't try very hard to cover my tracks, but I can't believe you went to the trouble to track her to *Acapulco*. She didn't really advertise where she was going for R and R. She didn't even tell her boss like she was supposed to."

Tino held up his hand to stave off Carlton's verbal lashing for spying on him, which he had expected. "It wasn't her we were watching out for, she just showed up. It was *you* we were watching, for *your* protection, my bold friend who—"

"My *protection*?" Carlton interrupted. "I may be a little crippled up, but I wasn't aware I needed a baby sitter." He shook his head again, then stopped to glare at Tino as a disturbing thought hit him. "Did you tell Paula? Dammit, Tino, men are supposed to stick together, even if she is your sister!"

It was Tino's turn to laugh at Carlton's distress and his use of an expletive, something he didn't often do. "*Half*-sister, Carlton. And I know that. Hell, if we didn't stick together, women would take over the world more than they already have. And the answer is no, I didn't tell her." When Carlton gave him a '*so, what's up?*' look, he quickly added: "Besides, I'm not aware of any arrangement between the two of you…nothing like a—well, you know what I mean."

"Yeah, I know what you mean. There is no *arrangement,* as you put it. You may recall that your lovely sister is a bit erratic in her behavior, making it a little difficult to commit to much of anything. Hence, no arrangement."

"Well, I'd bet your name wouldn't come up on a Google search for *'San Antonio's most wanted man for a relationship.'* You have a few quirks of your own, you know."

"Thank you, Doctor Phil," came the sarcastic reply. "But back to the original topic: so it was your idea? What did your crew use? Hidden microphones? Long-lens cameras? I'm afraid to ask what kind of pictures your spies took."

"No pictures," Tino replied glibly. "They might have been good, though, as long as your old ragged body hadn't been in them. That DEA girl is a lot prettier than you. I could see that in her newspaper picture."

"At last we agree on something."

"Good. And since you seem determined to know, it was Reynaldo who suggested you have a little protection, and I fully agreed with him. He's pretty attached to you since you saved his daughter's life, you know. And he knows more than anyone about what could have happened."

An eye roll from Carlton prompted further explanation from a finger-pointing Tino Perez. "You chose to go to Mexico instead of the Bahamas or the Caymans like any *sensible* gringo would have—just a few weeks after you gun down a big customer of the Gulf Cartel. Do you know how pissed off the *Golfos* are with you? And the DEA girl?"

Carlton flinched at the accusation. That part was hard to deny. Brujido Ramos may not have been the syndicate's largest customer, but certainly a valuable link in the illicit drug trade for a huge market just over a hundred miles inside the U. S. border. The cartel had to be livid over losing the outlet, especially since Ramos had been planning on pawning an under-age girl in his efforts to endear himself to someone big in the chain of command. Having spoiled both the financial relationship and the kidnapping plan, Carlton Westerfield was surely high on the cartel's *persona non grata* list, along with the DEA agent who had been involved in the Ramos takedown.

But Carlton, comfortable in his usual role of being non-descript and unnoticeable, hadn't worried about how the high-profile gun battle had impaired his life-long disguise of being the guy no one looked at twice… Mr. Ordinary. He simply liked *Acapulco*; he'd been there several times and chose it for some much-needed downtime. Inviting Heather seemed a good idea, and it had certainly turned out well. Now, hearing Tino explain the obvious, he realized it had been foolish to choose the West Coast of Mexico for a restful trip. While avoiding apprehension and discovery by the rabid news media following the shootout, his low-key identity was now blown among the underworld area he occasionally inhabited. Adding the hot-shot DEA agent (who hadn't escaped the media frenzy and, in defiance of her employer's resistance, was featured in a big newspaper spread) surely made the situation even more galling for the vengeful Gulf Group cartel.

Tino wasn't through. "You know how much manpower and technology they have at their disposal? You're lucky you made it back here at all, because I'm not sure we had enough people in place to cover your ass. I'm surprised you and Ms. Colson didn't show up in pieces, delivered to the DEA office by a FedEx driver. Just because the Gulf is across the country from *Acapulco*, and those Jalisco New Generation guys control the Mid-Pacific, they could have made a try to get you. *And* her."

Carlton was now aware of the mistake, but he was getting tired of hearing the rebuke. "Well, I appreciate the coverage, Tino. And it must have been adequate, since we're back, safe and sound. So can we drop it? Everything's fine."

"Oh, you think so? I guess you haven't talked to my sister."

"I thought you said you didn't tell—"

"I said I didn't tell her, and I didn't. But that doesn't mean she didn't find out, Lover Boy. Oh, and Reynaldo wants to talk to you. He wants to be a gun runner."

Carlton sighed and rose—slowly—from the rickety chair. "Okay, I'm headed home, so he can catch me there if he wants to meet in person. Right now, I'm going to take a nap. If my knee will quit aching."

"Take good care of it, will you?" Tino said, rising from behind the desk and walking toward the door with him. "Maybe some more heat will help," he added helpfully.

CHAPTER 2

Leaving Tino's office, Carlton wondered what Reynaldo had in mind. Months earlier, they had talked briefly about the possibility of getting weapons into Mexico, supposedly to arm a group of wannabe cocaine handlers with tenuous connections to the big guys. By creating havoc among the groups, Reynaldo hoped to end the monopoly of the Gulf Cartel, the ones he was currently doing business with, and thereby force prices down. Or something like that.

It sounded risky to Carlton, far too ambitious. This wasn't like showing a receipt at O'Reilly Auto Parts to take advantage of a "best price" guarantee. This was giving weapons to guys who might get their eyes gouged out with a rusty spoon for *thinking* about opposing cartel members. Plus, smuggling weapons could bring down a bunch of heat from the U. S. federal agency that prosecuted such activities, the Bureau of Alcohol, Tobacco, Firearms and Explosives, not to mention the Mexican government's dim view of guns in citizens' hands. The quick mental overview told Carlton he would advise Reynaldo Gomez to stick to what he knew best and pay a higher price if necessary. After all, he was supposed to give advice, right?

At his apartment door, he turned to look down on the patio deck from his second story railing. Blustery and cold, it was abandoned today except for the leaves blowing across the barren expanse of tiles. The pool furniture was stored under the cover of the empty pool, not to be seen again until April or May. He recalled the hot days of last summer and fall when the pool had been a regular hangout for him and Paula, and he wondered if those times were over for good.

Mercurial as Paula's temperament could be, she had qualities that drew men to her, and Carlton was no exception. Now he was concerned that his dalliance with Heather had ended the relationship—probably a good outcome—but he wasn't sure how to find out without a direct approach. He reached for his phone as he swung open the door. After four rings, he gave up, not knowing what to say if it flipped over to her voice mail. He hadn't put it back into his pocket when it rang in his hand, startling him. He nearly dropped it and chastised himself for his nervousness as he opened the cheap burner phone and pressed "talk."

"This is Carlton."

"Hello, stranger!" came Paula's seductive voice, sounding like they had spent the previous night together.

"Well, hi! I just tried to call you."

"So I saw. You don't give a girl much time to answer, do you?"

"Figured you were busy, out buying shoes or something. How are you?"

She laughed at their ongoing verbal jousting over her shoe-buying addiction. *"Not until tomorrow. There's a sale at every store in North Star Mall.*

"I heard you took some vacation time. Where'd you go? Acapulco again?"

"Yep. You know me, a dull creature of habit, no surprises," he answered cheerfully, steeling himself for what might come next. Then he took a deep breath and reminded himself of his earlier pledge to quit worrying about her reaction to his recent social activity. If she knew about Heather, so be it. If she confronted him, he'd own up to it and explain his actions in accordance with her approach to the subject. The best response might be—

His thoughts were interrupted by her next statement. *"Look, Reynaldo is here at my place, and he wanted to meet with you. Where are you?"*

"About seventy-five feet from you, in my apartment. I got home late last night, but I've been at Tino's office for the last hour or so."

"Oh! So you got home today, looked out at the pool and thought about me, right? Decided it was time to give me a call?"

Carlton was surprised again. Had she seen him looking at the pool and read his mind? He put the ridiculous thought aside and said, *"You've got me figured out, that's exactly right."*

"Carlton, I'll never have you figured out, but that's okay. Anyway, why don't you come over here?"

"Okay, give me thirty minutes."

Carlton snapped his phone shut and breathed a sigh of relief. He wasn't home-free just yet—Paula was the best actress he'd ever known—but at least there hadn't been a blow-up, not yet, anyway. And Reynaldo at her apartment—did that mean anything? They'd obviously had a thing going on about twelve years ago…

That would make the Big Departure a lot easier, wouldn't it?

Or maybe Tino had been jerking his chain; maybe Paula really didn't know about his vacation companion. He'd find out soon enough and try to handle it "using his big head instead of the little one," as Heather had admonished him repeatedly since he'd met her. Carlton showered and shaved quickly, mulling over the dilemma he faced.

The sporadic relationship with Paula had always been baffling, but in the days leading up to the kidnapping exchange, he'd learned of yet another facet to Paula's life which further illustrated that he might never know her completely: The young girl who had been kidnapped by Ramos was the daughter of Paula Hendricks—*and Reynaldo Gomez*. None of them had imparted this fact to Carlton while he was negotiating with Ramos for the exchange. When Carlton confronted them with the secret and how he'd learned it—on his own, thanks very much—Tino, Reynaldo, and Paula had all confessed it had been wrong to withhold the information. Given their intertwined past, being in the same room with all the parties could have been awkward, but Carlton chalked it up to lives lived fully, if on the edge, and decisions made on the fly. Plus, looking at his own history, who was he to point fingers?

Everyone, himself included, seemed comfortable with their linked histories, but it was the "one more thing" that concerned him. Going on three years, and he didn't know Paula Hendricks and never would. Maybe it was time to cut ties to the most mysterious woman he'd ever met and try to cultivate the thing with Heather, ignoring the age disparity between them. Oh, and she was a federal law enforcement agent, not what Carlton normally considered a viable dating prospect. On the plus side, Heather had never pointed a loaded gun at him and pulled the trigger, as Paula once had. That was a comforting thought.

He pulled on a cashmere sweater and headed toward her apartment, wondering if the limp in his gait would ever go away completely.

Paula opened the door and flashed The Smile, catching Carlton off guard for a second. Reynaldo stood behind her, his own brilliant smile reminding Carlton of Don de la Vega—*actor Guy Williams?*—in the ancient TV series, "*Zorro.*"

No one should be that handsome.

Paula gave him a big hug and leaned into him with all the right parts. "Hi! How's your knee?"

"Hello to you! It's much better, thanks. It's going to be a while before I run any races, though."

"Welcome home, Carlton!" Reynaldo extended his hand, obviously pleased to see his new friend and the recent hero of the hour.

Carlton disengaged his right arm from Paula's grip and shook Reynaldo's hand. "Hello, Reynaldo. How are y'all doing?" he asked, turning to include both of them in his inquiry.

Paula opened her mouth to speak, but Reynaldo beat her to it. "Everything's good here. Holidays are over and things have calmed down. As to business, everyone is back on track, as I'm sure Tino told you."

"Yeah, just that, not much else. He didn't go into detail, but I took it that business is running well, and everyone is breathing easier with our lunatic friend out of the picture."

"Thanks to you," Paula interjected. "Oh, and Cecilia is fine. Brenda says she really likes living in Mexico City."

Carlton smiled at the mention of the eleven year-old girl, the progeny of a past romance between Paula and Reynaldo. Having no children of his own, he thought himself ill-equipped to fathom the bond between parent and child, but he knew the entire shootout episode had been worth it to save her from the sordid plans of her maniac uncle.

Paula again reached for his arm and pulled him into the apartment. "Come on in, sit down. We just had coffee. Want something to drink?"

"Nothing for me, but I'll certainly sit down. The knee does better with no weight on it."

The three moved to sit down in the tiny apartment, with Paula and Reynaldo taking the small love seat and Carlton easing into an office chair by the door, the only thing that would fit in the sparse remaining space. As he'd done in Tino's office, he extended his right leg carefully and adjusted his butt to get comfortable. With everyone seated, five of the six knees in the room nearly touched, and they all laughed at the cramped setup.

Paula took the opportunity to excuse herself. "This is a bit close, and I know you boys need to visit. I'll go do a bit of shopping and leave you two to talk."

When the door closed behind her, Carlton chose to begin the conversation. He wanted to get right to the point, so he could pitch his advice not to engage in arms smuggling. "Tino told me you wanted to re-visit the subject of getting some weapons into Mexico."

His guarded tone didn't dissuade Reynaldo a bit. "Yes. I think it will give me a real advantage in my dealings down there, and I want your ideas about doing it. I've given it some thought since we talked about the cattle trailer I use at my Sabinal place, compartments in the roof or floor. The smell and distaste of climbing in would discourage checkpoint personnel from a hands-on inspection, but it's going to take a lot more, I know that."

"Have your ranch workers transported cattle over there before? Or back to the States?"

"Only a couple of times, and it's been a few months ago. Gus Painter—he's the foreman at Sabinal—hauled ten cows down to my place in Mexico on one trip and twelve on the next. A couple of weeks ago, I asked him about it, in an offhand way. He told me there was some paperwork and a short quarantine period, but I didn't ask him about what kind of scrutiny the trailer received going across, because I didn't want to explain why I wanted to know. At this point, the fewer people know what I'm planning, the better. Anyway, he got the cows to my place in Mexico without the trailer being dismantled, so the trip is doable."

Carlton nodded in agreement at the wisdom of keeping Gus in the dark for the time being. "So it was just cows going down and nothing coming back?" he asked.

"Right. We'd have to get a current look at what they do at the border and the interior checkpoint, the *aduana*, with another load of cows to see what goes on now."

"Cows *and* cow manure," Carlton corrected him. "Lots of the latter."

Reynaldo grinned at that. "The more I thought about it, the better the idea sounded."

Carlton held up a cautionary hand. "That idea was just shooting from the hip, Reynaldo, first thing that crossed my mind when I considered the people who are going to be looking for anything. Every time I've been around livestock for more than five minutes, they seem to produce lots of manure. And you're right: who wants to wade through manure to look for secret compartments?"

Reynaldo chuckled and nodded his agreement. "Sounds right to me, but I'm sure it's been covered before. A lot of the checkpoints—the ones coming into the States—use some kind of X-ray or imaging technology now, don't they? Even the most remote ones, I'm informed by my product movers. They're big drive-thru units, but they're portable. They can be moved to another location pretty quick."

"That makes sense," Carlton said. "Keeps everyone guessing as to where the tightest security will be set up. And yes, the manure trick, or something like it, has probably been tried.

"I don't know what they use going into Mexico, so let's look at the tightest possible scenario: if it were coming across *this* direction. The two countries are trying to work together, so there is a possibility that the Mexican officials are using some of the U. S. Border Patrol equipment, the imaging stuff. So the real trick would be fooling the imaging process—at least to some degree—plus having a deterrent or obstacle to discourage anybody wanting to look more thoroughly. Avoiding it altogether would be best, of course. On the plus side, a trailer would probably need to be pulled through an imaging device on a designated part of the checkpoint apron. A lot of cow shit on the trailer—and falling off the sides—is better, because the personnel will see they have to wade through it for the rest of their shift. So maybe, just *maybe*, they forgo the imaging procedure.

"Also, timing would be important. The slow traffic times seem like a poor choice, but the busiest time might not be best, either. In those cases, inspectors may have the trailer pulled to a separate area in order not to bog down the flow of traffic. Then they'd have time to take a closer look. So there's a fine line between, and it can only be determined by observation made during dry runs. Of course, law enforcement knows all this, and they periodically change their tactics to counter any intelligence learned by observers, at least on the U. S. side."

Reynaldo nodded in agreement with Carlton's quick assessment of checkpoint operations in general, telling Carlton where he needed to take the conversation. "But you already know all this, Reynaldo, so I'm not sure I'm the one to give you any insight into this. Unless there's something underlying this plan that you're not telling me—like the National Rifle Association has the contract to run border security for Mexico?"

Another big smile at the absurdity preceded a head shake before Carlton finished speaking. "No, nothing like that. I'm successful at this because I try to stay knowledgeable, and I'm just wanting to hear input from a different source. You've had good ideas for Tino—hell, that ambulance trick is still working. And the idea about inserting packages into cows like an artificial insemination process is far-fetched, but clever. I intend to try that soon, maybe on return trips from a weapons run."

"That keeps transportation costs down, not hauling donut holes or sailboat fuel on the return leg. But it doubles the risk to the driver."

Reynaldo thought about it for a moment. "Maybe it does, statistically. But a familiar rig and driver going back and forth has some value. It did when I had a pottery scheme going on, so it's worth considering in this venture. Checkpoint personnel are only human, and they get a comfort level with seeing the same guy, even though they're trained not to. But I'll listen to all the advice I can get. Sometimes success makes one blind to any other method of doing things. I don't want to be *that* guy, the one who refuses to see another viewpoint or refuses to try something new just because the old way has been working."

Carlton smiled. "Like the song line that goes '*don't let the sound of your own wheels make you crazy?*'"

"Exactly. Let me give you my take on this industry, Carlton, the smuggling industry. And it's basically the same, whether it's weapons or drugs or people—the smuggled commodity is contraband, and the successful smuggler makes money. The risks are high, but so are the profits.

"Everyone seems to think the big cartels are the only ones with the ability to pull off major smuggling operations and, in large part, that's true. Obviously, it's their livelihood, and they have the incentive to think of all the angles. But they also have the money to bribe law enforcement agents. Money is the big tool. And they got the money by being successful, so success begets success.

"The smaller smugglers, the less sophisticated ones, don't have the money to bribe officials or dig two-mile tunnels, so they try a bunch of tricks, some more ingenious than others. They try running bait cars in front of the real one. They use pregnant women as mules, pushing a baby carriage. They use old people and children, with bicycles and wheelchairs and walkers. And those methods…well, obviously, some work, some don't.

"Day in, day out, the big cartels are best at what they do because they have more manpower, more brains and more money. And that concept—the best of the best—has been sold to the public by all the news organizations. Plus, all the movies and books covering the drug trade highlight the big, glamorous operations. The workings of a nickel-and-dime operation wouldn't sell many books or movie tickets, but it doesn't mean those ideas are useless." Reynaldo ended his spiel by raising a single index finger, a cautionary gesture to emphasize his point against dismissing lower-level methods.

Carlton hesitated before posing his next question. "I mean no offense by this, but are you—that is, we—are we in the best-of-the-best, or the nickel-and-dime category?"

Reynaldo flashed his matinee-idol smile. "It doesn't bother me to admit my operation is nickel-and-dime, at least compared to the big cartel people. Like Tino, I do very well, as I'm sure you know. Players of our size get a lot less scrutiny because the DEA wants to be seen as taking down the big guys, the cartels who move tons—literally *tons*—of product all over the United States. Just like I said about movie producers and action-adventure authors, they're interested in the big busts, the big headlines."

Carlton looked doubtful, shaking his head. "Maybe so, but that doesn't make them careless when it comes to smaller players. I hear they were very proud of the recent bust on Brujido Ramos."

"Oh, I'm sure they were! Quite the coverage they got in the local outlets, and the casualties made it qualify for some regional coverage. It might even have gotten a mention at the national level as a fill-in piece, but I'm not sure."

Carlton waited a beat for Reynaldo to segue into something about the main DEA agent. He wanted to hear his take on his choice of "holiday" destinations and companions, away from Tino's input, and he wasn't disappointed.

"By the way, I hear your vacation was nice. Must have been pleasant, with that pretty DEA lass keeping you company." The last part was delivered with a questioning smirk.

Carlton smiled at the blatant opening. Although the pair were tough, ruthless drug traffickers and crime kingpins, Reynaldo and Tino sometimes acted like a couple of gossiping old hens on *Mayberry, RFD.* "Yeah, it was nice. She enjoyed it, too. Or so she said," he added, deciding to leave it at that. If either Reynaldo or Tino wanted a detailed accounting, they'd be waiting a long time.

A couple of beats went by before Reynaldo gave up and got back on point. "Anyway, I have located a guy in Mexico who's experienced in gun smuggling and firearms training, but in a different part of the world. His name is Clive Millstone, a British citizen from London. He did some work in Northern Ireland back when the action was hot there. Then, he operated in the Mediterranean for six years, and all over the Middle East. More recently, he's moved some weapons around South America before coming north to Mexico. He's currently living in *Monterrey.*"

Carlton didn't bother to hide his surprise. "He worked in the Middle East? Won't he draw a lot of heat? That part of the world has the attention of about twenty intelligence agencies, and all those guys share databases these days, or steal the info from each other."

Reynaldo waved off his concern. "Millstone has always been mid-level, under the radar of intelligence agencies. He's a hands-on operator, a worker, and he's not involved in the finance or planning end of it. He really just does grunt work, the actual transport part and hands-on training and has been that way for years. But he claims to know the trade, inside and out. I got the same endorsement from the two sources I have."

"So, did you check him out with anybody outside your usual sources? Get any information besides his occupational credentials?"

"I tried, and that's the best part: I came up with absolutely nothing. No information available on him at all. To me, that's a good sign."

Carlton couldn't find fault with that assumption, not on the surface, so he changed gears. "So what's he doing to put beans on the table now?"

"He's not doing anything at all in Mexico, just taking a break, traveling around the country as a tourist. I had him as a guest at my ranch for the first interview, and I explained how the weapons would be delivered to that location because it's very remote. He agreed, and he had some ideas for training that sounded good.

"He seems to have done well financially and wanted to take it easy for a while, but my proposal got his attention. I didn't have much trouble coaxing him out of retirement. Money has a way of getting things done.

"As far as gun smuggling or training, he's been inactive for over a year, so I don't think the agencies have any interest in guys like him. We discussed that. He says the investigative and enforcement agencies have plenty of current activity to keep them busy; besides, they don't bother with guys at his level."

Carlton thought carefully before continuing. He knew Reynaldo and Tino to be careful, professional, and generally risk-averse, and this was a departure from that philosophy. This sounded more like something the late Brujido Ramos would try: rubbing shoulders with the big boys, launching into something more glamorous, instead of sticking with what had worked for years.

Why would Reynaldo enlist the help of a guy, a Brit no less, with ties to Europe and the Middle East? No mention was made of any past experience with Latin America or its culture, and that was critical in dealing with anything in Mexico. Anyone who believed otherwise ought to try getting a fair price for a taxi ride in *Guadalajara* without speaking Spanish fluently, or even a plate of enchiladas on the far west side of San Antonio without a basic knowledge of the language. The thought gave him an idea. "Has Millstone lived in Mexico long?"

"About a month."

"Does he speak Spanish?"

"Yes. He spent some time in Spain and learned the language. Mainly, Spaniards speak Castilian Spanish, which is different than the dialects used in Mexico and certainly here in Texas, so he's probably not as fluent as he thinks he is. Anyway, he has a good grasp of the language and can converse well enough to pick up the nuances of Mexican Spanish and Tex-Mex. Plus, he knows a guy he can work with, a Mexican named Mendoza, who's supposed to be good with quick training programs on all kinds of small arms."

Carlton nodded at the explanation, but had reservations about it. It seemed Reynaldo was glossing over a critical job skill. Why use someone who had *any* deficiencies in the language department? A miscommunication in this line of work could be deadly, he knew that from first-hand experience.

Ask the gangbanger who hesitated when I asked him for change at the car wash.

Another thought occurred to Carlton. "Has Tino met this guy?" he asked, already knowing the answer.

"Yes. After I had him at my ranch, Tino and I met with him a couple of more times during the past month at *Villa Unión*, a little town about a hundred miles south of my ranch. We discussed this idea at length. Why?"

"I thought so. Tino referred to my vacation as "holiday," a common European term for vacation. The connection just now occurred to me." He shrugged away the event as simply an observation on his part, not mentioning that he had also caught Reynaldo's use of "lass" when he'd mentioned Heather a few minutes before.

Inwardly, he wondered how his bosses had picked up that much British slang if they'd only met with this guy—*Clive Millstone?*—a couple of times. Recalling his lesson from a few months earlier when Reynaldo and Tino had withheld information about Ramos, he figured he was now being sandbagged against knowing the full extent of their relationship with the arms-smuggling Brit.

Aloud, he decided to cut to the chase, do what he was paid to do. "Okay, Reynaldo, it seems you and Tino have faith in this guy. I'm sure he has some good ideas about methods to get guns across, since he's worked in some tough neighborhoods before. Weapons trade and covert training is not a business for amateurs, and since this Millhouse guy has stayed afloat this long, he must have an aptitude for it." He paused, waiting for Reynaldo to correct his intentional mistake.

After a few seconds, he continued. "But my take is this: You should stick to what you know best. Smuggling drugs is one thing, but smuggling weapons into a foreign country opens up a whole new bag of worms. That kind of activity starts looking like terrorism in the making, and every law enforcement agency in the world is on it like a hound dog humping a sofa.

"As to Millstone running below the horizon of the big agencies, don't bet on it. All law enforcement agencies can tap into the big databases. Even the police department in Podunk, Texas can get help from Homeland Security or Interpol if they play it right. So it would be naïve to think he's not going to show up if anyone gets even a whiff of his kind of activity on their turf."

Reynaldo nodded. "I know the technology is very good, and I respect that. I'd be a fool not to. But you're describing an ability to find someone who's probably not even in a database. How can any technology do that?"

"You can't really know if he's been entered into a system or not, much less if he's ever been observed, picked up, associated, or mentioned in a text, e-mail, or phone call between him and anyone he's done work for. In some cases, that's all it takes to get noticed and logged.

"Remember all the fuss over some big shots ending up on the TSA No Fly list? Those might have been errors, but it still happened. Their names got plugged into a log during some event. Maybe obscure, maybe innocent, but it happened anyway.

"The big agencies, the CIA, FBI, DEA, NSA, and the BATF all have access to world-wide data banks. And their analysts are able to fish those databases with name recognition software. It's time consuming and expensive, but taxpayers are footing the bill, so they don't care.

"I'll give you an example. Say Millstone gets a speeding ticket on Interstate Thirty-five, and he whips out his British driving permit or an international driver's license. All it takes is one conscientious clerk at Laredo P.D. to run his name on NCIC and get a hit on his name. Or it might get a hit on a somewhat similar name. Shady characters often change their operative name, but like to use something that's similar, has the same initials. That's worth a closer look at another database, putting in *both* names. A hit on that search would be cause to reach out to Interpol to get an international look. If anything hinky shows up—like anything concerning weapons—they might convince BATF to use its stroke to apply name-recognition software to thousands of phone calls during a certain time period and between certain points on the globe; that is, wherever this guy's been living, according to his license."

Reynaldo looked at Carlton with a pained expression. "How do you know all this shit? I mean, I don't doubt you, but where did you learn this?"

"Believe it or not, I read a lot and watch a lot of those crime and terrorism documentaries on television. That sounds like a flakey way to learn something, but the well-made documentaries aren't like some Oprah production that looks into the Kardashian's lifestyle, and it's not *Star Trek Next Generation* science fiction set three hundred years in the future. It's now, and it's real. They have interviews with the people who actually were involved in the cases—"

"I can't believe the agencies would allow their technology capabilities to be aired publicly," Reynaldo interrupted. "It seems that would defeat its usefulness, making everyone aware of it."

"You might think of it that way, but it makes no difference to people who think they can beat the system. A lot of crime goes undetected, and someone who avoids detection for a long time tends to get over-confident. They think it's their superior intellect that keeps them out of jail. In reality, it's because someone at a local P.D.—Laredo, in my example—failed to check the name as required for every stop of an international driver's license. For whatever reason…you know, maybe the donut shop was about to close."

Reynaldo laughed at the joke, but he realized Carlton was right: a lot of things came down to luck—a missed call, an unmade entry in a log, a failure to follow up on some protocol in a criminal investigation, no matter how minor.

Carlton wasn't through with his spiel. "When done correctly, it might not make any difference to be extra careful. The technology and tactics of modern law enforcement have plugged almost all the holes. That is, if law enforcement personnel follow through and use the full capabilities available to them. And records are important; even a traffic ticket shows up on every crime database."

"You paint a pretty bleak picture. How have you dodged the bullet? No pun intended," he added, pointing to Carlton's knee.

Carlton laughed at that. "Yeah, getting too old and slow to dodge the bullet, I guess. But as to avoiding arrest, or even being picked up, I have to attribute it to luck and a lot of caution. I don't use e-mail or buy anything online—"

"Damn, I use e-mail a lot, but I use yahoo and g-mail," Reynaldo interrupted. "Those can't be monitored, can they?"

"Yep. The only safe way to use e-mail is to have all the parties to the conversation use the same account. When anyone logs on, they open up 'drafts' and read the message in draft form, then delete it. If it's not sent through servers, there's no permanent record of it. Or so I'm informed, but I wouldn't stake my life on it.

"I use only burner phones, and I change them often. I don't keep any numbers in the address book, and I delete every call as soon as I hang up, incoming or outgoing. When I'm done with a phone, I make sure some homeless person gets it, or leave it where it will be found and used. Some hobo can do my cover-up for me by muddying the water after I'm done with it.

"I don't get into any confrontations on the road. I don't have unnecessary conversations at the gas station or in the grocery store. I keep a low profile; I don't overspend or over-tip or under-tip unless I *want* to make a point and be remembered. I pay cash for almost everything and use a cash-load debit card for anything I can't. I keep a modest checking account, and I file a tax return every year, paying Uncle Sugar his cut.

"Obviously, I don't use social media. The only pictures of me that exist are on my driver's license and passport. I don't have a handgun license, and I don't belong to any organizations or clubs. I don't go to the V.A. Hospital, even though I'm eligible, because I don't want to fill out forms and create a record that's easily accessible. Even though it's unlikely, I don't want to run into anyone who asks about my tour in Vietnam and my job while I was there. I've never contacted anyone I knew from the military, but that was years ago anyway."

Reynaldo shook his head in amazement. "I guess that recent activity in the parking garage caused you some concern, then?"

"Yes, it did. I didn't like being put in the spotlight like that, and I didn't like waving a heater around like John Wick. Not my style."

"You did very well for it not to be your style. But before that, how did you avoid all the situations where your name would get recorded somewhere? Like your example—what about traffic stops, a ticket for something?"

Carlton looked at him and smiled. "I've never had a traffic ticket, Reynaldo."

Nuevo Bayito, a "suburb" of Nuevo Laredo on Federal Highway 2, outside of the bustling border city in Tamaulipas, Mexico:

Just inside the small village, a single traffic light flashed yellow for thru traffic and red for side-street motorists. It was the sole traffic control device in this section of Nuevo Bayito, one the residents were quite proud of and justifiably so: most villages this size had only a lumpy speed bump to control the velocity of motor vehicles passing through. A real traffic light, even one that flashed instead of changing, was quite an amenity.

Nicolas was already driving slowly into the village and slowed even more for the light, then turned right down the side street named Lucio Blanco. After about three blocks of varying lengths, structures petered out completely, save a large tin warehouse just beyond the shabby houses populating the area. Nicolas pulled up to the front and sat while Isidro got out and went around back to a walk-thru door. His knock was answered by a much taller man, also Mexican, with a surly demeanor. He stalked out and brushed past Isidro, walking to the driver's side of the truck.

"You are late," he said to Nicolas in rapid Spanish. "Why?"

Caught off guard, Nicolas could only stammer. "Late? I drove here same as always. As you instructed, just under the speed limit. I drove steadily, and—"

"Did you stop along the way?" the surly man interrupted. "You know the penalty for stopping!"

Both Castro brothers knew full-well the penalty for stopping, or any other form of diversion from the specific route and speed: a brutal beating, and not only for the offender, but possibly his wife, mother, brother, father—anyone the cartel enforcers considered important to the worker. It was a harsh, brutal system of enforcement, one that ensured total subservience and adhesion to rules. To break any of the guidelines set out from the beginning of their employment meant swift, violent action.

Dirt-poor, uneducated, and unable to change their lives, the workers of Mexican cartels were treated as slaves and paid very meagerly for their efforts. When retribution for some minor infraction caused a death, there was always another poor soul in the community willing to step into the vacancy, since it was at least a way to make a living, bad as it was.

"No! I swear, I did not stop. After the big truck came in from the south, we unloaded everything and placed the bricks inside eight of the feed bags at the

farm. We mixed them with forty-six other bags in the manner we were told. Then we left and came the same way, the same speed, everything the same as always!" Nicolas insisted. He was becoming panicky now, the terror evident in his voice and on his face.

On the passenger side of the truck, Isidro had meekly approached and stood quietly beside the door, too terrified to add anything to the conversation. He couldn't understand the surly boss' accusation. They had done everything the same on this trip as every other time in the three months they'd worked for this bunch, a splinter group of Los Golfos, the Gulf Cartel. And now it appeared they might face punishment for something they hadn't done.

Like each of the thirty or so young men who labored at the horse farm and took part in the transport of illegal cargo, Nicolas and Isidro did their jobs exactly as instructed and asked no questions. All any of them knew was the horse farm was supposedly owned by a wealthy family with ties to Mexico City. Rarely, a few family members visited the farm and rode the horses around a grassy area for an hour or so, then left without saying a word to anyone. The visitors even saddled their own mounts and brushed their horses when finished riding. A pair of stable hands were employed to care for the horses, but the visitors spoke very little to them, if at all.

The main activity at the horse farm was the steady movement of livestock feed from a co-op grain warehouse in Monterrey, forty to fifty bags at a time. At some point in the journey to the horse farm—no one knew or dared ask where—a feed sack with bricks of cartel cocaine was added to the shipment, usually eight to fifteen bricks in a single bag. Apparently, the bribes required for that leg of the bricks' journey did not extend to the stretch between the farm and the last warehousing point on the Mexican side of the Border, the last stop before being sent into the U. S. at Laredo…hence, the multiple feed sack illusion.

Upon arrival at the horse farm, the bricks were deposited, one to a bag of feed, then stored among the dozens of bags containing only grain. This insertion process of the cocaine into some bags was, of course, carefully monitored by cartel overseers. All of the laborers had been engaged in the process, but no one ever discussed it while at work, not even among themselves.

The bags were stored in the huge barn until a specified time when it was loaded onto the horse farm's box truck and driven to the warehouse in Nuevo

Bayito. Busy times, like now, it entailed two trips a day—eighty or ninety heavy bags concealing eight to sixteen with cocaine—in order to mitigate the risk of losing all the product to a single highway stop. But at no time did a laborer mention the term "contraband," "cocaine," or "product." All horse farm and transportation activity was simply referred to in the context of "feed shipment."

Surly Man was closer to Nicolas now, face-to-face, shouting at the terrified driver. Isidro wanted to help his brother, but didn't know how he could, even if he had the courage to intervene. Just then, Surly Man reached through the truck window and slapped Nicolas hard across the face. Isidro knew he had to overcome his fear, find some courage to assist his brother, but his feet remained glued to the gravel on the opposite side of the truck. He was becoming nauseous with fear when the situation changed again, this time for the better.

"Haul this shit around to the other big door and get it unloaded!" Surly Man ordered, a nasty grin now plastered on his face. He stepped back and turned on his heel, heading to the far side of the warehouse, apparently to open the appointed door. As he passed by Isidro's side of the truck, he side-stepped quickly and gave Isidro a similar slap before laughing and continuing to the warehouse.

The Castro brothers had done nothing wrong, and Surly Man knew it. They had just been subjected to a scare tactic designed to keep them in line, to remind them up front that no infraction, no matter how slight, would be overlooked. And it reminded them who was boss. It was a favorite employment tactic of the Golfos, and not one that could be reported to the Secretaria del Trabajo y Previsión Social, the rough equivalent to the U. S. Department of Labor. A report to that agency would result in death to the whistleblower and his entire family.

Both men scrambled into the truck, glancing fearfully at each other, but saying nothing. What was there to say?

CHAPTER 3

The next day was Saturday, and Carlton managed to sleep in until after seven. Even with the beneficial aspects of his recent retreat, he was still tired from the trip, and his knee ached from too much walking through airports. He gingerly changed positions, and the resulting stab of pain told him he wouldn't be going back to sleep. Instead, he lay awake going over the conversation with Reynaldo Gomez again and wondering why he was so hell-bent to smuggle weapons to a group who may or may not be able to accomplish anything with them.

The meeting had carried on for a while, pausing when Paula returned, and the three of them went to a nearby *taqueria* for supper. Upon returning, she went to her apartment, shooing the two men away to discuss the matter further at Carlton's place. At that point, they left generalities behind and moved into the details of using the shipment of cattle between Reynaldo's two ranches as a means to haul the weapons: how to modify the trailer, when and how to load the guns and seal the compartments, and what could be done to defeat the imaging equipment. Carlton stressed the need to avoid the imaging process altogether, but admitted uncertainty as to how that might be accomplished and agreed to research the possibility of shielding.

A lengthy discussion followed over how to obtain the weapons, with Carlton giving his support for numerous, anonymous buyers, shopping estate sales and garage sales, plus checking Craigslist locally and as far away as Dallas and Houston. Gun shows would suffice, but weren't preferred. Plus, all transactions needed to be among individuals and for cash—using bills obtained as change from shopping, not from cashing a paycheck at the bank in order to avoid any sequential serial numbers being handed over and deposited to a seller's account…where a teller might notice and, who knew? That seemed a long shot, but if it were possible to avoid it, why not do it the safe way?

Reynaldo asked about locating a gun dealer who would falsify paperwork on a bulk sale in order to speed up the procurement process. Carlton responded by pointing out the publicity that every mass shooting had focused on the source of the guns involved. "Everyone's gone nuts over trying to stop the public shootings, like at schools and churches. The first thing they see on their TV screen is the horror of the shooting scene. Next, they show a close-up of the weapon involved—at least, that's what the narrator says. It might be a TV station file photo of a gun from two years ago. Then the scene switches to a well-stocked gun store with rows of assault rifles over a glass counter filled with handguns.

"So, unknowledgeable viewers first see the carnage, then they see the guns, and their first thought is ridding the world of guns must be the solution. The outcry begins, and they get their government representatives to lean on gun retailers with rules involving more paperwork and more scrutiny. Which gets done to save votes, not lives. Anyway, you have to forget that route."

"I see your point," Reynaldo agreed. "But I wish we could get the product without taking so much time by hunting up individuals on Craigslist or buying them piecemeal at gun shows."

"You can ask Tino, but I'll bet he can get people to do the buying. Believe me, this part of your plan I know better than anyone. That's how I've always gotten weapons, and it's worth the time to do it that way. Otherwise, I might have had plenty of time in the slammer to think over my mistake."

During the lengthy meeting, he tried several avenues to dissuade Reynaldo, but finally gave up and wondered why he'd been consulted in the first place. Reynaldo and Tino had extensive knowledge of their line of work, and Carlton had never assumed they really paid him solely for his expertise. Notwithstanding Reynaldo's claim that it never hurt to listen to another point of view, the crime boss surely knew that Carlton's forte was keeping a low profile and knowing when and how to pull a trigger, not planning a major smuggling operation. Carlton was certain that something else was in the works, something was being withheld. Or was he becoming paranoid because of the withheld information during the Ramos operation?

Both Reynaldo and Tino had survived by being the opposite of the late Brujido Ramos—they listened to reason and evaluated any logical suggestion that might solve or at least mitigate a problem. They firmly held to the tenet of not using violence until it was absolutely necessary. But Carlton was beginning to think the pair of crime bosses, during their temporary alliance—or perhaps, because of it—had decided to up their game. His thoughts moved to the possible scenarios at work.

According to Tino, the two had been boyhood friends, parting ways and establishing separate operations in San Antonio and Wichita Falls. When Paula's daughter was kidnapped, Tino contacted Reynaldo, citing his old friend's greater knowledge and resources for dealing with the situation. However, Carlton had seen nothing of the supposed superior manpower and resources; instead, he had arranged the exchange rendezvous himself, he alone had engaged the help of the DEA, and he had been the primary bag man. When the smoke cleared, everyone was happy—that is, except for Carlton. Although he'd been well-compensated for his work, pain, and injury, he hadn't liked being forced into the combat role, no matter the results.

But the two drug kingpins had lauded him as being "handier than a set of jumper cables at a Mexican wedding." Business was back on track and Tino's market area secure for the foreseeable future, with Reynaldo providing a large amount of the product and Tino using his marketing force on the street. So had the Ramos Elimination Project ignited more than this short-term partnership? Or had the temporary partnership given rise to an ambitious new venture? Taking on a drug cartel in a proxy war sounded like a strategy best left to the United States government—Carlton thought they needed Ollie North and Ronald Reagan for funneling weapons, not Carlton Westerfield.

His thoughts were interrupted by his phone. He recognized the number as Tino's latest burner and pressed "talk."

"Good morning, Tino."

"Good morning to you. How's your knee?"

"Pretty tender this morning. Slept on it wrong, I guess."

"You feel up to breakfast?"

"Depends on who's picking up the check."

An exaggerated sigh on the other end told Carlton he'd pushed the right button. *"I guess I could spring for an egg sandwich. As long as you don't bitch about your knee."*

"Just kidding. I think you bought last time, so I'll get the check. But let's get some gringo food. I've had enough Mexican food to last for a while."

"What, at some trendy place like the non-gluten place on Flores? What's the name of it, Local Hoity-Toity Five Tits?"

"Five Points Local, Tino. And it's gluten-free, not non-gluten."

"Point, tits, whatever. Gluten-free sounds like a German striptease act. No, I want to go someplace and order extra gluten."

"Extra gluten? Now that sounds like a German striptease act. Okay, you driving?"

"I'm in the parking lot."

"Give me five minutes."

Extra gluten was available at the IHOP on Southwest Military Drive, and both men seemed intent on loading up; Tino ordered blueberry pancakes and Carlton went for French toast.

Carlton sipped his coffee, waiting for Tino to get to the point. He knew from past experience that the invitation to breakfast was Faustino Perez' favorite ploy for launching into something which would entail Carlton's help, insight, or endorsement, if not outright participation. He didn't have to wait long.

"So, you and Reynaldo get a handle on the cattle trailer thing?"

Carlton finished pouring syrup on his toast before responding. "Somewhat. Lots of problems to be worked out, some research to be done. I don't know if getting the product into Mexico incurs the imaging process like it might coming this way. If so, I'm not sure the imaging technology can be defeated with lead shielding. I'd use some, just in case."

Tino nodded, recalling the lead-shielding step Carlton had advised. "I can't tell if it's worked in the Ford ambulance drive shafts, because none of my drivers have reported one being checked. I guess that's the benefit of using ambulances. They don't arouse much suspicion, no matter what."

"Yeah, and the drive shaft is a single, limited piece of pipe attached to the vehicle. I doubt many checkpoint personnel compare images of drive shafts on various vehicles. For all they know, all drive shafts may look like they have shielding in them. I think most of their training involves recognizing shapes of packages that aren't where they should be. But an entire lead-lined ceiling in a cow trailer might show up dramatically. If so, it'll really raise a red flag."

"So what do you recommend?"

Carlton looked directly at Tino to respond. "Abandoning the idea, that's what I suggest. Stirring up trouble among factions in that end of the pipeline seems like a good way to screw up the entire product source. If Reynaldo's suppliers catch on to his supplying their competitors with arms, won't that erode the trust a bit?"

"No doubt about it. That would really cause a problem. That's why Reynaldo needs a cut-out on this, someone who can't be connected to him. That's why he got a professional weapons guy, a trainer for the laborers. And he wants to hear some options for getting the guns and the actual transport."

"So that's where this Millstone guy comes in?"

Tino didn't answer immediately, catching Carlton's attention. He looked up to see Tino grinning at him, but the joke wasn't clear. "What?"

"*Millstone*. You got his name right, meaning I was right. I told Reynaldo you didn't forget the guy's name. You were just testing him."

It was Carlton's turn to grin, if sheepishly. "I *was* testing him, and he didn't call me on it. I wanted to see if he's become enamored too quickly with this slick Brit, along with you."

"Along with me? How do you figure that?"

"When I was in your office, you referred to my vacation as 'holiday,' and Reynaldo referred to Heather as a 'lass.' Those European terms tell me y'all have spent some time listening to this guy talk. Or somebody like him, with a British accent. Just because he's got an accent like someone in a spy movie doesn't mean he can accomplish the task, by the way.

"Anyway, I said his name incorrectly to see if it registered with Reynaldo. I waited for him to show me he's really familiar with the name, and that he's really done some checking on him. He didn't correct me, so I assumed he didn't know the guy's name all that well himself."

Tino smiled at the explanation. "Oh, it registered all right! He caught your misnomer and decided to let it slide, because he thought *you* didn't catch the guy's name, or forgot it during the conversation."

Carlton's mood changed with the implication. "I didn't forget anything, Tino! I'm just trying to evaluate this situation from an objective viewpoint. And I'm not sure either of you are doing the same," he added hotly.

"Okay, okay, chill out, will you? He—that is, both of us—were just concerned after you took a bullet and stayed in the hospital and rehab for what—six, seven weeks? They gave you some strong pain medication that might have affected your memory for a while. But I guess you quit taking that stuff when you started the heat therapy, right?"

His sly grin told Carlton that he and Reynaldo had, true to form, discussed his short fling in Mexico. It seemed the right time for an exaggerated eye roll, his only tactic for dealing with Faustino Perez, and in absentia, his friend, Reynaldo Gomez.

Shaking his head, Carlton had to laugh, in spite of himself. "You two old gossips are too much. You worry about my taking medication that fogs my memory—it didn't—and heat therapy that fogs my good sense—and it probably did."

"That wee lass would fog any man's good sense. And before you launch into your speech about fawning over the Brit and his corny accent, that was another test."

Carlton nodded. "And 'wee lass' is probably Scottish, not Londoner British. My two physiotherapists throwing out foreign phrases to see if my tired old brain could make the connection. I caught them, Tino, so I guess I passed."

"I never doubted for a second that you would."

"Okay. Can we quit dancing around trying to prove how clever we all are and get back on the subject? Reynaldo needs to give up on this plan before it causes him a lot of grief."

Tino shook his head. "I don't think he can be talked out of it, Carlton. He's firm about going forward with it. What we want to know is, will you help?"

Carlton sighed. "Sure, I'll do what I can. Which doesn't seem like much at this point. But maybe I'll be like Clark Gable in *Gone With the Wind*. He said something like 'I never back a cause until I know it's truly lost.' I just hope this isn't a lost cause, neither for Reynaldo nor those guys he wants to arm."

CHAPTER 4

Saturday afternoon seemed a perfect time to avoid contact with any of the Southside bunch, friends or not. Carlton had had enough of discussing how to run weapons into Mexico; besides, he wanted to take Tino's earlier advice and get more heat therapy for his knee. Trouble was, he wasn't sure if his therapy sessions would continue. Heather had texted him a couple of times since their return, but the messages had been generic and short, almost curt. In turn, Carlton had responded similarly, hoping the situation would eventually change, but not wanting to press the matter. All in all, he had to admit his future with Heather looked bleak.

Just before leaving Mexico, she had warned him that her return to everyday life would be different from his and she might not be "readily available," whatever that meant. She was returning to work at full-schedule, having completed her mandated ninety-day period of light duty. Her boss, Stan Ikos, was doing an evaluation of her performance as required by Administration regulations following a shooting event before giving the okay for permanent return to normal duty. She wanted to make sure she seemed fully engaged, and she explained that texting "kissy messages" back and forth wouldn't help her concentration. Furthermore, meeting with him was out for the time being, she'd explained. She hadn't documented him as her CI (Confidential Informant) as required by Administration rules and, even with her current celebrity status, Ikos could have her demoted or even canned for failing to get Westerfield on the official record. "Fame only gets you treated nice for a week or two at the DEA," she'd said. "And Stan knows you're not just some guy who overheard talk about Ramos' scheme to traffic drugs into town. He just can't prove otherwise."

Carlton had responded stoically to the news that her fame (and their torrid affair) was so short-lived, but he understood she had to buckle down and show she still had what it took to do her job as a gun-toting agent. Privately, he wondered if her explanation was a way to start the process of eliminating him—a nicer way than tossing him in the ditch, but just as effective. After all, he was considerably older than she, and the fling may have been no more than something the younger woman had on her bucket list. He felt himself circling the infamous Romance Drain. Ever the realist, he did a good job of shrugging it off, but didn't like the prospect of a long drought ahead…

Reprieve from the drought came in an odd form. When his text alert dinged, he cringed, thinking Tino or Reynaldo wanted to meet—again—to beat the gun-running horse a bit more. Finally peeking at the screen, he was delighted to see it was from Heather's burner number. He was less delighted when he read the message:

Can we meet tonight? My boss wants to take us to dinner. He has something he wants to talk with you about.

He frowned as he hit "send" on his reply: *Sure. Where and when?*

"Where" turned out to be the Jim's at Loop 410 and Broadway. "When" was scheduled for eight o'clock. Sitting in his car, Carlton watched the parking lot traffic ebb and flow, feeling like a jealous teenager waiting for his cheerleader girlfriend to show up with the starting quarterback. When he saw Heather's personal car, a late-model Honda Accord pull in, he sighed and got out of his car. A Ford Crown Vic pulled in across from Heather's Honda, and a tall man Carlton recognized as Heather's boss, Stan Ikos, emerged.

As he joined Heather and walked toward the entrance, Carlton reminded himself that Ikos couldn't know about the Mexico tryst and that he had to watch his actions and expressions while being near Heather. Given her dire predictions about returning to her job, she surely would put on the same act. It was unlikely he could advance his situation with Heather if he couldn't turn on his wit and charm, so he'd have to be satisfied with being near her and enjoying her company...which sounded pretty weak after their recent ten days together.

In truth, he wanted to get this meeting over and done with, go home and watch *Star Trek*.

Ikos, a solidly built guy with a commanding presence, pulled open the door for Heather as Carlton approached and gestured for Carlton to precede him through the door. Once inside, he extended his hand. "Hello again, Mr. Westerfield. I see you accomplished what you wanted about trading up in transportation."

Carlton recalled their previous meeting, a contentious lunch engagement where he had told the Special Agent in Charge that he needed reward money for the tip on Ramos so he could trade in his old Datsun pickup for a better car. Having noticed Carlton exiting from a late-model Cadillac, the government agent wanted to show Carlton his powers of observation and memory. "Yes, I did," he answered cheerfully as he shook Ikos strong hand. "My little pickup was okay, but it had a lot of miles on it."

"Kind of like its owner?" came the caustic reply, but it was accompanied by a big grin and Carlton responded in kind. He decided to wait a while before bringing up the subject of their earlier meeting in which they had haggled over payment.

Carlton turned toward Heather as a waitress ambled over to seat them. "And how are you Ms.—excuse me, *Agent* Colson? I read all about you in the paper. I hope your boss knows how valuable you are to the company and gave you a big raise."

Heather smiled and answered appropriately. "I wish it worked that way, but the DEA doesn't operate like that. I got a commendation letter in my file, but this line of work is like being a college football coach—you're only as good as your last season. Oh, and I got a reprimand letter the same day for agreeing to the newspaper interview, although I'm not sure how I could throw the reporter out of my hospital room with the stitches in my side."

Good, Carlton thought. She's on board with playing out our non-personal relationship by being her usual wise-ass self in front of her boss. His satisfaction was short-lived, however, evaporating with Ikos' first statement when they were seated and the waitress out of earshot.

"In the interest of saving time, I'll go ahead and cut through the bullshit, Westerfield. I know about your involvement in the shootout at the parking garage. I also know about you and Agent Colson meeting in Mexico, so we don't need to pussy-foot around here tonight."

Carlton hid his astonishment, wondering if Ikos only suspected and was playing him for an admission. Eyebrows raised, he turned to Heather as if to ask "*what's he talking about?*", but the deadpan expression on her pretty face told him nothing. He didn't know if she was as shocked as he and hiding it well, or if her lack of emotion was the way she chose to let him know that the cat was out of the bag. Either way, the revelation was a shocker, but he wasn't going to let it show to the big law enforcement agent across the table. "You and the Administration must have too much time on their hands if that's all you have on your agenda."

"As a matter of fact, we've got a lot to keep us busy. That's why I asked to meet with you tonight. I just didn't want to watch you acting smug, thinking you put one over on me or the Administration"

"I wasn't aware I was trying to put anything over on you. I simply took a trip, and who I meet at my destination is my business."

"Technically, that's true for you. But not for Agent Colson. She was supposed to document your involvement in the Ramos affair, have you officially tagged as a Confidential Informant. She's in a bit of hot water for failing to do that."

"Why didn't you do the documenting? You were aware of the information I gave you regarding a drug shipment. Which reminds me: when do I get paid for the tip?"

"You don't," came the quick reply. "You weren't listed as a CI, so I can't authorize paying you. You'll have to chalk that one up to performing your civic duty."

"Okay. Well, enjoy your dinner." Carlton rose from the table, turning to Heather as he lay his napkin down. "Sorry if I caused you a problem. I wasn't aware that DEA agents had no personal life, or I wouldn't have jeopardized your job—"

"Wait a minute!" Ikos barked. "You can't just walk away without hearing me out."

"Watch and see, Stan. As you just pointed out, I don't work for you, never did. So use your bully tactics on someone else."

"Okay, dammit, we'll pay you the money!" Ikos' remark was far too loud for the environment, and several diners turned to look at the commotion.

Carlton decided to make the most of the busted evening and enjoy himself. Matching Ikos' volume, he said, "Sorry, Stan, it's too late for that. Partial payment won't suffice, and my bank will have to go forward with the foreclosure proceedings on your home!" The remark caused even more curious diners to home in on the spectacle.

Glancing at Heather, he saw that she was about to burst out laughing, but she wiped the smirk from her face at Ikos' glare and cleared her throat. "Please wait," she asked calmly, taking over the failed negotiations from her boss. "Let's start over, okay? Stan wants to talk about something else entirely, so let's just get beyond this testosterone exhibit."

The last remark was accompanied by a hand on his arm which caused him to look directly at her instead of the fuming Ikos. A silent "please" was registered in her eyes, and Carlton hesitated in his exit for an awkward five seconds. He turned to address the nearest table where three people kept staring and waiting for the next salvo of words. Carlton didn't disappoint them. Instead, he gave his best smile and an apologetic shrug. "You can choose your friends, but you're stuck with your family...especially if you co-sign for them at your own bank."

Embarrassed, the trio went back to their salads.

Carlton sat down and forced a smile in Ikos' direction. "So Stan, what's on your mind?"

"What's on my mind is this," he hissed through gritted teeth. "You are a first-class jackass. But I think you can help us in this matter, so I'll put up with you—to a point."

"Agent Ikos, you'll find that I respond much in the same way I'm treated. Now, we had a discussion in the past about the people you usually deal with. I understand you're in constant contact with a bunch of low-lifes, dopers, grifters, con men, gangsters, and crooks—but I'm not one of those, so don't treat me like one and we'll get along just fine."

Ikos nodded his acquiescence, but said nothing in response, not directly to Carlton. Instead, he turned toward Heather. "I'm not seeing what you see in this old geezer, but open a file on him, establish him as your CI, and document every meeting you have. Maybe he can be useful."

"He's been useful in the past, Stan, don't forget that. Now, if we can all talk a little quieter, we can get down to the business at hand, okay?"

"Fine by me," Carlton said. "What's on *your* mind, Agent Colson?"

Heather took a breath and began what was obviously a scripted pitch. "Word on the street has a new player in our city, a bigger one than Faustino Perez. He's reportedly from somewhere in North Texas. You heard anything like that?"

"Nope," came Carlton's careful reply, hoping he was neither too quick nor too slow with the response. "But I don't go around inquiring about that kind of stuff."

"Think you could start? Inquiring about *that kind of stuff*?" It was Ikos, jumping into the conversation, but keeping the tone and decibel level of his voice in a reasonable range.

"I can give it a shot. What's up with this guy, anyway? He going to take over Ramos' action?"

"We're not sure at this point, which is why we need more intel on him," Heather began again, determined to get in her share of this meeting. "We've not been able to identify any new street personnel, but that's not conclusive of anything. He could be using an existing sales force, maybe Ramos' guys and gals.

"What we do know is prices at wholesale are creeping up. It could be due to this new player being willing to pay more to get his product. If so, we need to know. It tells us a lot about his financing abilities or other sources of income. Or it could signal a shortage in inventory coming through from South America. Most people don't realize that cocaine isn't a big production item in Mexico, but it's run through there, and the cartels get paid for transporting it."

"So I've heard. I always thought it was grown and produced there, but a documentary on NatGeo channel set me straight. Anyway, here in our city, getting rid of Ramos just created a vacuum? And you think this guy is stepping up to the plate?"

"Maybe. But we're more interested in his effect on the overall market, and why. Anytime there's a significant move in prices, it means a disturbance at some level of distribution. Like all businesses, the price finally flows down to the consumer on the street. And the higher prices are showing up on the street in the form of more muggings, carjackings, and residential B & Es. Crimes against persons and property are up almost fifteen percent in the last month, according to SAPD." Heather finished by glancing over at her boss, then back to Carlton.

"Well, I can listen up, but I can't think of any reason that information would be put to me—"

"We know you're connected with Faustino Perez." Ikos interrupted and held up his hand against Carlton's protest before he could speak. "Now, you may do nothing but work in his muffler shop, his warehouse, his ambulance business, or his junk shop out on Highway Sixteen. But he does other things for income, we know that, so don't waste our time denying it."

Carlton shrugged. "I'm not denying anything, because I don't *know* anything, except the workings at the 'junk shop' as you call it. But I'll listen up and see if anything comes up about a new guy from North Texas."

"That would be most helpful, Mr. Westerfield," Heather offered, her voice sounding official and stilted as she again glanced at her boss.

Carlton winced inwardly at the terse tone of the formal address, thinking back on the days in Mexico. Those days (and nights) hadn't been terse or formal at all, and he took this turn of moods to be a signal for him to leave this place, play their game, and go home to Kirk and Spock. "Give me a few days to see what I can learn," he said, using the same business-like tone as he rose to leave the table.

Ikos put his hand on his arm to restrain him. "Don't leave just yet. This was an invitation to dinner, remember? I've got to leave, but my star agent here, Agent Colson, will stay and pick up the tab. Try to earn your keep, Westerfield." With that parting shot, Stan Ikos, Agent in Charge, left the table.

Ikos was out the door and getting in the Ford before Carlton turned back toward a grinning Heather Colson. Taken aback by the change in her demeanor, he rolled his eyes and said, "I hope you enjoyed that."

"About as much as you did. But there was nothing I could do about it. He had me set up this meeting and warned me to play it his way, not tell you he knew about Mexico. He wanted to make that little power announcement himself."

"Well, I hope *he* enjoyed it, then, as well as you. I just wish I had had as much fun as my two DEA agent pals."

Heather narrowed her eyes and pouted. "I was going to make it up to you, but if we're just pals, you'll have to accept it as a prank among friends."

Carlton tried to look suitably hurt, but evidently failed, judging by the look of merriment she was unable to suppress. "Okay, one newbie DEA pal and my smokin' hot DEA lover?" he tried feebly.

"That's more like it. But he's set on getting you to perform as a CI, and it better be good, or he'll hand me walking papers to the office in Pierre, South Dakota. Plus, it's the only way you and I can have any contact."

"Really? Why? As I'm sure you know, I have no record of committing any crime, not even a parking ticket, so—"

"I know," she interrupted. "But Ikos has his suspicions about you and Perez, so he doesn't need an official record to designate you as forbidden fruit to one of his agents."

"Oh, yeah? I'll bet you're not forbidden fruit to Big Stan, not if he could get away with it. Who died and made him the big matchmaker referee over in Romance Control?"

"Forget it, Carlton. Jealousy doesn't suit you." The admonition was accompanied by a seductive grin, and Carlton decided to let it go. "And to answer your question," she continued, "the Drug Enforcement Administration has rules in place that give the local office AIC that authority. I know the rules, and I broke them."

"I'd put up with that for about six seconds. Guess that's why I could never hold a real job after I got out of the Army. Did you know they would follow your movements like that? On your recovery time off?"

She shook her head. "No, but it really doesn't surprise me. I should have known better, but I guess getting shot didn't do my judgement any good."

"It got you to Mexico, and I liked that judgement call just fine."

"It was fun, and it was exactly what I wanted to do. But I'm serious about having to get back in the thick of it and have another great bust to add to my name. My past performance has already been forgotten—"

"Not by me, it hasn't!"

The resulting smile was genuine, but she diluted it with an order. "Start thinking with the big head, Carlton. You have to find out something about this new player so we have a reason to see each other. Ikos will only give me so much rope."

Their designated waitress, who had wisely avoided the table, edged over to take their orders. Carlton wasn't really hungry, but since Uncle Sam was buying, he decided to eat anyway. Heather had the requisite salad that women, no matter their figure, feel compelled to order, while he ordered the biggest cheeseburger on the menu. It would give him more time to sit here with Heather, even if she wanted to talk some business between bites.

Kirk and Spock would have to get along without him.

Santa Monica, Coahuila, Mexico, a small village on State Highway 15:

Nicolas Castro pulled the box truck over on the dirt street that connected two paved residential avenues in his home village. His brother sat silently as he had for the long journey home from Nuevo Bayito and the confrontation with Surly Man. As they sat, engine idling, Nicolas felt he had to say something to Isidro, something to make him feel better about having done nothing to thwart the angry warehouseman's—his name was Jese Felan—violent harassment and humiliating slaps. It had angered him too, but he and Isidro, like the other laborers, could do nothing to confront any of the cartel's tough enforcers.

"Don't worry about it, Hermanito. You did the right thing by doing nothing. We can't do anything to upset those guys, or our families will pay with their lives. At least we have jobs and are making enough money to live on."

Isidro turned to face him. "It isn't enough, Nicolas! We both know the money they pay us is shit compared to the millions of dollars they are making while we take all the risk of moving la cocaína from the horse farm to the warehouse. We face the roadblocks, the federales, the risk of going to prison for life, and they treat us like peones—worse than peones, like slaves."

"But what can we do about it, Isidro? What can anyone do against the Golfos?"

A few minutes of silence passed before Isidro answered. "What about the meetings? We could go to the meetings and listen to what is said. There can be no harm in that."

Nicolas started to shake his head as he had done in the past when the secret meetings were mentioned, but something made him stop; he was torn between fear and pride. He was aware that a couple of the older laborers, Sebastian Chavez and Leobardo Muñoz, had allowed meetings to be held in their homes, right here in the village, only blocks from where they now sat. But a brief vision of what would happen if the meetings were found out caused him to begin his standard negative response to the idea.

Nicolas was married, with two young children. Isidro was not married and did not fully understand the risk to family as well as Nicolas did. Nor, apparently, did Sebastian and Leobardo. They were older, their children gone, wives content to spend all their time on Church matters and gossiping at the mercado. Besides, the older workers were treated less harshly than the younger men, likely because the surly overseers counted on the elders' wisdom to keep them in line. It was the younger men who needed harsh preemptory discipline.

Nicolas had heard that the meetings were being called and carried out by several of the younger men, some even younger than Isidro, but held in homes of the old ones, since they were less suspect of trouble and unconcerned about the ramifications of secret meetings being discovered. Nicolas did not share the old ones' attitude, but today's event made him pause in his vigorous head-shaking. He was sick of being treated like an animal by men who made millions of dollars while he and his family scraped by on what amounted to less than sixty American dollars a month. It was a living, but just barely. And today, as he drove the box truck home with shame in his heart for himself and his brother, he recalled a century-old call to rise up against oppression, a proclamation credited to one of Mexico's past heroes of the poor, Emiliano Zapata:

"Prefiero morir de pie que vivir siempre en arrodillado."

Indeed, today's humiliation had sparked that same idea in his mind, even if not so eloquently expressed as by the leader of the Zapatistas a hundred years ago. Nicolas Castro was ready to concede that he would rather die on his feet than spend the rest of his life living and begging on his knees. He turned to his brother. "When is the next meeting?"

CHAPTER 5

Carlton texted Tino that they needed to meet late Sunday, thereby managing to dodge everyone for most of the day. He took the opportunity to drive over to the north side of the city and meet Heather for a late lunch, ignoring her boss' restrictions. When he returned to his apartment, he didn't see any familiar cars and thought he might actually get to stay home for some evening reading or TV by himself before calling Tino to meet. It wasn't in the cards. His phone buzzed as he walked in the door.

"Are you home yet?"

"Just walked in the door."

"Can you come to my office? I know it's earlier than you wanted, but Reynaldo is here, and we can talk before Paula and Catarina get back from church."

Carlton suppressed a sigh. Just as well get on with it, he thought. *"Give me a few minutes, I'll be there."*

Tino and Reynaldo were engaged in an animated conversation in Spanish when Carlton walked in. The pair abruptly switched to English as a courtesy, but it didn't benefit him to hear them talk about someone they had known years before, so he took a chair in the corner and thumbed through a months-old magazine while they finished.

"So how was your date last night?"

Reynaldo's question shook Carlton out of his reverie, and he realized he'd almost dozed off. "Oh, great, if you consider sitting there with her boss being a good time. But once he got beyond scolding me for meeting her in Mexico, the subject matter was pretty interesting."

"Really? What did he want?" Tino asked. "More inside info on drug shipments of our rivals?"

"Better than that. They want me to find out about a big player from North Texas who's supposedly moved into the Alamo City."

Tino looked surprised as he turned to face Reynaldo, who looked stunned. "What did you tell them?" The question came from both of them simultaneously as though they had rehearsed it.

Carlton had known the news would be an unpleasant shock, but he had to laugh at the duo's harmonized response. "Nothing, Laurel and Hardy! I told them I'd listen up and see what I could find out about this mysterious new guy, but I wasn't likely to find out much."

He went on to tell them the DEA agents' theory about price movement and a new player in town, one from North Texas. He looked at each of them inquiringly, but both shook their heads. "Anyway, I guess that ties in with your plan to get lower prices by arming the competition, Reynaldo, but how did they hear about you? I mean, I only know you're from Wichita Falls because Tino told me. You don't go around with a badge that says 'I'm from Wichita Falls.'"

"I don't know, but it's disturbing. That part about rising wholesale prices is correct, and I'm impressed they're able to gauge that by crime at the street level. It's not like I send them a report on my supplier's price list."

All three fell quiet for a moment before Tino broke the silence. "Not a hint of why they think it's a North Texas player, not somebody from Miami or Chicago? Or Kearny, Nebraska?"

"Nothing. I didn't probe, though, because my position with Heather's boss is this: I don't know about anything illegal going on. I've insisted that the Ramos information was a one-off thing. Her boss, Ikos, knows that's a crock, but with him, I maintain that I just work at your market. I didn't express any interest or curiosity in their theory. I wanted y'all to hear this first and see if either of you knew how anything leaked about Reynaldo's home base. Plus, how you think I should approach the subject without being too curious, or if I just wait and see what they decide to tell me."

"Waiting would be the best way to handle it. They may be throwing out the "North Texas" angle just to see how much you know. I mean, North Texas could mean the Metroplex or the Panhandle, neither of which is near Wichita Falls."

Carlton shook his head. "Another test! I'll be glad when everyone figures out I haven't gone entirely senile yet."

The remark got a smile from Tino and an embarrassed chuckle from Reynaldo. "Okay, I know that was going overboard, but we...*I* was concerned about all the medication they gave you. My apologies."

Carlton waved a dismissal of the subject. "Forget it, both of you. Let's just figure out what this means and how it might affect current business as well as your plan to move those weapons.

"As to the North Texas connection, maybe they've spotted your car here at the flea market, maybe more than once. So they run the plates and find out it's registered in Wichita County."

"That's possible," Reynaldo said. "But I haven't done anything here to even warrant their checking my plates."

"So they just tossed out a red herring. Or, any car, especially a nice one, gets checked out for sitting here at Tino's place."

"Actually, it's registered to a friend of mine who's in the car business up there. I'll take it back this week and get a rental."

"That might keep their curiosity up," Tino said. "I'll get you something nice, something registered right here in town, and you can park the Lexus in one of the garages."

Reynaldo nodded his thanks and turned back to Carlton. "When do you meet with them again?"

Carlton chose his words carefully. "I've got a meeting with Heather set for Tuesday night. I told her it was the soonest I might be able to hear anything about the guy they're interested in."

Tino wasn't going to let him off that easily. "A meeting or a date, Romeo?"

"If I tell you, will you not send any watchers? Or people with cameras?"

"Okay, no watchers." The accompanying grin didn't convey much truth with the promise.

"It's going to be a meeting, and she's going to want something to give her boss. Now let's figure out what tidbit I can fork over so they'll keep thinking I'm valuable without getting our North Texas friend in trouble."

The next ten minutes were spent concocting a few mundane facts that a warehouse worker might come upon during the course of business, ones that could take a bit of effort to find, but nothing of any use in nailing down a new drug trafficker. The two bosses gave Carlton a few suggestions to get information from Heather about how much the DEA knew and the source of their information.

"With any luck, you'll find out it was just a guess, something they tried out to see the extent of your knowledge and involvement," Tino said.

"That would be the best outcome, if you can pin that down," Reynaldo added. His tone and the look on his face said he was concerned about the drug agency's information, fake or not.

All three went silent for a moment, thinking about the possible ramifications. Tino broke the silence with a complaint to his two companions. "Dammit, we can't keep a lower profile than we do now! Neither Reynaldo nor I do any hands-on stuff, not where the DEA could find out. So whatever they're doing, we have to find out the extent of it and react accordingly."

Carlton and Reynaldo nodded in agreement. Carlton thought Tino's sober tone matched Reynaldo's mood, evidencing what he had come to know about the two crime bosses: they were professionals, duly concerned over any event that might cause them a problem. The current example further fueled his confusion regarding Reynaldo's plan to smuggle weapons into Mexico. It seemed to fly in the face of the careful, guarded method of operation the two normally followed. His confusion wasn't diminished by Reynaldo's next comment.

"Let's go out to the ranch tomorrow," he suggested to Tino. "I'll get Gus and his sidekick to take a look at converting the cattle trailer. Then I'll give you the grand tour of the ranch."

He turned to Carlton. "Tino and I talked about getting the weapons, and he's able to help with that. As you suggested, it will be done with individuals, all cash, widely spread all over the state. He made some calls today, and we'll start seeing them show up in the next few days."

"I'll take care of the logistics on the weapons," Tino said to Carlton. "So you concentrate on finding out what the DEA knows and how they know it."

"Will do, Tino."

The three rose to leave and filed out the door, Tino last. As he turned to lock up, he asked Reynaldo to wait for him. Not included, Carlton walked to his car and waved to the pair as he got into the Caddy, wondering what was being said between the two still standing on the office porch. Whatever it was, it meant nothing at all to their advisor, none of his business. Probably continuing the conversation about some old friend from years ago, nothing to do with Carlton Westerfield or the business at hand.

Pulling out and heading toward his apartment, Carlton didn't believe that for a minute.

Watching Carlton's car turn right on Highway 16, the pair of crime bosses took up the conversation again, neither liking the news he had delivered.

"What the hell is going on, Tino? How did the DEA put all this shit together and come up with a 'new player from North Texas?'" Reynaldo asked his friend in a flurry of angry Spanish while making quote marks in the air.

"We're not certain they did. But it's better to know they're fishing around, that—"

"Tino, this couldn't be Carlton going into business with them..." Reynaldo interrupted, but the implication sounded wrong to his own ears, and he let the inquiry die in the breeze.

"No, I can't believe that. He's clever, but he's too direct to be devious. Besides, why would he do that? What would be the incentive?"

"The best incentive, the one that all men are faced with, my friend! The tender trap between women's legs! No one understands that better than I do." The rueful expression on his face revealed the last statement to be more accurate than he wished it to be.

"Reynaldo, if you're talking about the DEA girl, he doesn't need any help with her. It would seem that his recovery in Mexico went just fine without his dropping the dime on me, you, or our operations. If it had to do with that *chica*, he would just drop all of us and leave with her. He's probably got the money to do it, too, so there is no amount a government agency could pay that would turn him."

"But could the DEA have something on him he can't get out of? Wasn't he a button man for some fat gangster here in San Antonio?"

Tino shook his head. "Yes, but he was good at it, very low-key. And the DEA's first job is drugs, not murder. Even so, there wouldn't be a reason for them to set up a sting operation. They'd just have the local cops arrest him and sweat him for information in return for a no-bill by a grand jury, or something like that. Even if they had him on one of his old jobs for Big Mo, they'd just exchange it for a lighter sentence. Those hits he made through the years weren't on top-notch citizens, and cops didn't pursue most of them very hard, because they know he did them a favor with most of them."

Reynaldo nodded in agreement at Tino's evaluation; it didn't make sense in any direction. Besides, his own abilities at judging people had come into play the day he'd met the polite, reserved Anglo in Tino's employ. He was certain that Carlton Westerfield was exactly as he had first ascertained: smart, capable, too straight-forward and unfettered by anything or anyone to need deception for anything beyond doing his job—a job that paid very well. But still, the pretty DEA agent trying to make her career…

Tino changed subjects, breaking Reynaldo's train of thought. "Have you talked to Millstone and his training expert?" He knew his friend was staying in touch with the two weapons trainers in Mexico via the Brit's encrypted satellite phone and Reynaldo's cheap burner.

"Yes, that's why I've got to get the trailer converted and have a sit-down with Gus. He's brought Zachary Thomas over to the Sabinal ranch, and I've got to get both of them on board with the weapons movement."

"How are you going to do that?"

"The *second*-best incentive, Tino, money. Those two have extended families and girlfriends who need more than ordinary ranch workers can provide. So they're going to become gun runners."

"Okay, good. I ordered the guns to be bought with ammo when possible, so we don't have to chase around for it later. That's the thing about buying from individuals; they usually have ammo for it, and they're willing to throw it in to make the deal. And I'll get the stuff out to Sabinal personally. I'd send Carlton, but he doesn't like being around guns or ammunition."

Reynaldo looked perplexed by the confirmation of what Carlton had told him. "I don't understand that guy. The main tool of his trade, and he doesn't like to be around guns? How'd he get to be so good with one?"

Tino shrugged. "One of those guys who's got a natural talent, I guess. From what Paula told me about the car wash thing, he changes into a real gunman when he needs to. He gunned down those four gangbangers before they could clear leather. Or clear their baggy pants, that is."

At the mention of Paula, Reynaldo regarded his old friend carefully as he confided in him. "Paula and I are discussing longer range plans for us. She told me that she and Westerfield were through and seemed relieved that he hooked up with the DEA girl. What's her name? Heather?"

"Yes, Heather Colson. So…you and Paula…?"

"Maybe. I just hope Carlton isn't the jealous type. After hearing about his gunplay, I wouldn't want him to decide I was in his way." The last remark was made in a jovial tone, but there was no sign of a smile on Reynaldo's face. When he spoke again, another idea had occurred. "Maybe he's figured out how to get rid of me by using the Feds. He seems to like me, and that way, he wouldn't have to shoot me."

Tino disagreed. "No, no, he wouldn't get you sent to prison. And he *does* like you, so he wouldn't shoot you." After a moment, he added: "But he knows how to put a bomb in a car. I've seen him do it."

Reynaldo looked alarmed. "You *are* kidding, right?"

Tino didn't answer right away, causing Reynaldo's brow to knit even more. After five seconds of deadpan, Tino couldn't take any more and burst out laughing. "Hell, yes, I'm shittin' you! Carlton's on our side, and he's proven to be a stand-up guy a dozen times already. It's my crazy sister you need to be worried about, old friend!"

CHAPTER 6

The week started with a cold front that blew in at dawn on Monday with a strong wind and leaden clouds that looked like snow could be in store. Though it was early January, no one worried much about it during what passed for winter in South Texas, and by late afternoon, the wind died down, the sun poked through, and temperature managed to get into the fifties.

Carlton spent the day at the flea market, occasionally going back to Tino's office to unload packages from several cars that came and went. He carried the wrapped guns into the office and stacked them in a janitor's closet. At first, he was surprised at the quick response and the rapid accumulation of weapons. Then, recalling Tino's connection to this community, and the sway he held over the members' lives, it seemed logical that thirty or forty AR-15s and ten to twenty nine-millimeter handguns would show up magically in short order, along with ammunition.

He was glad to be clear of Tino and Reynaldo for a few days. They had both gone to the Sabinal ranch to oversee work on the cattle trailer conversion, but not before drafting Carlton into yet another discussion regarding the conversion project. While both had agreed with Carlton that building a "storage compartment" in the trailer would be simple enough, its existence, if spotted, might require some explaining to border inspectors. That opened up a new debate on the nature of the proposed compartment: hidden or obvious?

Carlton suggested an obvious one, with a visible door. Loading the compartment with plumbing repair materials, like water pipe sections or electrical conduit, could be used to blend with the barrels of weapons during an imaging process. Not perfect, he admitted, but ranches use a

53

lot of repair stuff, and it was better than a compartment filled with what clearly looked like assault rifles, no matter the quality of the imaging. And if there were no imaging equipment in use, a quick look would reveal only a bunch of water pipes shoved into the compartment. He also pointed out the suspicion a fully sealed compartment would raise if it were discovered.

However, Tino and Reynaldo were reluctant to outfit the new section with an external door and try passing it off as a storage compartment. They preferred a sealed compartment, "guns inside and cow shit on the outside." Carlton countered with the ease of extracting the weapons upon arrival via a door, but Reynaldo assured him that cutting the newly welded panel would only take minutes. The back-and-forth discussion went on for a while, with Carlton agreeing in the end, so long as it was sealed with welds identical to the rest of the trailer and the entire thing was given a coat of paint. When the paint dried and the work adequately plastered with manure, he said, it would be as good as could be fashioned on short notice. Reynaldo didn't like the extra step, but agreed that it was necessary.

The schedule for the conversion and shipping was another part of the operation that surprised Carlton. At the end of the conversation regarding compartment construction, Reynaldo had announced the weapons shipment into Mexico would take place within the next two weeks. Carlton argued for more time for the paint to dry and cure, for the trailer to take on a well-used patina. With usage, he said, a few weeks would have the thing looking like it a veteran of many cattle hauling trips, complete with dried manure covering the recent work. Reynaldo nixed the delay, assuring him that the ranch hands could simply keep some cows rotating through the trailer while sitting at the ranch in order to ensure the "manure patina" Carlton favored. Besides, he said, Gus would take one load of cattle to the Mexico ranch without any hidden weapons. "That will give the cows time to do their thing. One problem we'll never have is a shortage of cow shit, Carlton," he promised.

Not likely to be a shortage of *bullshit*, either, Carlton thought, but he smiled in agreement with Reynaldo's prediction. Nothing in this scheme looked entirely right, but he was through trying to get Reynaldo to see it differently. Besides, he had been tasked to find out what the DEA knew and how they knew it, which was going to be a lot more entertaining than debating the cure time for cow manure. As it turned out, Tuesday's date with Heather turned out to be more fun than he anticipated.

She wanted to meet at a quiet place where they could talk, and Carlton suggested Ernesto's on Jackson Keller Road, near the boundary of Castle Hills. For starters, Heather wanted a margarita, which she downed quickly, leading to another. While Carlton sipped on a beer and watched her, she proceeded to get tipsy and giggled like someone a lot more fun than a federal law enforcement agent. Experience had told Carlton what the second drink would do, and he wished they'd dispensed with the meal thing earlier.

Alcohol lowers inhibitions and generally boosts uninhibited talking, and the conversation soon turned to their relationship. Recalling his poor history with women, Carlton became wary at the outset of that subject; however, they parried around the difficult parts and ended up agreeing that it was just fine the way it was. Carlton was astonished, and he ordered a martini for himself to celebrate her proclamation that she was "happy with it just like this."

How many times has that ever happened in the history of the world—a woman happy with a relationship, no changes needed? Answer: Never!

Dinner was excellent, and topping it off with after-dinner drinks seemed appropriate—especially given what Carlton knew a glass of wine would do to his already-primed date.

"You're a funny girl," he allowed, watching her sip the wine without losing her smile. "And I *do* like that smile."

"Well, I smile when I'm happy."

"Me too. I should be around you more often."

"I'll remember that, and we'll try to work it out. Right now I'm remembering some fun nights in Mexico."

"Ah, Mexico!" He raised his glass and eased it toward hers for a toast. "We'll always have *Acapulco*, Sweetheart," he said in a miserable Humphrey Bogart voice, getting a thumbs-down for his performance, but tempered with a laugh of genuine enjoyment, by the sound of it. It made him wonder if there might actually be more to their strange pairing than he was willing to admit. Her next remark reinforced the thought.

"I hope it's me, not just the booze that's got you acting silly, Bogey. You'd better stick to your *Star Trek* references."

"Maybe a bit of both."

"Did I ever thank you for saving my life?" she asked suddenly, changing gears and surprising her date.

"We touched on it a time or two in Mexico, but I don't think I saved your life. We just helped each other out in a bad situation."

She was shaking her head before he finished speaking. "You're too modest, Carlton. Ramos had me lined up, I'd have been toast if you hadn't pulled your John Wick act, emptying your gun while falling backwards."

The recounting of the incident, though accurate, still embarrassed Carlton. "I think I just lost my balance and was pulling the trigger to hold onto something."

"Whatever you say, Mr. Wick. But I say thank you."

Carlton smiled and shrugged, hoping to change the subject. It was time to steer it in the direction he wanted—no, that Reynaldo and Tino wanted—without spoiling the mood of the evening...but another look across the table at her eyes sparkling in the candlelight changed that plan.

Forget Reynaldo's problems! This is going way too well to worry about him!

Later that night, Heather changed the subject for him, but not before some energetic Mexico replay. "I wish I didn't have to go to work tomorrow."

"Call in sick."

"More like call in exhausted," she giggled. "Or heavily satisfied. But Stan might blow a gasket over that, so I'll just go in a bit late. I'm allowed to do that, since I've been working with my CI tonight, trying to get information."

"Is that what they call what we've been doing? Guess I've been out of touch."

"Yep. Seduction for information, that's the name of the game."

"After this, I'd give you any information I had, gladly. I'd even make up some to give you. Unfortunately, all the papers I looked through had nothing to do with anyplace north of New Braunfels, and it's a long way from North Texas."

That got a laugh. "I don't want information, just some cuddling. I've spent days working on this, and I'm sick of Operation Esmereld—oops, I wasn't supposed to let you know the name we've tagged it with."

"Well, you didn't, because I missed it. Sounded to me like you said you'd like to try something kinky." That got him a punch in the ribs. "Ow! Guess I misheard you."

In truth, he hadn't misheard, but it wasn't clear enough to be sure if she had stopped short of saying "Esmerelda" or "Esmeralda." One was a name in a remake of an old song during disco times; the other meant "emerald" in Spanish. Neither meant anything to Carlton in the context of a drug trafficker from North Texas, but he knew nothing of how—or why—police and military operations needed names. The thought gave him an idea to draw out more information.

"Why do operations need murky sounding names? Why not just 'Operation North Texas Guy?'"

"Beats me. A few of us talked about it one day in the break room, and somebody said it was a way to promote secrecy while boosting morale."

"And I thought that was the purpose of a paycheck. Shows what I know. But how is the name picked?"

"That same person said the military actually uses a computer program to come up with something that's got a nice ring to it, describes the particular operation, and hasn't been used before. Oh, and it has to allude to success.

"Another guy said the DEA does it differently. He said they use an acronym of a phrase alluding to the investigation, one that refers to the information we use to start the investigation or even the name of the informant, or a coded tip about the subject."

"I wonder if it ever actually helps in a case or a battle."

"Who knows? This is the government we're talking about, it doesn't have to be logical or make sense."

Carlton nodded in the dark, agreeing with her viewpoint on anything government-related and pleased that he had gotten at least a hint at what might prompt a moniker like "Esmerelda." Maybe Tino and Reynaldo could make sense of it. If not…well, it would take some time and thought, but he had a basic plan on where to begin—and it could wait until tomorrow. Right now, it was important to be a good CI and give the agent what she wanted—cuddling.

Santa Monica, Coahuila, Mexico, inside the home of Sebastian Chavez:

The kitchen of the Chavez home held nine men in addition to Chavez, a few seated at the small dining table, the rest standing around the perimeter walls. The men, all laborers for the Golfos, had arrived singly or in pairs after dusk, and the home owner had herded them into the kitchen knowing that La Señora Chavez would be at the church with her friends until almost nine o'clock. That gave the men two hours to talk about their plight and what could possibly be done.

When the sporadic meetings began, talk had centered upon simply leaving the employ of the vicious cartel henchmen. One, a middle-aged man named Romero Cano, had immediately followed through by complaining to a higher-up in the organization, then failed to show up for his appointed shift on a Wednesday. On the Friday following, he and his wife were found in their home by an adult daughter, throats slashed. The local police were summoned, but nothing had come of the investigation. The final police report cited a home invasion gone awry, and futile resistance by the Canos apparently had met with violence from the knife-wielding robbers.

Thereafter, the talks became angry, the younger, stronger men arguing for a plan to catch the overseers off guard, a concerted effort to overpower them, then report the ongoing smuggling activities, as well as the atrocities, to authorities outside the local police district. Trouble was, no one really knew who to contact or what might happen if they followed through with such a bold course. Although unspoken, all feared ending up like Roberto Cano and his wife.

Tonight, however, the mood was different from the moment a young worker named Candelario Vasquez took the floor. "A big ranch that lies almost two hundred kilometers from here, southwest of Amistad Reservoir, is owned by a man who is from los Estados Unidos," he announced, proud to be the bearer of such worldly news. The statement meant little to the crowd, since few of them had ventured more than fifty kilometers beyond the immediate area. Only two even knew of the big water conservation reservoir on the border with the United States.

"My aunt and uncle work on the ranch, they are caretakers for the owner," he explained. *"His name is Reynaldo Gomez. He was born here in Santa*

Monica and managed to get to El Norte as a child. He became successful and bought the ranch back here in Mexico as a way to maintain contact with the country of his birth. He visits it from time to time, and our situation here became known to him after my uncle told him about Romero Cano trying to leave the employ of the Golfos."

The roundabout explanation raised a look of confusion on several faces until Candelario explained further. "Romero Cano and his wife also worked on the Gomez Ranch a few years ago. My Uncle Alberto was not sure, but he thinks this Gomez might have married a woman from the Cano Family, so he was shocked to hear the news about Romero and his wife being killed.

"When my uncle explained the situation here, Señor Gomez said he might be able to help, but it will be a big risk. We would have to do something very bold. Actually, 'very foolish' is how my uncle described it."

The crowd looked expectantly toward the speaker, anxious to hear of a possible solution, no matter that his uncle had proclaimed it "foolish." They were all sick to death of being treated harshly, for poor wages and with no prospect of change in sight. Bold, foolish…what difference did it make? It was time to take action, just as it had become time to do something during each of the many tumultuous periods of Mexico's history. The collective look of inquiry didn't fail to get results from young Vasquez, who grinned as he delivered the punchline.

"Señor Gomez is willing to provide us with guns."

CHAPTER 7

The small town of Sabinal lay beyond Hondo, about sixty miles west of San Antonio on U. S. Highway 90, and Reynaldo's ranch was to the south, about ten miles out of town. He left the city before dawn on Monday to avoid traffic and arrived in Sabinal before eight o'clock for breakfast. By nine, he was at the ranch going over the trailer and studying the ideal arrangement for a compartment.

Tino rose early too, but went by the office to arrange things for the next few days. He made a list of stall keepers to be contacted for inventory orders and wrote checks for payment of several bills. He composed a brief note of instructions for Carlton regarding additional incoming weapons, then put the first of the deliveries, three AR-15s and two military-style ammo boxes, in the well-secured office closet before leaving town.

Arriving about two hours behind Reynaldo, he found his friend in a deep discussion with two Anglos, one wiry, older man and a younger, stout-looking youth, whom he assumed to be the ranch foreman and his helper. All three were standing at the rear gate of a cattle trailer, Reynaldo pointing and gesturing at the interior ceiling while getting headshakes from the wiry man and a doubtful stare from the youth.

Tino emerged grinning from his pickup and walked toward the meeting. "Looks like we have full agreement on how to load cattle," he said, peering into the trailer. "You're going to have them line up in order, like people do at the airport, to cut down on pushing and shoving."

"And with just about as much success," the wiry man replied, returning Tino's grin. "Last time I took an airplane, the damn people paid no attention to their boarding pass number, they pushed and shoved like a bunch of damn cows. Couldn't figure out why they were so set on getting on the plane in a hurry, since it wasn't going to leave until we all got seated anyway. That was two years ago when I had to fly to Memphis for a funeral. Never again."

"I don't fly often, thank God, but it's always like that. Only thing dumber than cows are people."

Reynaldo ignored the banter and introduced the new arrival. "Tino Perez, meet Gus Painter, my foreman, and his assistant, Zachary Thomas." While the men exchanged handshakes, he wasted no time in getting down to business. "Tino's going to be helping on this project, Gus, so cooperate and give him all the help he needs if I'm not here. And Zach, if Tino can't get away from his business, he may call on you to go into San Antonio and pick up some things. He'll give you the address of the flea market on Highway Sixteen."

From the rapid-fire instructions, Tino surmised the ranch hands knew about the plan already; apparently, Reynaldo had filled them in as soon as he had arrived. "So what did you come up with on a compartment?" he asked, peering into the trailer.

"We were just talking about that. I like the idea of a ceiling mount, a dropped ceiling so to speak, about six inches in depth and all the way across. Gus and Zach think the floor's best."

"Nobody likes to walk through cow shit, not if they can help it. I think a false floor is the way to go." It was the younger hand, Zach, taking the opportunity to further his argument. "Plus, the process of building it goes faster. Just weld some channel steel down on the existing floor, and tack quarter-inch steel diamond-plate on top of it. I can do that in a couple of days."

Tino nodded at the logic and rapidity of the young man's plan, then turned to the older man. "Gus?"

"I like the floor, but would use some channel on the bottom and weld three-sixteenths plate to it. Leave the existing floor alone. Don't want to change the height by much, not more than six inches, anyway. I think that'd be noticeable to someone who's been around cattle trailers. Underneath would be harder to spot visually, but I don't know about any x-ray equipment or shit like that."

Tino thought over the men's viewpoints and looked at Reynaldo. "Well, it's your trailer and you're the boss, but these guys make good points."

Reynaldo frowned and shrugged. "They do. But I'm going by the old 'out of sight, out of mind' thing. Most people don't look up nearly as much as they look down. Especially if they're about to wade through a bunch of cow shit. They'll be watching where they put their feet."

Gus nodded in agreement with that. "You're right about that, Reynaldo. But we have to grind the welds, paint it, make it look pretty normal, in case somebody *does* look up. So there's some extra time there. And you'd still be able to see fresh paint. On this old trailer, that'd be a red flag."

Reynaldo sighed. "Hell, maybe we just flip a coin. But two days is better than three or four, and we don't have time to wait for the thing to look well-used. Put it on top of the floor, but only five inches tall."

"Top of the floor it is, Boss. Zach, get the tractor and pull this thing into the long barn. I'll go get materials while you're firing up the welder."

Reynaldo, pleased that the question was decided and the project getting under way, thanked his employees and motioned for Tino to follow him to the ranch house, just a cabin really. Within minutes, coffee was brewing, and the pair sat down at a well-worn table to talk.

Tino looked at his friend across the table and grinned. "Well, you got them started. When I walked up, I thought I was seeing the designing discussions for a new space exploration module."

"I know. I went overboard, but I wanted everyone to think this thing through, come up with ideas and tell me something. It's the same thing when I ask Carlton for advice. He knows that I'm aware of everything he's telling me, but sometimes, I just want to hear a different voice say it."

"He buying that?"

"I think so. Besides, what's not to buy? We're not holding back anything from him." After a pause, he amended his statement. "Well, nothing he needs to know, anyway."

"True, but he may be pissed when he finds out you're not really arming those people just to cause a market crash in cocaine prices."

"That will likely be a result, so the other doesn't need to come out. And a lower price on product doesn't hurt our feelings, does it? And it shouldn't bother him, our profit margin is where his paycheck comes from. Nothing will change for him."

"Cecilia being your daughter didn't change anything about taking down Brujido Ramos, but he didn't like being left uninformed."

Reynaldo glanced at Tino and shook his head. "I don't understand that! Why should he care about either thing: whose daughter Cecilia is, or why we're giving guns to cartel laborers?"

Tino shrugged. "I don't know, maybe it's that Vietnam veteran thing. I think a lot of those guys got screwed by misinformation every time they turned around, and it became a part of their mentality, to be suspicious about the boss' plans for anything."

"You think we should tell him? Maybe he'll be completely on board with it then."

"Your operation, your call, but I think so. He's a sharp guy, and he's wondering why you're off on this risky venture to get lower prices on product. He thinks you should just raise the street price. We're getting good product, we got Ramos and his diluted shit off the street, so we can continue to raise it without a problem."

"I know, he told me that. Except the increase in street crime that he heard about from the DEA girl could cause us grief if S.A.P.D. cracks down on our customers."

"There is that possibility. But the real problem with Carlton getting pissed and leaving doesn't lie with this operation. Hell, you and I both know all the stuff he's been telling us, and 'advising' us about. And he knows that *we* know. That's why he's suspicious about this weapons thing, because he's sure there's more to it than what we're telling him."

Reynaldo shrugged. "Well, he's your employee, so let's tell him if you think that's the way to go."

"I think Carlton is very useful in other business situations, even if not so much in this one. He will be helpful in future jobs, so I don't want him leaving us. We'll let him know this one is personal, but has a positive business twist to it."

"I hope that's not the same approach they used on those guys in Vietnam. He'll really be pissed then, and we don't want that to happen."

Tino rose and carried his cup to the sink. Rinsing it, he turned to his life-long friend. "No, we don't. I'll tell him when we get back to the city. Right now, I want a tour of this ranch, conducted by *el jefe* himself."

Tuesday morning, Reynaldo and Tino watched over the ongoing construction of the trailer compartment. True to his word, Zach was making fast progress by using the floor as the starting point of the compartment. By ten o'clock, five-inch channel steel crisscrossed the floor, and Gus was busy measuring and marking the steel plate material for cutting and attaching to the base channel. It appeared the major portion would be completed by dark, and Reynaldo expressed his appreciation by going into town and ordering lunch for the men. Just before eleven, he pulled into the yard area outside the barn and honked his horn.

"You guys take a break and eat an early lunch," he called out, carting the big sacks of barbeque lunches to a picnic table outside the cabin. "Call the others in, too. Time for a picnic."

"I won't argue with that, Boss," Gus replied, tapping Zach on his welding helmet to alert him.

While both men were washing up, Tino carried a cooler with soft drinks to the table and took a seat while Reynaldo looked over the trailer again. From his expression, it was clear that he was pleased with the job. "Looks like your trailer will be ready before we get all the stuff to hide in it," Tino remarked. "I called Carlton, and he's had a bunch brought to the market by the people I dispatched to make the buys. So far, we've got seventeen long guns and eight handguns, plus ammo for all of them. Not as much ammo as I'd hoped for, though. We may have to buy some."

"That's okay. We can go to any of the big sports stores and get cases of two twenty-three and nine millimeter without causing any concern. Hell, every shooting enthusiast I know does that, and the price break makes it commonplace."

"You give any more thought to lead shielding against imaging equipment?"

"Yes, I've had Zach split some old lead plumbing pipe we had in the barn, straighten it into sheets and attach it to the front part of the compartment. The rear part will get a door, by the way. I decided to use the back of the compartment to place a bunch of water pipe and plumbing parts, so an inspector can open it up and take a look if the imaging shows anything suspicious. The weapons and ammo will be in front of that. It would be a major pain in the ass for them to remove all the crap I'm going to put in there just to take a look in the front."

Tino nodded in agreement. "As we've learned through the years, all smuggling depends on good technique, but also on people thinking everything is normal. In this case, plumbing parts being hauled this way are fine as long as there's nothing that looks like you're trying to hide something."

"It's the best we can do on short notice," Reynaldo agreed.

Suddenly Tino burst out laughing and slapped his friend on the back. "*Short notice?* Do you realize how much time we spent beating this damn trailer thing to death? First one design, then another. Hidden compartment, then doors. Top side, bottom side. Hell, Reynaldo, if we spent half that much time planning our main business, we'd be rich, right up there with the *Golfos*! We wouldn't be trying to pull off this grand scheme of yours."

Reynaldo looked at him, embarrassed, then grinned. "You're right. But I want this thing to work, or at least have a good chance. And while we're at it, maybe it will help that piss-poor little community we came from."

"And help us with our bottom line at the same time," Tino reminded him.

"Yes, that too."

Lunch usually consisted of a quick sandwich eaten in fifteen minutes, followed by a twenty-minute nap, but today's meal turned into a two-hour affair. The boss and his buddy sat at the table and ate with them, conversing easily about ranch work, cattle, and the weather with the entire crew of seven men. The two trailer workers needed the long break before getting back to the job and working late, since Reynaldo had earlier decreed that the project had to be finished by the end of tomorrow. Gus, Zach, and the rest were happy to take advantage of his rare lunch delivery and the chance to sit and shoot the breeze for a while.

Near the end of the picnic, Reynaldo sprang another surprise on his men. He wanted the trailer to be loaded with cattle as soon as the floor paint dried and taken across the border to the Mexico ranch. He appointed Gus and one of the Spanish-speaking hands, Omar Guzman, to make the trip. During the crossing, the men were to pay close attention to every move, every word of the border inspectors. Any nuances in the paperwork, any new angles to insurance requirements, or any imposition of a quarantine period would be noted for the real delivery trip some ten days hence. No mention was made of the true nature of the trip, and Tino figured Reynaldo had laid it out that morning and banished the subject from everyone's lips. It was simply referred to as *viaje segundo*, the "second trip."

Lunch complete and orders given, Reynaldo and Tino prepared to leave for Laredo, traveling in separate vehicles. Tino was going to do some inventory shopping, then leave his pickup at the vendor's warehouse in order to ride with Reynaldo to an important meeting, one that was crucial to the success of the venture.

The trailer was moving along nicely, weapons were being gathered at the flea market, and word had been leaked to the bottom rung of *Golfo* cartel workers. The weapons shipment, *el viaje segundo*, had been scheduled, with a dry run beforehand to check out any problems in crossing. The multi-faceted plan was coming together.

But none of that mattered if the downtrodden cartel workers didn't know how to use the guns, and use them well. It was time to talk to the trainers.

CHAPTER 8

Laredo's most venerable hotel, *La Posada*, sits on the north bank of the Rio Grande overlooking *Nuevo Laredo* across the water, but the entrance and lobby face Zaragoza Street and San Agustín Plaza. San Agustín Cathedral stands nearby, looking like the centuries-old house of worship it is and sounding the part, with magnificent bells calling the faithful to prayer before each Mass.

Lacking much appeal to the younger crowd, *La Posada* still attracts the most discerning of guests—moneyed people from Mexico and older, wiser accommodation seekers from *El Norte*. Its rooms might be considered small and outdated by young hipsters, and occasional maintenance issues make it beneath the dignity of a generation that appreciates nothing but faster Wi-Fi connections; however, fine cuisine, manicured grounds and impeccable service make it the hotel of choice for the type of clientele management values most—the ones with real money.

It was late afternoon when Reynaldo pulled up in front and turned his keys over to a valet parking attendant along with a twenty-dollar bill and instructions to keep the vehicle handy. He and Tino strode into the lobby and turned right into the main dining area. Spotting his target at the front corner table, he flashed his trademark smile and approached the two men seated there, Tino trailing close behind him.

One man, older and bulky of build with a florid complexion, stood and extended a big, calloused hand. The other, a younger Latino, was smaller and slight, a fact made known after he half-rose and nodded timidly. To an observer, he appeared uncomfortable in the setting, perhaps lacking in social grace, but he was following his companion's lead in an effort to fit in.

"Reynaldo! It's the bee's knees to see you again!" Clive Millstone shook Reynaldo's hand vigorously before peering around him to make eye contact with Tino. "And Faustino! Likewise, it's dog's bollocks to lay these tired eyes on you!" The slang-laced greeting was delivered with a thick British accent, one that didn't fail to entertain the two drug traffickers. South Texas and Northern Mexico didn't lend much opportunity to hear a real-life Englishman braying like a character from a swashbuckler movie.

"It's good to see you, Clive," Reynaldo replied. He looked toward the smaller man. "I'm Reynaldo Gomez. This is my associate, Faustino Perez."

"Gustavo Mendoza." The man's voice, deep and strong, belied his slight physical build, and his strong handshake took both of them by surprise.

"Gustav has been a good chap, hauling me around his fair country, showing me the sights," Millstone said. Lowering his voice he added, "He really knows his onions, and some are quite a sight to see, I must say!"

Gustavo Mendoza smiled at that and seemed to relax a bit. "I have been trying to educate *Señor* Millstone in the ways of my—*our*—country," he offered, stressing the plural possessive pronoun to include Reynaldo and Tino.

"Did you gentlemen want to eat now, or just have a drink or two?" Millstone asked.

"Tino and I had an early lunch, so we're good. But you two go ahead and eat, won't bother us a bit," Reynaldo answered.

"Not a chance. Nosh is good here, I'm sure, but we're skipping lunch and headed for the steakhouse here in the hotel for din-din, a place called The Tack Room. You two must join us. Besides, if we have another pint just now, I'll be plastered and good for nothing but a kip."

Uncertain as to the meaning of Millstone's prediction, Reynaldo opted to move the meeting on to business, starting with a change of venue to something private. "Let's take a ride first, look around Laredo. We can talk first and decide where to eat later."

The men rose and headed for the door. Millstone stopped by a nearby table and exchanged jovial pleasantries with a middle-aged couple, then joined them in front where the valet was delivering Reynaldo's replacement wheels, a white Suburban.

Once in the car, Millstone changed gears, dropping the British accent a couple of notches and shifting the folksy slang over to language more befitting his occupation. "How's the transport schedule looking? Gustav and I would like as much time as possible with every bloke who's involved in this pissing contest, so we need to get started ASAP."

Tino and Reynaldo exchanged glances at the change. It wasn't clear why Millstone had begun the meeting sounding like Winston Churchill's uncouth brother, but both noticed the man's ability to change his persona quickly, no doubt a valuable skill in his line of work and probably something he often practiced. Nonetheless, Reynaldo's curiosity surfaced; he needed to know as much as he could about his new hire. Surprises were for birthdays, not gun smuggling operations.

"Everything is progressing nicely, Clive, but first I have a request: tell us about your over-the-top British act in the restaurant."

Millstone laughed. "Oh, that! The people at the next table overheard me talking at the front desk and asked me where I was from. I felt it best to play the tourist from London, so all of a sudden, I'm a successful car park owner, off on a lark to this side of the pond. Turns out, it was the right move. They hailed from Liverpool, of all places, reason they picked up my accent, even if they are from the wrong side of the Mersey River. Wanted to talk my ear off about Jolly Old England, like we all met for tea and crumpets with the Queen Mum last week.

"Gave them my story of long holiday in *Monterrey*, hiring Mendoza here to show me around Mexico and accompany me over the border for a quick look at the Yank side of the river and meet up with a pair of guys I'd met at the airport in Mexico City. By the by, you two are trying to sell me a car park in *Monterrey*."

Reynaldo nodded, admiring the gunrunner's fast verbal footwork with his overly friendly countrymen, then proceeded with a quick update on the readiness of the trailer and accumulation of weaponry. After clarifying a few items with Millstone, he opened his phone calendar to continue. "Today's what, the seventh? There will be a trial run in the next few days, hauling cows only. If everything goes smoothly with that, I'll direct the weapons to be taken to my ranch on Friday, the eighteenth or Saturday, the nineteenth.

"However, the first group of men will be at the ranch this Friday night, the eleventh, and ready to begin training Saturday morning. They can stay for four days. And there are enough weapons to train them with, though they'll have to share."

Mendoza had a question. "How many men in each group?"

"They will rotate in, seven or eight at a time. The way their shifts are scheduled, twenty or twenty-one men are on duty at any given time. They're on call twenty-four/seven, so out of thirty guys, only those off duty can take off and go to the ranch during their five-day break."

Mendoza issued a warning. "Those cartel bosses, I know how they operate. I've had experience with them, none of it good. They are very harsh, they don't like guys out of sight even if they are not on duty, and certainly not out of their home town for any extended time. Those seven or eight need to have a good reason to be gone, in case someone goes around to check."

Reynaldo shook his head. "That part can't be helped much. We've agreed the training cannot take place anywhere near *Santa Monica*, where they all live. Someone would see or hear of it. My ranch is two hundred kilometers away, very remote, which is perfect for our needs. But these men lead very structured lives, and they can't come up with a good excuse to be absent from their homes and families for any extended period of days.

"But the good news is, these overseers are an independent group working for the *Golfos* under contract. They are not very professional, not like the ones you know. More like a bunch of thugs. They depend on bullying tactics and intimidation to keep everyone in line. I'm informed that off-duty staff aren't checked on at all."

Mendoza brightened at that. "That's good, very good. Each small group has to get at least four days of training."

"And that's terribly inadequate, as we all know," Millstone warned.

Mendoza agreed. "Green, untrained men, even young, physically fit ones, need at least *ten* days of intense weapons training to become even marginally familiar with handling a weapon. And that's pushing it. Twenty days would be better, thirty days ideal."

Again, Reynaldo shook his head. "Rotating everyone through that much training would take months. And then, they have to be trained together for a short time, right? We—they don't have that much time. They're at their breaking point."

"Did you get a good count on how many in the cartel force?" Millstone probed.

"Best number I can get is eighteen or twenty. My brother-in-law worked there for a while, and he passed that number to my ranch foreman, Alberto, several months ago. Since then, I am informed that the total number of men does not vary. Some come, some go, but the force is steady at about twenty."

"No offense, but is your brother-in-law reliable as to numbers?"

"No offense taken. He's dead. Killed by those *Golfo* wannabes when he decided to leave their employ. But to answer your concern, I believe so. He was almost forty years old, had some education, not prone to exaggeration or falsehoods."

Millstone nodded. His expression said he was about to say something conciliatory, but he caught himself. No need for apologies, because the inquiry was valid. And the response did not surprise him, since death was a constant companion, for allies and foes alike. In this case, a man's death had probably been the catalyst for this operation, the final tipping point. Millstone understood that fact very well. Like all mercenaries, he knew the human race to be brutal and bloodthirsty, always primed for payback. He had gone to war before over the foibles of mankind, but these days, he provided the training to kill. It was how he made his living.

He looked to Mendoza, then back to Reynaldo. "So pure numbers are on our side. But we all know how fast it goes to shit when the firefight starts. One of your men panics, the rest may fly like quail."

"I'm fully aware of that, and—"

"We will be providing several experienced men," Tino interrupted. "Five, possibly six of my men will come down. And they are very experienced. They more closely resemble rattlesnakes than quail."

Mendoza looked confused by the comparison until Reynaldo turned to him. "*Viboradores de cascabeles.*" *Vibrators of bells,* he explained, the rather quaint-sounding term used in Mexico for the dangerous, aggressive diamondback rattlesnake, known for shaking its rattles in warning before striking…sometimes. "But occasionally," he added, "rattlesnakes strike without any warning at all."

Gustavo Mendoza smiled, pleased with Tino's commitment.

The meeting continued for another hour, both sides exchanging all known details and questioning possibilities, probabilities, and complete unknowns. The operation was, they agreed, a risky venture for inexperienced personnel. Millstone and Mendoza both knew that the laborers, no matter their anger and iron will, would not be the best men for an armed attack on cartel overseers. Even if they were mere *Golfo* wannabes, the opposition were likely trained and *definitely* more brutal and experienced in violence than a group of poor, hard-working villagers with families. Both men took turns stressing the dire situation to Reynaldo and Tino, but neither was moved by their reasoning and call for caution.

Before taking the men back to their hotel, Reynaldo raised the subject of payment. "I have the second portion of your payment with me, Clive." He removed a padded envelope from inside his shirt and passed it over the seat.

Millstone took it and tucked it inside his jacket without opening it, then turned to smile at Mendoza. "I like dealing with people in this hemisphere, Gustav. Good capitalist environment, money-minded folks, these Yanks. Not like those bloody wogs in the Middle East, always hedging, dodging, pushing for a discount, or whining about a delay in getting their money to pay me."

Mendoza returned the smile. "Yes, I like this method of doing business also. I am anxious to get started with the first group of trainees so I can begin delivering what we are paid for." Leaning forward toward the front seats, he amended his statement. "Believe me *Señores*, I can deliver the training, but it will be up to your men to learn it well and quickly. This job does not provide for on-job-training. On the job is too late."

Reynaldo glanced over at Tino, then up to his rear view mirror to address the back seat occupants. "That part we understand very well. And I am sure you gentlemen understand that getting to spend your bonus money depends on those laborers understanding it and doing a good job. So train them well."

"You can bet on that, Reynaldo. Remember, our arses will be on the line out there, too."

Business done, Tino changed the subject. "Let's go check out the Tack Room. I haven't eaten there in years."

"Good idea," Reynaldo agreed. "I happen to know a couple of guys with lots of cash who might buy us a steak."

CHAPTER 9

Reynaldo and Tino stayed overnight in Laredo, then decided to stay in the city the next day to visit mutual friends. On Wednesday morning, Reynaldo insisted that they both go back to the ranch to check progress before returning to San Antonio, drawing a groan from Tino. "Okay, I'll follow you back. But let's look it over and get back before dark. I need to unload this stuff at the vendors' stalls and collect some money."

They arrived to find the trailer alteration was done and the new paint already drying nicely. Reynaldo, of course, was anxious to load cows in it for the test run, but Gus persuaded him to wait another two days, minimum, complaining that Reynaldo needed to leave the project to him and Zach. "This is what you pay us for, so let us do it right, okay?" The boss relented and walked away grumbling.

Tino chided him for his antsy behavior. "Damn, you're like a kid before Christmas! Let these guys do their thing and load the cattle when it's good and dry."

"Okay, okay. Meanwhile, you can help me load some hay bales. I've got twenty bales sold to a guy in Hondo, so we'll drop them off on the way home."

"Of course. I knew there was another reason you wanted me to come back here with you."

Tino used his pickup to pull a hay trailer through the field, and the two loaded and secured the sold bales in less than an hour, "not bad for two old *peones*" as Tino put it.

After lunch, they left the ranch, but not before another smattering of instructions from Reynaldo and an eye roll from his foreman. "We got it, Boss, we'll take care of everything and make the test run on Friday. Just get that hay delivered will you?" Gus pleaded, earning a grin from Tino before a final wave.

It was mid-afternoon when the pair got back to the flea market. Tino distributed inventory and collected invoices while Reynaldo retired to the office building to check on weapons. Carlton had just finished putting another pair of AR-15s in the closet and opened the door again to show him the growing stack. "That makes twenty-one long guns and ten pistols, plus ammo for both. We'll probably need to buy a lot more ammo, unless some seller drops a bunch on us with the next five or six weapons we get."

"Tino said he would take care of that. It's amazing that his group of buyers have done this much, this quick. I thought it would take weeks to get enough weapons together."

"He doesn't lack for cooperation in the community," Carlton responded as the office door swung open and Tino entered.

"I heard the word 'cooperation.' I hope it's a good thing in this case," he said, moving to his desk with a handful of papers, checks and cash. "How's the weapons collection coming along?" he asked Carlton, gesturing toward the open closet.

"It's going well. I was just telling Reynaldo about the cooperation you get from the community. In this case, I was referring to the quick response on getting them bought and delivered. Faster than I expected."

"Yes, everyone does his or her share when it's time to step up. I've never had a problem with getting people in the community to get on any project I give them, no excuses or questions. In return, they trust me to make good decisions and look out for their welfare. I wish that part worked perfectly, but it doesn't," he added. "Oh, how did your date with DEA girl go?"

Coming on the heels of Tino's description of his role as a successful *patron*—which Carlton had witnessed before, he didn't need a tutorial—the quick change of subject caught him off guard. He did a quick mental replay of the previous night, and while he didn't answer immediately, the smile on his face was a giveaway to his two nosy companions.

"That look tells me how it went," Reynaldo remarked with a smirk.

"Okay, Lover Boy, all the juicy details," Tino quickly demanded.

Clearly, the two were piling on, but Carlton was already shaking his head. "No details for you two old gossips. I did try to get some info, though. She had a couple of drinks, but wasn't as tipsy as I thought, and she caught herself before divulging anything but the code name for the North Texas guy operation. And I barely caught it. It doesn't make any sense to me, so maybe I misunderstood what she said." He waited a couple of beats to get the reaction he wanted, looking from Tino to Reynaldo.

"Wait, let me guess," Tino said sarcastically. "They call it 'North Texas Guy Operation.' I'm glad you were able to pin down that critical piece of information."

"Nope. You're wrong. I asked the very question about why operations aren't just named aptly, as you just suggested. They aren't, she said, because it's a government thing, so it doesn't have to make sense. Sometimes it's related to the case, sometimes not. Sometimes it refers to the main informant or tipster, but not necessarily. It might be an acronym for the subject matter at hand. It only has to convey a mood of secrecy and success."

"Well, we're dying to hear what the DEA came up with for this one," Reynaldo said with mock sincerity. Like Tino, his tone said he didn't expect much of a revelation.

"Esmerelda." After uttering the word, Carlton continued to look at the pair and was surprised by their reaction—or lack thereof. For over five seconds, the silence in the tiny office was complete, almost palpable, while Tino and Reynaldo just stared at him.

Finally, Reynaldo asked the obvious. "Are you sure?"

"No, I'm not. I already told you, I barely caught it, had to play it over in my mind, because I didn't want to ask her to repeat it. Remember—"

"No, no, of course not!" Reynaldo interrupted, his voice sounding panicky. "But when she said it—"

This time, Carlton interrupted him and explained the setting, the mood, and his take on the inappropriateness of asking for a repeat of pillow talk. "Especially since she'd had a few drinks, wasn't supposed to be talking out of school, and wasn't going to say it again anyway."

"So you thought it over and came up with 'Esmerelda?'" Now it was Tino's turn to interrogate.

"That's about it. Could have been something else, but what the hell rhymes with Esmerelda? And what phrase would result in an acronym like that, with nine letters?" Carlton's tone told them he was nearly done explaining. "Why? What's so impossible about it being code-named Esmerelda?" he asked, again looking from one face to the other.

"Esmerelda is my wife's name." Reynaldo said it quietly, but his voice had a touch of steel.

Now, it was Carlton's turn to stare in silence. After a few seconds, he shook his head. "It's got to have an explanation, then, something other than the usual ways law enforcement or the military comes up with code names.

"Or it's another red herring. Maybe they got a list of spouses' names of suspects, and they threw this one out…" his voice trailed off as he realized the improbability of the ploy working. Besides, the atmosphere in the bedroom hadn't lent itself to watching his expression at the mention of… well, *anything*. He tried another tack. "Is Esmerelda a common name?"

Both crime bosses shrugged. "Not that common," Tino opined. "But not rare, either."

"I have only known two in my life," Reynaldo concurred. "And I married one of them. And now, an operation to bust me has the same name? After you find out they sometimes use an informant's name for the operation?"

"*Sometimes*, Reynaldo, not in every case. Remember the other ways of coming up with names—"

Tino interrupted him. "Whatever method they have of naming operations, this is not good news, Reynaldo. Could the DEA or the *Policía Federal* be putting pressure on Esmerelda with one of their joint operations? Is she involved in anything, any facet of your business that could get her compromised?"

Reynaldo shook his head emphatically. "No. I mean, it's not impossible that she knows about my other business, but she's only been exposed to the construction side of things. That's where the money comes from, certainly not the ranches, and she knows that. She makes a point of reminding me that she would live with me if we could live in Dallas, but not Wichita Falls. I tell her my business is centered there, I can't stay in Dallas. So, she stays in *Cuernavaca* at our summer home, or in *Mexico City* with her parents."

"So she has no other connection to anything in the States?" Carlton asked.

Reynaldo sighed deeply. "Only me. Her husband in Wichita Falls, which is in North Texas." His resigned tone said he wished none of the connected circumstances applied to him.

"Okay, so what do we do with this information, which may or may not have anything to do with your wife?" Carlton asked, hoping it was the latter, but suspecting otherwise. He had already calculated a couple of possibilities that he wouldn't share with them, not yet anyway.

"When will you see the DEA girl again?"

"This weekend, I hope. And remember, I need to feed her a tidbit or two so Stan Ikos will think he's getting something."

"Maybe we should come up with something that alludes to this code name, something that will get her to divulge something further," Reynaldo suggested.

Tino disagreed. "I think it would be best if he told her he did some more sneaking around, looking at my personal phone bills and correspondence, not just flea market stuff. Tell her you've been checking for *anything* related to North Texas, but nothing has turned up yet. That might cool their jets a little bit. Or better yet, it might get her to show more of the DEA's hand."

"Yeah, and hopefully that will satisfy Ikos' appetite for useful activity from Heather's new CI," Carlton said. "I don't want her jackass boss ordering her not to spend any time with me, so I'd better produce."

"Can he really do that?" Reynaldo asked, surprised.

"Maybe. He talks a good story about her job being in jeopardy because of my involvement in the Ramos shootout and her failure to document me then as a CI. He knows there was some joint planning, he just can't prove it."

Then he added the possibility he had mulled over several times. "Or it may be her way of giving me the door while laying the blame elsewhere—on her mean old boss and company policy."

"Wait a minute! You really think she's just using you to find out stuff? I thought she was hot for you."

Carlton grinned. "If not, she's done a good job of fooling me, but no matter what, I have to face the age difference. We do seem to click together, but I passed my 'sell-by' date a long time ago. Either way, she's pretty smart, so I've got to stay on my toes."

Carlton's wry response skirted the fact that he was almost certain she was using him, attraction or not. Regardless of their torrid times together, the attractive young woman could easily land a better prize than he represented, and furthering her career had to be higher on her list of priorities than sleeping with an older man. He knew he had to have realistic expectations when it came to this lovely, but unlikely, affair. Furthermore, he needed to keep a clear head—that is, think with the big one, not the little one—while he was delving for information about the Administration's interest in Reynaldo Gomez.

In summary, his relationship with a sharp DEA agent (plus her arrogant boss' demands) and the two drug kingpins before him made his situation akin to walking a tightrope.

At least it can't get any more complicated than it already is…can it?

CHAPTER 10

The answer to Carlton's self-query came later in the same day. After batting around the code-name mystery a while longer, they broke up to tend to other things—Tino claiming pressing business matters and Reynaldo not fooling anyone by leaving quickly after a muted phone conversation.

Carlton worked around the market another hour, then headed to his own apartment. He wanted to text Heather with his report of snooping around Tino's office (again) for any connection to North Texas and see if she responded with any hint of the DEA's source. Then he hoped for a quiet evening by himself, maybe watch old episodes of *Rawhide* and *Wanted Dead or Alive*, television from a time when it was easier to tell the good guys from the bad ones.

He smiled when he spotted Reynaldo's loaner car—another Lexus—in the parking lot next to Paula's Mustang, confirming his guess about his quick departure from their meeting. It appeared that being out of town for a few days had proven the old saying about absence and hearts growing fonder. That led Carlton to wonder about the wife in Mexico. What was she like, this faceless woman named Esmerelda? His unvoiced suspicions at the meeting asserted themselves again as he recalled Reynaldo's current pastime in the apartment across the way. It was an ugly possibility, and one that Reynaldo might easily be too blind to see. That much Carlton knew from first-hand experience.

If Paula Hendricks knew Esmerelda's name—and surely she did— could she be the DEA's informant? Would she do something as crazy as calling in a tip claiming to be Reynaldo's absent (and jealous) wife? A risky game to play with one's lover—he might go to prison—but not one Paula would be above playing. She had pulled a similar stunt with Carlton, diming him to Faustino Perez, drug kingpin, whom Carlton had clipped for a lot of money at their first encounter. Only by leaving the country for a year did he avoid becoming another statistic in the city's murder tally. The bizarre circumstances that eventually led to a prolonged affair with her, plus his current employment and friendship with Perez supported the insane idea that she could be the informant, the instigator for the DEA's investigation.

What a tangled web we weave...

Abandoning the ongoing drama around him, Carlton propped his feet up, turned on the television, and texted Heather's burner phone about his sneaky efforts around Tino's office failing thus far to reveal evidence of any business north of San Antonio itself. He ended by asking if she or the DEA knew the specific town or city from which the "North Texas guy" hailed and promised to concentrate on any documentation to or from that location.

Homework done, he surfed for westerns, but found *Star Trek* and *Star Trek Next Generation* episodes back-to-back and settled in for what he hoped would be a peaceful evening. It wasn't to be.

Around eight o'clock, a knock at the door roused him from a nap that might have extended until three in the morning, his usual wake-up time. He stumbled to the door and found both Reynaldo and Tino smiling, apparently at having caught him in a natural bachelor environment, clad only in underwear and asleep before the TV.

"Getting your beauty rest?" Tino asked. "You sure need it."

"I had a hard day," he yawned. "The boss is a slave driver. Come on in and tell me what's so important in the middle of the night."

The two walked in, and Carlton ushered them toward the kitchen barstools, the only place in the small apartment that would accommodate visitors. He swiveled the recliner toward them and looked inquiringly at the pair, who had suddenly fallen silent. "What's up?"

Tino and Reynaldo exchanged glances, alerting Carlton that *something* was up, and it probably spelled trouble. Reynaldo started to speak, but Tino cut in. "We wanted to give you more information about the gun shipment. I told Reynaldo you needed to know the entire story, because you got your panties in a wad the last time you didn't have all the information."

Carlton shifted uneasily in the chair, trying to wake up and choose his words carefully before speaking. "Yeah, well, I *did* wonder why everyone chose to leave me in the dark about the entire Ramos story. I had to find out everything for myself…which turned out okay, since my homework is *my* responsibility. That way, I can only blame any problems on myself."

Reynaldo spoke up, sounding careful in his wording as well. "Would it have made any difference in the way you handled the exchange for Cecilia? I mean, if we—I—had told you about me and Paula, our past relationship…" He left the sentence hanging, as though unsure how to phrase it any better.

"I don't know," Carlton confessed. "And we never will know now, will we? But there might have been some options for consideration."

Reynaldo nodded in agreement, but Tino cut in. "Look, Brujido Ramos was a maniac. He loved violence, or at least the concept of being like the big boys to the south of us. It was going to be a gun battle, no matter what you knew going in. And you knew that going in, right?"

"Oh, it occurred to me, yes," came the sardonic reply. "So maybe it wouldn't have changed my plan. You'll have to excuse my being upset over getting my ass shot up, though."

Hearing the use of a crude word told Tino that Carlton was getting steamed, and he moved to steer the conversation away from the fact that he, Tino, had lied to Carlton, telling him that Ramos had insisted on him being the bag man, although he'd done nothing of the sort. He set out to bolster his case and cover the tricky maneuver. "I certainly didn't want you to get shot, Carlton, not in the ass *or* your knee. But you made yourself the obvious trigger man by your performance at the car wash shootout. It wasn't going to be easy, but we don't have anyone else who could shoot that well."

"Oh, I think I get it now! But let me guess: if it were easy, you'd have sent a girl scout with a note pinned to her shirt, right?" Tino's smirk told Carlton he'd only succeeded in validating his subterfuge with his sarcastic response. "Anyway, that's done, but what's this information about the weapons deal that will keep my panties from getting wadded up in my crotch?"

"It's about more than getting better prices on product." It was Reynaldo, speaking up as though taking full responsibility for the past panty-wadding. He took a breath and began. "Tino and I were born in *Santa Monica*, a little town—hell, just a village, really—where the entire labor force lives. The cartel bosses—they're not really members of the *Golfos*, they're just a splinter group who contracts the job—treat them like dirt, using brutal scare tactics to keep the workers in line, whether they need it or not. My brother-in-law tried to quit, and they killed him and his wife. That was the final straw. We're going to help the workers retaliate before anyone else gets killed for nothing."

Carlton blinked. "This way, they at least get killed for *something*?"

Reynaldo didn't hesitate in replying. "Exactly."

"Okay," he said slowly. "So you're taking on a drug cartel for personal reasons, and if your townsfolk should win, it will result in lower prices too?"

"That's the plan. But I—Tino and I—would have done this anyway, even if the prospect of getting a better deal on product weren't possible."

"Won't the main group, the real *Golfos*, be the ones controlling your pricing, not the laborers?"

"The shitheads running it now are skimming and pumping up *my* prices to cover the shortfall. In other words, I'm paying to have a bunch of poor people treated like slaves and my relatives killed. I've had it up to here." His voice rose an octave as he drew a line across his forehead.

Carlton didn't know Reynaldo that well, but it was clear that the man, drug trafficker or not, was set on a humanitarian act of avenging the mistreatment. Whether or not it affected the price of his product purchases might be a lesser factor in the equation. Still, it seemed a dangerous route, taking on a group of cartel enforcers with a bunch of amateurs. He thought a moment before speaking. "Would it be a better option to pass the word along to the big guys that their contractors have been skimming? From what I've heard, the payback would be swift and final."

Reynaldo shook his head. "My brother-in-law—his name was Romero Cano—tried that about a week before he decided to quit. He may have approached the wrong person, or the *Golfos'* representative didn't believe him. Or maybe the guy he talked to went straight to the enforcers and asked them 'what the hell was going on, what was this Cano guy talking about?' Whatever took place, it cost him his life. And his wife's too—Esmerelda's sister.

"You have to understand, Carlton, there is absolutely no honor among this bunch. The one Romero approached may have been taking a cut from the enforcers himself and tipped them off, or he may have killed Romero and Ana himself.

"There's not a way to do it without an overwhelming show of force; in fact, killing all of the enforcer crew. Even if I were to approach the head of the *Golfos* personally, he would just think I was another small player trying to cause a problem, to oust his contractor group, or carry out my personal vendetta. I am, of course, but he doesn't care about that. He only worries about the profit. Anyone else's problems are just that—someone else's problem.

"Believe me, if there were a bloodless way to do this, I would be all for it. But the laborers are sick of it, and they are trapped into the job, they can't quit. I'm afraid they will try something on their own, even with sticks and rocks if they can't get guns. That would really be a massacre, so they are going to get guns."

Carlton nodded in understanding. The explanation made sense, more sense than the half-baked idea of an armed uprising to effect lower prices. At least the revenge angle was logical—Carlton himself had pulled off an act of revenge years earlier, one that had been observed by Randall (Big Mo) Morris, a local thug. Impressed, the fat gangster had approached him about employment the same night. The informal interview on a dark San Antonio back street had resulted in his long career of killing people for money.

His old memory was interrupted by Tino. "Look, Carlton, we're small players compared to even the minor cartel groups in Mexico," he explained. "It's not often we would have a chance in a situation like this, but the group handling that area aren't very professional. They have guns, they're untrustworthy and plenty dangerous.

"But they aren't in the same league with the *Golfos*. The reason the *Golfos* put up with them is because the area isn't a hotbed of activity. No one else really wants to be stuck there, running product from a small town in the middle of nowhere to a warehouse in *Nuevo Laredo*. So the *Golfos* let them do as they please, as long as the product gets moved to the warehouse when it's ready for transport."

"How are the laborers going to pull this off? I mean, is your guy Millstone going to show them how to shoot and attack? Can he train your guys in time?"

"Remember, I told you he has an associate—his name is Gustavo Mendoza—who's going to train them," Reynaldo interrupted. He briefly explained the training schedule, the shift workers going to his ranch for intensive training in groups before a final dry run with all present. Carlton listened intently and tried to maintain a neutral expression, but a doubtful look crept onto his countenance as the plan was described.

Seeing the look, Tino took over. "We know this sounds shaky to someone as careful as you are. You would have these guys training for a couple of years. We—the laborers—don't have that long.

"This Mendoza is tops in his field, just like Millstone. He knows the training period is short, but says he can do it. We are paying a lot of money, and those two are involved right up to their eyeballs, even in the attack.

"They have two incentives. One, they will be paid a big bonus if they are successful, and those two know all about that incentive. Two, if they aren't successful, they are probably going to die in the effort, so staying alive is the other incentive."

Carlton looked at him in surprise. "They're *that* dedicated? Or so hard up for money they'll go into a gun battle with undertrained partners? That's just nuts, Tino! I didn't ask you before, Reynaldo…where did you find these two maniacs?"

Tino gestured back toward Reynaldo, who smiled at the apt description of his two newest employees. "It took a lot of research, a lot of very *quiet* research. I found Millstone first, and he recommended Mendoza as a guy he'd done a lot of work with."

Carlton took the vague non-answer to be a subtle dodging of his question, but he managed to keep his face devoid of expression. Besides, it didn't make any difference where his bosses had come upon the two mercenaries, but it was clear that they were planning to reenact *The Magnificent Seven*. It was an old story, done many times in every culture: poor, downtrodden folks assisted by a gutsy band of guerillas in order to bring justice and righteousness to the masses, against huge odds…the eternal story of good triumphing over evil. That's just what everyone wants, right?

Yeah, great entertainment in the theater, but in real life? Good luck!

CHAPTER 11

The end of the week had seen a great deal of activity in weapons delivery. By Friday evening, Carlton had stored thirty-one long guns and fourteen pistols in the closet, along with hundreds of rounds of ammunition. The next day, Saturday, Tino and Reynaldo took separate vehicles and ferried about half of the arsenal to the Sabinal ranch and placed them in three outbuildings. The rest stayed in the city; however, at Reynaldo's instruction, a few remained locked in the janitor's closet and the rest moved to various storage rooms throughout the flea market until the date for smuggling them to Mexico drew near. By spreading them out, he contended, a search and seizure, fire, theft—any unforeseen event—wouldn't involve all the guns, and the operation could go ahead as planned.

Carlton thought loss of the weapons by theft was unlikely—who would break into the private office of Faustino Perez?—but he had to admire Reynaldo's commitment to the success of his venture by guarding against every possible problem or delay. It reminded him of his earlier career, when careful planning was his utmost priority, almost an obsession. It had served him well.

Although unbidden to do so, Carlton kept a list of the weapons, ammunition, the procurer, and the date delivered in case Tino wanted to check on how his money was being spent. The exercise was mainly to satisfy himself of doing his job, because his observations over the past couple of years told him that any misuse of Perez' money was out of the question. The relationship between members of the community and *El Patrón* was symbiotic; they depended on each other and, quaint as the term might seem these days, loyalty between the two was unquestionable.

Despite the expanded explanation they had given him, he continued to wonder about the near fanaticism Reynaldo and Tino exhibited over this project—bad one that it was, in his opinion—and what had driven two smart, no-nonsense crime bosses to conjure up such a plan, embrace it, and most importantly, finance it.

The cost of the weapons probably wasn't much, maybe twelve or fifteen thousand dollars. Then there were expenses involved in shipping them via the ranch: cattle trailer conversion, disguising the movement with cattle hauling, and paying the ranch foreman and others a nice bonus for the risk in hauling the stuff to Mexico. But the two mercenaries—trainers?—whatever Millstone and Mendoza were—had to be charging a hefty price to take part in this heady proposition.

It still eluded Carlton as to why the pair of experienced drug traffickers would take such a chance with this bold plan to overthrow cartel gang bosses, even if they weren't the most professional bunch in the business. The altruistic angle of helping their old home town citizens just didn't seem like enough incentive, even if a successful conclusion resulted in better working conditions *and* lower product prices. However, he wasn't in any position to question the matter further. He'd voiced his opinion, given a few helpful tips on the details, and was keeping up with procurement of the tools to do the job.

Of greater importance, he thought, was the nagging question of the DEA's interest in the "new player" in the city. By all appearances, the federal agency held some information about Reynaldo Gomez, and those appearances became a lot more serious when the operation to uncover his activities had the same name as his wife. Whether a mistake, an intentional red herring or a coincidence, the mystery needed to be solved before the powerful law enforcement agency flexed its muscles in Reynaldo's direction.

He'd arranged to meet with Heather on Saturday evening, when he hoped to learn a few details of the DEA's knowledge, but he didn't count on it. A slip-up like revealing the operation name probably would not happen again. At best, maybe he could learn the actual town or city the new player supposedly hailed from, and if it turned out to be Wichita Falls, Reynaldo would do well to cease activity and disappear for a while. The thought gave him an idea, one he would put to Reynaldo when and if he learned more from Agent Colson.

After a few text exchanges on Saturday afternoon, they agreed to meet at the old beer and burger joint on Broadway, right where Mulberry crossed it and entered Brackenridge Park. The venue was fine for an informal date, and the noise level assured privacy, no matter the subject discussed or how loudly they discussed it.

Carlton had a deuce table by the window facing Broadway when Heather arrived, running a few minutes late and looking a bit harried. "Sorry, I went by my office to get shoes I'd left under my desk. Stan was there, going over files, and I couldn't get away from him. He wanted to talk, and I finally just had to make a break, or I'd still be there."

Carlton half-stood as she plopped down opposite him before he could pull out her chair. "Glad I missed out on that meeting. What was old Stan so wound up about this time?"

"Oh, the usual," she replied, exasperated. "'*Drug-related criminal activity is running rampant in our city, and what are we doing about it?*' This is while he's pounding on the table, his voice getting louder by the second." The look on her face said the question was an ongoing mantra from her boss.

Carlton had experienced Ikos' verbal delivery first-hand, and he smiled at her expression. "Okay, I'll try to be nicer about asking the question than he was, but what *are* we doing about it?"

"What the Administration always does: follow up on leads, check our sources, form a new task force, invent a new approach to figuring out who's who…business as usual on all fronts." Her look said she had just quoted the party line response fed to every over-zealous Agent in Charge throughout the agency.

"You ever think further about a change in careers?" he asked, recalling that she had alluded to a possible career change many months before, not long after he'd met her and her partner. She'd had a different boss then, a dirty cop, a real hard-ass named Tim Hunnicut, who was milking an informer who worked for Tino Perez. He'd taken early retirement in the form of a car bomb, along with the informer. Her new boss, this Stan Ikos, was a blowhard, but nothing like Hunnicut, so maybe her chagrin at the job was temporary.

Griping about your job is an American tradition!

She sighed before answering. "Not really. I mean, I think about it, but not seriously enough to take the first step."

"And what would that be? The first step?"

She grinned at him. "Deciding I can live on less money than I do now, for starters. Plus, I'd be giving up a lot on my retirement by quitting now. This isn't a bad gig in those two departments. I make decent money, a lot more than I could by going into a completely different field, because I'd have to start over, learn to do something else. And the retirement is good, but I have to stay to make it worthwhile for spending the last thirteen years at it."

"So you'd have to go into something different? Something besides law enforcement?"

"Yes. It wouldn't make sense to take another law enforcement job. The DEA is a big organization, with all the best tools, the best technology, the most prestige—it's the best there is. Anything else would be a step down and just doing the same work with fewer resources. I'd just as well stay where I am." The last statement sounded resigned, almost forlorn.

Carlton nodded at her logic, then moved to change the subject. "Well, let's forget about all that for a while. Are you hungry?"

"Starving. What's good here?"

"I always have a burger and a beer, but I expect everything is edible. This place is pretty popular, as you can see. So I don't think they put out anything terrible."

They both settled on burgers and beers, skipped the fries, then ordered dessert instead. The conversation turned to family history—hers, not his—which resulted in a few laughs as he learned more about the agent's personal life.

They'd covered the basics in Mexico—born in Oklahoma, a sister and two brothers, parents still living in Tulsa. Now she expanded the story: for the most part, it was typical middle-class America, Oklahoma style. She'd grown up in Tulsa; her dad had been a cop, and mom was a nurse. The four kids led normal Midwest lives, even while dodging tornadoes and going to rodeos, "being regular Okie hillbillies," as she put it.

She'd attended Oklahoma State and majored in Criminal Justice. Following up with two years of post-graduate work in related subjects, she was a shoo-in for a job with the Oklahoma State Police. After a year of clerical work, she was sick of it and applied with the Drug Enforcement Administration. Again, the right education and grades resulted in a job interview, followed up by an acceptance letter two weeks later. Determined not to be stalled in the same mundane tasks again, she managed to get on the fast track to be a field agent from the start.

"And I've been at it for almost thirteen years. So, there you have it, the life and times of Heather Colson. Pretty boring, huh? Especially after you suggested we forget it for a while."

Carlton smiled at her, pleased that the cruise on Memory Lane had subtly brought them back to her job, as he wanted. Getting her to the subject of "North Texas guy" couldn't happen without her job being somewhere in the mix. "*Boring*? Aren't you forgetting an action-packed day in Park North Mall a few months ago?"

She grinned at him. "Yeah, I guess boring is the wrong word. I just mean it—my career, that is—has been so...*textbook* in its progression. And now, it's *predictable*, even when I have a successful bust. Because no matter how many victories I get, the boss is predictable; he always wants more points on the board."

"That's what all bosses do. And your job's secure, even if your boss is a piece of work sometimes. I can attest to that. But that goes with any job.

"I think your problem is this: you're an adrenaline junkie. No matter the amount of action, you keep waiting for the next buzz. In your case, it's the next bust, the next arrest. It's your form of intoxication, Heather. That's why you barely hesitated before agreeing to help me with the Ramos handoff."

She thought about it for a moment. "I did go for it pretty quickly, didn't I? Even though I knew it was against Administration protocol."

"And you didn't have qualms about getting Rex and Cho to help you. You talked them into taking the same risk in order to perform the mission. In the military, that shows leadership. And I'm certainly glad you and your two co-workers were there to help me out. I'm just sorry we got holes shot in us in the process."

She didn't respond, but sat quietly, obviously reliving the life-threatening events in the underground garage that led to a hospital stay and painful recuperation before enjoying the accolades and celebrity of the successful bust.

"So maybe you've got a future in a leadership position with the Administration," he continued. "You could do the Agent-in-Charge job, couldn't you? That might stave off boredom for a while. And you could be the first AIC to be unpredictable."

She laughed at that. "Maybe so. I'd have to really think that one over. AIC is a big deal, with lots of perks, but lots of problems."

"Oh, I'm sure! Look at Ikos. He's got a major perk just seeing you every day."

That brightened her. "That's sweet, and I'm glad you think that." Turning mischievous, she added, "With that perk, what *problem* could he possibly have?"

"Um…just seeing you every day?" he asked with a pained expression on his face.

She reached around the tiny table to jab Carlton in the ribs, but he deflected the shot and grinned at her. "Just kidding. Seriously, I understand what you're saying about your career being textbook, almost following a script. But it happened because you had good parents, a good education, good grades, and the drive to get where you are now. Seems to me you've got things pretty well in order."

She shrugged. "Maybe now. But I hit a few rough patches along the way that didn't have anything to do with a career."

Carlton waited for more, but she seemed hesitant to elaborate. He looked at her questioningly. "Want to tell me about it?"

"I was married by my second year at college. He was in pre-law, determined to be a hot-shot defense lawyer like his dad. We had some pretty intense discussions about the justice system, how it works—or *didn't* work, in my opinion. It was okay for a while, because we both enjoyed verbal contests."

Carlton was surprised. "I didn't know you were married! Guess we didn't get around to that in Mexico."

"Guess not. You didn't mention that you ever married, so I didn't bother to bring mine up. Thought it might spoil the mood."

"The mood in Mexico was perfect, Heather."

"Yes, it was. I think it was exactly what we both needed." She looked at him closely, getting a smile as both fell silent for a moment before she continued.

"I soon found out how argumentative he could be, so he was probably going to be a good lawyer. But along with that, he turned surly when any discussion didn't go his way. That tactic extended to talking about our future, and I saw I'd made a mistake by not finding out more before we married, like he wanted a whole bunch of kids. That wasn't what I wanted, certainly not right away.

"Anyway, after a while he turned downright mean. He became a bully, even shoved me around a few times when we had a disagreement. That did it; we were divorced after less than a year."

Carlton looked at her, feigning surprise this time. "Wow! You almost made a whole year? Why so long?"

She laughed bitterly. "I couldn't get out sooner, that's why. Anyway, enough of my story. I want to know more about Carlton Westerfield."

"So do I. But except for a few exciting interludes, he qualifies for boring. Or maybe just mundane. Besides, I'd bet you've used the DEA's substantial clout to check up on me, so you already know all about me."

She again displayed the mischievous look. "Well, I might have run a check or two, but I didn't find out nearly enough. Oddly, even the stuff I found was pretty thin, generic—"

"Boring, you mean. Not much to know beyond what you saw. And I have to keep a little bit back, try to stay a mystery man, or an adrenaline junkie like you will drop me like a bad habit."

"That's not true! I want to know more about your personal life, Carlton, and not about the military, or your temporary job at the newspaper after that. For instance, why you never married. Or, apparently, never wanted kids."

Carlton looked up at her with a sly grin. "You can ask that after just telling me your experience in that department? What a mystery!"

Undeterred, she continued, albeit in a different direction. "You really are a bit of a puzzle, Carlton, and not just your personal history or your love life." She paused, looking at him intently.

"Oh? Like what?" he asked cautiously, wondering where this line of inquiry was headed.

"For instance, how about the fact that you have no record for a hospital admittance in your entire life, though I know your knee had to entail a few surgeries and rehab. Care to explain that?"

"Faulty recordkeeping? I don't know." Carlton kept a straight face, but was alerted by the quick segue from long-past history to a few months ago.

She pouted at the non-answer, and he marveled at her ability to shift and change in seconds. It also renewed his vigilance against revealing anything he didn't want her to know. She was very good at probing and finding out on her own. He had to be careful about bringing up North Texas; in fact, wait until she did, he decided.

By seven thirty, it was dark outside and Carlton asked her what she wanted to do. "We could go to a movie, but you'll have to pick it."

"I checked already and didn't find anything I wanted to see. I guess we could call it a night and go home."

"Or I could have a clever remark like 'your place or mine?'"

"Oh, Carlton, that's the most romantic thing I've ever heard!" she gushed, leaning toward him and batting her eyelashes like a pole dancer seducing a drunk businessman out of a hundred-dollar bill.

"Yep, that's me, Mr. Romantic."

"Okay, smooth talker, let's go to your place. Mine might be bugged. Or worse, Stan might come over and want to talk shop again."

"My place it is, then. You remember how to get there?"

The rest of the night went well, a replay of earlier in the week. By midnight, Carlton decided his plan to get DEA information had to wait until morning, which was fine with him. He wasn't about to spoil the mood by bringing it up just now…

Dawn was barely breaking when Carlton awoke just after seven, surprised he had slept that long. He gingerly moved his leg, testing the morning's knee pain and found it tolerable, diminished from the past several mornings. He took that as a positive sign, almost as good as last night—no, wait, not even close. He stopped moving the leg and turned his head carefully, not wanting to awaken her.

Curled up in a ball beside him, Heather was snoring softly, and he watched the rise and fall of her bare shoulder in the dim light seeping through the curtains. It seemed a profoundly intimate activity, even though he was the only one doing anything. Watching her sleep was like another type of lovemaking—seeing her unaware of his presence, unaware of his eyes gazing at her, but feeling a closeness he'd never experienced. He enjoyed this new level of intimacy and hoped she would keep on sleeping for another hour or so. But as his brain stirred awake and started to process more information, he became aware of the contrast between this and their previous encounters, and he wondered what it meant to ignore the reality behind their relationship.

He had retained that reality during their date on the previous Saturday. Of course, after the opening act with her boss, it was simple to keep the evening's conversation—and feelings—away from anything serious. Then, their private dinner date last Tuesday had progressed and ended fabulously, but again, the atmosphere didn't lend itself to self-examination of personal feelings.

So why was this morning different? Maybe it all had to do with timing or last night's revelation of more of her background that made it seem so intimate to lie beside her and watch her while she slept, breathing in and out, and causing a flutter in Carlton that felt much like the first time he'd kissed her on the beach in Mexico.

Okay, bud, first-kiss flutter is acceptable, but you better be on your toes with any woman you want to watch snoring!

About seven fifteen, Heather moaned slightly and straightened from the fetal position while her eyelids fluttered a few seconds before settling back into snooze mode. Carlton homed in on her delicious warmth, and she responded by wrapping him up in a tangle of arms and legs.

Clearly, this was not going to be a day to hit the floor early.

It was after nine o'clock when they left in separate cars and met for breakfast at the Jim's on Broadway, near where they had eaten the night before. She seemed somewhat subdued as they walked across the parking lot, looking down at the pavement as though trying to spot a lost earring. The transition had occurred during the drive, and Carlton wondered if she had received a phone call en route that changed her mood. He glanced at her surreptitiously, trying to detect what effect, if any, the past twelve hours or so may have had on her.

Once inside and seated, he made an attempt to jump-start the conversation, but she seemed noticeably quieter, almost withdrawn. After a couple of tries, he settled in to eat, not about to inquire about her mood and certainly not about the DEA's investigation. She didn't seem to mind the silence and set into her pancakes with a gusto usually found at a picnic with fried chicken.

He wondered if she was harboring regrets about confiding in him, allowing a closer look at her past life than she had in Mexico. Or maybe the regrets had to do with an internal review of her past—he'd had plenty of those himself and recognized the possibility. Maybe she was contemplating how to spend Sunday, or she was already anticipating Monday morning like many people did, allowing it to color the rest of the weekend. It had been decades since Carlton had had a real job, so he couldn't relate to the phenomenon any better than that of Friday afternoon's wave of happiness around the workplace. Or maybe it was nothing, just his imagination. That train of thought reminded him that he knew very little about women, so he was wasting his time trying to figure it out.

The answer came after he had walked her to her car and opened the door. She turned to him and said, "Look, Carlton, there's something I need to tell you." She was looking him squarely in the eyes, her own blue ones exuding a look of...of what? Honesty? Forthrightness?

Carlton had to admire the look, but immediately dreaded what he knew was coming. When it came, he had to fight to control his expression, to stifle the look of surprise that should have come to his face.

"We found out about the player from North Texas. He's from Wichita Falls, and he's an associate of Faustino Perez; in fact, the two of them go way back to childhood. We think they're working together now, here in the city, trying to up the ante with their suppliers. Our analysts have determined that they may have plans to take over a segment of distribution in Mexico from the *Golfos,* but we're not sure."

"*Analysts*? The DEA uses *analysts* to determine what drug dealers are planning? How can that *possibly* work?" he asked heatedly, knowing she would have an explanation that would reveal his ignorance. Worse, it might be an explanation he (and Gomez) wouldn't like. He was right.

"Yes, we use analysts who input all known information and activities of the subject and compare those factors against a database of historical events for similar players in like markets. And all of those guys' recent activities point to *something* of that nature being in the works. It would take weapons and a lot of money, so we've been trying to determine how much stuff they have access to, not only in drugs, but money and arms, because all three are so interchangeable in their sphere of operations."

"Sphere of operations? The flea market on Highway Sixteen is now a *sphere of operations?*" He didn't bother to keep the sarcasm from his voice.

Heather ignored the tone and continued with her tutorial. "Yes, here as well as in Mexico. We've got sources on the ground down there, and we're waiting on more information. It's hard to make contact, and we can't push our informants any harder, or they'll be exposed and killed. Then we won't have anything to go on.

"Anyway, I know—the DEA knows—about you and Perez." The protest was already on his lips when she raised a hand to silence him. "Carlton, don't bother to tell me anything, or try to explain it away. We don't know all the details, but we have enough to connect you to him and, by association, this other guy—his name is Reynaldo Gomez—so you're automatically off-limits for any further personal contact with me. That's DEA protocol, and I can't change it. I can't ignore it, or I'll lose my job, maybe even face some criminal charges myself."

Carlton didn't try to say anything, but took a deep breath and exhaled, a grimace on his face. This revelation explained her mood change, the non-verbal breakfast. He waited for more and was quickly rewarded.

"Look, why do you think I was in such a state about my job last night? Ikos wasn't just going over files when I walked in to get some shoes. He called me down there and proceeded to give me all the information I just gave you—which may get me fired, by the way—and to tell me you are now *just* a CI. No more personal contact whatsoever. And what did I do? Got in my car and met you!"

He waited a few beats for her to continue. When she didn't, he took his cue to say something, anything that didn't leave him here in the parking lot with a dumb look on his face. "It's a good thing you don't want an explanation, because there's nothing to explain. My connection to Perez is being a worker at his flea market. I haul boxes of Mexican crap to the vendor stalls and haul off the trash when the crowds leave. I happened to overhear the Ramos kidnapping and ransom thing, but it was a one-time event. I'm not a button man for Faustino Perez, I'm a stock boy.

"I've tried to explain this to your boss, but it doesn't register; instead, I guess he expected me to dig through the trash to find a connection to this North Texas guy. The only thing I have to go on is the name of the operation: Esmerelda, or something like that, which you didn't volunteer, by the way. Instead, you accidently let it slip out the other night—or was it an accident? Or another clever DEA trick?" He waited to see if she would rise to the bait or clam up completely, now that she was in her DEA agent mode. Her answer delivered another surprise.

"Oh, that!" she exclaimed, rolling her eyes, as if he were the most naïve person on the planet. "It's supposed to be an acronym for the title of a San Antonio Office directive to identify Gomez. I saw the heading in bold print. It was something like 'Establish Source of Merchandise Held or Exported by Land: Drugs and Arms'. That was too long to include in every intra-office memo, so somebody came up with a single word."

This time, Carlton couldn't hide his surprise. "*That* got turned into a woman's name—*Esmerelda*?"

She shrugged. "Take the first letters of the words, throw in some phonetic trickery, and come up with one word that says it all. I told you the origination of operational names was iffy at best, downright goofy at times. Guess that one qualifies as a real boner. But it doesn't change the information that's been gathered on Perez and Gomez. And your connection to them," she added.

"I can't defend myself by refuting the information the DEA has on him; I simply don't know, so I can't verify it one way or the other. But I do have a news flash for the DEA: Big-time drug traffickers don't confide in the guy who puts trash in the dumpster and sweeps the floors. Oh, and what about the other hundred or so people that work for Perez in some capacity? Are *they* all on the DEA suspect list?"

"Carlton, you know why you're singled out on this," she said, exasperation creeping into her voice. "The parking garage party you reminded me of last night? Well, I'm reminding *you*: Ikos knows you set up the exchange with Ramos, and an interesting connection has come up that has him re-thinking the entire thing.

"For starters, he's figured out you were involved a lot more than he first thought. If he decides to have the slugs re-examined and compared closely, he'll know I didn't fire all the shots into Ramos. They'll have his body exhumed and look for more bullets. Internal Affairs will re-open the case and brace Rex and Cho again. Ramos may have been a slime ball, but it won't keep you from facing murder one charges—"

Carlton was nearing the end of his patience, his feelings for her notwithstanding. "And where are they going to find the gun that fired those mystery slugs? Out behind the grassy knoll?"

The look of confusion on her face told him that she either hadn't considered the necessity of the weapon for prosecution, or her training hadn't included details of one of history's most debated murder investigations. Either way, the look quickly disappeared and she continued her troubling prediction. "If they conclude there are different bullets, it'll open up a whole new school of thought, Carlton."

"Speaking of school, I was in the third grade when Kennedy got killed."

She ignored his remark, since it was absolutely nonsensical to someone her age. "And the connection Ikos is looking at is this: four gangbangers got shot at a car wash a few days before the parking garage incident. It's taken months to do it, but all of the victims have been connected to Ramos. All were killed with the same gun, a gun that's also missing." She paused, obviously waiting for a response. Doing his best to keep his expression neutral, he waited her out.

"The gun used was a .45 caliber, probably a Colt, not a Glock, so that's not the connection. It's the fact that all four were gunned down so quickly, none of them got off a shot. Four of Ramos' thugs taken out by someone very good with a handgun."

When he didn't respond, she finished the explanation, such as it was. "Ikos doesn't know this, but I've seen you shoot, Carlton. You're that good."

Now he opened his mouth to protest, but she cut him off. "I know, it's a big circumstantial leap, but believe me, the science is there to substantiate these things, and the DEA uses it. Ikos has grilled me several times lately about how I took Ramos when I'd been shot in the side. It was a pretty bad wound for me to be playing Annie Oakley, and he knows that. He didn't want to shed doubts on my story while I was the wounded heroine of the hour, but now, he's even mentioned having Ramos' body exhumed to do angle-of-entry assessments on every bullet hole in his worthless corpse.

"Oh, and your sketchy past could come back to haunt you. Our office has recently acquired tons of old stuff—*paper* files, for God's sake—on Randall Morris. Ikos has two people working to find any connection between "Big Mo" and—guess who?—Carlton Westerfield."

Carlton didn't bother to attempt a response to her latest news. He was certain that no connection would be found between him and the obese gangster he'd worked for all those years. He'd been extremely careful, a lot more so than he had been in the last two years, he thought ruefully, before meeting Paula Hendricks and now, Heather Colson. Not even the vaunted DEA could find a connection if there wasn't one to find, right?

That thought led, of course, to the possibility of a manufactured connection, something the big government agency was not above using in order to achieve its goals. He began a mental rundown of his caches of currency, currently holding something well over a half-million bucks. *It would take about two hours to recover the three cash-filled PVC pipes…*

Heather's voice interrupted his thoughts. "You don't need to deny anything. I'm not your adversary, Carlton. I'm just telling you what we know and what the DEA can do with that information. Plus, the rules I have to follow. And the reason I'm telling you is because I care for you."

Reynaldo Gomez' Mexico ranch, some fifty miles west-southwest of Amistad Reservoir:

The Castro brothers, Nicolas and Isidro, were in the first group to arrive at the training site. They were staying in the bunkhouses near the cattle pens, eight of them altogether, intent on absorbing all they needed to know in order to overcome their harsh overseers, but wondering now if it were possible. The other six men of the group shared their feelings.

Early on the second day, it all remained frightfully foreign to the young men. Every aspect of the training was strenuous and demanding, both physically and mentally. The physical part was not as hard as the mental concentration required to follow the endless shouted demands of the two trainers. They were accustomed to hard work, but the rapid-fire instructions covered more than could be absorbed and obeyed by most of them. Oddly, the younger Castro brother, Isidro, seemed more adept than anyone at keeping up with the ever-changing orders being shouted at them. But for all of them, the experience was traumatic, something they could never have imagined as peasant workers in Santa Monica.

And the trainers themselves—from the screaming, demanding Mendoza (no rank, no given name, just <u>Mendoza</u>) with his short, powerful jabs to the chest of anyone who did not immediately catch on, to the stout, red-faced man speaking miserable Spanish in the strangest accent anyone had heard—were no less harsh than the very men they hoped to overthrow! In fact, so harrowing was the first day of training, three of the men gathered the first night and quietly discussed quitting and simply returning to work for the vicious gang bosses.

Their ad hoc meeting in the bunkhouse was discovered by Mendoza, who apparently had been lurking nearby, almost as though he had anticipated such activity. He roused everyone in the bunkhouse, turned on all the lights, and lined them up against one wall, then began to berate the three malcontents as "cowards, unfit to serve with the others." By the end of his rant, the three were on the verge of tears. One by one, they were ordered to stand before the others and request to be re-admitted to the group for the next day's training. The remaining five men, co-workers and associates of the accused and full of their own doubts, were embarrassed by the process, but mumbled approval for the act of forgiveness. Mendoza ended the session by shouting derisive comments at *the entire group, asking them "how had their mothers raised such egg-laying chickens with not a fighting rooster in the batch?"*

By the end of the second day, the terrifying experience was slowly being accepted by the recruits. Constant repetition of the shouted instructions finally dulled the shock to their temperaments, as well as their eardrums. The orders for loading and charging the rifles began to seem possible to follow, almost normal. By noon of the third day, everyone was able to load a weapon, pull the charging handle and fire into hay bales arranged against the gigantic mound of dirt that had been piled up beyond the cattle pens. Mendoza and the other one, Millstone, still grumbled at their performance, but not as loudly as they first had. And, the sound of the rifles being fired began to sound comforting, though accuracy of the shots fired was another matter.

None of them had ever fired a weapon, though it was rumored that two of their companions scheduled for a later session had served for a while in the military and received rudimentary training. Those two men, though absent from this session, began to command a new respect among the others for enduring hardship such as this training!

Each man knew the importance of this intense learning session, the absolute necessity to ignore the hardship and do it again and again until it was right. All of the young men understood that this was their only chance to gain the knowledge and firepower needed to win freedom from the hated overseers. Such was their devotion to that thought that, by the end of the fourth day, Mendoza actually smiled at them as they boarded the bus for home.

Tired but happy, they didn't see the looks of exasperation and doubt exchanged between him and Millstone as the bus disappeared in a plume of dust, on its way back to Santa Monica to pick up another load of trainees.

CHAPTER 12

Carlton decided to wait until mid-afternoon to tell Tino and Reynaldo about Heather's surprise announcement. He knew the delay might be risky, but he was anxious to sort through the information and gauge its impact before contacting his employers.

After leaving the restaurant parking lot, he drove to nearby Brackenridge Park and parked near the zoo. For ten minutes, he sat in his car and tried, unsuccessfully, to digest the events, then got out to wander around the public grounds. It was a good day for it, the weather having cooperated with temperatures nearing the mid-sixties by noon. He skirted around the zoo entrance, then walked toward the miniature train station. Surprised to find it open, he bought a ticket for the thirty-minute ride around the park, then sat in the waiting area mulling over the same facts he'd failed to decipher in his car.

The blunt announcement of her feelings for him stood in stark contrast to the stern, almost scolding, tone she'd used to convey the extent of the DEA's ongoing investigations of both Reynaldo and himself. For a while in the parking lot, an immediate kiss-off wouldn't have surprised him. Though she griped about some aspects of her job, he knew how she valued her career and her status with the Administration. The developing hints of his connection to illegal activity and two drug traffickers had to be a cause for concern for her job. Plus, being the daughter of a cop and following his footsteps into law enforcement, it was a reason for downright rejection of him from a personal standpoint. Notwithstanding her professed fondness for him, Carlton Westerfield wasn't catch of the day, that much he understood.

Then, just when he'd been contemplating the need for a disappearing act (certain that she had come to a conclusion that didn't bode well for Carlton) she changed his entire outlook for their relationship with a few words. The surprise revelation, coming on the heels of his own mental tug-of-war regarding his feelings for her, reinforced his opinion that women simply operated on a different wavelength.

A bigger problem, at least for Reynaldo and Tino, was the damning information about their plan to move up a few rungs on the drug trafficking ladder…providing it was true. He pondered the supposed findings regarding a takeover of some magnitude, whereby Reynaldo and Tino would go up against the *Golfos* to secure a piece of the Mexican cocaine distribution network.

Could that ambitious plan be a result of the new relationship with the British gunrunner? Clive Millstone had spent time in South America; perhaps he had contacts with the Colombian producers, a necessary connection to pull off a distributorship. Or maybe the market was ready for a change, and Reynaldo had seen this opportunity coming months ago, then roped his buddy Tino into it.

In any event, it didn't jibe with their recent explanation of simply stirring up the process by elimination some over-zealous slave drivers, contract help that wouldn't be missed by the big cartel so long as product and profits kept flowing. When the pair visited him—when, last Wednesday night?—Reynaldo had passionately explained his reasons for supplying the labor force with guns as being altruistic, with a bit of revenge for his brother-in-law's death thrown in. Sure, it would result in a better price by eliminating the skimming overseers, but the main thrust was to help the poor, downtrodden workers…*what a crock!*

If Heather's stunning report could be believed, Carlton thought, he'd once again been lied to—albeit by omission—by the two crime bosses, much like they had left out details of Reynaldo's relationship to the young kidnapped girl he had rescued. And now, they were planning a full-scale war under the guise of something altogether different.

Mulling over the two events, he had to smile at their shenanigans, a reaction that brought up two questions: *Did it make any difference?* After all, it was simply omitting the full scope of the plan to lower prices while helping out their old hometown buds, right? No need for Carlton to know

104

the details beyond how many weapons to gather and lock up. Being fully informed wouldn't alter the plan or its outcome any more than knowing the young kidnapped girl's parentage would have made any difference in the way Brujido Ramos was eliminated.

The second question was short, but a lot more puzzling: *Why?* He wasn't about to head to Mexico with Millstone and Mendoza to join the fight, so there was no need to sugar-coat the plan. The pair could be financing Teddy Roosevelt and his Rough Riders to do the deed, and Carlton wasn't going into battle. So why soft-peddle the plan by withholding the real reason?

The Brackenridge Eagle rounded the last curve with a whistle blast before sighing to a halt in the station, and Carlton gave up on the riddles swirling through his head. He boarded the train and leaned back to enjoy a few minutes of scenery in the park without worrying about anything. Tino and Reynaldo could wait a while to hear the latest from the DEA; meanwhile, he was looking forward to seeing the look on their faces when he once again confronted them with information he'd had to learn on his own.

It was after three when he got to his apartment. He called Tino first, then Reynaldo, asking them to meet in his apartment, judging that it was as safe from prying eyes and ears as anywhere. His Cadillac sitting at his own address couldn't cause much of a problem, could it? And the configuration of the building didn't lend itself to easy surveillance. In any event, he told both of them to watch their backs and arrive fifteen minutes apart.

"So she just blurted all this out in the parking lot?" Reynaldo asked. He and Tino had taken their usual spots on the couch while Carlton related Heather's report to them from the kitchen counter. It was the second time he'd gone through it, Tino having insisted on a preview before Reynaldo arrived. The looks on their faces shifted from the obvious—surprise—to doubt, then worry.

Privately, Carlton was enjoying their distress, payback for being left in the dark. Aloud, he stuck to her exact words as best he could recall, conveying no expression with the narrative. After rehashing every facet of it a couple of times, he spread his hands and looked at the pair questioningly. "So now what?"

"Now we owe you an explanation, that's what," Tino said after a quick glance at his partner, who was nodding in agreement.

Carlton shook his head. "Nope. I don't want to know any more than I already do. It seems the DEA is a step or two ahead of y'all on this venture, as well as liking me for a murder charge. If they drag me in, they'll try to cut a deal by offering me a free pass for information on you two. If I don't have it, I can't give it. And if your whole deal comes crashing down, you can't blame me for singing a song I don't know the words to."

"You think they might be close to taking you in for questioning?" Reynaldo asked, the worried look returning.

He shrugged. "Who knows? I'm not worried about the long-ago stuff, but if they dig Ramos up and find holes in him from different angles, they'll know Heather had a little help taking him out. And they won't be looking for the helper to give him a Good Citizen Award."

"Probably not," Tino agreed, smiling at the wry assessment. "But explaining our plan doesn't give you any more than what you already know, Carlton. The end result is just a little more ambitious than what we told you about, and—"

"It started out to be exactly what I told you the other night," Reynaldo cut in, his voice taking a defensive tone. "But when I learned more after my brother-in-law was killed, I saw that eliminating the contract overseers would create a temporary vacuum, and I could fill it permanently.

"The *Golfos* would be served very well by having somebody in place who has skin in the game. Of course, they'll meet with me—two brothers, Israel and Gilberto Rendón, run the show for the Benavides family—and want a full explanation before they would agree to parcel out a piece of the action, but when I tell them what's been going on and give them the numbers, they'll see that those guys have been stealing from them for months, and that *I've* been the one making up the skim in the form of higher prices.

"Plus, those contract guys enforce discipline the wrong way, too harsh even for the drug business. Killing Romero Cano and his wife was *way* out of line. Regardless of what you hear about the violence and the harsh discipline, it has some new unspoken rules. Even the occasional murder of an innocent to make an example is now being frowned on because of the increased heat from the government. And that heat is coming from U. S. government agencies that subsidize Mexico's war on drugs."

"U. S. agencies are willing to let business go on as usual, as long as they dial back the violence on bystanders?" Carlton asked, knowing the answer and its bitter irony.

Reynaldo shrugged. "Everybody needs a job and a paycheck, right? But nobody likes ugly headlines that might get the assistance money and equipment cut off."

"Well, wiping out the *Golfos'* enforcement team will entail a few bodies, won't it?"

"Yes, but they're not bystanders. The police will make a half-assed investigation, then say 'good riddance' and close the case.

"Besides, we've learned from the laborers that the local police are being paid to stay clear of that section of *Nuevo Bayito* by the *Golfos*. The enforcers don't realize their bosses are going to help us out in that regard. No matter how much ruckus we cause, the police won't be quick to answer any calls to the warehouse. They'll wait until the shooting stops, maybe even a day or two later, then send in a few cops to check things out. They'll find the same workers as always, but without the enforcers."

"Just some enforcers' bodies—if all goes well, and your team wins."

"If all goes well, there will be time to dispose of them. If not, I promise you the investigation will be perfunctory, just as it is every time a bunch of cartel guys get the bad end of the action. The police will look at it as someone handing them a small victory."

Carlton was quiet for a moment, wondering how to pose the obvious follow-up question, but there wasn't a gentle approach. "And if it goes badly, and your team loses?"

"Then I guess you can say you told me so. Or tell me I should have confided in you, given you the entire story, so there would be a better outcome."

Carlton shook his head in disagreement. "That's not what I meant to imply, Reynaldo. The only *better outcome* I can envision is calling it off—which is what I advised from the get-go. Knowing the entire plan wouldn't have made any difference in my advice. I just have to wonder why I wasn't brought completely into the loop because, believe it or not, I'm a team player."

Reynaldo hesitated before responding. "I know you're a team player, so I can't give you a good explanation. I can only apologize and ask that you continue to help on this. Like I said, it started out a lot simpler than it appears now, but the action plan is the same."

Carlton, too, thought for a moment before responding. "I'm on board with helping. But in the future, maybe you two could let me decide what I need to know in order to be of any use."

"Agreed. Oh, and just so you'll know: the deception is on me. Our friend Tino over here said I should tell you the entire plan. I should have listened to him instead of being an ass."

Carlton looked at Tino, who gave his customary eye-roll at his friend's candor. "You can take a horse to water, but what do you do with a horse's ass?"

Carlton laughed and the uncomfortable conversation was over.

The three sat quietly for a minute, Reynaldo and Tino pondering the news report from Heather and the possible crisis it represented. Carlton thought about the impact of going forward with a plan to take out a team of armed thugs with a group of poorly trained laborers, especially with the DEA knowing of the plan, if not the exact timing.

Unable to see anything positive from it, he broke the silence with a change of subjects. "I do have one piece of good news, Reynaldo. The code name for the operation, *Esmerelda*? It's not your wife, has nothing to do with her." He proceeded to tell the origin of the moniker, getting a laugh from everyone, then tried to quote the directive title as best he could recall, but ended up writing it out in order to see how someone could come up with it.

It was a good piece of news, and Reynaldo was visibly comforted by it, although he and Tino both shook their heads over the distress it had caused. "That acronym doesn't make much sense, but more sense than Esmerelda informing on me to the DEA," he declared, glad the mystery had been cleared up.

As for Carlton, he was glad he hadn't brought up the possibility of Paula being the actual source for a pair of reasons: one, it wasn't true; and two, it would have made him look like a jilted lover, jealously trying to seed doubts in her new lover's mind.

That train of thought took him back to his current paramour and what had occurred a few hours before, both the good and bad parts. The good part was her declaration of caring for him, (whatever that meant). The bad part was, of course, they couldn't even be seen together. And trying to circumvent the DEA's rules was out of the question. The huge federal agency had all the manpower and technology needed to form an effective chastity belt around its pretty star agent.

Tino brought him out of his reverie with questions that made Carlton suspect his mind-reading abilities. "So where does this leave you with Heather? She can only call you, right, you can't contact her?"

"That's the last thing she said to me before driving off. And between the investigation and her boss' suspicions, that's not too likely. She could lose her job, or maybe even be charged with something."

"Do you think her report is accurate? Does the DEA really have people on the ground, trying to get more information?"

Carlton shook his head. "I just don't know, Tino, but it sounded legit to me. After all, they got this far, right? So somebody is leaking info, and somebody at DEA is getting it. What we don't know is whether their people 'on the ground' can get anything more, and when. And if they can get it quickly, how does that affect the plan?"

Reynaldo made his decision known. "I'm going forward with the plan. It only affects us if they can get the full scope of it in the next few days, and maybe not even then.

"The attack timetable will be known only by me, Tino, Millstone and Mendoza after they determine a time when all the overseers will be at the warehouse. The laborers will be informed as late as possible to prevent accidental leaks. And none of those people I just named have any incentive to get killed."

Carlton thought about it for a minute. "That's a good idea, because one of your laborers could be the informer. If so, he could get sick or disappear just before showtime. That would tell you who the informer is, but too late to counter it." He let the suggestion hang for a moment.

Reynaldo looked at Tino. Both of them considered the possibility, then responded, Reynaldo speaking first. "That works in theory, but I just can't see it. I learned a lot from Romero before he was killed. He stressed that every one of his co-workers would be committed to a plan to do this. Besides, they're a close-knit community, and not one of them—even if enough money were dangled to turn one—would trust an outsider to pay them to betray the others and bail them out of danger at the last minute."

Tino nodded in agreement. "I've spent some time there in the past few years, and I know some of them, a few of them pretty well. It's hard to convey what Reynaldo's telling you about their loyalty to each other and their commitment to family and friends, but we've seen it with our own eyes. I just can't believe one of those guys is the leak."

"It's not the type of action that can be called off once it starts," Carlton warned. "Is there an escape plan in case it goes badly from the beginning? If not for the participants, how about their families? If they lose, the surviving enforcers could make it hard on the families."

One look at Reynaldo and Tino told him the pair had not made any contingency plans for wives and children. Reynaldo shifted uneasily on the couch, and Tino's face took on an even more impassive expression than usual. Finally, Reynaldo responded. "I can get a bunch of people out of *Santa Monica* on the bus they're using to go to the ranch for training. But it would take three or four trips to evacuate everybody."

"What about the cattle trailer? Will it be at your Mexico ranch?"

Reynaldo brightened at the idea. "After delivery of the weapons, I can get Gus to leave it hooked up to the truck and return to Sabinal in another vehicle. I can have Alberto standing by in *Santa Monica* with the trailer ready to load up and haul them to the ranch. That might attract more attention than the bus, but it will have to do."

"That's good thinking, Carlton," Tino said. "But I hope the families don't mind all the cow shit they'll have to wade through if it comes to that."

Carlton looked at his two scheming friends, the ones who insisted on leaving their advisor in the dark, and shook his head. "Tino, I don't think they'll care. They don't know it, but they're already in shit up to their eyeballs."

Reynaldo Gomez' Mexico ranch, Wednesday, January 16, 7:30 a.m.:

The second group of laborer/trainees stepped off the ancient bus, squinting in the bright light of early morning. Fresh from their shift, all of them were tired, but eager to receive the training, snippets of which had been passed along to them by the returning first group as they passed each other the previous night.

They had been warned about the trainers and knew a little of what to expect: yelling, shouting, repetition, and run, run, run. Further fueling their concerns, one out of this group had served in the military and was fairly knowledgeable in the rigors of basic training, rigors that he inflated in his stories during the trip. The warnings and stories had served to excite the men and make them anxious to start training, to see and hold weapons, to prepare to do something about their plight.

But the best incentive of all had been provided by the overseers during the recent work shift. Two of the laborers had been beaten, one badly enough to require medical attention from the local doctor in Santa Monica. Both of them were in the current group of trainees, stoic and determined to learn all they could in the next few days. When the conflict began, those two would surely be ready to exact a full measure of revenge against their tormentors.

Training began the moment they stepped onto the hard gravel lot in front of the bunkhouse. The two trainers introduced themselves as Mendoza and Millstone, no titles, no other names or identification given. The Hispanic, Mendoza, took over after the quick introduction. He briefly explained what the men were to do in the next four days, then laid out a timetable, beginning with carrying their small bags of personal items and clothing into the bunkhouse and claiming a bunk.

After that, he explained, work would begin in earnest, so everyone must be ready and alert. You must listen carefully and respond instantly, he told them before pointing to the bunkhouse door and ordering them to get started. All of the men turned and headed toward the door, each thinking he was following the dictate and performing well thus far. It was the last time any of them made that mistake.

"Move, move, move!" he screamed at the shuffling bunch. "This is not a picnic! You are not going inside to give your wife and children a hug! Hurry up! Act like men, not a flock of chickens!"

The bigger one, Millstone, raced to the door ahead of them and commenced shouting at them individually in a strange dialect. He had a different comment, none of them kind, for each one as they tried to squeeze around him and get inside. His accent sounded like some telenova star from Spain the women gossiped about at community gatherings, but the comparison ended with his cultured Spanish. Red-faced and screaming, his size and demeanor frightened the men even more than the maniac in the parking lot. He was screaming descriptions of what he was going to do to them, their mothers, their sisters, if they didn't haul ass and do what they'd been told.

On the second day, those descriptions would be transferred to the enemy, and the overseers would be described as doing those unspeakable acts. But for today, the two angry trainers were intent on indoctrinating the young men to the ways of a very violent world by shouting horrible things in their faces.

Another tactic was inserted into the program with this bunch. A verbal barrage regarding secrecy was unleashed at the end of the first day, while the men ate quietly in the dimly lit bunkhouse. The tongue-lashing started when Mendoza stepped inside, carrying his own plate of simple food, beans and tortillas with a small piece of chicken breast comprising the entire nutrition plan of the program.

"Okay, listen up, men! We have learned of a possible problem, one that might be with us right now. There is possibly a talker, if not in this group, maybe among the ones you work with, the ones back in Santa Monica.

"Remember, you were instructed at your meetings about this, and how important it is to remain quiet, not gossip like a bunch of old women. And now it seems someone has disobeyed that instruction! That can get every one of you killed, but not before I personally kill the talker myself."

The threat silenced the entire room to less than a whisper. The hungry men ceased eating. Forks quit rising to mouths and lowering to plates. No shuffling of feet, scraping of chairs. Even breathing became quieter.

Mendoza's eyes roamed the room, taking in each man individually for a couple of chilling seconds before continuing. "Let me inform you how dangerous this is. Señor Gomez has given you this chance to free yourselves, and he will not tolerate failure. But I promise you it will fail if anyone—ANYONE—hears of it. This training program is supposed to be kept secret, but it is difficult because several of you must be here for four days. Absences like that are noticed, so your wives and girlfriends must not offer a single word regarding why you *are absent, or what you are doing. If asked, they just say you are out of town visiting friends. No discussions! Discussions lead to questions, such as why several of you are gone at the same time.*

"The entire attack schedule is a secret. Not even I or Millstone know the details, but nothing must be divulged to a single person about an attack, not even your priest. If I find out that a priest has heard such a tale, I will kill him and the person who thought the confessional box was a sacred place. Then I will burn down the church. <u>During Mass!</u>"

At the delivery of that threat, the room became even quieter, if that were possible. Millstone chose that moment to make his entry and begin the next phase. Beans, tortillas, and chicken grew cold on the plates as each man warily eyed the big Anglo leaning over the head of the table, saying nothing, just glaring at them. Meanwhile, Mendoza eyed each laborer, his dark eyes seeming to penetrate their souls.

"You will listen carefully to what I say," Millstone began, using precise words and a grammatically correct delivery, albeit with the strange-sounding accent. Furthermore, his tone did not convey any alternative to listening carefully. "Mendoza has told you what may have occurred. If any of you know of such a talker, whether it happened by accident or purposely, you must tell us. TELL US NOW! If you do that, nothing will happen to you; we will simply deal with the talker. But if we find out later that any one of you knew of a leak regarding your training or an attack, I will kill the talker <u>and</u> the withholder of his or her identity in a most unpleasant manner."

To accentuate the speech, he went on to describe how he would slay the perpetrator and the non-informant. The day's training regimen had left no doubt that the big man would do as he promised. By the time he was through, the cold meals were left untouched. Apparently, the tired men weren't as hungry as they thought.

For three more days, the trainees would be goaded, threatened, cajoled, begged, and persuaded to catch on to every aspect of the drills—while maintaining operational silence—as though their lives and the lives of their families depended on it.

Because for the next two weeks, that would be the stark reality.

CHAPTER 13

The next week sailed by for Carlton, mainly because he found tasks around the flea market to keep him busy during the day, then headed off to a different place to eat nearly every night. He saw Tino and Reynaldo almost daily, but the pair were so engrossed with preparing for the final trip with the weapons they didn't spend much time talking with him. That suited Carlton just fine; he was willing to help if needed, but remaining in the dark about weapons smuggling seemed a good idea.

What was inevitable though, was hearing the name of the next trip, the one with the weapons, dubbed "*viaje segundo*," the second trip. Reynaldo's ranch hands, Gus and Omar, had made the first trip, a run with cattle only, on the previous Saturday and encountered no problems. Now it was Friday, and the weapons transport was scheduled to take place. After hearing the first trip had gone well, Carlton felt the trip would unfold without a hitch, but he cornered Tino and Reynaldo on Thursday evening to remind them of the DEA's purported surveillance of them.

"How many of your ranch hands know about this trip?" he asked Reynaldo.

"Only Gus and Omar know the details. I sent the welder, a guy named Zach, on a trip to Uvalde to buy a load of feed and told him to stay there with his family for a long weekend. Those three are the only ones who know anything of *viaje segundo*, and I had Gus and Omar load the weapons in the trailer while everyone else was out working."

"That's about as quiet as you could keep it on this end. Now you have to worry about a reception at your ranch. Still nothing to indicate who might be a tipster?"

"I had a long discussion with Clive and Mendoza, told them to listen up and watch carefully around the ranch to see if they could learn anything. Mendoza suggested planting a few seeds about snitches during the training sessions, see if anyone cracked or gave a sign of being dirty. I told him to do it.

"I've learned a few things about him since this started, and he's got some skills in interrogation that sounded pretty ugly. Like it or not, I think he's the right guy to train those laborers in short order, plus find out if I've got a mole.

"Also, my ranch foreman down there, an older guy named Alberto, drives the transport bus for the groups of trainees. He's been inquiring around *Santa Monica*, looking for any person who doesn't fit in, anyone who might have a grudge against me or any of the laborers. He was to report anything to Clive, and so far, nothing."

Carlton thought it over. "We don't know who their 'people on the ground' are, or how many; actually, we don't even know if they exist. If they are real, it's possible that the information they got was a one-off tip, or someone's lucky guess as to your end game. Even so, they don't have any real knowledge of a time schedule."

"Tino and I have used all our contacts to check, and so far, nothing's come up. But I'm worried about the absence of seven or eight workers at a time. In a town that small, it might be noticed, but we've seen nothing to indicate anyone's suspicious."

"You sure you can you keep the attack timetable secret from everyone?" Carlton persisted.

"Absolutely. The DEA contacts down there—if they exist—won't get the schedule from those four, and neither can any drug interdiction force in Mexico. Hell, I might change the schedule at the last minute, anyway."

"That's good, because only one group could be worse than the DEA getting wind of it, or the Mexican federal force for drug interdiction. The *Golfos'* enforcers."

"That's for sure," Tino said. "Any law enforcement group wouldn't be sure of identities and probably wouldn't shoot without provocation anyway. But those assholes working for the *Golfos* know every one of the laborers and would gun them down without a word."

The grim assessment settled on their minds for a full minute before Reynaldo stood up and announced, "We've got to get out to Sabinal, Tino,"

Carlton stood, thinking he had just witnessed the last discussion before the weapons were to be loaded and driven to Mexico. He was relieved and glad he didn't have to hear any more about the guns, the trailer, the risks, or anything else. But he hoped it wasn't the last discussion he would have with the two men who had become his friends, friends who were now talking about which vehicle to take, apparently unworried about the pending task.

He took his cue to head for the door, but Reynaldo's voice stopped him with door handle in hand. "Sure you don't want to go with us, Carlton?"

He turned to the pair. "I think I'll pass. You don't need me hobbling along. Maybe next time?"

Reynaldo flashed his movie-star smile, and Tino used his deadpan countenance to face their advisor. It was Tino who spoke. "But you'll come bail us out of trouble if we call you, right?"

"Of course. But this time, try to leave the body bags out of it, okay?"

PART II

CHAPTER 14

Alberto watched as the big Ford pickup pulled through the front ranch gate and turned left, in the direction of the bunkhouse. Closing the pen gate behind him, he walked toward the pickup, which was pulling to a stop a short distance from the front door of the weathered structure. Two men got out, looking stiff and tired from their trip. When the passenger turned, he smiled and waved, then turned to say something to the driver before turning back to the old ranch foreman with another wave of greeting.

Reynaldo strode toward Alberto and extended his hand. "*Hola, Berto! Que tal?*"

"*Hola Jefe! Como está?*"

"I am fine. How are things going here?"

"It's been busy. Gus and Omar got here late on Friday with the cattle. They put the trailer with the weapons in that shed," he added, pointing to a small, low-roofed building beside the bunkhouse.

"Good! And they left in the old pickup?"

"*Sí*, and both were complaining the whole time about driving it back to Texas."

Reynaldo laughed and gestured to the other man coming around the pickup. "I found this hitchhiker and picked him up. He says he can help us. What do you think?"

Tino grinned and shook Alberto's hand. "It was the other way around, *Berto*. You can see that I was driving and it is my pickup, not this *peón's* I saw sleeping beside the road."

"Ah, Faustino, you should *tién cuidado* about picking up people on the road. One never knows what they have on their mind."

"Okay, I'll be more careful. Now show us inside and tell me that Henrietta has some food ready."

The men continued their bantering all the way to the ranch house, where they were greeted by the ranch cook, Henrietta, who bade them to sit at the table and eat while they talked. The smells emanating from the kitchen enticed them to obey her instructions, and within minutes, she had the table set and food on the way, but never ceasing in her running commentary. It was as though she was as hungry for company and conversation as her guests were for food.

The men switched to the serious matters at hand while she dished out food, lots of it, but not much different from what was prepared for the trainees while stationed in the bunkhouse. Tino and Reynaldo ate heartily while Alberto picked at his plate and gave the pair an update on the recent activity. "Mendoza and Millstone went with Agapito to take the second bunch of men back to *Santa Monica* and will bring the next group in immediately. They should get here early tomorrow."

Reynaldo nodded, pleased that the training was almost half complete. Two more groups to be cycled through the ranch, then a quick joint session in *Santa Monica*, just before the attack, if possible. "How has the training been going so far?" he asked his old ranch foreman, probing for some news of the abilities of his two gunrunning/commando-training employees.

The old man bobbed his head up and down as he addressed the question, an exuberant signal from the normally taciturn ranch caretaker. The gesture pleased Reynaldo, who had little previous insight into the trainers beyond reputation. "They seem to take charge immediately, and the young men listen carefully to what they say, especially the big one. But maybe it is because they have to listen closely in order to understand his speech, the strange accent.

"The smaller one, Mendoza, has no trouble making himself understood. He is a harsh one, that man. From the moment they get here, the young men are frightened of him, maybe more frightened than they are of their overseers in *Nuevo Bayito*." He proceeded to relate the story of Mendoza's threat regarding a snitch among them, how he would burn down their church during Mass if a guilty one was left unreported.

Reynaldo frowned at the report, but inwardly he smiled. He knew the impact such a threat would have on the men of *Santa Monica*, where the

Church constituted the center of everything in their lives: spiritual, social, and of the town itself. Mendoza had picked the right subject to illustrate the importance of exposing a snitch, a betrayer among the group.

"The training looks hard, *muy dificil*," Alberto continued. "All day long, they are running around in the fashion the two *jefes* tell them. Sometimes in groups of three or four, with individual ones spread to the sides. Sometimes, they spread out in a single line and run for the pens or the house, then split and go around it, while the single ones step aside and kneel with their weapons pointed ahead.

"They practice for hours, then gather in the bunkhouse while the big one explains it, over and over. He also draws pictures on a big paper on the wall. He draws lines and arrows all over it. It means nothing to me, but it must be a way to attack and be protected. Whatever it is, by the time they go back to *Santa Monica*, they should be able to do it while sleeping."

"And the guns, Berto. What about the weapons' training, the actual shooting?"

"They shoot the weapons at hay bales, but only after many times of loading and pointing, loading and pointing. The first group had to take turns with the three rifles, but when Omar and Gus brought the rest, the second group each had a gun, so the training went better."

That got a smile from both men; neither Reynaldo nor Tino had to disguise their emotions upon hearing this description of the training. Both knew the value of repetition, both physical and auditory, to instill automatic actions and reactions in men. It was critical that the young, sparsely trained men act without thinking when the attack began. Too much thought would bring on fear, the reality of what was happening, and untrained men might flee the battle, or worse, freeze in fear. Either way, it would doom the attack.

It appeared that hiring the gun runner and his mercenary helper had been a good move, Reynaldo thought, as well it should be, with the price they charged. With the third batch arriving tomorrow and the fourth and last group coming on Thursday, he and Tino would have an opportunity to see the training regimen first-hand.

For now, the report was encouraging, and Reynaldo set forth to encourage his faithful ranch crew in turn with well-deserved praise. "That's good, Berto, very good. It seems the trainers are doing what needs to be done, and they need your help to do it. I want to thank you and Henrietta and Agapito for carrying out my instructions for this project of mine. The extra work it caused will not be forgotten."

Overhearing the remark, Henrietta beamed in appreciation of the boss' compliment. The trio had worked at the ranch for many years while others came and went during periods of more and less activity. It had been four of them, she and her husband, Agapito, plus Alberto and his wife, Maria, until Maria died some years ago.

More recently, a man named Romero Cano and his wife, Irma, had worked at the ranch until deciding to go to *Santa Monica*. About two months ago, they received the terrible news that Romero and Irma had died, murdered in a horrible way. Without knowing all the details, she surmised that their deaths had something to do with this strange new activity, this military-type training going on here at the ranch.

The presence of ten or eleven more mouths to feed meant a lot more work for her and Agapito; however, their loyalty to *Señor Gomez* sufficed to make the extra work bearable, and especially upon hearing his praise and his mention of "this project of mine." The increased activity provided a measure of excitement not seen at the ranch since many years earlier, when *El Patrón* had been severely injured in a helicopter crash and brought to the ranch by two young Anglos named Mike and Sandra. For two weeks, she, Agapito, and Alberto had nursed all three back to health while overhearing vague stories of murder, drugs and money. The memory caused her to cross herself and murmur, *"Ay, Dios mío! My boss has too much excitement in his life for me! I pray for Him to protect us all from whatever is going on."*

Just after sunrise the next morning, the transport bus pulled up to the bunkhouse and rattled to a stop. Millstone emerged first, followed by Mendoza, then the next group of trainees. Sleepy but excited, they stepped onto the hard gravel and gazed around at the ranch buildings and the surrounding area. For most of them, it was the farthest they had traveled beyond the *Santa Monica* to *Nuevo Laredo* route, and the trip held the promise of a huge change in their lives, so the drowsiness evaporated quickly in the bright sunlight.

Then the training began.

Watching from inside the ranch house, Reynaldo and Tino were able to witness the action closely, getting a good overview of the near-ritualistic program carried out by the two mercenaries. After a couple of hours, both of them were wondering about the need for such brutal verbal lashings, but it only took a brief thought of what the young men would be facing to remind them of why the two professionals were hired.

"I'm glad it's them he's screaming at, not me," Tino commented, turning away from the window, his impassive face giving away nothing while his words and tone left no doubt as to his unwillingness to be treated in such a manner.

Reynaldo laughed good naturedly at his friend. "That's because you and I are old, not as able to take abuse as those young men are. That's why *young* men have always fought wars. Old ones are too wise to engage in such foolishness."

"If you say so. But we're going to have to be involved in this one, aren't we? I talked to six of my best guys. Four of them were with me on the Laredo massacre. All of them are anxious to be on the attack, but I won't let them be involved without being there myself."

Reynaldo nodded in agreement, in contrast to the frown of worry on his face. "Of course. Both of us need to be in on this thing. It is the only way I can face the Rendón brothers afterward and ask for concessions for the *Santa Monica* operation. They would not listen to anyone who would send his men into a battle without being there himself."

"I think you are being too charitable in your opinion of the *Golfos*, Reynaldo, including Carlos Benavides. They don't have an ounce of loyalty to anything but money," Tino commented dryly.

"I don't mean they have loyalty or bravery as traits themselves. But I think they have more respect for one who takes action. Or maybe fear. They have to know that whoever plans to take over the *Santa Monica* transport section is unafraid—not of them, or anything else. They also have to be shown that we will do whatever is necessary, and I cannot think of a better way than to be in on the elimination of their piece-of-shit enforcers personally."

Tino nodded at the logic and took it one stage further. "Then we have to be able to do that in a fashion that instills *fear* instead of respect. It's time we talked with Millstone and Mendoza about a solid plan for the attack.

One that eliminates every single one of the overseers in such a way their mothers will not recognize them at their funerals."

The unnecessary death of Romero Cano and his wife, plus the stories of horrendous mistreatment of some of the young men now training yards away made Reynaldo smile at the suggestion. Inwardly, he toyed with some ideas to make his point known without causing grieving mothers even more despair.

The pair watched the training throughout the morning session before making an appearance. Lunch break had been announced, and the men quickly crowded through the bunkhouse doorway, now afraid to do anything slowly lest they suffer the wrath of the screaming Mendoza. Tino and Reynaldo strode into the bunkhouse behind the trainees. Each was carrying a tray with several meals stacked on it, which they placed on the long dining table. Henrietta and Agapito followed with insulated boxes holding drinks and containers with more food.

Stepping aside, Tino and Reynaldo acknowledged the curious glances of the laborers with nods and greetings before turning to greet Millstone and Mendoza, who were the last ones to enter. "Ah, I see our commander-in-chief and his aide-de-camp have joined us!" Millstone bellowed. "So good of you to come! And bringing chow, no less!" Addressing the tired men who remained standing around the table, uncertain as to what to do, he introduced both of them, causing the curious glances to turn to outright stares and a few shy mumbles of greeting and appreciation for the opportunity to change their fortunes.

Mendoza took over, barking at the men to sit down and eat. It was the first order of the day to offer any relief from the hard training, and the men gratefully grabbed chairs and dug in, while Henrietta circled the table and dished out additional food and big glasses of ice water. About midway through the meal, she made another round, this time distributing big ice-cold bottles of Coca Cola, a favorite beverage in rural Northern Mexico. The cokes were far better than any dessert she could have concocted, as evidenced by the smiles of gratitude on the grimy faces.

Within twenty minutes, plates had been scraped clean of second and third helpings, and the big Coca Cola bottles drained of the last drops. Henrietta and Agapito set about to clear the table while Millstone and

Mendoza moved to the end wall to the left of the door. The wall had several big sheets of paper, some containing drawings, and a couple left blank. The trainees turned chairs to face the wall, wondering what lessons they were going to hear from their new leaders, or perhaps from their mysterious benefactors, *Señor Gomez* and *Señor Perez*.

It was the big one, Millstone, who grabbed a marker and stepped up to the wall and launched into a speech about the necessity for the men to work together. He drew a rectangle in the center of a blank sheet and labeled it "warehouse," then asked for locations of doors and windows. After drawing in the details, he proceeded to illustrate several modes of attack, various angles from all sides. He went on to explain that final assignments for the attack would be given when all of them met for a final training session— only a few hours' worth—and each man must remember his position and route into the warehouse.

The men listened intently, as did Reynaldo and Tino. After a while, Millstone took a seat and Mendoza stepped up to the wall. He reiterated some of the points made by Millstone, then concentrated on tactics and details, such as running, kneeling, coverage of each other's backs. Lastly, he described a heated battle at close quarters, leaving out no gory detail of the horrible sights, sounds, and smells of a battleground. Such were his descriptive powers that some of the young men looked ready to lose their recently-acquired lunch by the end of his tirade. Like Millstone, he had talked for about ten minutes when he paused and let silence punctuate the next segment. The men visibly relaxed in their seats, clearly shocked by what had been related to them beforehand and a little nervous about what was next.

Pointing at Reynaldo, Mendoza made a declaration to get their attention refocused. "That man is angry! Angry that a friend and relative— as well as your co-worker—was killed by the overseers in the *Nuevo Bayito* warehouse. Oh, and his wife was also murdered. So he is spending a lot of money to extract revenge for those murders, as well as for the mistreatment suffered by each of you.

"So we are going to extract that revenge in the manner *Señor Gomez* wishes, which is to kill every last one of the overseers. And I think I am correct that he wants to leave no false message that this attack was simply to get rid of some cruel overseers; he wants a firm lesson sent to the ones who put them in place. And it is going to be a harsh lesson," he added, looking about the faces in the room.

He paused to turn again to Reynaldo. "Am I right, *Señor Gomez*?"

Reynaldo stood and moved in front, turning to face the group. "Tino and I talked earlier about the need to make a point, show everyone involved how angry I am about the deaths and mistreatment of my friends. In the past hour or so, I have envisioned many ways to do that, some as violent as anything you see or hear about in these violent times here in Mexico. I thought about beheading and castrating every last one of the overseers as payback, and mailing the pieces to their families. But I have changed my mind. Such acts would only place us—you men—on the same level as the ones we are going to eliminate.

"Instead, I want every one of them killed, the bodies stacked in a pile, then burned. I'll see that plenty of gasoline in available, enough that not a single body part is left for burial."

If the men had been shocked by the first option, the one he had discarded, they looked completely aghast at the directive they had just gotten. Catholics all (and regardless of recent Vatican rulings easing restrictions about cremation) the men in the room still saw cremation as a sin. Burning human bodies would amount to a massive crime against the Church, their beliefs, and almost certainly against God!

Reynaldo let the idea sit in the room for almost twenty seconds before speaking again. "I see that your beliefs—and mine—are offended by such actions. So we are *not* going to burn the bodies. But we are going to kill every one of the overseers and anyone who steps in to help them during the attack.

"I suggested the atrocity to show all of you my anger and my resolution to do away with the *Golfos'* contract overseers. But we are not heathens. We will not perform any acts beyond what is necessary to protect ourselves and our families. You are here to learn how to do that, and it will be a very unpleasant and upsetting event in your lives. You will remember it for the rest of your days. But as you know, it is absolutely necessary.

"These men who are training you—Mendoza and Millstone—are very good at their job. It is important that you do everything in the manner prescribed by them. If you do that, you will be able to defeat the overseers."

With that, Reynaldo sat down, choosing not to embellish his comments with any encouraging statements, no pep talk language. Instead, he hoped his remarks adequately conveyed his commitment to the project as well as emphasizing his goal to eradicate the source of oppression they had endured for months. He knew Tino would question his decision, but watching the faces of the young men, he felt it had been the correct course of action.

CHAPTER 15

Reynaldo and Tino stayed around for another day, watching the training, participating in the bunkhouse meals, and listening to training lectures. That night after lights out, they discussed the options for the actual attack and its aftermath with Millstone and Mendoza, who had been gathering information from the trainees on operations and schedules inside the *Bayito* warehouse. One important factor was revealed: laziness on the part of the *Golfos'* enforcers enabled a couple of senior laborers to communicate with the *Bayito* warehouse as to product availability and transport needs. Either of those two, Leobardo Muñoz or Sebastian Chavez, would be able to draw the entire contract workforce—about twenty men—to the warehouse with a single phone call. An enforcer was not required to verify the need for such a request. The trainers were elated to have that critical information.

On Tuesday, the pair returned to Sabinal, where Reynaldo talked at length with Gus and Omar, thanking them for a well-executed *viaje segundo* and driving the decrepit old truck home. He explained the need for the dependable truck to remain in Mexico, attached to the cattle trailer, in case the families of the laborers needed to be evacuated. Turning to Zack, he likewise praised the welding job and his contribution to the successful arms smuggling venture.

Then, he stressed the need to erase all of it from their memories. "I don't have to tell you three the importance of this, but I will anyway. We did all we could to mask the trailer conversion by buying steel plate and welding materials at different places and using cash. And Zack, that was a good idea to use the truck-mounted welder so our electric bill wouldn't have a spike in it for those two days.

"Keeping the others out in the pasture was probably enough to keep a lid on our project. I don't think any of them have much interest in the activities here beyond working the cattle, repairing fences, and getting a paycheck, but I want you to keep your ears tuned for anything. If anyone is curious, tell them the trailer needed to be strengthened and temporary partitions added for hauling bulls. Oh, and let me know if that doesn't seem to satisfy their curiosity."

All three nodded at the directive and hoped they wouldn't have to report anyone voicing too much interest in the trailer conversion. Reynaldo's tone said he wouldn't be pleased to hear of such curiosity, and none of them wanted to find out how it might be handled.

The next day, Wednesday, both returned to San Antonio and went straight to the flea market, where they found Carlton engaged in moving inventory from the storage sheds to individual booths, billing it out as he went. In addition to a hand truck, he carried a clipboard and was meticulously listing every item, along with its destination and the booth owner's name. He looked up when Tino and Reynaldo sauntered up, grinning like two schoolboys about to try out a prank. "Well, look who made it home! How was the trip?"

"Very successful," Reynaldo replied. "Things are going well, even better than I'd hoped for."

"And I see things are going well here," Tino remarked. "I'm glad to see you're so good at doing the invoice paperwork. Now I know who to get when I don't want to do it."

Carlton frowned. "I knew I shouldn't have let you catch me doing it. And I shouldn't have looked up when you two came in."

"It's the first important thing you learn in the military after basic training. *'Carry a clipboard, look busy, and* _don't look up_ *unless someone calls you by rank and name.'* That way, everybody is convinced that you're important and busy, so they leave you alone."

"Well, you get old, you forget some of life's lessons," Tino said, as though quoting a philosopher known only to him. "And I was going to bother you to take a lunch break, but I guess we need to leave you alone with your work and your forgotten memories?"

"Nope, I'm tired of working and I haven't forgotten how to eat. You buying? You can give me the whole story while we eat."

The three went to the snack bar where Beatriz, the silent eatery operator, served them enchilada plates and lemonade, while Reynaldo quietly updated Carlton with an overview of their excursion to Mexico. "The weapons made it through without a glitch, Gus and Omar made it home in the ranch pickup, and the training is going well."

He and Tino pitched in to give details of the ranch activities and the methods being used by Millstone and Mendoza. Carlton nodded a lot, surprised at the depth of the training and wondering if he could change his mind about the possibility of success. When the subject of uncovering the tipster arose, he gave his own report on his DEA contact. "I've talked to Heather a couple of times, and it's been all business—mostly about research they're doing to find out about bigger cocaine movements or news about a changing of the guard at the cartel level. Pretty generic stuff they do day-in, day-out, I'd guess.

"But I was surprised that she didn't say anything specific as to *your* cartel suppliers, or *your* plan to take over. And nothing about their 'sources on the ground in Mexico' or any news about the 'Esmerelda' study on Reynaldo Gomez. I tried to steer the conversation that way a couple of times, but she avoided it. That makes me wonder if she was just testing me that day at Jim's, wanting to see if it would be passed along and turn up elsewhere, or if later developments indicate you've changed your plans. That would point to me as a leak in their investigation. Either that, or I'm already identified with the opposing team, so they don't trust me to sneak around for information."

"So Lover Boy is on the back burner?" It was Tino, his tell-tale sly grin saying he was angling for a snippet of gossip.

"*Way* back. Like on the way to the land fill. On the plus side, she said the research being done on Randall Morris hadn't turned up anything on yours truly. That may be the only reason she's still able to talk to me at all—I'm no longer a person of interest for past sins.

"She mentioned that a further investigation might be pending for the parking garage shooting, but not anytime soon. That's good news, but probably because Ikos and the San Antonio office have their marching orders to concentrate on this rumored cartel shakeup—which is *bad* news."

Reynaldo nodded, frowning at the implication that full resources might be brought to bear in uncovering his plan. "Best we can hope for is they learn nothing in the next ten days or so, when it will be too late. Besides, I'm less worried now, since the guns are already in place at the ranch. Even if the plan is blown, I don't know what they could do except wait for the attack and try to intervene."

"True, but maybe the idea is to give the info to the enforcers so they'll be ready to wipe out your force. That would kill your plan to bring more product in at a higher profit margin, which accomplishes what the DEA is tasked to do—reduce the availability of drugs—without risking their own personnel. Or maybe the DEA wants to have Mexican drug forces join in the fun and use the confusion to take out both groups—yours and the *Golfos*. Because of those possible scenarios, I think it's critical to uncover the tipster and squeeze him or her for what the information is going to be used for."

"Well, as I described a while ago, the trainers are leaning hard on the men to give up any informers, or even anyone expressing doubts about the plan. Plus, I have other people working the town, listening for gossip, or speculation about the absences, or anything being leaked, either by accident or on purpose. So far, not a word. Everyone is doing exactly as I'd hoped."

"So training is almost over?"

"Yes. The last group will arrive tomorrow and stay until next Tuesday, the twenty-ninth. We're headed back soon, and four of Tino's men are going to follow us down there. Those four will train at the ranch until time for the attack, and Millstone and Mendoza will use them in as squad leaders, since they have battle experience.

"As soon as the laborers are taken back to *Santa Monica*, Millstone will try to schedule one joint class, but it's doubtful he can do it with all the men. Some of them are on duty at all times, and he can't risk suspicion at this stage."

"So how is he going to coordinate the attack?"

"He and Mendoza gave me and Tino a long lesson on how they conduct the training. They explained that they are training each group to do exactly what they're supposed to do, and expect their co-workers to do their part. *'Coordination by training'*, they said, using drawings of the warehouse—the *objective*, that is—for each group and putting together an attack plan that requires each man, each group, to do his job. *'Independent training, joint execution'* is what Mendoza called it."

"Sounds like you two got your fair share of education. I hope the trainees retain all of it as well as you have."

Tino pointed out an additional tool used by the professionals. "Millstone asks members of each group for descriptions of the warehouse and surrounding grounds, then draws it onto the classroom wall. When the class is over, he takes down that drawing and puts up a blank sheet to draw the next group's description. Then he and Mendoza compare the drawings, checking for any big differences in what the men are observing."

Carlton thought it over and felt his earlier change of heart might have been premature. "I'm trying to extrapolate that to a football team training each player separately without ever running a play as a group of eleven men."

"So that's what's wrong with the Cowboys!" Reynaldo quipped. "No extrapolation!"

"Quit using big gringo words, and tell us what you mean," Tino said crossly. Before Carlton could respond, he grinned and added: "I'm just pricking with you, Carlton. I get it, and I agree with you. Sounds risky as hell, but that's what we've got to work with."

All three sat quietly for a minute, thinking about the situation. Finally, Carlton took a deep breath and tried to sound encouraging. "From what you've told me, those two trainers know what they're doing. What they're preparing your laborers for is guerrilla warfare, so it's probably not like any military training I've had. It may go exactly as they plan it, no problems at all. It's what we've got to hope for. Meanwhile, what do you want me to do?"

"Keep doing the inventory distribution around here," Tino interjected before Reynaldo could answer. "Oh, and the invoice work, while you're at it."

Carlton groaned theatrically. "Why did I ask? Oh, okay. What about bank deposits and payroll?"

"Paula and Caterina will handle that stuff here at the market, but they may need you to run a few errands, or make the bank run."

"Will do, *Jefe*." He gave a mock salute, then turned serious. "I hope this goes well, and I hope you all return in one piece."

Both men nodded—too somberly, Carlton thought—and he paused a moment to choose his next words. "Look, I'd be less than honest if I told you I was enamored with the plan, but it sounds like chances for success have been greatly improved by those two gunrunners you hired. And from what you've told me about your young workers' situation, they have the incentive to make it work.

"So *vaya con Dios*, my friends, and I'm here if you need me. Unless I'm writing up invoices, of course," he added, trying to lighten the mood, which had suddenly become subdued.

Reynaldo laughed. "Sure you don't want to go to Mexico with us?"

"Instead of doing paperwork? It's sounding better all the time."

CHAPTER 16

Once again, Carlton was left to his own company at the flea market and, like before, it gave him a sense of security. With Reynaldo and Tino gone (along with the weapons) he didn't have to worry about Ikos pulling a raid in order to grab the now-identified "North Texas Player" and his childhood bud, Faustino Perez, and their arsenal—something he had considered a possibility since hearing Heather's startling report. Plus, if the law enforcement agency came knocking in the next several days, he would have a perfect opportunity to demonstrate the work he claimed to do for Tino. And if questioned about either of the absent men, he could honestly say he didn't know; neither had mentioned further contact, so Carlton hadn't either. If they needed him—God forbid!—they could call.

As to Heather, she had in fact called twice just to chat, calls he'd left out of his report to Reynaldo. While his depiction of her "all business" calls were complete and accurate, he felt no duty to give his bosses more opportunity to rib him about his personal life. The business calls came from a blocked number, which he suspected was a DEA line that was being monitored or recorded. Maybe she was supposed to contact her confidential informant a couple of times a week and see if the conversation would reveal anything new.

The personal calls came from a new burner phone number, and Carlton didn't miss the chance to tell her she was taking up his quirky phone habit. "Well, I see you've taken my advice to change phones from time to time," he quipped.

"The other one quit working," she lied. "I see why you go through so many of these things—they're flimsy."

"Hard to get good equipment these days."

"I could reverse those adjectives and sound really clever…but a bit slutty."

It took Carlton about five seconds of grammar manipulation to rearrange his sentence and laugh at her risqué remark. "That's good! I like a clever woman. And slutty isn't a deal killer."

The conversation had ended with a question he'd wanted to ask since the episode in Jim's parking lot—would he ever see her again? Her answer had been cryptic, alluding to a challenging work schedule, but Carlton figured his future with her actually hinged on the results of the DEA's ongoing investigations, the ones about which she was now close-mouthed. As he had determined days before, no matter the attraction, his market value was questionable.

That bleak assessment was still on his mind on Friday when his phone rang a little before lunchtime. He saw the number was Heather's new one, and he stepped into Tino's vacant office for some privacy.

"Hi, clever girl!"

"Hello yourself. What's going on with you today?"

"Same stuff as always. I'm delivering goods to the booths at the flea market."

"Sounds exciting. Do you get to take a lunch break?"

"Certainly. Would you meet me for lunch?"

"Sure. What's good on your side of town?"

"Oh, we have dozens of Mediterranean restaurants, plus several with fine French cuisine, and a sprinkling of Scandinavian bistros, all within two miles of the flea market." He continued the ridiculous tale in an airy voice, sounding like a snooty tour guide playing to a busload of retirees. *"Actually, three of the French places are located on the all-pedestrian promenade stretch of Applewhite Road."*

"Carlton, have you lost your —"

"Tacos or enchiladas," he interrupted. *"Or both. Take your pick from about thirty places within a half-mile of here."*

"That's more like it," she laughed. *"One o'clock okay?"*

"Yes, perfect."

"I'll pick you up at the entrance gate and we'll find a place."

Lunch turned out to be almost a mile away, on Zarzamora, but he was accurate on the menu items. Both dug into their food with little chatter, but nothing like the silent, uncomfortable breakfast at Jim's. Carlton started to mention the pleasant change, but kept quiet, thinking it might break the spell. Then he abruptly chastised himself for worrying about her moods, career challenges...or anything else he couldn't control, for that matter.

"Why the serious face?"

The question shook him from his thoughts, and he laughed to cover his vacillation. He decided to test the waters. "I was just thinking how nice this is compared to our last meal together—if 'together' is the right word."

She thought for a moment. "Oh, you mean at the coffee shop. Well, it wasn't our happiest time, was it?"

"Took me by surprise, that's for sure. Quite a change from the night before."

That got a brief smile. "I knew it had to be done, but why spoil a perfectly good night?"

"One with hard equipment?"

They both laughed at that and rose to leave. Once in her car, Heather put the key in the ignition, but turned to face Carlton without starting it. He tensed for what was coming and was mystified by her words and actions.

"I certainly enjoyed lunch. And I appreciate your efforts to find out about Perez' old buddy from North Texas."

The momentary look of inquiry on his face prompted her to raise a finger to her lips for silence. Just as he started to ask, she moved the finger to her ear, then pointed to several locations in her car: the glove box, the console, under the seat.

He scolded himself for the two or three seconds it took for him to catch on; she thought the car was bugged. He replayed her opening line in his mind and tried to give the appropriate response. "Well, efforts are good, but I wish I'd been able to get something more concrete." He punctuated the lame sentence with raised eyebrows that asked for approval and was relieved when she gave a thumbs-up and rolling motion for him to continue in the same vein. "I'll keep checking the incoming mail, since

I'm the one to get it each day at noon. I'm not sure what you expect to find, though, unless it's something addressed to Gomez that looks interesting."

She nodded her head and answered. "Yeah, just note who and where it came from and deliver it as usual. Can't raise any suspicions by taking it. Besides, stealing U. S. Postal Service material is another problem you don't need." A sly grin and chopping motion of her hand told him the ruse was over, or so he hoped.

She started the car and he said, "It's hard to turn left out of here, you might want to turn right and go around the block to catch that light." Pulling to the parking lot exit, she looked both ways and voiced agreement with his suggestion.

The drive back to the flea market was punctuated by small talk, none of which sounded authentic to Carlton. However, little could be done about it with the elephant in the car, and he had to hope their listeners had overheard dozens of similar post-lunch conversations that sounded just as canned.

As she pulled into the flea market, he had an idea to salvage the performance. "Pull up over there, and I'll show you some of the stuff I do every day."

She responded with her own eyebrows raised, but parked where he indicated and both got out of the car. He walked around it to guide her onto a raised boardwalk, which fronted a long row of vendors' booths. Only when they were ten feet or so from the car did he start to breathe again. "My boss is gone, so let me give you an extended tour."

Before she could comment, he took her hand and tugged her along the walkway. Only after passing a couple of booths did she speak. "That was perfect, you played it just right. I'm sorry, I should have given you a heads-up in the restaurant, but I didn't think about it until I started talking in the car. And I really do appreciate your efforts at getting intel for me, but I realized you might have a reaction that would get me canned. And maybe worse for you."

"Your employer has your car wired?" Carlton couldn't keep the astonishment from his voice.

"I don't know for sure, but as I said, I just happened to think of the possibility in the car and didn't want you to start a conversation that I would have to respond to without editing. Any questions you asked could have revealed that you know more than you should."

"Good thing you did, because I was about to ask. You've been evasive about the stuff you told me in Jim's parking lot, but I assumed it was because we were on telephones you couldn't be sure of. I didn't think about your car being bugged."

She took a deep breath and turned to him. "This is what I talked about in Corpus Christi, months ago, remember? The time Rex and I came down for a Come-to-Jesus meeting and braced you about stealing Hunnicut's service weapon?"

"I recall meeting with you two on the beach, and we had a nice chat and a couple of beers, but I don't remember stealing anybody's gun." The last part was delivered with firm conviction, but accompanied by a grin that said otherwise.

Ignoring his mixed response, she continued. "Anyway, Rex and I both hinted that we were tired of working where every day is a mystery: who's doing what, and why; what your boss is trying to do; who he's trying to manipulate. Oh, and wondering when you're going to be the next victim.

"It came up again before we met at Good Time Charlies the other night, except now it's Stan Ikos instead of Timothy Hunnicut. At least Stan's a decent guy, but this is more of the same crap, and I'm not sure I'm up to the challenge."

"Seems like you do pretty well at it. Your sign language in the car told me what I needed to know, even if our conversation sounded a little lame."

"I don't think it matters, because I have no reason to think I'm wired… seriously, I don't. I'm just being careful. For both of us."

"I certainly appreciate that, both the action and the sentiment behind it, being careful for both of us." He paused, knowing he needed to tread carefully in these waters. "Is there anything I could do to make things go better with Ikos? I mean, since I'm not likely to find a letter from a cartel boss addressed to Gomez with 'finance proposal' written on the envelope?"

She laughed at the silly remark, then turned to face him, instantly serious. "Sure, you could make things better. You could flip and give me Perez and Gomez. You could give me all the details of the plan to knock over the *Golfos'* Laredo branch. You could flip that crazy slut Paula

Hendricks, tell me how she's involved, what she does to stay connected—besides wiggle her butt, that is."

He opened his mouth to speak, but nothing came out. Luckily, she didn't see the hesitation and continued with her heated diatribe. "But you're not going to do that, and I wouldn't expect you to, no matter what it would do for my career or our relationship. And I know that; I knew it when I met you in Mexico."

She paused, but Carlton didn't know what to say. He settled on something apropos, intelligent-sounding, maybe even profound.

"I don't know what to say."

"Then don't say anything. Just listen to what I have to tell you. Our people in place down there have managed to come up with information on your buddies. Pretty interesting stuff, when you consider their beginnings. First, Faustino Perez: Born, *Santa Monica*, Mexico, in the state of *Coahuila* on May 5, 1965. His father was a professor of geology in *Monterrey*, his mother was an American school counselor from the East Coast, possibly Virginia. Seems the couple was traveling on a research assignment to the Border Region when the very pregnant Mrs. Perez decided to give birth to baby Faustino, who joined the family with his six-year-old sister, Marta.

"The assignment lasted a long time, and the young Perez family made *Santa Monica* their off-and-on home for several years. Then they went back to *Monterrey* for good when Professor Perez became ill. He died in 1969, and Widow Perez came back to the States with young Faustino, but Marta stayed in *Monterrey* with her aunt, a sister of the late professor.

"Back in the States—Houston—Widow Perez soon marries Virgil Hendricks, a petroleum engineer with Enco, now Exxon. They had two children, a boy who died young and a girl named—you ready for this?—*Paula*!"

Carlton was nodding in acknowledgment before she finished the sentence. "Yes, I know that part. Remember, I told you the relationship when we met to talk about taking Brujido Ramos. Tino is Paula's half-brother."

His comment was met with a grin. "I didn't say *all* this information came from our Mexico informants. I'm supposed to contribute something at my shop—you know, something to earn my paycheck.

"And I remembered; I was just testing you to see if *you* remembered what you told me. Apparently, you do."

"I'm really getting tired of people testing me and my memory."

"Huh?"

"Nothing. It seems everyone I know wants to check out my mental capacity with a clever test…which I always pass, by the way."

Heather let the remark slide and continued her tutorial on Faustino Perez. "Mr. Hendricks moved his family to San Antonio where Faustino—who then started going by *Tino*—excelled in school, first, on the south side of town; and later, in Castle Hills, where he attended Antonian Prep School on West Avenue. Seems he was an outstanding member of the debate team, known for his linguistic skills. But after graduation, he goes into business peddling flea market crap, which leads to peddling not-so-legal stuff, like stolen goods, which leads us to now."

"All that detail of his early life, but just a hazy, general knowledge of his recent life? That doesn't seem logical, given the current environment of snooping technology, especially with your employer's budget."

"Not logical at all, Mr. Spock," she answered with an impish grin, poking fun at his earlier admission of being a Trekkie. "You are very astute to have caught that. Actually, we have some details of his current MO that I won't bore you with, but believe me, the files are full of information on Perez' many operations. He runs a good-sized network, probably a lot bigger than you know about—"

"All I know about is this flea market." Carlton gave a broad sweep of his arm, as though there was a question about which flea market held his interest.

Ignoring the interruption, Heather pushed ahead. "With lots of people engaged in the physical distribution and payment collection end of it. And whatever you know—more than you're telling, of course—you probably *don't* know about a lot of his activities. But the Agency does, and we're trying to get a lead on why he's hooked up with Gomez and what they are planning, because it could be big.

"Which brings me to Reynaldo Xavier Gomez: also born in *Santa Monica*, on September 16, 1965. Little is known about his parents, except they were successful merchants in the town, ran some kind of general merchandise store and made decent money. They managed to get him to the States when he was about twelve, to Dallas, where he lived with an uncle and aunt. He applied for citizenship, went to good schools, ended up near the top of his class, excelling in English Literature."

She paused, a quizzical look on her face, and Carlton rose to the cue. "So he and Tino have the same background, split up, but end up in the States as top students with language—the English language—being their strong points. Oh, and both born on holidays."

"What? What holidays?"

"May 5 and September 16 are both national holidays in Mexico. September 16 is actually Independence Day, and May 5 commemorates the Battle of *Puebla* in 1862. Anyway, maybe that or being from the same little town forms some kind of kinship for ex-pats from Mexico, makes them lean toward the same things."

"Maybe so. Some quirky thing like John Adams and Thomas Jefferson both being Founding Fathers, then both dying on the same day, Independence Day of the nation they founded. I wouldn't put these two guys in the same league with founding fathers, but it seems they have exactly the same view on importing contraband drugs."

"Not only pretty, but smart too! Oh, and clever," he added, genuinely impressed with the historical tidbit.

She smiled, but waved her hand at him in a dismissive manner. "You're supposed to be listening, not talking. But if you cared to give me additional information…?"

Arched eyebrows over her blue eyes gave her an inquisitive look—and alluring to boot, he thought, smiling at her school teacher demeanor. It was a look he'd encountered when they first met: very appealing and… dangerous. "Information?" he asked innocently. "Okay. I don't know about Gomez, but Perez speaks excellent, unaccented English. I suspect his boyhood friend does, too." He went on to explain Perez' penchant for proper diction and his professed desire to emulate successful Mexican-Americans.

Heather nodded and seemed to make a mental note, causing Carlton to question his contribution to her Perez Biography file, but he soon dismissed it as inconsequential. Speaking well wasn't a crime, not yet anyway, and it appeared that she—or the DEA—had already focused on that facet of their two investigation targets.

And speaking of investigation targets—which Agent Colson was doing in fine fashion, sounding like she was reading from a printed report—why was he hearing all this detail now, when she had been mum for the past two weeks or so? Had the 'sources on the ground' only recently gathered all this info? Or was this another test for Carlton Westerfield, CI to Agent Colson of the DEA?

Whatever the reason, he hoped she would continue and impart some information that would be helpful to the pair. Then it struck him that passing the information to the men might be a small problem, since they hadn't made arrangements for contacting each other. Carlton had considered asking about it, but decided against it, not wanting any connection to a project in which he had serious doubts. Now, he might be faced with the task of reaching them in rural Northern Mexico…he'd have to get a phone and card with Mexico capabilities, and he wondered at the DEA's ability to trace such calls, even if made by a burner phone. Maybe the powerful agency tracked every call between the two countries, especially ones made from throwaway phones…maybe a loophole for dodging wiretap warrants?

His musings were interrupted by a question mark in Heather's voice, a question mark following a question he had missed. "Are you okay?" she asked, concern in her voice and on her face.

"Sure! Top of my game, never better," he lied. "I was just thinking about what you said and missed the part you asked about. I'm sorry, what was the question?"

"I asked you about Gomez, the half of that duo we don't have as much on. We've discovered he owns a construction company in Wichita Falls, a very successful one, and legitimate on the surface. It's bound to be the vehicle for laundering his drug money, so no doubt he'll lose it when he's convicted of drug trafficking.

"Anyway, I know you won't say much, but what's he like?"

Carlton was shaking his head again, realizing he did a lot of that lately. "I don't know that I've ever seen him, Heather. It would have to be here at the flea market, and Perez doesn't introduce his hired help to everyone who comes in here."

Now Heather was shaking her head in real disagreement. "A car registered to Reynaldo Gomez has been seen on several occasions, both here *and* at the apartment complex where you live, Carlton. Are you going to tell me that's a coincidence in a city with one-point-five million people?

"Look, I'm not asking you to lead me to your neighbor and help me handcuff him. I just need to report some background, something that's not in the file, even if it doesn't assist in his conviction."

"I don't know my neighbors, Heather. Most of them speak Spanish when we meet in the parking lot, or just nod a greeting, like you do when *you* bump into *your* neighbor.

"Oh, wait, scratch that! When *you* bump into *your* neighbor, you whip out a recorder and ask him where and when he was born," he added, smiling to blunt the accusation.

The smiling delivery worked. She rolled her eyes, then pouted and leaned back, arms folded in front of her in a classic woman-spurned pose. "I can see you're not going to give me anything, even though I've told you the bulk of what we know about those two."

He thought for a moment about something, a tidbit he might proffer to keep her talking. Briefly, he considered telling her that Reynaldo Gomez was the father of the kidnapped child they had effectively rescued from Brujido Ramos by shooting him multiple times. But that would indelibly cement him to Paula who, not being his legal wife, might be forced to testify against him at some point. Not knowing the full legal implication, he decided against it. "Heather, I'm really sorry, but I can't give you something I don't have. I just don't know the guy. If I've ever seen him, I didn't know it."

"Oh, okay," she said airily. "You're no help, but thank you for lunch. I enjoyed the French cuisine and walking through the gardens on the Zarzamora Promenade."

They both laughed, then Carlton got serious for a final stab at information. "Glad to show you the sights and fine food. But tell me: after being so hush-hush for the last two weeks, why tell me all this today? I mean, the stuff about those two guys is entertaining, but—"

"I'm telling you again: the DEA has information, a *lot* more than I'm telling you," she interrupted. "Information about what they're planning to do in Mexico. Not all the details, but we know it's going to be soon, maybe around the first of February. So whatever you do, don't be anywhere near them around that time."

Carlton struggled to hide his excitement and moved to cover it with a theatrical sweep of his hand. "Well, Tino's not here today, and I wouldn't know Raymond Gomez if he walked up to me right now."

Another eye roll. "I happen to think Tino's only a flip-phone call away from you. And it's *Reynaldo*, not Raymond, but you already knew that. A nice touch, though."

He inhaled deeply and began an eye-roll of his own when she stepped forward and poked him in the chest. "Just be careful, okay? Everyone involved down there is going to die, Carlton. Don't be one of them."

CHAPTER 17

On Friday morning, after a one-day delay in *Santa Monica*, the fourth and last batch of trainees arrived at the bunkhouse door promptly at six, while Tino and Reynaldo were crossing the border in Tino's pickup. A carload of four young men following six car lengths behind them was stopped briefly and waved through with a minimum of fuss. Once through the checkpoint, the car closed the distance enough to keep Tino in sight, but never too close.

It was almost nine when the two vehicles arrived, and training was well under way in the large gravel expanse beyond the pens. Hay bales had been arranged against pen railings, and men with rifles took turns charging the pens, stopping to kneel and point at the bales when Mendoza shouted a command to do so. Time after time, four-man groups charged, kneeled, and pointed; then they rose and rushed the pens again, splitting into pairs to run around the ends of the pens before stopping to kneel again and point at the bales.

All the running, kneeling, and pointing resulted in not a single shot fired, not yet. While basic weapon operations and handling had been covered during the trip by Mendoza using a large picture of an AR-15 assault rifle, only after a few hours of intense hands-on training would the trainees actually pull the triggers of weapons with live rounds in the magazines, something that would be a first for almost every one of them. For now, it was only run, kneel, and point. The trainees were tired and sweaty—and wondering if this was the right way to train for overthrowing the hated enforcers. Right now, it surely didn't seem so.

The newest arrivals were met by Millstone and introduced by Tino only as David, Daniel, Freddy, and Enrique, no last names given or needed.

"All of these young men have been under fire; in fact, they have more than a couple of times," Tino explained. He elaborated with a quick replay of the helicopter attack from months before, giving the trainer basic facts of the minutes-long air attack and its tragic outcome before ending with an endorsement of the four silent men standing before them. "We lost four men that day, including brothers of David and Enrique here. Throughout the entire attack, these four kept up steady return fire and managed to take out at least two aircraft shooters, as well as wounding the pilot. That was the only thing that kept us from being completely wiped out, because the pilot had to pull away to safety before he lost consciousness."

The Brit gave the four an appraising gaze, then turned to Tino. "Then these men know the confusion of a firefight. Just as important, they know the cost of losing a battle, or even breaking even, as they did that day, from what you've described just now." He turned back to the men who had, until now, been standing silently and hearing their histories being told as though they weren't present. "Glad to have you blokes join us. As you know, the men we are training have no experience beyond charging and shooting at square blocks of grass—hay bales, I think they are called—and they don't shoot back."

All four men smiled at the truism, with the most outspoken, David Avila, speaking up. "Nothing is as scary as being shot at, but especially now, after being in a firefight in which you see ones around you being hit. And dying."

Millstone nodded in agreement. "And your jobs, as squad leaders, will be to convey that feeling to the young men out there jousting at grass bundles like some Don Quixote poking at windmills. But the trick is to convey confidence, not fear. They have to be fooled into thinking they will be victorious if they just listen to what you show them and follow orders."

The group turned to watch the run, kneel, and shoot exercise for a few minutes, while Millstone explained that the drill, simple as it was, needed to be ground into the new trainees' minds until it was an automatic response. Later, he explained, more intricate drills would be introduced, but for now he wanted to hammer home a basic three-part drill and get the men to coordinate with each other and with the other groups. "Perform without thinking," he called it.

He led the four to the training area and called a brief halt while he introduced them to the group. Mendoza lectured for a few minutes, then matched each of the new men with two of the trainees. The newly placed squad leaders were issued weapons, handed over unloaded, along with a box of ammunition and empty magazines. "Okay, squad leaders! At my signal, I want nine rounds placed in your magazines, magazines inserted, first round in the chamber using the charging handle in unlocked position, just pull and release, no locking back the bolt.

"Then we will commence the same exercise a few times with squad leaders placing one round into each of the hay bales at each called stop. Trainees, watch your leaders and try to copy their movements, including pointing and squeezing the triggers of your weapons."

At Mendoza's signal, the four leaders squatted to the ground, opened the boxes and quickly stuffed nine rounds into their magazines. Freddy was done first, and he slapped the mag home, flipped the rifle over and jerked the charging handle back, releasing it crisply at the right second. The retracted bolt picked up the round on top of the magazine stack and slammed it into the chamber. The other three finished loading and racking a round within seconds of Freddy, then stood with the rifles in something akin to a port-arms position.

The other trainees watched the leaders in awe. The slick maneuver had been something the young men had only seen on TV...and now they might actually learn to do it! Mendoza, who had not heard Tino's introductory spiel, was surprised and pleased. He stole a glance at Millstone, who was nodding in appreciation. These four were definitely going to be an asset to the group, and their impact would be much greater if they could train, even briefly, with the rest of the men now back in *Santa Monica*. Mendoza looked over the entire group for five seconds before giving the command to charge the hay bales.

The charge of the first group went well for about twenty feet, until Mendoza screamed for the kneel position. Freddy and David performed flawlessly, Enrique and Daniel less so, but adequately. The problem arose when Freddy cranked off three quick rounds, swinging the AR-15 smoothly between the hay bales. The other squad leaders, impervious to the sharp crack of the fast-moving bullets, rose and dashed toward the next kneeling point, while their underlings seemed to forget mimicking their leaders,

Instead, most of them cringed back at the noise while a few actually turned the other way, disoriented by the unexpected noise. None of them mimed firing their weapon as instructed.

Before the second kneeling position was reached, Mendoza screamed for a halt. He stalked to the middle of the practice area and glared at the men. "Did you think we would fight with rocks? This is not your school playground! I told you earlier, the gunfire is loud, so don't flinch and cringe away like a girl! Besides, you have heard nothing until you hear it going on all around you—with half of it coming your way!

"This group wins the prize for being the most startled by gunfire. But you will get over it, that I promise you. How long it takes is up to you, every one of you."

The drill continued for another hour before Millstone called a halt and herded the group inside for classroom training before lunch. Tino and Reynaldo retired to the ranch house where Tino managed to filch a tiny sample of the lunch Henrietta was preparing, and Reynaldo went outside to use his phone. A recently acquired piece of equipment, Reynaldo's new satellite phone was the only sure method of communication out here, short of driving more than ten miles to the tiny community of Tule. A single land line existed there, but its functionality was sporadic at best.

Agapito arrived at noon, and the four prepared to deliver and serve lunch to the trainees and instructors. Afterwards, Tino and Reynaldo moved away from the others to speak privately, going over possible scenarios of the coming attack and the aftermath. By mid-afternoon, the pair had covered every conceivable outcome they could imagine and hashed over the next action required to counter it or take advantage of it.

"Damn, I think we need to write all this stuff down," Tino complained. "I can't remember all of this crap of 'what ifs' and 'where tos'."

Reynaldo glanced at his friend and grinned, knowing he would remember every single thing they had discussed. "Don't forget the 'how manys' and 'what next', old friend. We can't forget any of it, because we sure can't write it down. And we've got to go over it all again with Clive and Gustavo. Maybe this evening after supper."

At the mention of the mercenary trainers, Tino frowned and changed gears. "I think our trainers are pleased with getting my four gunmen."

"Of course. No doubt, those four have increased the chances of success beyond their expectations. And mine, too, to be honest."

Tino thought for a moment, mulling over the performance the four had put on. Simple as it was, the trainees had been impressed. That bode well for the plan, since each of the untrained young men would undoubtedly do his best to copy their experienced counterparts from north of the border. He could only think of one other asset which would boost morale and the odds for success. "I wish Carlton weren't hobbling around—and wanted to come help out in the gunfight."

"Well, both parts of that wishful statement rule him out; he *is* hobbling, and he *doesn't* want to be in another gunfight."

"I know. You going to call him and see if he's heard anything from the DEA girl?"

"I don't think there's any need to. From what he told us, it sounds like he's out of the loop with her. That may have cooled him off for trying to get information from her. Or even trying to see her."

Tino looked at him. "You know about their little vacation in *Acapulco*. Your watcher said they were two regular little lovebirds in Paradise. And I told you what she looked like. Would a little shove-off cool you down?"

"Hell no! You?"

"Absolutely not. And he may still be knocking her lights out, but I'm not sure how that helps us to get information on the DEA's investigation."

"Look, we're still not sure there's any information to get. If they had those 'sources on the ground' here in Mexico, we'd know about it by now. Antonio's still working on it, and nothing gets by him or that nosy wife of his."

"He called in lately?"

"No, he can't call me on his cheap phone out here, but that was him I called during lunch with my sat phone. He hasn't heard of anyone asking the wrong questions in *Santa Monica*. The only thing out of the ordinary was some tourists traveling through there a few days ago. Their car broke down, and they knocked on a couple of doors, asking about a repair shop. He said they ended up getting it towed to *Nuevo Laredo*."

"Tourists? In *Santa Monica*? They must have been lost!"

Reynaldo shook his head. "I asked Antonio about that, he checked it out. Said they were on the way from *Monterey* to *Piedras Negras*, then decided to turn south to *Nuevo Laredo* to cross into the States, taking the long route. He saw them, said they were two middle-aged couples, nicely dressed, talkative, but polite. They ate lunch at Benny's while they waited for the tow truck, then walked around the *zócolo* and took pictures, mostly of them standing in front of the church."

"Doesn't sound like anyone involved in spy work for the *Golfos*, but I don't know what type of people the DEA uses. Maybe older, polite couples who are slick enough to have their car break down, call a tow truck, take pictures? While driving through *Santa Monica*, garden site of all of Mexico?"

Reynaldo smiled at his friend's ominous, but unlikely, scenario. "Well, if they didn't ask any odd questions and they're gone, I guess we can forget about them."

"So what's next? Figuring out how to have a joint training session?"

"We'll talk to Millstone after today's training, but I don't think it can be done with all the men. Remember, as soon as this group gets back on Tuesday, they will have to take over for the shift getting off work. If they don't show, those *Golfo* assholes will know something is wrong."

Tino thought about it for a moment. "Yes, and they will send someone to check. Maybe two or three guys."

The suggestion floated in the air for a moment before Reynaldo saw where he was going. "That might work. Even if they send eight or ten guys to rough up the missing shift…"

"Our entire force will be in *Santa Monica*, armed and waiting for them, and eight or ten fewer to defend the warehouse," Tino finished the thought. "Of course, that leaves the one shift still stuck in the warehouse, unarmed. The bosses won't let them leave without the next shift walking in the door."

"And they will walk in the door, just a bit late. And armed to the teeth."

"Yes, but every single one of the guys sent to check will have his phone out, ready to report what they find. We can't count on taking out all of them without somebody getting word back to the warehouse first."

Reynaldo thought about that scenario. "The two senior guys, Leobardo and Sebastian? One of them—hell, both of them—can make panic calls to the warehouse saying all hell's broken loose, get the entire enforcement group to come to *Santa Monica*."

Tino shook his head. "No, even if they didn't smell a trap, our guys have all been training for an attack on the warehouse, not in their hometown, with women and kids everywhere."

Reynaldo sighed. "You're right, that won't work. We'll ask Millstone, but I think he's going to have to make do with training just three of the groups jointly. And when the new shift goes to the warehouse, they can take weapons to the ones inside."

"Or the new shift that goes in—right on time, of course—consists of three times as many as needed to work." The idea was accompanied by Tino's sly grin as he finished. "Plus Millstone, Mendoza, you, me, my four men, and all the weapons."

Reynaldo mulled it over. "That seems to be the only way to maintain surprise, doesn't it?"

"Sounds like Tuesday is going to be a surprisingly busy day at the *Golfos'* warehouse."

CHAPTER 18

Reynaldo and Tino ate supper with the trainees, chatting amiably with a couple of the more talkative ones whose families they knew. Millstone and Mendoza mostly listened, inserting a couple of questions about the warehouse operations and daily duties of everyone, laborers and overseers alike. The men seemed willing to talk freely between bites of Henrietta's plain but satisfying meal, unaware that each group before them had been subjected to the same subtle interrogation.

After eating, the conversation began in earnest, and Tino and Reynaldo sat back to listen. Both trainers used tablets to record their findings, scribbling notes in margins and drawing indecipherable diagrams to illustrate their findings. They had also done this with each of the groups, accumulating information about the warehouse activities and the overseers throughout each shift. Now, with the last group's input, they could begin comparing all of it, probing for inconsistencies or weaknesses in defenses, or anything else that might be exploited to aid in the attack.

Along with the obvious strategy-based questions, both threw in a few inquiries about life in *Santa Monica*, listening intently for any hint of subversion, real or suspected, among the thirty-one laborers. Tino and Reynaldo paid particular attention to these inquiries and the men's responses, hoping to uncover the DEA's supposed "sources on the ground."

After over an hour, the questions waned and men started yawning, exhausted by a long day's training that had begun with the pre-dawn journey to the ranch. Now, combined with full bellies, the men wanted nothing more than to retire to their cots and get some sleep before the second day of hard work.

Reynaldo asked the trainers to come to the ranch house for a meeting. "I know you have been at it all day, same as the others, and need to sleep. This won't take long."

Millstone, red-eyed, with bone-tired weariness sketched on his face, managed a grin. "Part of what you pay us for, Reynaldo. If I wanted sleep, I would have chosen a different occupation."

Gustav Mendoza, looking just as exhausted, put on a look of concurrence. "Not a problem, as long as I don't have to shout the same instructions at anyone for the third time."

The four went to the ranch house kitchen, where Henrietta served coffee and left the men at the rough-hewn table. Tino spoke before Reynaldo, leaning forward to look at each trainer in turn. "I wanted to tell both of you that I am pleased with your training program. Hearing your instructions and seeing the reactions from the men, it is clear you both have skills to make men follow your lead.

"I brought my four best men for a firefight. I wanted to tell you, out of their presence, that they are bright and dedicated to getting the job done. As you saw, they are quite familiar with weapons and how to use them. They know what they are here for, the dangers, the risk, and so do their families. Don't hesitate to use them in any capacity you need."

Millstone glanced at Mendoza before responding. "We both saw that, Tino. Those four lads will be a boon to this operation, and we won't be shy about calling on them to carry a heavy load. Right, Gustav?"

Mendoza agreed and carried it one step further. "The attack will be heavily dependent on those four. The rest of them are trying hard, but we simply don't have time to get across the harshness of a gunfight, certainly not one against seasoned gunmen."

"Do you have reservations about our chances of success?" Reynaldo asked. "We need to know now, not a few hours before the attack."

Mendoza cast a wary glance at Millstone, a move not lost on either employer. Millstone nodded in return, then turned back to his audience. "This group is the last. We've seen all the recruits, but had precious little time for a real evaluation. But Gustav and I talked today about it, and we have to tell you something: there are going to be a great many casualties, even if we soundly defeat those blokes in the warehouse.

"Now, the addition of your four chaps greatly boosts our odds, but the other men simply can't be changed from sheep to lions in four days. They are going to make mistakes, possibly panic under fire, and many—I'd venture to say half—are going to be wounded or killed. And in this environment, we have no capacity for handling the wounded. In fact, the wounded should be…well, you both know." A mimed gun-shooting hand, index finger pulling a trigger ended his message.

The implied solution hung in the air for a full minute before anyone spoke. What Clive Millstone was saying was all too clear: anyone wounded to an extent as to be immobile should be shot by his own men to avoid capture. In the event of losing the battle, or worse, law enforcement intervention, interrogation and torture would be used to identify everyone involved—specifically the four seated at the table.

Tino took a deep breath and addressed the trainers, looking back and forth between them. "I wish we'd known that earlier. I could have brought some more of my men. They might not be as proficient as David and the others, but certainly better than what you are describing. Time is getting short for any changes now."

Gustav Mendoza leaned forward in his chair to field the mild rebuke from the boss. "Tino, we felt we had to see all the recruits before saying anything. I thought it was possible that this entire last batch might be a pleasant surprise, change the dynamics of the overall group. So did Clive. But the truth is, none of the laborers is a true killer, not in the natural sense. With more training time, maybe a week or two with every man, we might uncover several with real talent and a desire to kill. We could train them to use it, along with the weapons, spread confidence to the rest. But we haven't seen it yet and, as you said, time is short."

Tino looked at Reynaldo, then back to the trainers. "I can contact at least three others who are very good. One of them is older, but very capable and physically tougher than any of them. In fact, he and his wife fought with the Cuban Resistance against Castro. But there will be no time for training with the rest. They will simply be an addition to the number in our force."

Neither trainer hesitated, another cause for concern for Tino and Reynaldo. Both mercenaries nodded vigorously, Millstone immediately voicing their joint approval. "Yes, Tino. That would be most helpful. I'm afraid we're dealing with a group that's subject to come up short in the firefight. If they don't perform better than what we're seeing, we're all going to take it in the knickers.

"Today is what? Friday? The twenty-fifth? When could your additional men be here?"

Tino looked to Reynaldo. "Can we call tonight? Or should we?"

"We can call anytime, anywhere with this phone," he explained. "But sat phone traffic is likely to be monitored between Mexico and the States, especially at this time of night. I recommend we wait until tomorrow, when calls to Texas will attract less attention."

Millstone agreed. "Sat phones are less likely to be used to call Aunt Gertrude about her geraniums and more likely to be used for more serious matters. All agencies know that, of course. In some parts of the world, *all* the calls bounced off a satellite are targeted, especially during late hours."

"I can have them get here on Monday," Tino promised. "But they can't miss Mass at their own church on Sunday, not these three. Their wives would castrate them."

Mendoza smiled. "If they are like me, they prefer having their balls intact. I definitely think they should attend Mass."

"Since it might be their last one, a confession would also be in order," Millstone muttered, making Tino wish he'd not offered up the lives of three more of his friends.

The next day's training went better, thanks to David Avila's outgoing manner in dealing with the trainees. In every group situation, he exercised the mandate given by Millstone when they'd arrived, speaking out to the laborers, addressing shortcomings, giving advice, and encouraging ones who deserved praise. By afternoon, the other three squad leaders were doing the same, and the run, kneel, shoot exercise came off without a hitch.

The change was not lost on Millstone and Mendoza. "I wish we had time to train all of them together with those four leading separate squads," Clive murmured to his partner as the men re-grouped and ran the hay-bale attack again.

"I agree with you. However, we may have given our employers a worse view of the situation than was necessary. I think it is possible that these peasants will perform better than they appear here in a gravel parking lot. When facing those enforcers we've been hearing about—"

Millstone interrupted the other man's prediction. "Oh, don't I know it, Gustav! These young blokes are stark raving mad at those boffers running the warehouse, and that will help. And as you and I both know, when following a few good lads like Tino's lot, it could all turn out much better than we think. But I didn't want to present a rosy picture before the canvas dries. Better they be happily surprised than otherwise, eh?"

"Agreed. As for this bunch, enough fighting hay bales. I'm giving them real rifles, real ammunition, and letting them shoot for real. Let's go set up some targets on those bundles of grass, as you call them."

The next few hours were spent on firearms, hands-on training that fascinated the young recruits. When the shooting practice commenced, the trainers were again surprised by the results. Several of the men shot well, hitting the targets within inches of the bullseye, and none of them missing the backup hay bales entirely. As quitting time neared, spirits were buoyed by the day's events. The young men of *Santa Monica* were feeling better about embarking on an attack that would, hopefully, change their lives for the better.

Meanwhile, Tino was engaged in locating and speaking with three more possible gunmen in San Antonio: Fernando Campos, Ramón Espinoza, and Raul Vega. By noon, Tino had talked to Campos and Vega, and both had readily agreed to come. As for Ramón Espinoza, his wife promised to give him the message as soon as he came home from his job at an insurance office where personal phone calls were prohibited. "Tell him to call Raul Vega as soon as he comes in, Juana," Tino instructed the wife. "It is important, and Raul can explain everything to him."

Reynaldo took his phone back and started to put it in his pocket. "Do you know any more that might be good for this operation?" he asked Tino, halting in mid-gesture and proffering the phone back to him.

"Not that I want down here. I thought about the Estrada brothers, Sergio and Estéban, but they perform so much watch and guard duty for me, I don't want them down here. They've worked well as guards, but I don't think they are particularly great trigger men."

Reynaldo held his phone for a moment, looking at Tino. "I know we went over this yesterday, but are you sure we shouldn't call Carlton, see if he's heard anything?"

Tino shook his head. "No, I guess not. Hell, I'd rather call him to see if he'd come down here with the others. He's met Fernando and Ramón, and he's worked with Raul. He has a lot of faith in the old man, and vice-versa."

"Tino, there's no way is he going to come down here, not even as a backup. And I can't say I blame him. He's still limping pretty badly."

"Hope he heals up soon, We may need him for another day."

"If we don't win this one, there won't *be* another day, old friend."

CHAPTER 19

Carlton had planned to spend Saturday doing his typical bachelor regimen of housework, laundry, and washing his car. Instead, it turned into a quest to contact Reynaldo and Tino, a fruitless effort as it turned out. The new burner phone with international capabilities, something he'd had no use for in the past, seemed to work fine, but neither man responded to repeated calls. By mid-morning, he was frustrated enough to go to his last resort: asking Paula if she could contact them.

That call was met with a voicemail, further stoking his concern. Checking the parking lot, he saw her Mustang in its usual spot, so he took a chance and knocked on her door. She answered with a big smile that was partially blocked by her own phone, explaining the voicemail. He gestured an apology with his hands and started to back away from the door, but she quickly wound up her call and motioned for him to come inside while promising the other party she would call back later.

She flipped her phone shut and tugged him into her apartment. "Hi! How are you?"

"Oh, I'm fine. Look, sorry to barge in, but I tried to call—"

"No problem," she said, waving aside his concern. "That was Caterina Vega, I can call her back later. She was just telling me about Raul and the other two guys who are going down to Reynaldo's ranch—"

It was Carlton's turn to interrupt. "*What?* Who called Raul? I tried to call Tino and Reynaldo, but neither one answered his phone. I figured service was sketchy at his ranch, but I really need to reach them."

"He has a new phone, a satellite phone that has good service, but he only calls out on it. And he doesn't leave it turned on, he says those phones are more likely to be monitored."

"Good thinking on his part. I don't know for sure, but it makes sense that an expensive phone and expensive minutes aren't used to make casual social calls. Law enforcement figured that out a long time ago."

"He called me yesterday, and he said he won't call again until Tuesday. You need to talk to him before then? Is it important?"

Her inquisitive tone revealed a trait Carlton had encountered several times in the past; she had always wanted to know what was going on with Tino, what he was doing, down to the details. It was the curious streak in her that ran contrary to Carlton's sense of "need to know," and now it sounded as though she had zeroed in on Reynaldo's activities as well. That wasn't surprising, since they were keeping close company these days, but it didn't sit well with Carlton to let her in on the intel he'd gotten from Heather. If Reynaldo wanted her to know, he could tell her himself. "Pretty important," he replied. "It's some information they asked me to get, and I think they need it sooner rather than later."

"I can ask Caterina. Maybe she and Raul have a way of getting in touch with somebody down there, and they can relay a message to him."

Carlton thought about it for a minute, not liking the idea of more messages, more phone calls between the two camps. Heather's warning might have been pitched out to him to see if it raised any flags, such as an increase in communications, even unmonitored ones. Again, he chastised himself for not setting up a means to communicate with the pair—but that should have been their responsibility, not his, he reasoned.

His response to her suggestion was guarded. "I think it would be best to get the info to Tino or Reynaldo without any intermediaries. That was the impression I got from Reynaldo." In truth, he'd been given no such impression, but it seemed a mild fabrication to ensure compartmentalized intel.

Paula's next suggestion made him realize he'd set himself up. "Well, Raul and two other men—Ramón Somebody and another guy—are going down tomorrow, I think right after morning Mass. You could go with them and deliver the message in person."

Carlton must have let his guard down regarding his facial expression. She tilted her head and looked at him closely. "Not what you wanted to do, is it?"

He shook his head. "No, not what I had in mind for Sunday afternoon." Thinking quickly, he amended the comment. "My knee's still not up to riding in a car for hours. When I'm working, I can more or less move like I want to and rest when I need it." He hoped the half-truth masked his real reason—he simply didn't want to go to Mexico and end up in a gunfight over something he viewed as a poor cause—and a very risky venture, for sure. *The Magnificent Seven* only works for so many re-makes, he thought darkly.

"Well, short of writing up a message and sealing it for delivery by Raul to Reynaldo, I don't know how to get it there quicker."

The thought of writing a vaguely worded message with "Eyes Only" on a sealed envelope and handing it to Raul Vega sounded too dramatic, almost comical. It smacked of something from a low-budget spy movie... ridiculous...or was it? He mentally ticked off possibilities that might occur: *One*, although Raul Vega was Tino's long-time employee and trusted beyond doubt, there was no way to ensure the other two would not learn about its existence, if not its content. They would surely be curious about a sealed message, perhaps innocently passing along the wrong comment to wives or girlfriends by phone as they headed toward Mexico. *Talkative, gossipy* wives or girlfriends...*Two*, what if the three men were stopped for a routine search after entering Mexico, a place where Reasonable Cause had no standing? Or had a traffic accident in either country? What would investigating officers make of such a piece of intriguing correspondence?

Then there was the matter of the yet-uncovered leak...

Carlton knew he was over-thinking the situation; however, the result from any of a hundred scenarios might not be so trivial, he reasoned.

Not for the first time, he wished for the old days when he'd worked solo, performing contract work for Randall "Big Mo" Morris. His work had been completely independent of outside assistance or intervention, to the degree that Big Mo often had to see the results of his contract in next day's newspaper.

Now his "employment" was as an "advisor," or so Tino had claimed, the recent firefight in a parking garage notwithstanding. Carrying the analysis one step further, Carlton realized that this line of work called for absolute discretion, and the only way to achieve that was by making a trip to Mexico and delivering the message himself. Cursing his sense of duty to the men who paid him a thousand bucks a week to stick doo-dads on shelves in vendors' stalls, he looked at Paula and delivered a delayed response to her last proposal.

"Damn! When does Raul plan to leave?"

Seeing the expression on Paula's face told him that his rare use of an expletive had boosted her curiosity, but she didn't ask. Apparently, she knew better than to grill him about it. They'd had discussions in the past about his penchant for channeling information strictly on what he termed a "need to know" basis. Not once had he budged from his position, and this time wasn't likely to be an exception.

"I'll call Caterina back now and find out." She hit re-dial and gave Caterina a quick run-through of Carlton's need to go to Mexico with Raul and the others. Within a minute, she had the information and folded her phone shut. "Like I thought, they're leaving in the morning, right after Mass. Ramón Espinoza is going to pick up Raul and Fernando Campos in his car. I can take you to the Vega's house if you want me to."

Carlton sighed. He knew the older man, Raul Vega, fairly well, but didn't like the idea of taking a trip with the other two, whom, to his knowledge, he'd never met. "Okay, that will be great if you would do that. Do you know the other two, Ramón and…?"

"Uh, Fernando Campos. I know who they are from church. Fernando's wife is on a committee with Caterina. I'm not sure I'd recognize Ramón, though."

"And we're going in his car? Espinoza's?"

"Yes, because they keep Mexico insurance on it. The Espinozas have family in *Monterrey*, they drive down there sometimes."

That part made Carlton feel more comfortable, since driving in Mexico without proper insurance coverage was an absolute no-no. Most U. S. policies provided coverage a few miles inside the border, but driving into the interior required Mexico-based coverage. It could be purchased at any border town, but that obviously created another documentation trail, one that would be avoided by using Ramón's car.

"Okay, good. I wish it were only Raul and myself going, but I guess I'm going to get a road trip with Fernando and Ramón to boot. At least he's got the right insurance already in place."

Paula's face brightened with another idea. "I could give you Reynaldo's satellite phone number, and you could keep trying it. Or just text him, and he will see it when he uses it again."

"No, after thinking it through, phone communication is not good for this. I'd better just go down there."

"That serious, huh?"

Carlton saw through the thinly-veiled attempt to get him to reveal the information. "Paula, you know I can't—"

She raised her hands in surrender. "I know, I know! It's 'need to know' only. And I don't need to know, right?"

He smiled and shrugged to lessen the impact of outright denying her any further news. She was, after all, an insider—even Reynaldo's lover. Divulging the message probably wouldn't hurt...or would it?

He couldn't forget that he'd earlier suspected her of being the informant during the period when the DEA's Operation Esmerelda had raised so much concern among the two crime bosses and their advisor. Although cleared on that count later, Carlton still recalled his own experiences with the attractive woman now smiling back at him, her defeat already forgotten. A few of those events still remained unexplained.

He'd deliver the message in person.

After thanking Paula for her help, Carlton left to salvage what he could of Saturday afternoon. By eight that evening he had done all his chores and began packing for the next day's trip. Pulling his medium-sized carry-on bag from the closet, he suddenly realized the difficulty he faced in determining what to pack. Not knowing the length of time he'd have to spend made the task harder. He decided to include enough for a couple of days, counting on delivering the dire warning message and coaxing Reynaldo and Tino to return to Texas—and give him a lift. With the attack plan abandoned, Espinoza might want to take the opportunity to head on down to *Monterrey* to visit family.

Smiling to himself at that overly optimistic outlook, he added a few items in the event he had to make his own way back to the States: his hiking boots, three pair of hiking socks, and a small backpack with energy bars tucked inside. Not enough for a long trek, but better than relying on calfskin loafers for a hike across the desert.

Hefting the full bag, he wondered at the wisdom of doing this, getting involved with a project in which he had little faith, even if it was only to deliver a message. Shouldn't he trust his own instincts, the ones that had kept him alive and out of prison all these years? That fact alone was reason enough to think he might be smarter than a lot of other people in his line of work. In this case, perhaps he was wiser than the two men he was trying to warn—and certainly more cautious.

From the beginning, he'd felt the drug lord duo had made a poor decision, launching this half-baked plan to take over distribution to increase their product flow. That line of thinking led to recalling an earlier tutorial from Heather: that the DEA's primary goal was to slow the flow of drugs into the U. S.; stymie the efforts of importers and distributors; and finally, shut off the flow altogether by eliminating the players and their financing.

Replaying the conversation in his mind, he wondered if he was being tricked into doing the DEA's job for them: in effect, calling off Reynaldo's grand scheme to take over a distribution branch operation, thereby limiting his ability to ship more drugs into the States. It wouldn't be unheard of for a government agency to use propaganda—or an outright lie—to further its agenda. Maybe that was what Heather's grave—and false—warning had been intended to accomplish.

But the impact of her earlier lessons on DEA policy paled in comparison to the words she'd said just the day before, standing in front of her car at the flea market and looking up at him with striking blue eyes. Staring at the zipped-up travel bag, he felt her finger poking him in the chest and recalled her words verbatim:

"Everyone involved down there is going to die, Carlton. Don't be one of them."

CHAPTER 20

Monday morning dawned clear and cold at the Mexico ranch, a typical Northern Mexico winter day. By six thirty, the men had eaten breakfast and were already doing a few exercises to loosen up for the day's physical activities. Being young and fit, the trainees hadn't had much trouble adapting to the long, strenuous days, since they had worked all their lives at some sort of physical task. Plus, life in slow-paced *Santa Monica* included sandlot soccer as a pastime for all the young men of the town. They weren't strangers to running.

But the four newcomers, though workers themselves and fairly young, were less accustomed to running, kneeling, standing quickly, and darting from one objective point to another. It made for good-natured ribbing from the less skilled, but younger, more nimble trainees, who had quickly become friendly (and a little less awe-struck) with their San Antonio companions. The banter was taken in stride by David, Freddy and the other two, who handed out a few friendly barbs of their own.

Watching the men, Millstone and Mendoza saw the interaction as a positive factor that made the men feel more comfortable with each other and formed a basis for group cohesion. Both trainers wished the camaraderie could be extended to the rest of the men who had already trained and returned to *Santa Monica*, but they knew it was pointless to try to convince Reynaldo to alter his attack schedule. The previous evening, he and Tino had made it clear that the attack must occur on Tuesday, when the replacement shift went in to work.

On its surface, the attack schedule was sound. The sooner it happened after the final group's return, the less chance of a leak revealing where the men of the village had been, and why they had been leaving and returning in groups of eight or nine for four or more days at a time. Training at the ranch was nearing its end; in fact, today's schedule was to be a shortened one, with weapons familiarity being the focus, and only a few sprint, kneel, and aim exercises. The trip back to *Santa Monica* would begin late in the afternoon, after the other three men promised by Tino arrived from San Antonio.

The trainees would be encouraged to spend time with their families, little as it was, since the Tuesday shift change would occur at four in the afternoon. They had been told a full rehearsal and a short joint lecture session was in store for Tuesday, and the actual attack would be later, probably on Wednesday, or even Thursday. However, when the men were already seated on the bus they would they be informed that the attack would occur in a few hours, a ploy designed to eliminate a leak of the attack or anyone changing his mind. Tuesday's warehouse shift change, at four o'clock, would be the time of the attack. With that shift change would come a hellish experience such as the young laborers had never witnessed, of that the trainers were certain. For some, it would likely be their last shift.

At mid-morning, a green Ford Escape pulled into the front gate and proceeded toward the ranch house. It stopped at the garden fence, and Carlton climbed out first, anxious to find Reynaldo. He almost stumbled, his knee being stiff after the long ride, and he had to hold on to the door for a moment and flex his injured leg a few times before walking. Even then, his limp remained more pronounced than in recent days, reminding him that the seemingly thin excuse he'd given Paula regarding his reluctance to take this trip wasn't so silly after all.

In fact, it hurts like hell!

Raul Vega and the other two men took their time getting out, then stretched their legs and gazed curiously toward the pen area where over a dozen men were arranged in a loose group. By their collective stillness, they appeared to be listening intently to the individual sitting on the top fence rail, demonstrating a weapon he was holding aloft. Raul headed toward the gathering and motioned for the other two to follow him.

Carlton's knock on the screen door was greeted by a familiar voice. "Carlton? Damn, I knew you couldn't stay away! Come on in." Tino opened the door with a smile and extended his hand, genuinely pleased to see his friend, but wondering what had caused the change of mind.

"I got sick of writing up invoices, so I thought I'd come down and do something pleasant."

"Something pleasant like helping us with the attack?" Tino asked with his trademark sly grin.

Carlton responded with a frown, trying to get the conversation headed in a serious direction. "I'm afraid I don't have any help for the attack. In fact, I have information which will put a stop to it. Where's Reynaldo? Both of you need to hear this."

If the terse announcement surprised Tino, he didn't show it. Instead, he answered the question by nodding in the direction of the group gathered at the pen. "He's out there with the last group of trainees. I'll get him and we can talk in the kitchen." He gestured to his right, the area of the open floor plan used for meals, the scarred wooden table and several chairs sitting in the middle.

Carlton hobbled to a chair and eased into it, extending his leg in an attempt to relieve the ache. A woman was busy over the stove and barely looked up at the interruption. Her preoccupation with cooking told him that one more stranger, one more mouth to feed, made no difference to her. However, she finally smiled and greeted him in Spanish, getting a smile in return, momentarily replacing the grimace of pain he wore. *"Buenos días"* was the best he could do on short notice, and it seemed to suffice.

Within a minute Reynaldo appeared, followed by Tino. Both wore expressions of concern. "Carlton, what a surprise this is! We discussed calling you, but you didn't leave us with much hope you would come down here. In fact—"

"I wish you had," Carlton interrupted. "My knee would have appreciated it."

Reynaldo ignored the medical report and asked, "Any trouble finding this place?"

"Not a bit. As Tino suggested, we stopped by your place at Sabinal and talked to Omar. Apparently, he gave Ramón good directions, because this is pretty remote."

"That it is. Makes it the perfect place for getting off the grid, doesn't it?"

The comment again reminded Carlton of his bosses' failure to arrange communication, and he struggled to keep irritation from his voice. "It's way off the grid, alright, but you've got a satellite phone, so we should have set up a schedule for you to call me and check to see if I'd heard anything."

Reynaldo nodded in agreement. "Clearly, that is evident now. At the time, though, it seemed you had run into a dead-end with your information source. But now that you're here, what's the big news?"

Carlton proceeded to relate the story of Heather's invitation to lunch, the odd drive back to the flea market, carrying on a forced conversation that she thought might be overheard, and the final admonition on the front walkway of the vendors' stalls. In recounting the meeting, he included specifics she had given him about the DEA's knowledge of the two men, along with details of their earlier lives which, he hoped, lent credence to the DEA agent's story and thus, to her warning at the end.

During the minutes-long tale, both drug lords alternated between staring at him intently, nodding at some dates and events, and glancing furtively at each other. Finally, Carlton paused, then repeated what he felt had been the crux of her report. "Her very words were *we know it's going to be soon, maybe around the first of February.*' Today's the twenty-eighth, right? I don't know what date you've set as D-day, but we're closing in on the first day of February.

"And her final line, just before she got in her car and left: *'Everyone involved down there is going to die.'* No prediction of 'dozens of arrests' or 'drug ring busted' or any of the usual headlines the DEA likes to bask in. Not even a comment about taking a huge load of product off the street.

"That indicates they may have handed off the job to the *Federales*. Or whatever Mexico's equivalent of the DEA is called. Maybe they even handed it over to the *Golfos* themselves, hoping for a hands-off, double victory, where they don't even get their hands dirty wiping out everyone at the scene. In either scenario, it sounds like your group is being set up for a massacre."

Reynaldo inhaled deeply and blew it out in exasperation. "Yes, we talked about those possibilities, and the tone of her warning makes something like that sound plausible." He threw a look at Tino, who shrugged, but said nothing. However, the look of concentration on his face indicated he was organizing his thoughts on the matter.

Carlton kept quiet, looking back and forth between both men while keeping his expression neutral. He had rehearsed delivery of the long sought-after news, and while it was not as succinct as he had wished for, it carried enough detail to justify calling off the attack. But he knew it needed to be a decision arrived at by the two men before him, not influenced by any theatrics on his part, and without an opinion or suggestion—yet.

A long minute passed in silence before Tino cleared his throat and spoke quietly. "We've beaten this damn horse to death. And now we keep on flogging it. We've considered everything from a completely false report to one she and her bosses hope will simply throw a wrench in changing anything down here that might increase product flow in San Antonio. To do that, it would have to be something drastic. And what you just reported damn sure sounds drastic. But is it real?"

"Or it could be that we are missing something completely, that something entirely different is being played out here?" Reynaldo countered. "Believe me, we haven't been lax in trying to find out something on our own, and the people I used in doing so are good at keeping ears to the ground and finding out what's going on, what's being said." He gave Carlton a rundown of Antonio Sanchez and his wife's efforts around *Santa Monica*, including the single dead-end report of two couples breaking down and spending a couple of days in the village taking pictures of the church.

"Millstone and Mendoza have grilled every single one of the laborers, trying to get any indication of a leak, whether by accident or otherwise," Tino added. "Later, they try to trip up that individual with the same question asked another way. So far, nothing. There simply isn't proof that *anything* is leaking out of *Santa Monica*, and that's where it would have to come from to raise suspicion of a pending attack on the *Nuevo Bayito* warehouse."

Reynaldo raised a finger to emphasize a point. "If the training activity continued for much longer, I have no doubt there would be a problem. The absence of the men is out of the ordinary, and that has been going on for three weeks. Any longer, and Sanchez and his wife would tell me that it is being noticed, being discussed. In a small town, speculation about anything out of the ordinary is a risk, even if it doesn't cause a leak right away.

"But today is the last day. This group is going back to *Santa Monica* this afternoon. The attack is scheduled for tomorrow afternoon around four o'clock." He looked from Carlton to Tino, then back to Carlton before continuing. "That decision was made final last night in a discussion between us and the two trainers. Not even the men know of it, not for certain, even though they know they are the last group.

"They have been led to believe there will be a joint training session—a rehearsal for loading the bus and a lecture—in *Santa Monica*, one with all the men taking place in the attack. Unfortunately, due to the shift-change schedule, that will not be possible. When everyone is gathered for the joint session, they will be informed that it's actually the real thing. That way, no one has a chance to get cold feet, or to inform the wrong party about the attack."

Carlton waited a beat before asking the obvious question. "So you're going forward with the attack?"

"Yes."

Another beat, then two. "Reynaldo, this—" He paused and started over, determined to keep his voice even, devoid of plaintiveness or confrontation. "I know you're the boss, and the final decision is yours to make. So please don't take it wrong when I question you. I'm not questioning your authority—I'm questioning the wisdom of going against fresh intel that specifically warns against going forward with the attack." He glanced over to Tino, including him in the statement.

Reynaldo was shaking his head before Carlton was through talking. "No, no, I don't mind your questioning me. That's what Tino pays you to do—advise us about certain matters. So neither of us is going to be upset at your advice, no matter what it is." He stopped to let that sink in.

The pause gave Tino an opening. "Carlton, is it possible that Heather is trying to keep *you* clear of this by painting a picture of Armageddon? Can she be looking out only for *your* interests in trying to separate you from…us? Me? Reynaldo? The drug business?"

Carlton shook his head. "I don't know, Tino. I thought about that, of course. I think she's concerned for my welfare, but not in the way you're thinking. She's not that enamored with me, and—"

"And you are too modest, my friend." It was Reynaldo, and the compliment, if that was how it was intended, sounded more like a scolding.

"I have a source that tells me you are quite the ladies' man. But only when you want to be."

Carlton, sensing he was losing by allowing the discussion to wander off-track, continued his point in a louder voice. "Maybe back in the day, but the age difference keeps this from being what you two think it is.

"She gave me the info out of concern for me, but you have to remember, Heather Colson's a DEA agent. A high-profile agent, as a matter of fact, who has access to ongoing operations. And I think this information is payback for putting her in the spotlight with the Ramos bust. I gave her a bone, and she's tossing one back. Nothing more, nothing less."

The ensuing outburst of laughter confused Carlton until he thought about his last statement. One look at Tino told him he'd lost any chance to change the crime boss' minds; instead, his efforts had turned on him with the use of a metaphor, one his friends had taken far too literally.

"You said it, not us, *bone-thrower!*" Tino quipped, while Reynaldo tried to keep from joining his partner's laughter without much success.

Carlton had to grin at his own carelessness. "Okay, you two old gossips. Bad choice of words. But a couple of prep school nerds like y'all should have gotten the point."

"I know you were speaking metaphorically, but I've always thought that was the silliest one in the world. So in this case, you left yourself wide-open to being taken literally."

"I'll know better next time. But back to the subject at hand: can one of you explain to me why you're going to ignore the warning—the basis for which I've been trying to discover for weeks?"

It was Reynaldo's question to field. "I think my sources on the ground are better than the DEA's, Carlton. Plus, the DEA doesn't know the exact date, but I do. It's as simple as that.

"But don't think we don't appreciate your efforts to get the information and deliver the message. And don't think we're ignoring the warning. We're going to have a discussion with Millstone and Mendoza, give them everything you've just told us. They will be better prepared for whatever might be in store, even the worst-case scenario, which is the warehouse enforcers being forewarned and contracted to take us out without facing any legal fallout later."

"I have another thought about this," Tino offered. "I think Agent Colson might have been hedging when she said 'maybe around the first of February.' I think she was trying to justify the breach she committed by being a little vague about the date. I think *someone* is going to be prepared for *something* to happen on Friday, the first day of February. I think that's the *exact* date they are expecting us. But by then, the attack will be over.

"However, I want to join Reynaldo in thanking you for coming down here—bad knee and all—to deliver information that is absolutely critical. As he said, you didn't sound like you wanted in on this at all, so we decided not to call you. We are at fault for not setting up a fail-safe communication method."

Carlton took a deep breath and released it slowly while trying hard to calm himself. Clearly, the pair didn't believe the calamity predicted by Heather, or they felt they could avoid it by beating the deadline of February 1. Either way, it appeared they didn't have any faith in the giant agency's ability to gather intel, analyze it, and act on it. Reynaldo's comment about his sources being superior to theirs might be valid in some situations, but it seemed a huge risk to think its unlimited budget and dozens of contract informers couldn't outwit a gaggle of hometown busy-bodies who snooped and gossiped for entertainment. Even with a home field advantage, Reynaldo's informers lacked the true expertise and, more importantly, the technology, to wage a war of intel-gathering in the twenty-first century.

He opened his mouth to lodge another protest, but thought better of it. He was sure both of the crime bosses were sincere in their faith in him and their expressions of appreciation for doing his job. Best to go with the flow. He'd said his piece, and now it was time to give it up. He looked back and forth at both of them. "I was going to try again with something to change your mind, but I can tell it wouldn't work. I respect your knowledge in this environment, and I know you've put a lot into getting this thing done.

"So, since I passed on the convenience store breakfast the others had, let's get something to eat and drink while y'all tell me all about it."

Reynaldo's magazine-cover smile and Tino's grin told him he'd made the right choice. They both said something to the woman, then introduced her to Carlton. This time she stopped, smiled and let loose a flurry of Spanish, which Carlton tried gamely to follow. He failed, but saved the day by extending his hand and saying *"Mucho gusto, Henrietta. Yo tengo hambre y la comida parece muy deliciosa."* His clumsy effort to tell her he was hungry and the food looked good did the trick. Another flurry of Spanish accompanied delivery of a plate of food, albeit a small one. He smiled broadly and thanked her profusely before digging in to much better fare than his traveling companions' stale breakfast pastries.

As it turned out, Carlton's snack was only a preview of the big lunch in the bunkhouse. Sitting between Raul Vega and Fernando Campos, he didn't have any problem cleaning another plate of Henrietta's food while listening to the trainers' sporadic reminders of the past few days' training and the banter among the last batch of trainees.

Looking around, he couldn't help but notice the youth of the group and he wondered at the content of their conversation, of which he understood little, save a smattering of words or phrases. Whatever their topics, the young men all laughed and joked with each other, making Carlton wonder what the mood would be if they truly understood the danger they would face in less than twenty-four hours. Had they been informed of the possibility of their deaths? In this case, the *probability*? If so, did it simply not sink in on young men? Wasn't that the reason *young* men were sent away to war? How could they be that naïve? The young are not really beset with ignorance, he decided, just a lack of the wisdom that comes only with experience.

They reminded him of another group of soldiers from a half century before, and he wondered if they were as scared as that bunch had been.

CHAPTER 21

By four in the afternoon, the trainers had finished with the men, but continued to lecture while they packed for the trip home. A short discussion between Tino and the trainers had resulted in a suggestion that Vega drive a vehicle during the attack, so he would make the trip to *Santa Monica* tomorrow. For now, the experienced resistance fighter would stay and join in the evening's discussion. At five, the bus pulled out, leaving Millstone, Mendoza, and Raul Vega at the bunkhouse. Mendoza talked a lot while Vega nodded and asked a few questions.

The evening had been set for an extensive strategy report from the trainers to Tino and Reynaldo, along with a final overview of the tactics of the attack, some of which had been questioned by the pair while watching the training. Clive Millstone had listened carefully, but waved aside their concerns, as did the other military tactics trainer. So long as the assault was carried out in the fashion taught during the run, kneel, and shoot exercises, Mendoza claimed, the men didn't need to know the timetable or any details, because the squad leaders had been thoroughly instructed in those matters. *'Compartmentalized need to know'* he'd called it, the best defense against last-minute leaks, fear, or confusion.

Hearing Tino describe the theory, Carlton understood the reasoning, but wasn't sure if it would work well in an action where forty or fifty men were shooting at each other. He didn't comment, and his silence must have alerted the pair to possible doubts. He didn't miss Tino's quick glance at his partner, and he wasn't surprised by what came next.

"Come on, sit in on this, Carlton," Reynaldo urged him. "You can evaluate what these guys are telling us as well as anyone, so don't be afraid to speak up if you hear something that sounds wrong to you. Remember, those two work for us, me and Tino. I hired them for their expertise, but their words aren't scribed on stone tablets. Besides, you're here now, just as well help us out with this so we can get done and go home."

Though delivered with a smile, the quip nevertheless drove home the gravity of their situation. Just as the possibility had occurred to him on the trip down, Carlton was now stranded fifty miles inside Mexico at a remote location. Until the attack was completed—successfully—he had no prospects for a way home. And if the attack ended otherwise…he recalled his hurriedly-packed travel bag and pushed the thought from his mind. There was no point in worrying about something that hadn't yet happened and that he couldn't alter anyway.

He felt foolish sitting in on the strategy session, but there was nothing to do in the gathering darkness outside and very little inside the small ranch house to occupy one's time or thoughts. The kitchen was the center of activity, and Tino gestured to an empty chair as the meeting began with Carlton being introduced to the mercenaries as an "operations advisor." Sitting beside Raul Vega, he leaned back and hoped the others would overlook his presence.

After a brief recap of the training program and its effectiveness in similar settings, Mendoza opened with an explanation of the plan to get all or most of the overseers in the warehouse at one time. "Among our group are two senior men, uh, Sebastian Chavez and Leo Muñoz, who report directly to the warehouse boss, Jese Felan, or his helper, 'Gordo' Carillo.

"Those two, I am informed, are the most hated of the overseers. Each shift, they slap, hit, or otherwise demean three or four of the laborers for no reason whatsoever. Therefore, they are *personal* targets for the men, although I stressed that it was impossible to take time trying to single them out, a fact they will soon see for themselves when the shooting starts.

"The good thing is, all the trainees claim they know every overseer by sight. Apparently, months of mistreatment and fear have ground their faces into the men's memories. So there should be no confusion over identification of the enemy. All of our group have known each other for years, but we still ordered them to wear a green bandana around their necks for quick identification of friendlies."

He referred to his extensive notes before continuing. "We have learned that either of the two older laborers, Leo Muñoz or Sebastian Chavez, can call for more overseers in the event of a problem, or when an overly large load has been delivered to the horse farm by calling directly to Felan or Carillo. In the past, Carillo has always called in the entire enforcement crew in those situations. Of Felan, we didn't get any intel concerning his handling of such a problem, but it is assumed to be the same."

He raised a finger to make a point. "Tomorrow, before the scheduled shift change, Leobardo will call Gordo Carillo and inform him that a huge shipment has arrived, with instructions to get it all to the *Nuevo Bayito* warehouse by doubling up on personnel and vehicles. He will offer to send an additional load by means of an old bus—*our* old bus—kept at the horse farm, along with a crew of men to speed up the unloading and sorting process.

"If history holds, Carillo will readily agree. When the bus pulls up to the front door, only a few men can be seen sitting in the seats, the rest must be below the windows. They will all be armed with long guns. Three of them—Freddy, Enrico, and Daniel—will also have handguns, as will Clive and myself." He finished by looking to Tino for approval for the use of his three men to lead the assault and was answered with a satisfied nod.

Millstone took over by tacking a sheet on the wall depicting the *Nuevo Bayito* warehouse, complete with driveways, surrounding streets, and the highway from *Santa Monica* shown out-of-scale in the margins. "This is the highway coming in from the horse farm," he began. "The trucks all take this street to the warehouse, they always pull around to the back roll-up door, and shift changes always occur via this walk-in door," he explained, pointing to each item in turn.

"We've interviewed every single man among the trainees and come up with the same setup again and again. So there was no need to get caught up in over-researching roads and streets. We're going to access the warehouse just like a normal delivery of product. The truck will contain a standard load of feed sacks but will be manned by six men instead of the usual three. Five will be the expected laborers for the oversized load, and the sixth will be Freddy Castro. All will be using long guns when the action starts, but weapons will remain tucked in by the feed sacks until the last minute in case the greeter wants to take a peek inside. Oh, and weapons for the six men coming off shift will be in the truck, too. Throughout the training program, every trainee has been told to head for the truck to get a weapon if they are on shift when the attack occurs."

"Another example of the simplicity of our training," Mendoza injected. "We stressed *'if you don't have a weapon, go straight to the delivery truck.'* That has been drilled into every single man, regardless of his shift, in case something changes on the warehouse schedule."

Millstone nodded emphatically and continued. "The bus will be carrying twenty-four men, four squads, plus leaders. It will pull up to this front-facing walk-in door. As commanders—myself and Gustav—we will direct those squads out of the bus, some through the front door, but most out the back. All doors will have their hinge bolts removed, so when thrown open, they will simply fall to the ground to speed up the unloading process.

"The individual soldiers have been briefed on exactly where to go and what to do. We have used these same drawings and instructions, so every man who's been here knows what to do. The only thing they don't know is who their squad leader will be, and they will learn that at the last minute.

"Oh, and if possible, might I see Mr. Vega drive the bus?" He looked at Raul, then to Tino who passed the decision back to Raul with a hand gesture.

"Of course I will drive," he responded without hesitation. "So when all are unloaded, I should drive around to the roll-up door to pick up the men?" Clearly, the older man had studied the paper and foreseen his duty before being told.

"Exactly," Millstone confirmed. "You will be able to tell from the tempo of the gunfire how it's going, when it's over. But I will tell you when the survivors are all loaded. If I don't make it, Mendoza will do the honors. If neither of us make it, one of the squad leaders—Tino's men from your city—will inform you. If all those fail, use your own judgment by listening to the men climbing into the truck. Or just leave when you know no one is coming back." He paused to let the enormity of a complete failure sink in. Raul Vega's face didn't change; evidently, his time in Cuba had included such experiences.

He turned his attention to Tino. "The next question is, how are you and Reynaldo going to arrive? Or do you really think the two of you should be in on this?"

"We will be going in with my men," Tino answered sternly.

Millstone frowned and glanced to Mendoza before speaking. "Not to question your ability in a firefight, but your blokes will be busy directing their respective squads, and I prefer they not be distracted by having their boss in the same spot." He let the comment lie, and the look on Mendoza's face said he agreed, but neither elaborated or offered an alternative.

Reynaldo spoke up. "Clive, your point is taken. Tino and I are not *pistoleros*. However, as we have talked about before, this entire operation is aimed at getting an arrangement with *Golfo* officials. They would have little respect for me or Tino if we did not participate in the actual battle.

"But I take it you want us to have our own way to and from the action, so we will have to arrange that. And we will be wearing green bandanas, just in case," he added with a grin.

Several seconds of silence went by before Tino surprised everyone by turning to Carlton, who had been sitting quietly, listening to the strategy discussion with more interest than he thought it would hold for him when it began. "Would you take us and drop us off at the walk-in door as soon as the bus is unloaded and the men are inside? We'll come out the same way, alive and in short order, I hope."

In truth, Carlton was less surprised than anyone else in the room. He'd silently agreed with Millstone and Mendoza's observation regarding the pair going into the battle since it could distract the young men. But more importantly, his own body told him that two middle-aged men, tough crime bosses or not, had no business in the middle of a fast-paced battle of run, kneel, and shoot. What did surprise him was his guarded response. "Before I would even consider it, I want to know what our exit strategy is. Oh, and how and when we're going to get back to the States."

Tino waved aside the concern. "Reynaldo and I talked about our participation. We're carrying handguns, of course, but we're following a force of capable young men—*well behind them*, by the way. We've watched the training, and it looks like these two have a sweep strategy set up for the inside of the warehouse that will keep two old guys from having to do much in the way of shooting.

"Anyway, to answer your question, we'll go in my pickup, taking our stuff with us. When this is done, we'll head straight for the border. And home. So don't forget your toothbrush and panties, we won't be coming back to the ranch."

Reynaldo added. "I've checked the quickest route from the warehouse to the nearest border crossing. The old bridge, *Puente Numero Uno*, is closest to *Nuevo Bayito*. It feeds into Laredo at Convent Avenue, right at the *La Posada* Hotel. With luck, we can stop there for dinner."

Seeing through Reynaldo's light tone, Carlton wasn't convinced. "What about traffic at that time of day?"

"Heavy, but not any worse than any weekday evening."

Millstone, who had been listening closely to the exchange, intervened. "I think it would be best for you two chaps to go in the roll-up door, after the feed truck has backed in to unload. The action will be between the walk-in door and the back of the delivery truck, so you will be somewhat shielded from it instead of trapped between factions. But you would be there to make your presence known at the mop-up," he added, clearly trying to sell Reynaldo on the safer entry point.

Tino and Reynaldo both shrugged in agreement to the suggestion. Carlton nodded his acquiescence; it didn't matter to him which door he delivered his friends to. What *did* matter was the fact that he'd possibly— make that *probably*—not see them emerge alive. Unlike Tino and Reynaldo, he couldn't dismiss Heather Colson's dire warning. Thinking of which, despite Reynaldo's vow to inform his mercenary leaders, it hadn't occurred yet. Carlton thought it should have been the first order of business for the strategy conference. Then he recalled similar briefings in Vietnam where vital information was left until last: *By the way, about six hundred NVA regulars are entrenched at our objective, possibly aided by some VC…*

Or worse, left out altogether: *The mission to capture Ah Fuk Me commences at oh-six-hundred and mop-up ops should be over at oh-nine-thirty… Questions?*

Like now, Carlton had been just a grunt who took orders, "ate shit and liked it" as the enlisted men's expression went. *Unlike* now, he was just a kid from Texas who hadn't known any better and couldn't change it. Now, being a lot older and hopefully—thanks to Heather Colson—a lot wiser, this seemed like a recipe for disaster, one he hadn't been drafted into, grunt or not.

He wondered if he had officially agreed to be their driver simply by insisting on hearing the exit strategy and timetable and receiving it, however weak it had sounded coming from his flippant friends. Thinking back to his first realization that he would have to deliver Heather's warning in person, he had known that getting back to Texas might be a problem, and it surely would be if he were at the scene of a bloody firefight—even waiting outside in a pickup like a getaway wheelman in a gangster movie. Being that close to a pitched gun battle was not his idea of wisdom in action.

But what else was he going to do while the attack was happening? Sit at the ranch practicing Spanish with Henrietta? Begin walking back to the Border? While those options seemed a lot wiser, he knew it wasn't in him. Loyalty to the mission had been forced in the military by authority; here, it was forced by knowledge that it was the only thing to do, right? However…

How long could it possibly take to hike back to Amistad? And San Antonio's only two hundred miles in…

His reverie was interrupted by hearing his name in the conversation. Reynaldo was telling Millstone and Mendoza about Heather's warning. "Carlton's relationship with this agent has been long and valuable," he continued. "We would be foolish not to discuss the possibilities this opens up."

Carlton listened closely while the men discussed her report. He was pleased that both men contributed to the narrative, including exact verbiage and leaving nothing out. Of course, he recognized that by voicing the report themselves, the men who were paying Millstone and Mendoza weren't likely to get any doubtful feedback, no matter the content of the message.

After relating the entire warning and describing its source in descriptive terms ("smart, pretty, and dangerous") Reynaldo and Tino gave their viewpoints, then sat back and waited for a response from their mercenary hires. And soon after Millstone started talking, Carlton knew he'd been right—none of the other men in the room wanted to call off the attack.

"That's bloody interesting, indeed it is," Millstone intoned, looking to Mendoza, who nodded somberly. "I've heard similar tales before attacks in almost every dust-up I've been in. Some of the sources were trustworthy, most were not. And some of the predictions were correct, most were not.

"However, the correlation between trustworthiness and accuracy wasn't always evident. I've had the best of sources be completely wrong and a shilling-mongering snitch turn out to be spot-on. I've had to live with both scenarios, but unlike my countryman Churchill and his debacle at Gallipoli, I never regretted with going ahead in the face of a dire warning. If you're asking, I say go with my string of luck."

Mendoza pitched in, giving a different viewpoint, but leaning toward the same response. "I haven't had as much direct battle experience as Clive, but all training regimens cover misinformation and bad intel, and their effects on battles. The problem is, either one, intended or not, can cause a change in momentum of a battle, so the idea behind good training is to minimize the effect of bad intel. Well-trained troops can overcome bad intel or misinformation if the battle plan is basic. Since we're not absolutely sure if this might be either, I would recommend relying on our simple battle plan: A rapid, overpowering sweep without hesitation; no taking of prisoners; and making sure of no survivors in the opposition force."

Listening to both accounts, Carlton was inclined to agree with Clive's take and disagree with Mendoza's, but with both men in favor of proceeding as planned, he knew for certain that nothing was going to persuade Reynaldo to change the current battle plan or its timetable. Nevertheless, he appreciated the accurate presentation of Heather's news and the opportunity extended to the mercenaries to evaluate it.

The discussion of unplanned intervention reminded him of another topic, one he'd briefly discussed with Reynaldo. He'd thought about it again while riding down with Vega and the others and wanted to hear the topic covered by someone else. He waited until he was sure Mendoza was done to bring it up. "What about law enforcement? Won't someone call in if they hear shots being fired?"

"Good question Mr. Westerfield, but all the trainees have told us the warehouse is completely ignored by law enforcement, just as we suspected it would be. They told us the enforcers often take target practice out back, and no one ever shows up. The operators pay dearly to be left alone."

Carlton wasn't convinced, just as he hadn't been when hearing Reynaldo's similar take that night in his apartment. "I figured the warehouse operation itself is being protected by the *Golfos* buying off the authorities; in fact, Reynaldo and I discussed it. But a full-scale battle is a bit more than target practice. Won't the local citizens be curious, maybe call for the cops to come take a look?"

Millstone grinned. "No, because they all know what curiosity did to the cat. Besides, the battle is going to be over before anyone determines it's more than just another day of target practice."

Carlton nodded and said nothing, but didn't like the idea of relying on the enemy's well-funded protection plan extending to anyone else, especially himself and his friends. While the finality in Millstone's voice and lack of dissent from Reynaldo told him the matter was closed, he filed away the knowledge under "Leaving ASAP." Local cops in Mexico probably didn't give verbal warnings or fire warning shots at fleeing gringos, whether on the pad or not.

The meeting continued for almost two more hours. Millstone and Mendoza left nothing out, not a single shred of the planned action. When it seemed that every possible contingency had been addressed, a lull settled over the group for a minute or two as Millstone looked at each of the attendees in turn as though soliciting any further questions. Then he stood and stretched, apparently signaling the strategy session was over. Suddenly he raised a hand to signal another matter, something forgotten until now. "Two more items: there may be slight variations of what we anticipate that arise as the action commences. Don't be alarmed if there is a change of some minor detail. If it happens, I'll call it as I see fit."

A second finger signaled the other of his points. "We've ordered all the men to leave their cell phones behind. They won't be needing them, and if they lose them, there's personal information that would undoubtedly endanger their families.

"For operational security, I insist that all of you—and myself—do likewise, or take proper precautions. That means removing the battery, not just turning it off. Even when a cell phone is turned off, there's some technology out there that can do amazing things with the faint signal that keeps your clock right when you cross times zones. Since we've gotten news of a possible muck-up, there's no sense in taking any chances with being tracked. Those of us in this room can use phones while we're en route to *Santa Monica*, but we have to disable them before we even start for the warehouse." The others nodded, and everyone rose to stretch tired bodies.

No matter what tomorrow brought, thankfully, the strategy session was over.

Carlton had paid close attention to the goings-on since, if he were to be involved, even at the periphery of the action, he needed to know as much as possible about the plan. The compartmentalized, need-to-know form of training might be the correct method for the young trainees from *Santa Monica*, but to Carlton, it seemed a lot like a long-ago plan, one doomed to failure for a large number of its participants, as illustrated by the fifty-eight thousand-plus whose names adorned a black granite wall in Washington, D. C. Having dodged that fate, he didn't want his name scratched crudely on a piece of wood over a shallow grave in Mexico.

Following the rest, he carried his travel bag to the bunkhouse and picked a cot. Rummaging through the bag for his toothbrush, he decided to set out his hiking boots for tomorrow, plus a hiking vest with several pockets. It seemed sparse preparation for what had been discussed for the past several hours, but there was nothing else he could do.

PART III

CHAPTER 22

Driving the Texas ranch truck, Raul Vega towed the modified cattle trailer with its cache of weapons toward *Santa Monica*. His passenger was Reynaldo Gomez, the titled owner of the rig and in whose name the Mexican insurance policy was issued, a policy that listed the holder's occupation as "rancher." At Carlton's suggestion, Reynaldo had checked with neighboring ranchers and learned that cattle could be sold in the area around *Santa Monica*, hence the six cows along for the ride to provide at least slim cover for the hidden weapons.

The cowmen followed Tino's Ford Crew Cab pickup carrying Tino, Millstone and Mendoza, with Carlton at the wheel. It was mid-morning on Tuesday, the twenty-ninth of January, another cool, clear day with sun that promised to warm the afternoon into the seventies. All of the men in the small convoy were silent save a few stray remarks concerning the passing countryside. Strangely, not a word was uttered about the upcoming afternoon.

Arriving in *Santa Monica* just before one o'clock, Millstone consulted a hand-drawn map and directed Carlton from the highway onto a smaller side street in a residential area. The old bus that had ferried the laborers to the ranch was parked in front of one house, and Mendoza jumped out to knock on the door. It opened immediately and Alberto came out, followed by Isidro and Nicolas Castro. The four men split up and began knocking on doors up and down the street. Meanwhile, Millstone looked at the map again and took the opposite side of the street. He began knocking on doors and leaving without waiting for an answer, then moving on to the next house. Within a minute, eight more laborers had emerged from their respective houses and hustled off to summon their co-workers in an adjacent neighborhood to this, the staging area farthest from *el centro*, the center of the village. The quiet residential area was predominately occupied by the warehouse laborers and, hopefully, short on curious eyes and loose tongues.

Millstone returned to the pickup while Mendoza remained on the cracked sidewalk anxiously peering up and down the street for his troops. Within five minutes, the street looked like the scene of a group of concertgoers, green bandanas in their hands like so many tickets. Glancing down at his watch, Millstone noted that a little over nine minutes had passed since stopping in front of the younger Castro's house. The carefully prearranged (and repeatedly stressed) call to assembly had come off without a hitch—and without a single phone call going over the local airwaves. Only one more neighborhood to visit and rally the rest of the laborers.

At a subdued two-word command from Mendoza, the men jostled into two lines behind the cattle trailer, where Raul and Alberto had already isolated the cows into the front section and opened the compartments to begin handing out loaded weapons. When everyone had received a long gun, Mendoza distributed handguns to certain of the trainees and to each of the squad leaders. He gave one to Millstone, who suggested he take an extra one for each of them. "I'll put ours in the truck while you get the rest of the men rounded up. Don't want to frighten the mums and kiddies by knocking on a door with a gun in your hand, now do we?" he quipped.

The first group's arming complete, Mendoza gave a quick order to board the bus. As soon as the men were seated, he stepped aboard and stood at the front, raising a hand for silence. "This drill was to have been in preparation for a final training session, with everyone working together. But things have changed, and we do not have that opportunity. This is the real attack. I repeat: *This is the actual attack!* When we get there, unload as we did in practice, look for your squad leader, and remember your training." He sat down without further explanation and without soliciting questions.

The young men looked stunned for a few seconds, then seemed to take the announcement in stride. A few of them began talking with their seatmates as Raul revved up the bus and pulled away. The convoy, now three vehicles strong, pulled out of the neighborhood to another area on the opposite side of the highway where the process was repeated. With only nine laborers there, the men were armed and on the bus in less than five minutes. A minute later, they too had been informed of the change in status for today's session and began talking with the rest. Their chatter became louder, voices tinged with excitement. Clearly, avoiding another training session in return for the real thing suited most of the trainees just fine. Only a few had wistful looks that indicated they had not properly said goodbyes before departing, but within a few blocks, the looks disappeared. The young men were ready to fight.

With Raul and the bus now leading the convoy, he pulled out of the residential area and back onto the highway, heading east toward the horse farm, with Carlton and Alberto trailing him at quarter-mile intervals. During the trip, a short phone call from Millstone to Leo Muñoz revealed everything to be in good order at the farm, better than anticipated. Currently, only two of the cartel overseers were on duty there. Two others had not shown up, leaving the farm lightly guarded, he reported. Having received only a normal shipment from the south the previous night, it had taken little time to distribute the cocaine bricks among ten of the feed bags and make a discrete mark on each of them. Now, the remaining overseers watched as Leo's crew of six laborers loaded the ten bags on the box truck floor, then proceeded to cover them with another forty-two of the heavy bags filled with nothing but high-quality feed, bound for the warehouse in *Nuevo Bayito*.

It was half past noon when Carlton pulled Tino's pickup over to the side of the road leading to the horse farm a quarter mile short of the entrance, soon followed by Alberto in the ranch pickup. Still leading the convoy, Raul continued ahead, pulling the bus into the horse farm lot. As a precaution, only eight laborers—David Avila among them for the moment—were visible through the bus windows, the rest crouched in the floorboard lest one of the overseers be outside smoking and notice the arriving shift to be larger than usual. Creaking to a halt, the eight scheduled shift members trundled off the bus as usual, taking care to hold the poorly attached door in place as they disembarked. Spreading out, the leader of the group, young Isidro Castro, stepped inside and strode determinedly toward the loading action, followed by the rest of the arriving shift.

All seemed entirely normal to the working crew and the two overseers until Isidro walked closer and pointed to the two *Golfo* employees. "Those two!" he shouted, pulling a handgun from underneath his baggy shirt and shooting twice at the one nearest him. Only six feet or so away, both shots hit the man square in the chest. He was dead on the way to the dirt floor. At the same time, David Avila had pulled his handgun and shot the other overseer from a longer distance, about fifteen feet. His second shot was unnecessary, but made anyway to ensure no cell phone panic button was pushed by the dying man.

The sound of four quick gunshots inside the barn was deafening. Every one of the men flinched, then recovered quickly and stared in amazement at the bodies on the floor. The smell of the smoke hanging in the air was familiar from the training exercises, but the dead men with blood pooling and soaking into the dirt was a new experience. In seconds, the scene changed from utter silence to a cacophony of jabbering voices, commenting on how Isidro Castro had single-handedly started their quest for victory, how the shots had come so quickly and deadly, how these two *cabrones* had gotten their just rewards…

It took David a minute to quieten and calm them so he could give Leo final instructions for his phone call to the *Nuevo Bayito* warehouse boss. "You guys shut up and listen!" he hissed, then turned and grabbed Muñoz' arm. "Leo, call the warehouse and tell Felan or Carillo that last night's shipment was three times larger than usual. Tell him you are sending a double shift of men in the bus, plus another crew in the box truck and urge him to get all the overseers in there before the four o'clock shift change."

While Leo stepped away to make the call, David again turned to the excited men around him. "We need to bury these bodies. Dig a hole big enough for both…" He looked around frantically, then continued, "Hell, right over there is fine! Inside that stall. The horses will shit and piss on it and stomp it down soon enough." Orders given, he quickly turned away and went outside to report the good news to Millstone and Mendoza, who passed the word along to Reynaldo by phone. Concerned that this action was taking too much time, he dashed back into the barn to find utter chaos.

The men had started talking again, laughing nervously at the appropriateness of the grave site, and no grave digging had started. Furious,

David silenced them again and harshly ordered them to get on with the burial detail "before I kick all your asses." That did the trick, sort of. Stifling giggles, the men got shovels and took turns digging into the hard-packed earth. Working hard with the adrenaline rush, the hole was quickly over four feet deep, good enough to hold two bodies. At David's direction, the bodies were dragged to the edge and unceremoniously dumped in, one atop the other. Four shovels made quick work of covering the grave. The grisly task complete, even David was unable to suppress a grin as three of the men pissed on the freshly tamped ground, "getting them ready for Hell," they said, setting off another round of nervous laughter.

Leo's call was met with the expected response, plus a terse order to "quit fucking around and get your asses over here." Closing his phone, Leo smiled as he repeated the order to the expectant men around him. Pumped up by the last hour's action, they immediately declared they were more than ready to "quit fucking around" and go. As they loaded, David addressed each of them at the doorway of the bus, sternly reminding them of the sheer luck that only two overseers had been on duty, and just because they had been eliminated by quick ambush did not mean victory was in sight. Every man nodded in agreement, but David could see they were still running on adrenaline, anticipating a glorious victory in the next two hours or so, and paying little heed to his warning.

Recalling his own baptism in a bloody firefight against a superior force in a helicopter, he hoped the excitement and optimism worked to their advantage today, better than it had for him shooting his way down IH-35. On that day, David had felt the adrenaline rush through his body and experienced enough excitement for a lifetime in the span of five minutes. He had fought with everything he had, firing and reloading as fast as he could, then struggling to reacquire the enemy in his sights and start firing again.

It was a heroic effort, but in the end, he watched while his brother and three of his friends died.

It was almost eighty miles to the warehouse, about one and a half hours for the loosely-spaced convoy traveling east on Federal Highway 2. Leading the way, the feed-laden box truck was driven by Leo, with David Avila as his front-seat passenger. The entire horse farm crew, plus Ramón

Espinoza and Fernando Campos, sat in back atop the bags of feed, along with spare weapons for the unarmed shift already at work inside the *Nuevo Bayito* warehouse.

Following a hundred yards back was the fully loaded bus, with nineteen laborers, plus Freddy, Enrico, and Daniel. Clive Millstone and Gustav Mendoza brought the total to twenty-four, as planned. A last-minute change by Millstone called for Mendoza to be the fourth bus squad leader, while he, Millstone, would oversee the assault from the right front flank and "take care" of any wounded men. If anyone picked up on the order's vague verbiage, it was quickly forgotten by the scared, excited young men.

Tino's pickup lagged behind another two hundred or so yards, Carlton still at the wheel, Tino and Reynaldo aboard. Last in line was Alberto in the pickup and trailer rig, still hauling six cows in the trailer, and hanging well back from Carlton. Before leaving the horse farm, Reynaldo nervously joked that he might yet find a buyer for the decoy load before sending the old ranch foreman back to *Santa Monica*, where he would await word on the battle's outcome. In the worst case, he would unload the cows and go to the home of one young man left behind who would help him make an effort to evacuate families of laborers, at least those who wanted to leave.

In the end, that contingency plan had largely been left untended due to the inability to inform family members ahead of time without risking a leak. Also, as Mendoza pointed out, if the attack failed and all the laborers were killed, it was not likely there would be any further retaliation against families. The *Golfos'* enforcers would be too busy trying to recruit replacement workers to take time murdering unsuspecting family members, he said. Reynaldo had finally agreed, but insisted on making the trailer escape available. Carlton, figuring it was done to give Alberto a way back to the ranch, wished he were riding with the old ranch hand.

Almost everyone in the vehicles had traveled the route before; the laborers had done so many times in recent months. Tino, Reynaldo, and the others were familiar with the area from past forays into Mexico. Even Millstone and Mendoza had made a reconnoitering run after delivering the third batch of trainees to *Santa Monica*. Only Carlton had not made the trip, and his trepidation grew with every passing mile for some reason he could not put a finger on.

He had been impressed with the gathering and loading of Reynaldo's small army, a testament to Millstone and Mendoza's training skills, no doubt. As they approached *Nuevo Bayito*, he hoped the training extended to the men's fighting skills, that they would follow orders from the trainers by sticking to the simple attack plan, stay the right distance behind the squad leaders, and that no one got scared and created mass panic among the troops. Several possibilities for problems went through his mind, all of them capable of creating a setting for failure; however, none of those approached the feeling of foreboding that something simply was not right.

Recalling his days in Vietnam, he tried to put the feeling aside, knowing that every man here, including the experienced ones, Millstone and Mendoza, had likely felt the same at some time. Though he had been involved in very little combat, Carlton had experienced the feeling of unease to some extent with each waking hour for thirteen months. Now, he couldn't help but wonder if this mission, though tiny in size, was destined to end like the years-long war several nations had endured a half-century earlier—no clear victory and lots of dead soldiers.

Glancing at his passengers, he wondered if they sensed his doubts, or if they harbored some of their own. To his right, Reynaldo appeared stoic and determined, though perhaps a bit nervous, judging by his continuous handling of his pistol, a Glock 19. In his mirror, Carlton saw that Tino, as always, was impossible to read. His flat face remained impassive, his hands unmoving, seemingly unaware of the gun in the seat beside him.

Seeing the two men's weapons reminded him of his own vulnerabilities: first, his weakened knee; plus, being the driver, his value as a target was high. Not as bad as being a squad radio operator in Vietnam, he thought, but a prime target nonetheless. He cleared his throat and addressed both men without looking at either of them. "Think you guys could come up with a spare handgun? Like a Colt forty-five?"

"Thought you'd never ask," came the reply from behind him. Tino, leering like a schoolboy peeking into the girls' dressing room, leaned forward around the driver's headrest, and offered him exactly what he'd jokingly requested.

Lowering his eyes from the mirror to look at the proffered gun, he saw Reynaldo beside him, also grinning from ear to ear. "*What?* What the hell is so funny?"

"You didn't think we'd leave you unarmed, did you?" Reynaldo asked, the grin still plastered in place. "I'd really like to see some of that gunplay you're famous for. Today would be a good day to show me."

Carlton didn't answer for a minute. When he did, it was a cautious response. "I was thinking more along the lines of protection, but I'm hopeful I don't need it."

"Just the same, maybe you could pretend you're at a carwash…"

"I'll keep it in mind, but it'll be a last resort. Afraid I'm not up to any gunplay today." Getting no response from either, he amended his declaration. "Looks like I may have picked a poor crowd to be with today, though."

That got a brittle laugh from his friends. Carlton hoped they were still laughing when this day was over.

CHAPTER 23

At Millstone's brief telephone order, the convoy slowed considerably during the trip to time their arrival correctly for the shift change. Everything needed to look normal until the minute the new "shift" barged in the door, so it was ten minutes before four o'clock when the bus rolled into the parking lot of the warehouse in *Nuevo Bayito*.

Raul Vega, with a ball cap pulled low over his eyes, eased the bus to a stop about fifteen feet before reaching the front walk-in door. The eight men scheduled to take the upcoming shift rose from their seats in unison, keeping their weapons below window level. Rising from a front seat, David Avila stepped into the foot well and shoved the bus door outward quickly and with considerable force. This time, it sagged on the two remaining loosened bolts and fell to the ground. He turned to motion for the eight standing men to follow him, but they were already crowded into the front section, ready to go. Within a few seconds, all nine men had rushed down the steps and headed for the door. David signaled for them to line up along the wall and await the rest.

At the rear of the bus, out of direct line-of-sight from the warehouse, the disembarking process was to have been executed simultaneously, but it went slower. Millstone threw the doors open; one fell off as planned, the other one sagged, but hung on by a single bolt before reversing directions and swinging half-closed again. Without pausing, he jumped out and frantically waved for the men to exit. All fifteen men lurched forward at once, momentarily clogging the doorway, until Millstone finished jerking the door from its hinge. The blockage cleared, men jumped to the ground and broke into rough groups, but the look on most faces said they had been confused by the slight delay. Squad leaders were supposed to split off and raise their hands to signal their groups to rally behind them, but it was going slower than Mendoza wanted, as evidenced by his hissing order to "hurry the fuck up."

And hurry they did. Within seconds, the replacement shift disappeared into the walk-in door, followed immediately by ten more men comprising the extra shifts sent over to handle the larger shipment. The remaining five, led by Clive Millstone, dashed around the barn to the roll-up door as the box truck was easing back to it. Its backup alarm was beeping loudly, a good covering noise for the extra footsteps, a possible diversion, just as Millstone had mentioned in the strategy session.

Meanwhile, Carlton had accelerated the pickup around to the roll-up door and slammed on the brakes, sliding to a stop just in front of the now-stationary box truck. Tino and Reynaldo jumped out brandishing their handguns and stepped up to the roll-up door, which was slowly grinding open. Standing on the opposite side of the enlarging opening were Millstone and his squad of five laborers. The two groups looked at each other across the fifteen feet or so between them and waited for the laborers inside the box to throw back the truck's tarp flaps in preparation for what normally signaled unloading the feed sacks. This time, it would signal an added barrage on the *Golfos'* crew.

The door was excruciatingly slow. From his vantage point in Tino's pickup, Carlton could see past the back of the box truck, but not into the darker warehouse interior. The heavy door was rising slowly, too slowly to accomplish a simultaneous entry of more than thirty-five armed men. The men who had entered through the walk-in door on the other side were surely inside and fully engaged with the overseers, he thought, but he could not hear any gunfire.

Then he recalled Millstone's words regarding unknown factors and adjusting to them on the fly. Judging the speed of the door, Carlton hoped he would see this as a possible tactical advantage: By having the first men inside already engaged and drawing fire, the smaller group coming through the roll-up door seconds later would have the overseers completely flanked at their rear, with no escape possible from a cross-fire. Of course, the danger lay in the possibility of friendly-fire casualties, but the advantage over the enemy might be worth the risk…or was it? Being no military tactician, Carlton had no idea how this would play out, but it didn't take a military genius to know something would happen very soon.

The thought was barely formed in his mind when he saw the tarp flap being thrown out toward the driver's side. It slapped the receding warehouse door, then flopped back before a hand reached around and pushed it back against the side of the box and tucked it behind a metal bar attached there for that purpose. Without being able to see the passenger side, he figured the same action was happening over there.

Again, Carlton saw the unexpected motion as a possible advantage. Anyone inside the warehouse would immediately be drawn to the movement of the tarp and the appearance of the workers inside the truck. Whether it provided a distraction from the men coming through the walk-in door or not, it would signal a new threat, one that couldn't be ignored. This might just work, he thought, marveling at the turn of events, planned or not, and realizing that Millstone and Mendoza may have foreseen what he was only now witnessing.

But at that point, less than one minute into the attack, everything changed. Within seconds, it seemed as if the action until now had been a false run-up, a feint to something entirely different from what was taking place. The grinding sound of the roll-up door motor was instantly drowned out by a fusillade of ear-splitting gunfire, a precisely timed barrage that had started on an unknown cue and was immediately at full pitch. Either the attackers had opened up at a signal from squad leaders—or the overseers, being forewarned, had ambushed the laborers. Heather's warning again rose into Carlton's consciousness, but in the ongoing din he couldn't recall her exact words. *It was something to do with everyone dying.*

Gunfire from within the warehouse was deafening, coming in waves and bursts, punctuated with louder, single, boom-like explosions, which Carlton's mind subconsciously interpreted as large-bore shotgun blasts. It took several more seconds before it occurred to him that the laborers didn't have any shotguns, so the deadly blasts had to be coming from the *Golfo* enforcers. Cognizant of the firepower of auto-loading shotguns in confined areas, he wished he had recommended a few scatterguns to be carried by the first ones to enter, but it was too late for that.

Instead, he could only hope Tino and Reynaldo, being closer to the action, would see what was happening and make the right decision. He gassed the pickup forward to get a better view. Millstone was leaning back against the warehouse door jamb, shielded from the interior, with a two-handed grip keeping his pistol pointed up. At a slight lull in the firing, he nodded to the five terrified men crouching to his left along the side of the warehouse and jumped around the corner, his pistol extended and trying to acquire a target. Apparently successful, he unleashed four or five shots quickly, then screamed something to the still-cowering men. The first one rose hesitantly, followed by the second and third, before all five rushed around the opening, rifles blazing.

Carlton couldn't spot Tino or Reynaldo from this side, so he jammed the pickup into reverse and backed up, watching for the sliver of a view he hoped to get down the passenger side of the truck. Seeing Tino's back, he stopped to watch him dash forward into the warehouse, his pistol at the ready but not yet firing. Reynaldo was nowhere to be seen; perhaps he had entered before Tino and was in front of him, placing him somewhere in the vicinity of Millstone. At least that was a good sign, he thought. The Brit gunrunner seemed knowledgeable in his field and, hopefully, both older men would stick close to him in the maelstrom.

Impossibly, the noise level rose even more, and Carlton realized the men in the back of the feed truck were firing from within the box. It seemed odd that they had only now begun shooting, but he knew that time and events during a firefight became warped beyond the brain's ability to decipher the relationship between them, so maybe they had been firing all along. Depending on their field of view, it might not be a bad position, he thought, given the mounded feed bags stacked throughout the back of the truck. Better than the guys on foot, dashing through the open doorway, shielded by absolutely nothing.

A movement in his peripheral vision caused Carlton to flinch, then look to his right, out the passenger window. The bus was wobbling over some ruts in the driveway, ones made by countless trips of the feed truck as it backed up to the roll-up door. Raul was at the wheel, cap still pulled low, his face hidden from view. But the old fighter's determination was evident in the speed and direction of the decrepit passenger carrier as it slammed over the ruts and veered left toward the opening Carlton had just vacated. As planned, he was at the pickup point for the laborers exiting the warehouse, supposedly to be bidden there by signal from Millstone or

Mendoza…or, worst case, because he had seen absolute failure from his previous vantage point and was here to gather up any survivors who could get to the bus.

Trying to determine which, but unable to tell, Carlton's frustration grew with each passing second. Discounting the time-warp factor of every gun battle, it had to have been going on for a minute or two, maybe three. The quick victory anticipated for the surprise attack was overdue, leaving only one explanation—it hadn't gone well. As Heather's warning elbowed into his thoughts again, he made a decision. He had to find Reynaldo and Tino, get them out of there.

He took several deep breaths, steeling himself for what was next. With the Colt in his right hand, he opened the door with his left and bailed out of the pickup, bracing for the pain in his damaged knee when his foot hit the ground. It wasn't as bad as he'd expected, so he sprinted forward down the passenger side of the truck, where the gunfire from within was so overpowering he could feel the percussions inside his chest. He crouched down, ever mindful of the ongoing barrage scant feet to his right, the thin sheet-metal sides of the feed truck providing the sole divider between him and a hail of metal-jacketed lead. A stray friendly round could easily take him out before he ever got to the opening to look for his friends.

He reached the door jamb of the warehouse and crouched lower. The gunfire from the box truck was now almost overhead, the individual muzzle blasts wreaking havoc on his eardrums. Trying to ignore the pandemonium, he scanned the interior for any sign of Tino or Reynaldo, but with no success.

What he saw was a nightmarish scene straight from Hell.

Bodies littered the floor in front of him, and he expected to see Reynaldo's crisp white shirt or Tino's faded denim work shirt among them. However, the dead all seemed to be dressed similarly, and Carlton suddenly remembered the green bandanas. Another quick scan revealed every one of the bodies to have the tell-tale headgear. Recalling the position of attackers on this side of the warehouse, he figured them to be the group led by Millstone, the reluctant five or so who finally rose and dashed around the opening a minute or so ago. Apparently, they all had rushed directly into enemy fire; as evidenced by the closely-grouped bodies, it appeared they hadn't had time to split up and take any kind of crouching posture. But where was Millstone? He had motioned them around the corner and into the fight, and he had been leading with his handgun at the ready. Even so, Carlton couldn't see how he could have escaped the slaughter displayed in front of him.

The answer came a few seconds later.

Incredibly, the crescendo of sound slowed, then stopped, almost as suddenly as it had begun. Carlton realized the shooters inside the box truck had been silent for a while, though he'd not noticed until the rest of the warehouse's bombardment abated. Daring to raise his head a few inches, he spotted Millstone hobbling toward him and the open roll-up door, albeit at an angle that prevented him from seeing the extent of his obvious injury. Directly in front of him, Tino and Reynaldo also stumbled along, their hands empty. Amazed, he couldn't see any blood on either of his friends or the British mercenary. As they drew closer he saw why, but his thought process was interrupted by a movement to his left.

Three men were quickly approaching the doorway, one with a shotgun slung loosely by his side and the other two holding short machine pistols, which instantly labeled them to be members of the enforcer group. At the same time Carlton made the connection, a surprised look on the shotgun-wielding one's face told him that he'd likewise been made as the next target. Shotgun Man jerked the weapon up, bringing the muzzle around toward Carlton while his right hand sought the trigger guard. It was a practiced move and, judging by its speed and fluidity, one he'd done many times before.

As the shotgun muzzle rose toward him, Carlton raised the Colt and swung it up toward the center mass of the man in one smooth motion. Squeezing the trigger just before reaching the target area, he heard the sound and felt the punch against his palm just as his brain registered the sight of the man's arms flinging aside and the shotgun muzzle falling away from its target. Without pausing, he adjusted the upward movement to one going left to right, squeezing the trigger at intervals which should place two rounds into each advancing man. Of five rounds fired in about three seconds, four hit their mark, or close enough to do the job. All three men went down, weapons clattering on the concrete floor in quick succession. One man emitted a shrieking sound that turned into a low moan before going silent; then he lay on the floor twitching, but unable to breathe. Within another few seconds, the twitching ceased.

The silence was absolute for a few seconds, then the roar of two or three over-revving engines sounded outside the roll-up door. Taking his eyes from the scene before him, Carlton saw two panel vans race by the opening, followed by a larger enclosed truck. All three flashed past the box truck, then sped away, the sound of their engines receding quickly. Only then did Carlton notice that the bus was nowhere in sight, and he wondered if Raul Vega had taken on a single survivor or had left alone in the escape vehicle. From what he had witnessed a few minutes before, the latter seemed most likely.

He eased the pistol down slowly and tried to recall all that had happened in the past few minutes, but before he could organize his thoughts a grating voice broke in, one with a strong British accent. "Bravo! I swear by all the saints above me, I've not seen a bloody Yank that could shoot like that! I could've used a bloke like you many times over, what?"

Carlton turned toward the voice. He still held the Colt in his hand, finger on the trigger, but knew he wouldn't have a chance to use it against the turncoat mercenary/trainer. The trio stood about fifteen feet away, Tino looking only slightly better than the haggard-faced Reynaldo Gomez, who looked stricken with horror at the scene around him. Standing inches behind them, Clive Millstone had a pistol jammed into Tino's neck, just under his left ear, and another stuck into Reynaldo's ribcage.

Seeing his friends' precarious situation—held at gunpoint by their recently-hired laborer trainer, Carlton realized who the DEA had "on the ground" down here, but his tired, sound-battered brain couldn't process the details of the deception. He simply couldn't connect the dots between last nights' almost cozy strategy session and the tensed-up formation standing before him. More importantly, he didn't know what was coming next, but it didn't take long to find out.

"Just toss the piece, lad! Nice and easy, now! You can stoop down and toss it gently, no need to scuff up a fine one like that. I may want to keep it for myself, eh? In fact, I know I will, so toss it easy, Yank." He followed the directive with a laugh that sounded like a horse snorting, obviously proud of his cleverness and full control of the situation.

The impact of Millstone's treachery suddenly rolled over Carlton like an incoming tide, and his anger roiled to the surface, making him unable to control his actions, no matter the consequences. On impulse, he pitched the Colt toward Millstone with a distinct upward arc. It landed with a loud metallic clatter, then bounced and skittered across the floor just as the three *Golfos'* guns had done less than a minute earlier. It came to a stop near Millstone's feet, and he stooped to pick it up, his face growing crimson with rage while his gun's muzzle never moved from Tino's direction. He picked the Colt up carefully and stared with disgust at a scuff mark now marring the barrel. Glaring at Carlton, he thrust the Colt into his waistband, while his gun went back to Tino's neck.

Having recovered a bit from his shock at this turn of events, Carlton couldn't resist countering the mercenary's swaggering claim on the weapon. "I don't care if it gets scratched up, it's a rental," he intoned with a shrug and nonchalance he didn't feel.

Millstone's face clouded over as he jerked the gun from Tino's neck and thrust it in Carlton's direction. "Bloody Yank wiseass! I heard you were a shit-sharp bloke, but you'd be wise to lay off me with your crap! The pay's the same for me whether I turn you over in one piece or fifteen. That goes for all of you blokes. Which will it be for you, Yank?"

Carlton didn't respond; he'd pushed the Brit as far as he'd dared, maybe too far. Even now, he or his friends might pay for his actions, but it didn't seem overly important at this moment. He used the strained silence as an opportunity to look around at the carnage and was stunned—make that *shocked*—to see and smell the results of a few minutes of concentrated gunfire inside a confined place. Smoke still hung in the air, dense as fog, the sharp smell of it permeating every cubic inch of the warehouse interior, along with the smells of violent death—blood, urine, and shit, all combined into an odor apart from all others. He'd smelled it in Vietnam only a couple of times, but its distinctiveness made it instantly identifiable for what it was: savagery inflicted on humans by fellow humans.

And that was just the smell. Seeing the results first-hand would be worse, he knew, and he dreaded it. But knowing the circumstances that had precipitated this horror, he was certain that experience was coming.

CHAPTER 24

"Now just step over here and join us, laddie," Millstone said, gesturing with his right-hand pistol for Carlton to come forward. "And be quick about it, but not too quick, mind you," he added in a voice that had lost none of its venom since seeing the auto-pistol tossed high and crashing onto the floor, contrary to his order. As Carlton neared the trio, Millstone made a twirling motion with the muzzle. "Need to check you out, front and back, Yank, and as you can see, I'm a bit overworked here, so don't do anything foolish that might cause my finger to twitch."

Carlton turned around and stood still while Millstone stepped around his two other captives and ran a gun barrel up and down his legs, being none too careful in the crotch area. Carlton winced, getting another horse laugh from his tormentor, but he resisted any further reaction. As Millstone had indicated, he was busy holding three captives, so any sudden move would be met with a bullet, no doubt about it. And the remark alluding to getting paid whether the three of them were delivered alive or dead didn't sound encouraging.

"So where's your mobile, then?" he asked. "You leave it behind, like I told the rest of your lot to do? That's what your mates here did, good lads that they are."

"I left it behind," Carlton confirmed simply, not wanting to elaborate. In fact, he'd left it in his travel bag with the battery removed, just as Millstone had instructed. In the unlikely event they got out of this, he thought he could get back into Tino's pickup, even with the key removed, as he was sure it would be soon.

Millstone stepped back and ordered all three of his captives to move forward, deeper into the warehouse. Within twenty feet, their progress was slowed by visual products of the carnage. Bodies lay strewn across the floor, some lying across others in a profusion of arms and legs that indicated not a battle, but a mass execution. Clearly, the attackers had been ambushed in a professional manner—not immediately as they entered, but after all of them were inside and committed. Also, it appeared that not a single survivor lay on the floor; there were no twitching, moaning, crying men calling for their mothers, for their God, for mercy, for water, for a quick death. That none still cried out or at least whimpered was almost an impossibility in a gun battle with so many participants, but in this case, it was proof of the brutality and harsh efficiency of the enforcers— or whomever had wielded the extreme firepower he had heard during the battle. Even as the laborers lay wounded and dying, an unrelenting barrage of lead had continued to pelt the fallen bodies, evidence of which was verified by the horribly shredded corpses and blood-soaked floors and walls of the warehouse.

Seeing the pattern, Carlton knew the laborers had never stood a chance. Their arrival, which had been kept secret until the last possible moment, had somehow been leaked by their own leader, the man the young laborers had listened to, learned from, trusted, and followed into battle. The same man who was now prodding three men along with two guns trained on them. Carlton had no idea where this situation was headed, but it couldn't be good.

"Turn to the right just ahead, around the stitching machine," Millstone ordered as a large steel table with a sewing machine atop it loomed before them in the dense smoke. "We're going between the conveyor belt and that stack of feed bags, so stay spread out from each other where I can see you. And keep your hands behind you!"

Obeying the order, Carlton stepped away from Reynaldo to lead the way, and Tino moved a few inches in the other direction enough for the three of them to proceed as directed. After moving only five or six steps, Carlton stopped and stared at the mangled body in his path, the only one in this particular area and lying apart from the others. It was the other trainer—Mendoza?—the one who had spoken at length during the strategy session…or what was left of him. His left arm was draped over the bottom frame piece of the sewing table, and barely attached to his body, which lay face-up and appeared to have been shot dozens of times with a large-bore shotgun. His head hung back, slack and barely attached to his neck by a tiny piece of vertebra that shone white in the gloom. Oddly, his face had mostly escaped the damage, providing what was possibly the only identification among the dozens of bodies in the building.

A handgun lay in the puddle of blood soaking into the dirt floor, its magazine half-ejected from the grip housing. It appeared he had been in the process of re-loading when he was cut down, reminding Carlton of the dead trainer's observations regarding pre-battle warnings and misinformation being surmountable by a simple battle plan and adherence to training. Sound as his viewpoint might have been in past events, it had failed him miserably this day.

The pause in progress was noted by Millstone, who limped around the other side of the sewing table, keeping both handguns trained on his captives. When he reached the other side, he looked down at his dead co-trainer and cocked his head to one side. "Ah, Mendoza, my lad! Too bad that you had to go, eh? But your plan just didn't fit mine." Looking up at the three men, he explained the statement. "Gustav was going to give you over to the DEA chaps, so I had to put a stop to that in order to deliver Reynaldo to some other blokes who offered more money. Unfortunately, when we began discussing how to get the pair of you separated from the action in here, he took exception and pointed his gun in my direction. He got off one shot as I dove away, but damn the luck, I banged my old knee pretty good when I hit the floor and lost my weapon.

"Anyway, he wasn't done with it. He took another shot at me while I was scrabbling around on the floor, trying to find cover. Then his weapon jammed on him, but he didn't panic, good soldier that he was. He just squatted down to fix it. Alas, it seems the magazine had a problem he was trying to remedy when the shotgunners saw my dilemma and took care of it." The look on Millstone's face said the problem with the gun's magazine had been orchestrated to suit his needs, just as this entire bloody scene had been.

Reynaldo, who hadn't uttered a word until now, glared at Millstone. "So both of you sold us out to the DEA, and you sold out to a higher bidder."

Millstone nodded, but didn't elaborate. Tino took over, going into interrogation mode to learn the extent of his treachery. "With your history, you wouldn't have any problem working for the *Golfos*, but how did you go to work for the DEA? They have the ability to check out anyone who works for them, I'm sure. Why would they deal with you?"

Millstone laughed. "Ah, Tino, they don't care how they get the job done, they just want it done—with as little risk as possible to their own fuckin' hides, I might add."

Reynaldo came back with another question, keeping his hands behind him, but looking around the interior of the warehouse. "Where did all the enforcers go? Or did you get all your men killed with somebody more professional than that bunch of scum the *Golfos* had in charge here?"

"Oh, it was those enforcer lads, all right! They weren't the best I'd seen, but with a little time to prepare, they got the job done, I think you'll agree." He winced as he turned on his damaged leg, motioning toward the carnage with the pistol in his left hand. The right-hand weapon never wavered from covering his three captives. "That was them what left a bit ago—without three of their group, thanks to Mr. Westerfield here. A sure-shit shot he is, that one! I'm surprised neither of you informed me of that bit of tattle."

"Why don't you toss his gun back to him to get a better exhibition of his skills?" Tino asked.

Millstone looked at Carlton and smiled, raising his eyebrows in mock surprise. "Take on this hot-shit Yank in a gunfight? Like a shootout in one of your western movies?" Turning back to Tino, the smile faded. "I'd wager you'd like that, Tino."

"Yes, I would. But if I bet on anything, it would be Carlton blowing your lying ass to Kingdom Come. So don't be offended if I put my money on him."

The grating laugh came again. "Thanks, but I'll pass on that, Tino. Unlike some people, I know my limitations." He directed a smirk in Reynaldo's direction to make his point.

"I see there's no limits to your cowardice and betrayal, Clive," came the response. "And what is it with your accent? You practicing going back to being a loyal British citizen? Or just being an ass who can't even spell loyalty?"

The offhand remark hit a nerve. "Best watch your mouth, Reynaldo! Don't worry your pretty head about my loyalty—of which I have none, by the by. You'd do well to save your worrying for your upcoming chit-chat with the Rendón brothers."

At the mention of the name, a look of confidence passed over Reynaldo's face. "Then let's get on with it, Clive. I had already planned to talk with Israel and Gilberto, so getting me to them will speed up the process."

If the apparent knowledge of the Rendón brothers' given names made any impression on Millstone, he didn't show it. Instead, he directed his attention back to Carlton. "It will be interesting to see what the big men will want to do with you, Yank. They may want to hire you for your trigger skills. Or they may be really pissed at your depleting their gun crew by three men in just a few seconds."

Carlton didn't answer; he'd heard of the Rendón brothers, only in the context that they were involved in leadership of the *Golfo* Cartel. In any event, things weren't looking good for any of them at the moment, and Carlton wished he had opted to hike back to the States when he had the chance instead of driving here to deliver all of them to what was likely to be a very unpleasant death. Better yet, he should have listened to Heather Colson and stayed away from this entirely, instead of delivering a warning that went unheeded. It was a little late to ponder that option, he thought bitterly.

His reverie was interrupted by Millstone. "Okay boyos! Enough explaining and reminiscing, we've got to move on, because I have work to do." He gestured with his right hand pistol toward the gap between the sewing table and the feed sack pallets. "Just move it on through there now, around our departed friend. I've got to get you blokes into something comfortable and secure so you can be rested up for your interview. You'll just wait while I run a few errands, what?"

The procession continued toward what appeared to be the storage area for building supplies and equipment used on farms and ranches. Two tractors stood side by side, and a few small plowing and harvesting attachments sat in a row beyond them. Millstone herded them between the farm stuff and a row of pallets on which rolls of fencing wire and metal fence posts were stacked and bound with metal straps. Beyond the materials section, a medium-sized, fully enclosed trailer stood, something like one used to haul expensive cars across the country.

"Go over to that car hauler," came the next order, verifying the trailer's usage. "Open the door, there's a good lad," he said, the clipped British accent sounding almost cheerful. "Now pop on inside and move up to the front. I don't want to have a problem while I'm closing the door, now, so move on up. But keep your hands on your arses, mind you, don't get cheeky!"

The trio walked up the sloped gangplank, which also served as the rear door when lifted on its hinges to the closed position. Before they reached the front of the trailer, Millstone was heaving on the gangplank/door, and what little light had been available dimmed, then disappeared altogether as the door closed the gap.

CHAPTER 25

The dim interior of the warehouse had been gloomy enough, but now, inside the enclosed trailer, the darkness was like being inside a cave when the tour guide turns off the lights.

As the door neared the fully closed position, Tino reached out to Reynaldo and grasped his right arm to keep from bumping together in the blackness he knew was coming. Sensing the movement rather than seeing it, Carlton reached back and grabbed his left hand. All three instinctively knew the trailer was the last holding pen they would see, a temporary prison before they died, and whatever plan they devised to escape would involve working together quietly and quickly, not stumbling around like the Three Stooges.

Standing together in the blackness, the trio was quiet for a long moment, listening to the metallic sounds outside as Millstone sealed their fates as solidly as he sealed the trailer with its hasp and lock-bar mechanism. No doubt, each had his own thoughts regarding the past several weeks, which had culminated in the past hour's horrific results. Carlton heard Tino clear his throat and an intake of breath in preparation to say something, but he stifled it for reasons known only to him. Closest to him, he could feel Reynaldo's pulse hammering through his hand and his breathing sounded hoarse and labored. He too, inhaled and sounded as though he wanted to say something, but the words apparently died in his throat. As for Carlton, he couldn't think of a single thing to say; besides, what would be the point?

All of them had known this could be the result. That Reynaldo pressed ahead with the attack and Tino condoned it by acquiescence didn't mean the two drug kingpins were wrong in their reasoning. It simply meant they had been beaten by a powerful enemy, compounded by treachery of two key players they had paid well and trusted. Carlton didn't feel any smarter for having taken Heather's warning as a sufficient reason to abandon the plan. His personality and history simply guided his actions toward caution. Life's lessons had served him well in the past, and ignoring—make that *overriding*—them today had been a huge mistake, probably a fatal one.

As Millstone's footsteps faded, Carlton turned to his right, where he had fixed in his mind the nearest wall to be, three or four feet away. Gripping Reynaldo's hand and holding his free hand in front to keep from smacking into it face-first, he moved tentatively. At first, he could feel Reynaldo and Tino resisting, but he pulled harder and they shuffled along with him without comment. When he touched the wall, he turned right, heading toward the front, but moving slowly and feeling along the side of the trailer, trying to find a seam, a crack, any point that could be exploited.

"Where are we going?" Reynaldo finally asked.

"Just exploring. Tino, you back there?"

"I'm here, being tugged along by my two friends. But I'll ask the same question another way: *What* are you exploring?"

"Trying to find any joint in the sheet metal, or any weakness or seam we might use to get out of this thing."

Nodding uselessly in the inky blackness, Reynaldo immediately mimicked Carlton's actions, then voiced a better idea. "I'm taller, so I'll work the top third, Carlton, you get the middle, and Tino can work on the bottom third of the wall. We can use both hands and just bump along together so we stay at the same speed."

Shuffling into the proposed positions, they started the process that might locate an avenue of escape. To an observer, the team would have appeared to be the three blind mice from the nursery rhyme and quite a ludicrous sight. Under other circumstances, the trio of mature men would surely have howled in laughter at themselves, but the past hour's horror had eliminated any humor from their lives for now and a long time to come.

They worked along the wall, shuffling slowly at first, then picking up the pace as each became familiar with the smooth texture of sheet metal and row upon row of round-headed rivets that bonded it to horizontal bands of heavier steel. After what seemed to be about ten feet, the wall made a sharp curve to the right, indicating they had reached the front end of the trailer. So far, they'd not found a single fissure or the slightest indention that might yield to any amount of pushing or hammering, but they had little choice except to continue and hope for something to present itself.

Carlton was still leading the team through the darkness when his foot touched something lying in the floor. "Wait, stop here. Something's on the floor." He moved his foot along the object a few inches in each direction, then pushed against it. It moved, and its weight told him it was metal, at least several pounds. When it stopped moving easily, he reached down and ran his fingers over the find. It had nudged against another object, this one easier to identify, and a smile crossed his face. "Here's a piece of lumber, feels like a four-by-four block for jacking up the trailer. This other thing must be the jack, but I can't tell which end is which. Sit tight a sec." He ran his hands over the objects again and picked the jack up to examine it closer, feeling a renewed empathy for sight-impaired people.

A relatively simple piece of equipment, vehicle jacks came in various configurations and operated differently, though with the same result. A quick visual examination would indicate how this one worked, but that wasn't going to happen. The darkness was so complete Carlton could feel his pulse quickening in frustration as he moved his hands along every surface of the tool. "Here, one of you see if you can figure out this jack while I see if there's any more blocks." He turned slowly and found Reynaldo's—or was it Tino's?—fumbling fingers take the jack from him.

Kneeling was a problem for his injured leg, so he found the board again and used it to probe the floor in front of him. Within another foot, he found what he had hoped for, another piece of lumber, this one larger and longer, maybe a landscape timber. He placed the two together against the curved wall of the trailer and used his feet to continue the search. After moving a few more feet without finding anything else, he turned to his right and made a sweep back toward where he had found the jack—he hoped. His left foot touched something much heavier. Stooping to examine it, he recognized the shape and bulk as a heavy metal tool box, the type used by mechanics or carried around in the back of a service truck, not the flimsy household variety. It took a minute to figure out the lid; it had a thick steel hasp, which folded over a rotating lock ring. Luckily, there wasn't a lock through the ring, but it was turned to a position that held the hasp firm against the lid. He struggled to turn the lock ring in order to open the lid, but no luck. Apparently rusted or just stuck, he called out to the others to bring the jack to him.

"Okay, we're headed your way," Reynaldo answered. "What have you got?"

"A tool box. The lock ring holding the hasp is stuck, so I want to use the jack to get into it."

"Okay. Keep talking, I think you're about six or seven feet away, but I can't tell for sure."

Carlton instead chose to whistle something tuneless, but it sufficed to get Reynaldo and Tino homed in on him. Reaching out clumsily, Tino touched Carlton's arm at the same time he stubbed his toe on the tool box. He handed over the jack and reached down to explore Carlton's find. "I found the lock ring. I don't think it's rusted, it's just tight. Bring the jack down here."

Crouching with the jack, Tino set it down on the tool box, then reached for Carlton's hand and guided him to the jack. Both of them explored the jack, and it was Tino who found what he thought might work "Here. Can you use this slot to turn the ring?"

"That's what I had in mind. Careful with our fingers here. Try to get the slot down over the ring."

"Okay, it's over it, but barely. You got it?"

"Yes, I have it centered over the ring. Which way should I turn it?"

"Either way, ninety degrees. Go easy, though. You've got a lot of leverage with that."

Carlton pivoted the jack and felt the lock ring turn slightly before stopping. He increased the pressure slightly, felt it give again, then break with a metallic snap. Muttering a curse, he set the jack down and felt around for the hasp. If the lock ring had not broken off cleanly, the hasp might still be blocked. Getting two fingertips under the end, he pulled up, wriggling it at the same time. The hasp popped up and folded back, allowing the lid to be raised.

"What happened?" Tino asked anxiously. "You break it?"

"Yep, it broke off, but the hasp came up. Watch out, I'm opening the lid."

Feeling around the inside carefully, he found several heavy bars, perhaps wrenches or some kind or pry bars. On one end, he found a very heavy steel object about a foot long, square on one end, then tapering to a dull point at the other. It seemed to be some type of anvil, and the point, though dull, gave him an idea. "Did you figure out the jack?"

Reynaldo answered from a few feet away. "It's a hydraulic type, a small version of a house jack. We need a handle, something to stick in this sleeve and pump up and down. That works the hydraulic pump, which pushes the shaft up, along with whatever is sitting on top of it."

"Let's hope it works sideways, too."

"How's that going to get us out of this box?" Tino asked.

He explained what he thought might work, and the other two squatted on the floor to help arrange the pieces. First, he pushed one end of the tool box against the wall. "Okay, where is that longer four-by-four?" It took a few minutes for Reynaldo to relocate the two pieces of lumber and guide them in Carlton's direction. He placed the longer timber against the tool box end and extended it with the shorter one. Fumbling around in the tool box, he panicked for a second when he couldn't locate the anvil, or whatever the heavy piece was. Then he remembered he'd set it aside, but it took another few minutes before Tino found it. By then, it was difficult to find the end of the wood block again, but he finally placed the square end in line, but a foot or so away. Reaching for the dull tip, he found it to be a few inches from the opposite wall. "Okay, Reynaldo, do you have the jack?"

"Right here."

Another minute went by while the two of them coordinated to get the jack in position between the short block and the anvil's square end. Carlton scooted along the chain of various parts and discovered he needed something to fill a six-inch gap. Back in the tool box, he found what he needed in the form of a solid steel hammer, a massive thing of indeterminate use. "I don't know what this is, but it's made for this job...I hope."

Then he dug around in the box for a handle to operate the jack. The best he could do was a big screwdriver. Carrying the two items, he scooted back to the jack and arranged the parts in a continuous line, each one touching the other. With the jack laid down, its plunger was about a half inch from the anvil. He felt along the jack's side for the sleeve and inserted the screwdriver. Working the action, he kept his finger on the plunger, but didn't feel it extending after eight or ten pumps. "Damn! All this, and the jack doesn't work?"

Reynaldo came to the rescue by finding the closure valve and turning it to the right. "To the right closes it, and the jack goes up," he explained. "Turn it left, the pressure releases, and the jack comes down. But we probably need pliers to make sure it's shut tight."

Another fumbling excursion in the tool box produced a pair of channel-lock pliers, which tightened the valve considerably. This time, Reynaldo took a turn at working the screwdriver-turned-jack handle, poor substitute that it was. After two or three strokes, Carlton felt the plunger end move toward the anvil, and he moved his fingers as the gap closed.

"Okay, hold it right there. We've got to get a hand on all these pieces and make sure they stay in line as the pressure increases."

"And any one of them could pop out and knock hell out of us, right?" came the jaded observation from Tino's direction.

"Exactly. But if this were easy—"

"I know, I know. Girl Scouts could break out."

It was the first utterance from any of them that hinted at humor, likely due to the past hour or so fumbling around in complete darkness, working together on a project that might save their lives, instead of viewing the carnage that had taken so many.

By the time Reynaldo had pumped the jack ten or twelve times, the tip of the anvil had dug into the sheet metal an inch or so. A few more strokes caused the metal skin to pop some rivets, then break open as the tip pierced through to the outside.

Even though it was dusk outside, the dim light seeping through the edges of the split seemed bright as a searchlight to the trio, allowing them to readjust the components easily and dig in the tool box for additional items to expand the rent in the metal skin. It took almost another half hour of moving the jack and its string of bases before the hole was large enough to insert the longer board and rock it side to side, enlarging the hole enough for Reynaldo to squeeze through. Finally, he managed to get free of the jagged metal with only a minor scrape, then cautiously stepped around the back of the trailer to check out the lock situation. When he returned, the news was bad. "It's got a padlock. You'll have to come out the same way I did."

Another fifteen minutes of grunting and pushing with an awkward array of pieces made the hole large enough for Carlton, then barrel-chested Tino. All three stood beside the trailer, silent except for labored breathing, which made listening for any movement in the warehouse impossible. As their breathing settled down, nothing but silence enveloped them, and they quietly contemplated their next move.

Santa Monica, Coahuila, Mexico, outside the Nuestra Madre de Merced Catholic Church.

The bus wheezed to a stop against the curb only twenty meters from the church's front door. Raul Vega was in the driver's seat, his lined face devoid of expression as he checked on his few passengers in the mirror. Among them were David Avila and Ramón Espinoza, Tino's men, both with slight wounds. Stretched across two of the seats were Isidro Castro and Sebastian Chavez, more seriously hurt, but awake and stable. Standing and watching over the pair was Leobardo Muñoz, the older laborer who had phoned the warehouse to report the excessive load of product and set up the attack.

They numbered only five, the survivors of almost forty men who had left this village about eight hours ago. Counting himself made six. A piss-poor showing, Raul thought, as bad as any of the battles he had fought in years ago as a young man in Cuba. But once again he had survived. Was it for some purpose God had delivered him? Maybe to be the driver of this bus, he thought. What more could an old guerilla fighter be good for if not to transport the fortunate few who had escaped?

Leobardo, still carrying his phone against the trainers' directive to laborers, had made a single call to his wife, giving her the basic news and instructing her to arrange for the priest to be summoned and the church designated as the rendezvous point. Her arrangements must have been effective, since it appeared everyone in town was gathering around the bus, staring at it and shuffling closer as it idled in the street. Some were crying, some were praying, and all were wearing faces of pure anguish after learning of the massacre moments before in a chain reaction of frantic phone calls and conversations in the streets.

As the community's spiritual leader, it would be up to the priest to inform the wives and families of the details of the tragedy, as well as lead prayers for the souls of the dead and for the community. Hopefully, here at Our Mother of Mercy Church, the people could meet in safety to hear about their loved ones, to pray, to plan funerals, and to discuss what to do with the rest of their lives. Surely even the godless cartel members would not violate the church's sacred grounds the common thinking went, but after witnessing the day's horrific ambush and slaughter, Raul wasn't so sure.

His thoughts turned to his boss and long-time friend, Faustino Perez, and his more recently acquired friend, Carlton Westerfield. How he would miss

Tino, as would his wife, Caterina, along with the entire population of the community! And the polite, likeable gringo, Carlton, whom his wife adored. He had become well-known for his competent assistance to Tino and would be sorely missed by all the young men involved in the trafficking business. Suddenly Raul wondered if word of the massacre would reach anyone at home first, or if he might be the unlucky bearer of the bad news…that is, if he ever got home himself.

That thought made him wish he had gone with Alberto, driving the pickup and pulling a cattle trailer back to Reynaldo's ranch, instead of agreeing to drive the bus. He had known the day would be bad, with dead and wounded from the battle bleeding and shitting everywhere, some of the survivors perhaps dying on the bus ride home. Back in Cuba, he had been involved in several such missions, all of them bad—none of them were easy or pleasant—but today's butchery had exceeded anything Raul Vega had ever seen. It set a new record for man's inhumanity to fellow man…

Of course, the battle could have gone the other way, as Reynaldo and the trainers had planned for and predicted. If so, the inhumanity would have been inflicted on the Golfo contract workers, and they would all lie shredded to bits on the warehouse floor instead of Reynaldo, the trainers, Tino, Carlton, and the laborers-turned-soldiers. What would happen now to the families of the laborers? Or the families of those who had come from San Antonio at the behest of Tino and Reynaldo? What would happen in the community where Faustino Perez employed dozens of workers in his many business enterprises and served as El Patrón to several hundred people? And what of Reynaldo's own community, the ranch and his employees? What would become of all that?

Raul's head swirled with all those thoughts and many more, each interspersed with a jumble of whys, what-ifs, and hows—useless interrogatories with no answers. Suddenly, he felt very tired, very old, and very useless. He was relieved to see the priest emerging from the church, stepping onto the sidewalk and heading toward the bus. The crowd parted momentarily for the holy man to pass, then closed around him, seeking solace from the only one they knew who could function at times like these. Hands went to his robes, faces moved toward his, lips formed questions and pleaded for answers and begged for mercy and relief from this new hell that had been cast upon them. Clearly, it would take a while for him to reach the bus.

Raul reached to open the door, but remembered it had been rigged to fall off in order to facilitate exiting the bus for the attack. As it occurred, it had only facilitated exiting the bus to die. The door was gone, in its place a gap, an emptiness where a protective door had once been, reminding him of the gap created this day in dozens, or even hundreds, of human lives. From Raul's viewpoint in the driver's seat, the gap looked as wide as Eternity.

He switched off the engine and waited for God's emissary to get there and make things right.

CHAPTER 26

Tino led the way out of the warehouse, choosing the walk-in door where the laborers normally entered, rather than the big roll-up door. At first the trio had discussed searching the warehouse for survivors, but quickly dismissed the idea as a waste of time, or worse, attracting unwanted attention. Heading for the door, Tino said, "I think we've seen enough to know there isn't a living soul in here. Millstone made sure of that, so let's get out of here while we can still include ourselves in the survivor category." Recalling the mangled bodies in the main storage area, neither Reynaldo nor Carlton could disagree.

It seemed like hours had passed while trapped in the pitch-black trailer, but it was still light outside when Tino eased the door open a thin crack. Seeing no movement, he pushed it open with his foot and stepped back to take in a wider view of the parking lot, which was empty. He stepped forward and peeked around the door jamb, then around the wide-open door. No one was in sight on this side of the building, and he turned to the others. "I know this is a bad time to think of anything else but our current problems, but I have to say something, inappropriate or not: If I get out of here alive, I'm going to donate some money for eyesight research and help for blind people. How about it, are we together on that?"

If the comment seemed inappropriate to the other two, they didn't voice it. Instead, Reynaldo answered immediately. "I'll match whatever you give. Carlton?"

"Count me in for a serious donation. That was a frustrating *nightmare*. I can't imagine what it would be like to face a lifetime of groping around in absolute darkness."

The philanthropy matter settled, they listened for a minute, then moved quickly around the building. At the second corner, Tino peeked around the loading area and saw nothing but his pickup sitting where Carlton had left it. The box truck was gone, apparently taken by Millstone. Happy to abandon their earlier awkward stumbling in the dark, the trio strolled toward the pickup almost casually, albeit swiveling their heads warily in every direction. The entire neighborhood appeared deserted, proof of the cartel's hold on local police. Now, over an hour after an intense firefight, the industrial subdivision still seemed as quiet and deserted as it would early on a Sunday morning.

Reaching the pickup, Tino opened the door and leaned inside. "Key's gone, dammit! I knew that sonofabitch—"

"Our friend Millstone thinks of everything, even when he's locked us up in a trailer," Reynaldo said irritably. "Why would he take the key?"

"He just wanted to make sure no one else took it while he's delivering the box truck goods for safekeeping. I'm sure he intends to come back and take my pickup."

"Move over, Tino," Carlton interrupted, squatting gingerly in the door opening. "There's one under here, I hope." It took a minute of groping around before he found it, and he handed the magnetic box up to Tino. Favoring the bad knee, he struggled painfully to his feet and met Tino's questioning look with a pained grimace. "You kept leaving instructions to haul something around the flea market, but sometimes you left with the key in your pocket. I had a duplicate made and put the key box under here weeks ago."

"Carlton, your usefulness never ceases to amaze me."

Carlton shook his head wearily while he massaged his knee. "I haven't felt more useless since I joined the Army, but we'll see. By the way, where are we going?"

Tino and Reynaldo exchanged glances, and he realized the matter had been settled previously, without his input. Reynaldo cleared his throat and answered. "We're taking you to the border. We'll cross over where I said, since the bus station is only a few blocks from there. You can be back in San—"

Carlton put his hand up, interrupting him in mid-sentence. "That's not the way it works, Reynaldo! I'm in this with you two, like it or not, and I'm not leaving y'all here in the mess."

"Yes you are, Carlton!" Now it was Tino weighing in, his voice a few decibels above Carlton's angry outburst. "Reynaldo and I will come back and go to *Santa Monica*. We have to go face the music on this, but there's little we can do right now. And absolutely nothing you can help us with there, you don't speak Spanish well enough."

"You've done a lot more than your share already, my friend," Reynaldo added. "Just get back and lie low for a couple of days, and we'll be back to handle what's left on that end."

"Look, we talked about this earlier," Tino said, his voice ratcheted down, but still firm, cross sounding. "Reynaldo and I discussed what we would do if it went to shit. Well, it did. You didn't want in on this in the first place, but you came down to warn us anyway. I told you we'd get you home, and that's what we're going to do."

Carlton looked back and forth between the two and saw he was defeated. No matter that everything had changed in the past few hours, the pair facing him had already decided to get him out. For a brief instant, he wondered what his reaction would have been fifty years ago, if he had been offered a way back to San Antonio earlier than his tour in Vietnam called for. It was a no-brainer. "Whatever we're going to do, let's do it now. Reynaldo, you know the way to the border crossing, so you want to drive?"

"Sure. Let's go. I've had enough…" The comment trailed off, apparently because he realized the futility of voicing something all of them had experienced to a degree, an experience that defied being put into words. Looking embarrassed, he turned away and climbed into the driver's seat with the key in his hand. After a few seconds, he put it in the switch and started the engine, then sat staring out the windshield, waiting for the others to get in. Tino got in front while Carlton clambered slowly into the back seat and stifled a groan as he closed the door. His knee was killing him. Reynaldo put the truck in gear and accelerated away from the blood-soaked scene. No one said a word.

As Reynaldo had said, the route to *Puente Numero Uno* was fairly direct from *Bayito*, and within fifteen minutes they were traveling east

225

on *Avenida 15 de Junio*, which led to *Avenida Vicente Guerrero* and the old international bridge. He turned left on Guerrero and paused while Mexican Border Police directed vehicles into various lanes leading onto the bridge. At a signal from one of the cops, he shifted over to take his appointed lane and began the slow creep across the heavily traveled bridge, a major point of entry into the United States.

Judging from the snail's pace of the lines in front of them, it was going to be a while before they reached the United States and relative safety. Carlton took the opportunity to retrieve his small travel bag from under the rear seat and replace the battery in his phone. Inside his shaving kit was his passport, which he tucked into his front cargo pants pocket. Not seeing any other bags, but recalling Tino's reminder to bring everything along, he asked, "Didn't y'all load your bags in here? Are they in the bed, inside the toolbox?"

Looking in the mirror at the same time Tino turned around in his seat, Reynaldo let fly with a string of curses in his native tongue. Tino didn't need to interpret for Carlton; instead, he voiced his own angry thoughts in English. "That bastard took our bags, as well as the key. Now he's got everything of ours from socks to cell phones, and—"

"Your passports too?" Carlton nearly panicked, foreseeing a long delay as the least possible problem in store when they reached the U. S. entry point. Even though both men could eventually get documentation that would provide proof of citizenship, it wasn't going to be the smooth way to get home...but what of this day had been smooth?

"Nope, we stuck those inside our boots," Tino said with a hint of triumph. "It seemed a bit silly at the time, but looks like the only damned thing we've done right so far." He reached down and fumbled for a minute, then produced his passport with his trademark sly grin.

Seeing the passport made Carlton wince inwardly, ashamed that he had worried—unnecessarily, as it turned out—about a small inconvenience in his trip home, when about forty men wouldn't be returning home at all. The thought brought to mind the individuals he knew personally, the ones from San Antonio—David Avila, Freddy, and others. Plus, the ones he'd made the trip to the ranch with, Ramón Espinoza and Fernando Campos. Had they been among the slaughtered men lying on the warehouse floor? And what about Raul Vega? He'd been driving the bus and pulled around to the roll-up door to await survivors just before he decided to go in after Tino and Reynaldo. Of all of them, it seemed Raul might have had the best chance of surviving. But the rest? Without taking time for a body count it wasn't possible to know, but the overall scene had left the impression of—

The others had been having the same thoughts, and Tino interrupted his musing. "God, I wonder if anyone got out of there alive. There must have been, what? Twenty-five or thirty in that area in the center? Maybe we should have taken time—"

"There wasn't time, Tino," Carlton reminded him. "And you pointed out there wasn't any use in looking, which was correct. No point in second-guessing now. We all know no one inside the warehouse survived, so if anybody survived, it was early on, when somebody saw it going badly and got out. Maybe they grabbed a few others and didn't get caught in the ambush."

"Carlton?" It was Reynaldo, looking at him in the mirror, his voice sounding weak. He took a deep breath, then exhaled without saying anything for a few seconds. When he finally spoke, it was in a subdued voice, one that sounded on the verge of catching in his throat. "You just witnessed the biggest mistake in my life. And if I'd listened to you, it wouldn't have happened. But I still owe you for making the effort—more effort than anyone I've ever known would. And I ignored it, and now…"

Again, his voice trailed off, leaving Carlton embarrassed at the man's rambling attempt to say something meaningful in the face of today's nightmarish result. He wanted desperately to respond, to say something that would make Reynaldo feel better, but he couldn't think of anything at all, and certainly nothing that would be of any value. How could it? Reynaldo was correct in his self-assessment: It had been a huge mistake, and completely avoidable. How does one address that with words of comfort?

Tino came to his rescue. "Reynaldo, I was on board for the entire thing. You saw an opportunity to get a better deal on product, move up a rung to control another part of distribution. That part made sense from a business perspective.

"And both of us were anxious to help the young men of our home town by getting rid of that bunch of thugs the Rendóns had working for them. The combination blinded us to the situation. We know these things happen in our line of work. The violence, the greed, the treachery—it's no surprise to us, not at all."

All three fell silent after that, looking around the packed bridge, watching the crush of humanity on the sidewalks and in vehicles around them, but each harboring private thoughts far from the normality of the busy border crossing. Carlton searched his mind for something to say, if not in a consoling vein, then something to let the others know he wasn't taking an "I told you so" stance, no matter the horrible outcome of this day. Nothing came to mind.

By constantly dealing with the crowd, experience had taught the border guards on both sides of the river to work efficiently, and Reynaldo steered to the appointed entry gate less than forty-five minutes later. All had their passports ready for scrutiny by the guard, but he took only a cursory glance while the drug-sniffing dogs circled the pickup, then waved them through. Carlton breathed a sigh of relief. Without voicing his concern to the others, he had wondered if driving the pickup around the drug warehouse might have contaminated the tires, wheels, or wheel wells with even a trace of contraband, enough to put the dogs on alert.

Reynaldo pulled out of the checkpoint onto Convent Avenue. After a few blocks, he took a left on Farragut in order to approach the bus station on Salinas Street from the right direction for its one-way status. Just like in *Nuevo Laredo*, getting to anything in Laredo took a knowledge of which one-way streets to take in order to reach one's destination. It was one of many features *Los Dos Laredos* had in common.

Another common occurrence was vehicles pulling in and out of lanes, continually jockeying for position on the narrow streets. Miraculously, few accidents occurred. Residents and visitors alike seemed to adapt to the haphazard driving environment with some horn blasts, but few of the rude hand gestures and road rage instances found in other U. S. cities. So Reynaldo thought nothing of the furniture van that angled across his lane, causing him to brake just before turning on the bus station's street. But the big Lincoln SUV that bumped into the pickup's rear made him jerk his head to the rear view mirror, then right and left at both side mirrors.

At the impact, Tino turned around in his seat, then back to the furniture van which had come to a complete stop for no apparent reason.

Carlton mimicked the head movements of his companions and saw that they were sandwiched between the two. All three knew instantly what was happening, but before anyone could react, men burst from the back doors of the Lincoln and the side door of the van. Within seconds, they were surrounded by six or seven Hispanic men who didn't bother to pull out weapons—they didn't need to.

Lastly, from the front passenger seat of the SUV, Clive Millstone emerged, his ruddy face even redder than usual. He sauntered up to the driver's window and looked around inside at his three escapees, now recaptured. "Well, mates, long time no see, eh?" he said, the cocky British accent now delivered with a snarl, only inches from Reynaldo's face. "Don't tell me you've forgotten your appointment with Israel and Gilberto, because I promise you, they haven't!

"I assumed you would find a way out of that old trailer. Not that solid, I knew that, but just didn't think it would be so soon, knackered out as the lot of you are. Good thing I arranged a way to check on your arses, right?"

He turned his angry look on the back seat occupant. "And there's the shit-hot shooter, the Yank! Bet you were the one what's helped the three of you out of the box, right? And without any fancy shooting, I'll wager! I'll be learning how you managed it soon enough though, mark that in your little black book."

Carlton didn't respond, but from the front passenger seat, Tino spoke, his voice laced with sarcasm. "This little reunion is very nice, Clive, but the middle of the street is a piss-poor location to bring up old times and issue threats. Unless you've stopped us to return our bags, you should move along, go somewhere else with your poofter accent."

Barely turning his head, Millstone shifted his eyes toward the voice at the same time he was pulling a Colt automatic pistol from his waistband. Carlton recognized it as the one he'd pitched toward the Brit gunrunner about two hours before from the scuff mark along the right side of the barrel. At this moment, he regretted the childish move; the angry man might recall the insolent gesture and take it out on all of them with the now-scratched weapon. Carlton was evaluating if he could lunge forward, grab the scuffed barrel, and twist it out of the extended hand when Clive suddenly raised the handgun and shoved it through the window, past Reynaldo's face, and pulled the trigger.

Upon hearing Tino's acerbic tone, Carlton had wondered what the Brit's reaction would be to the caustic interruption—especially the derogatory-sounding slang term—but before he could guess its exact meaning, he felt the muzzle blast from the Colt and saw Tino's head explode in his peripheral vision. The blast inside the cab was ear-shattering.

For a fraction of a second, the surreal event unfolded with only the horrendous carnage a big chunk of fast-moving lead can impart to its target. At over eight hundred feet per second, the two hundred thirty grain slug is possibly unmatched in its effect on a human skull, especially at close range. Blood and tissue splattered against the passenger side glass and ricocheted around the entire cab of the pickup even as the glass itself bowed outward, still intact, but starred by a thousand fissures in the safety glass. Carlton felt a few drops of gore hit his face, but couldn't react to it. His brain was simply unable to process what was happening.

The action slowed as the horrific event registered on his consciousness. Like a slow-motion scene, he saw Reynaldo jerk his head back, his face contorted in pain as the hot powder blast scorched him, and flecks of glowing gun powder spewed between him and the windshield and upward toward the headliner. Then Carlton's eyes were drawn to movement of the Colt's muzzle pulling back, retracting from the open window. He had the vague thought that Reynaldo's head was next, and he struggled to come up with a reaction that might change the inevitable outcome, the one he'd just witnessed with Tino. For the third time in as many hours, reaction failed him; nothing came to mind.

He was relieved of the dilemma by Millstone's snarling order, delivered with a twitch of the Colt and leaving no possibility of anything but compliance. *"Out of the fucking car, Reynaldo! And you, Yank, get your arse up here and drive! Follow the sodding van, we're going for a little ride we are, and you're going to drive nicely, right in between us. Any muckup on your part, and I'll do the same to Reynaldo, then you! Remember, I get paid whether you blokes live or die. Got it, Yank?"*

"Got it." The faraway sound of his own voice startled him at first, before he realized the percussion from the gunshot had distorted his eardrums. Nothing was going to sound right, not for quite a while, maybe never again. And there would be no future in which to hear anything if he didn't do exactly as the maniacal gun-wielding man ordered. As Reynaldo opened the door and staggered out into the waiting hands of two of the men, he pushed the seat back forward and clambered out as fast as his damage knee would allow.

While Reynaldo was hustled into the Navigator, Carlton pulled the pickup in gear and held his foot on the brake, waiting for the van to lead him wherever they were going. Beside him, Tino's limp form had slumped against the dashboard, and a brief glance was all he could stomach. He tried to tell himself that the sight was merely a continuation of the brutal slaughterhouse scene at the warehouse, but this time it was his friend whose body was mangled and lifeless, still leaking blood from the massive hemorrhage site that had been his head a minute ago. He swallowed hard, fighting against the rising bile that threatened to erupt from his mouth. He began sucking deep breaths into his lungs and exhaling through his mouth, anything to draw attention away from what lay beside him—a friend massacred and gone forevermore, taken by the same method with which Carlton had made his living for most of his adult life. Despite the stress of the moment—or perhaps because of it—the irony didn't escape him.

This day had been worse than any he could recall, even worse than witnessing the aftermath of a firefight in Vietnam, his first. His unit had not been directly involved in the battle, but was summoned to the scene minutes afterward to take charge of some captured ordnance. He was eighteen years old, and the sight of shot-up bodies had shaken him badly; he had been scared witless and couldn't stop an odd quivering in his facial muscles. Only when he dared look into the face of the grunt next to him did he realize he wasn't unique in his reaction to his first brush with battle deaths. The guy, an FNG from Wyoming, was crying like a child, his choking sobs heard above the sound of frantic calls for medics and help. Only later did Carlton realize that his face hadn't really been quivering—the sensation was caused by tears running down his cheeks, but he hadn't realized he was crying.

Yes, this day was worse than that one years ago—and it wasn't even close to being over.

CHAPTER 27

The furniture van pulled away quickly, and Carlton gassed the pickup to stay close. Behind him, the maroon SUV stayed right on his bumper, leaving little opportunity to evade Millstone and the others, even if he wanted to. With Millstone holding Reynaldo, he was in control, no question about that. Miserable human being that he was, Millstone knew his business and wasn't likely to make a second mistake if, in fact, the escape from the trailer hadn't been foreseen or even staged by the gun runner. Carlton wasn't sure; maybe the jack and tools had been left intentionally, but pulling them over before seeing where they would go seemed contrary to that line of thought. Why bother? And why kill Tino over a verbal barb, no matter how offensive? Where was the van leading him? Where was Reynaldo's meeting with Gilberto and Israel Rendón going to be held? More questions swirled around in his head, but went unanswered.

For now, the best Carlton could hope for was to be stopped by a cop. Maybe another driver had witnessed the argument and execution and called the police. Or, even with the noisy traffic, someone on the sidewalk may have seen what was happening. Not that likely, but not impossible with the shattered side glass covered with blood and brain tissue. However, that hope faded as the van led him straight to the interstate and turned north without incident, staying in the outside lane. There, no one could see the passenger side door glass, while the Navigator stayed glued to his rear end. He settled in to the drive as best he could and avoided looking to his right.

The drive didn't last long. Six or seven miles north of the border bridge, Laredo's outskirts consist of several industrial subdivisions, mostly storage facilities that house the huge amount of goods shipped between the three

North American nations under the NAFTA. Row upon row of trucks, trailers, and shipping containers line the expanse of concrete drives adjacent to the warehouses. It amounted to the American version of the area around *Nuevo Bayito,* only cleaner, bigger, newer—and continually expanding. In addition to the growth along the interstate corridor, a growing number of transfer and storage facilities are located to the northwest of the city, outside the north loop designated IH-69, along Mines Road, an old route which winds parallel to the border and accesses several big ranches of Webb County.

When the furniture van exited at Mines, Carlton figured they wouldn't be going much farther. Their destination had to be one of the outlying ranches or, more likely, a warehouse in the industrial suburbs. Beyond those possibilities lay only the vast expanse of South Texas, not a likely spot for a meeting with powerful cartel bosses like the Rendón brothers… or was it?

He grew more apprehensive with each passing mile. Whatever their destination, it would be a one-way trip for him. He was of no use to the cartel guys, and therefore, no use to Millstone. As for Reynaldo, it was anyone's guess, but these guys would surely kill Carlton Westerfield and bury him with Tino in a shallow grave, or simply toss the bodies to the buzzards that patrolled the ranchland. Or possibly the blood-soaked pickup would be torched in order to destroy evidence that two murders had taken place. In either case, his demise was near, both in time and distance. As to the method of his death, he didn't have to look toward the right side of the cab to be reminded. He could take solace in the speed and finality of his end…or could he? With Millstone behind the trigger, who knew? The prospect of lying only wounded but incapacitated, next to his dead friend, in a burning vehicle? It made his skin crawl—

His macabre brooding was interrupted when the van braked sharply and turned left across all lanes of Mines Road, into an industrial area which, according to the sign, was called TransAmericas Distributors. A checker-board network of streets serviced the big park, and the van made several turns, both left and right, before pulling up to a smaller warehouse with twin roll-up doors facing the street. A third, larger roll-up sat farther to the right side of the structure. Looking beyond the building, Carlton saw they had neared the edge of the warehouse complex, since the area ahead was covered with South Texas scrub brush and mesquite instead of asphalt and concrete. The street ended abruptly, evidenced by a steel barrier with a sign that read "Dead End." The apropos warning message wasn't lost on Carlton.

As the convoy neared the building, both smaller doors rose, indicating one or both of the captors' vehicles had remotes and that this was their destination. Carlton began to feel a little better, less nervous about being burned alive—at least for the moment. That was a process for a ranch, not inside a warehouse. But what was about to take place was a looming mystery, one that he didn't want any part of.

He drove in behind the van as the Navigator peeled to the left and entered the other door. To the right, in the larger bay, sat the box truck, confirming Millstone's transportation method from the *Bayito* warehouse. Checking the rear view mirror, he saw the door closing behind him, barely clearing the pickup's rear bumper. As the door lurched downward, some interior lights flickered on, illuminating the entire floor area. Daylight was apparently fading fast, something he hadn't noticed during the drive. When the narrowing band of outside light narrowed to a strip before disappearing completely, he wondered if he'd just seen his last day on Earth.

Movement to his left shook him from his reverie. It was Millstone and three of his helpers approaching his door. He reached for the handle, but Millstone beat him to it, jerking the door open with his left hand while his right shoved the Colt into his face. The look of pure rage on his face told Carlton he'd been mistaken about the warehouse interior being wrong for another bloody shooting. It was coming now, within seconds, and he could only brace for it.

Well, three score and ten's pretty close, anyway, he thought, recalling some ancient lesson from Vacation Bible School regarding a man's allotted time on Earth.

"Get your arse out of the fockin' truck, Yank!" Millstone screamed at him, the British accent sounding harsher than ever.

He complied as quickly as his stiff knee allowed, prompting one of Millstone's sidekicks to grab his arm and jerk him from the edge of the seat. Pain shot through the knee and he grimaced, barely stifling a groan of pain as the guy shoved him forward, toward the SUV.

Reynaldo was standing beside an open rear door, scowling and blinking in the bright overhead warehouse lighting, apparently still feeling the effects of the hot gunshot residue that had seared his face. He raised his head and squinted in Carlton's direction, but it was hard to tell if he could see or not. Three more of the guys stood around Reynaldo, glowering at him and turning to give Carlton the same treatment as he stumbled forward. None of them uttered a word, however. Apparently, the loud-mouthed Brit was the sole voice of the group.

"Enjoy your little trip with your mate, did you?" Millstone asked, a snide grin on his face. "Bet you had to carry the conversation, eh?"

Carlton thought of several clever comebacks to the asinine questions, most of them regarding the gun runner's parentage, but dismissed the idea as puerile, useless, and life-threatening. Such dialogue sounded good in tough-guy movies, but this was real life, and he had recently seen the reward for a smart remark. He hadn't been executed yet, and it appeared he might be included in the meeting with Reynaldo and the Rendón brothers, so waiting to see what took place—without asking for a bullet—seemed the best plan of action.

Two more guys were now exiting the furniture van, and they joined the entourage as Millstone led everyone toward the rear of the building. Narrow glassed-in offices lined the back wall, and the still-silent men herded Reynaldo and Carlton toward the left-hand corner one, where a dim light barely illuminated its interior. Leading the group, Millstone flung the door open and flipped a switch, bathing the room in incandescent light instead of the harsh glare of the florescent warehouse strips. He stood to one side of the door and motioned for entry without saying anything.

His helpers obviously had been previously instructed about the seating arrangements. Reynaldo's three guards pushed him into a chair facing the desk while Carlton's keepers shoved him toward an ordinary door near the back corner facing the parking lot. Carlton now saw the office was larger, still narrow, but much deeper than the others, extending all the way to the back side of the building where a wide plate-glass window revealed a black Range Rover parked in back. The waning daylight and dark window tint prevented his being able to see if anyone was in the car, and no other vehicles sat in the lot, not within sight, anyway.

As his guards led him by the desk, he glanced at Reynaldo, who seemed to be recovering somewhat. The incessant blinking had slowed, and he was leaned back in his chair with arms on the chrome armrests and his face expressionless while the three men hovered near him. Observing him more closely however, Carlton watched his hands flexing and gripping the armrests tightly enough to turn his knuckles white. Neither one of us is going to relax for a while, he thought, wishing the cartel bosses would show up. No matter what happened then, it had to beat sitting here waiting and anticipating something bad—or did it? It was hard to imagine the day getting any worse, he thought, as one guy opened the door and flipped a light switch before the other two shoved him inside and slammed it shut.

The door had opened to a closet—it now appeared to be more of a storage room—which was about five feet wide and fifteen feet long. A couple of filing cabinets sat against a wall, and a well-worn secretary's chair was shoved into a corner. Otherwise, the room was empty. He checked the ceiling corners for cameras, but the small room had apparently been deemed unimportant, giving him hope that he could engineer an escape.

His knee was hurting big-time, and he pulled the chair out, spun it around and plopped down with a groan; really, it was more of an exhalation of breath he had been holding since having the Colt shoved into his face by the raging Millstone. Being isolated in here—or anywhere—was better than that tense moment.

He looked around the sparsely-occupied room, wondering if there might be an avenue of escape. The ceiling appeared to be painted drywall, not drop-in tiles that might be pushed up to reveal HVAC ducts or a ventilation fan with a duct to the outside wall of the building. The interior walls were likewise sheetrock, and no other door accessed the room. Without walking past everyone in the office, there was no way out of here.

He had to hope the upcoming meeting with the Rendón brothers went a lot better than he thought it would. Otherwise, he could only hope that his insignificance would result in his being released when the meeting ended, or being moved elsewhere, even for a short time—not a likely scenario for a witness to a murder. That left waiting for a lull in the meeting, maybe a bathroom break or some type of interruption, when he could open the door and run for his life. A slim chance of success, but better than any alternative Millstone had in store for him.

He was contemplating the quickest route out of the building when he heard the unmistakable sound of a key turning in the deadbolt. It told him all he needed to know about leaving any time soon. He shook his head in frustration and wracked his brain to come up with something else. Three or four fruitless minutes went by before a vague idea came to mind, and another minute passed while he organized his thoughts into a plan.

It began by pulling out his phone and punching in what had become a favorite number. He hoped the text made sense, and he hoped the phone-tracing technology he'd heard about extended to his burner.

In Laredo, off Mines Rd, TransAmerica Distributors warehouse. Golfo cartel guys here, plus drugs, holding me and Gomez. Black Rng Rovr in back. Can u track this phone? HURRY

CHAPTER 28

Fifteen minutes had crawled by when a door at the rear of the office opened. Two men entered, both wearing casual, but expensive-looking clothes: dark slacks, dress shirts with cufflinks, and gleaming cowboy boots. Neither wore jackets. Judging by their appearance, they had to be the Rendón brothers, and they appeared to be unaccompanied, save Millstone and his companions out in the warehouse. That was an unusual situation; cartel higher-ups were always guarded by a contingent of heavily armed men, and Reynaldo wondered about the deviation from standard practice.

Reynaldo knew of the pair, but he had not met them face-to-face until now. They reputedly ran the northern portion of the *Golfo* trade area and answered only to the Benavides family. He had to look closely to determine they weren't twins and finally saw that one was heavier and a few years older.

They strode into the room abreast, neither displaying leadership over the other. In fact, neither displayed much of anything that would give away their moods or intentions. A look of mild interest could describe their countenances, and silence seemed to be their trademark opening gambit. On the surface, it was better than the maniacal Millstone's ravings, but Reynaldo wondered if this were the calm before the storm. Each pulled a chair toward the desk and positioned them on either side of Reynaldo, but remained standing. Only when one of them spoke did a hint of leadership appear.

"I am Israel Rendón, and this is my brother Gilberto," the older one announced, looking at Reynaldo like a beggar who had shown up at the back door. "And you are Reynaldo Gomez, the fool who thought he could take over our *Nuevo Bayito* operation."

Reynaldo took a deep breath and leaned forward in his chair, still blinking in reaction to the burning in his left eye. The entire left side of his face had been singed by the powder blast from the shot that had killed Tino. Also, his hearing was impaired; he heard everything with a tinny-sounding distortion, and his capacity to think clearly was not in good shape. In addition to watching his life-long friend die, he had signed a death warrant for thirty or forty other men and discovered the turncoat treachery of a well-paid associate—all in the last few hours. But he had to put those events aside for the moment and use every ounce of his negotiating skills, politeness, forthrightness, and downright courage in dealing with these dangerous men. This was a time to respond very carefully in order to stay alive.

He turned to face the speaker and talked quietly but forcefully. "No, Israel, I am the fool who has been paying higher prices for each purchase in order to cover the amount your enforcers were stealing. They knew they couldn't get by with stealing it directly from you, so they started charging me a surcharge on each shipment. This has been going on for over six months.

"Now, since I paid the higher price, you—and the Benavides family—would have been receiving more money for the product had those thieves not been taking it for themselves. Therefore, they were, in effect, stealing from *you and Carlos Benavides*. So while I am the fool today, who has been the fool for the past six months?"

A furtive glance exchanged by the brothers told Reynaldo what he had suspected: they hadn't known of the surcharge going into the enforcers' pockets. "And how do you know this 'surcharge' as you call it, was not an ordinary increase in the market price?" the other one, Gilberto, asked.

"The idiots had the balls to brag about it to their workers. One of them was my brother-in-law, Romero Cano. He reported it to the appropriate man in your chain of command. As a result, he and his wife, my wife's sister, were both murdered the next day. That indicates that he was on the take also. In addition, after those murders, the enforcers began to treat the other workers with extreme harshness, far in excess of ordinary discipline: unwarranted slappings, beatings, and threats of more to come—"

"So you took an immediate interest in all this brutality for what reason?" Israel interrupted. "An excuse to take over and run things more diplomatically? Maybe out of the kindness of your heart and not the welfare of your pocketbook? Like us, you are a drug trafficker, Gomez, not a priest, not a good Samaritan."

"I was born in *Santa Monica*. And yes, in addition to my brother-in-law, I do know the families of some of the workers. And while my interest in this matter was initially financial, what I heard about the treatment of the men was enough to tell me they needed help."

"And what of this Perez? Another good Samaritan?"

"Faustino Perez was also born there, in *Santa Monica*. He was gunned down in cold blood an hour ago—by Clive Millstone, while in our employ, *as well as yours!*" he added, the first raised voice in the meeting. "Exactly the kind of senseless violence that went on for years until higher-ups like Carlos Benavides saw that such stupidity only brings more attention from law enforcement on both sides of the Border.

"Like your warehouse workers, Millstone is drawing pay from two sources, possibly a third. That should verify what I told you about the quality of men in your employ, even if Romero and his wife had not been killed. So you may want to watch your back around Millstone, since he's known for killing his employers by shooting them at close range."

"So, the good Samaritans—Gomez and Perez—train my workers to rise up against my management team in order to take over the *Bayito* transfer sector," the younger one stated, ignoring Reynaldo's descriptive indictment of Millstone.

Reynaldo didn't respond immediately, but evaluated the course of the conversation. The "Samaritan" statement came from Gilberto, not Israel, who had first used it. The tag-team nature of the interrogation was being employed to make Reynaldo turn back and forth due to the seating arrangement. The intended effect was to keep him off-balance, unsure of where the next question or comment was coming from. It was a tactic Reynaldo himself had used on occasion in other business matters and he took it in stride.

He turned to face the younger Rendón. "Yes. That is what I planned to do. And had it succeeded, you would have been pleased with the results, if you had even bothered to notice. Your profits would have stayed the same, and you might have picked up some additional trade due to the *Bayito* operation being well-run. For example, Tino Perez would have been a good prospect, had that idiot not killed him. Adding a customer would have been good, since you lost your outlet in San Antonio—"

"What do you mean, 'lost our outlet in San Antonio'?" Gilberto snapped, forgetting the tag-team tactic and telling Reynaldo he had struck another nerve.

"You didn't realize that Brujido Ramos is no longer in business? Thanks to *his* idiocy, he is not among us, not for several months. If your product movement has not suffered, it is because the thieves you have employed at *Bayito* have taken over his product share. Since it is certain that you and your brother, or even Carlos Benavides himself, must approve new wholesale movers, they are undoubtedly moving it someplace at retail, thus forcing their street customers to pay the surcharge. Again, your bottom line does not suffer, but the effect is theft of the profit margin between wholesale and retail. And I am certain that you do not approve of employees at the wholesale level moving into retail without your consent."

"How do you know this about Ramos?" Israel asked in his calm, measured voice. "We pay well to remain apprised of every event in our market area."

"Because I personally commissioned the elimination of Ramos, Tino and I did, but news of his demise was in the newspaper, Israel," Reynaldo said, his tone almost gentle, but not as in explaining something to a child. He knew it was dangerous, but he hoped walking the tightrope between audacity and honesty would keep him alive. "There was a shootout during a kidnapping exchange. He was killed by…" Reynaldo let his voice trail off, feigning a lapse of memory. It was intentionally a poor act, and it got the desired response, if from the undesirable brother.

Gilberto jumped in. "Was killed by who? Don't just make something up, Gomez, we're going to check out this story of yours—"

"So I suggest you tell the truth," Israel ended for him, his senior position revealed by his tone of voice.

Reynaldo didn't hesitate. "The Anglo you have locked in that closet." He gestured toward the back of the room. "If you check out the official newspaper account, it will say a DEA agent, a female, killed him. She was there because he gave her the tip, so she may have fired a shot or two to get the credit. But I paid *him* to do it, and you can be certain that he is quite capable by asking Millstone."

"Why kill Ramos? Was he operating in Wichita Falls? Oh, don't look so surprised, Gomez! You think we don't know all about you? *Do you know who we are?*

If Israel had shown his leadership of the sibling team, Gilberto was now showing why he would never achieve the position by displaying unnecessary arrogance, a trait that surely infuriated Israel. Reynaldo knew he had to tread carefully here in order to placate the younger man while keeping a civil tone in this conversation that was quickly becoming unraveled and off-subject.

"No, he wasn't encroaching on my North Texas turf. He kidnapped my daughter. My *eleven-year-old* daughter, Gilberto!" he said, his voice rising at the end. "He held her for a ransom of several kilos of cocaine and two hundred thousand in cash. Tino and I employed that Anglo to handle it." Reynaldo again nodded nonchalantly toward the closet. "His name is Carlton Westerfield. He was the bag man for the exchange. It turned out to be a bad day for Brujido Ramos, the day he learned not to kidnap young girls.

"And to answer your other questions, yes, I am sure you know all about me. You should, because I have been a good customer for over four years. Consequently, I know who the Rendón brothers are, and right now they are wasting time by interrogating a good customer instead of cleaning their house of thieves."

"You are painting a bad picture of Ramos, one of our better customers in the San Antonio market," Israel said. "Why would he do such a thing when his business was doing well and showing increases all the time?"

"You would have to ask him, and that won't be possible. However, he had supposedly planned to sell my daughter to a higher-up in the cartel structure, somewhere in the Mexico City area."

"The *Golfos* are not operating in *Distrito Federal*," Israel said, referring to the Federal District surrounding the capital city of Mexico.

Reynaldo shrugged. "Perhaps Ramos was courting someone in another cartel, wanting to change suppliers. It would make sense, since he was probably incurring the same surcharge as I was, and looking for a better price. But I did not hear the name of any individual, and I am not familiar with Mexico City cartel structure. I only heard that my daughter was destined to be sold..." Again, his voice trailed off, this time without putting on an act.

"If what you say is true, then Brujido Ramos was engaged in a very unsavory practice," Israel observed. "And you had every right to have him eliminated.

"As to your accusations regarding our contract crew at *Bayito*, it will take some time to check out."

Apparently feeling the need to have some input, Gilberto spoke up. "We will check out all this you have told us, not only about Ramos and the *Bayito* operation, but this mysterious gringo we now have locked in that storeroom."

Israel leaned in closer to Reynaldo. "Gomez, you talk very well and you tell a convincing story for your actions. But you realize we cannot let this thing go unanswered, regardless of what we find out about Ramos or our enforcement team. If we did not retaliate by making an example of you and the gringo—" He stopped, a frown creasing his brow as he tried to identify the sound reaching his ears.

A faint background noise had suddenly become louder in a matter of seconds, enabling all three men to recognize the dull clatter of a helicopter rotor which was now accompanied by the sound of feet running across the concrete floor of the warehouse. The door burst open and Millstone shouted an unnecessary warning to the brothers before flinging the door back and withdrawing into the warehouse. As the door slammed shut, Israel and Gilberto were sprinting toward the back door of the office, the one leading to the parking lot and the Range Rover. As they reached the door, headlights were reflecting off the Rover's gleaming black paint job, along with the red and blue strobe of police lights. The helicopter was hovering, its blinding white spotlight raking across the parking lot, eliminating the cover of darkness for a hundred yards in every direction.

Reynaldo didn't move for a few seconds. Sitting in the chair for the past half hour had disguised the extent of damage, both physical and mental, he had suffered from the day's brain-numbing events. It had taken all his concentration to carry on the tense conversation, and its sudden interruption confused him. Then his brain processed what was happening, and he saw a chance to escape this deathtrap.

He pushed out of the chair and tried to run for the same door the Rendón brothers had just exited, but his tired brain wasn't the only thing impaired. His legs didn't want to move with any coordination and his balance was poor, almost non-existent. He fell to the floor immediately, stunned, but unhurt. He stayed down for a minute, flexing his legs and arms to restore circulation. When he rose to his feet again, his coordination seemed slightly better, so he blinked and shook his head again, trying to clear his vision. Aiming for the door, he glanced to his left and detoured toward the closet near the back of the office.

He had seen Millstone's three men push Carlton inside, but hadn't realized the deadbolt had been locked with a key. He grabbed the handle and turned it, jerking it toward him, but the deadbolt held the door firmly shut. This close, he could hear Carlton pounding on the door and yelling something, but his hearing didn't work well enough to tell his brain what was being shouted. Undoubtedly, it concerned getting him out, which he intended to do—but how?

Looking around the sparse office, he couldn't see anything that might break the door or sheetrock walls. He was considering going into the warehouse section to look for a tool when his eyes were drawn to the desk and its drawers, their chrome pulls now facing him. He wobbled back to the desk and jerked the drawers open, starting with the top left. Behind him, he could hear Carlton's voice and loud pounding on the door. He vaguely wondered whether his hearing was getting better or Carlton was getting louder.

The spare storeroom key was in the right-hand drawer, on a ring with several others. He grabbed the ring and made his way back to the storeroom, a long twenty-five feet from the desk. The deadbolt responded to the fourth key he tried, and Carlton burst through the door, almost knocking Reynaldo over in the process.

"Let's get out of here!" Carlton shouted over the din of the hovering aircraft. "That's the DEA and probably every other law enforcement agency in the state. We have to go on foot, get out into the countryside."

Reynaldo pointed to the back door and yelled back. "From the way the Rendón brothers left here, they're going to be a lot more interested in grabbing them than a couple of U. S. citizens."

"You want to bet your next twenty years on that?"

Reynaldo took all of two seconds to respond. "I'm right behind you."

CHAPTER 29

Carlton dashed for the door, Reynaldo on his heels. As they neared the rear exit, Reynaldo veered to one side and turned off the light, trying to put them in relative darkness, save the strobe light show outside. However, the light coming through the big window still turned everything into a kaleidoscope, even the office walls around them. Hopefully, it would be hard for anyone to see them from outside, because it was impossible to tell what was going on in the rear parking lot. An army of law enforcement officers might have guns drawn and trained on the door, but they had to get out. As Tino had done at the *Bayito* warehouse few hours before, Carlton cautiously pushed the door open a few inches and leaned his head against the door jamb, then the door itself, peering left and right and hoping he wasn't going to run into a hail of gunfire.

The sight, at least what he could see, was encouraging. The Range Rover was gone, and the helicopter was moving away from this side of the building, crawling low over the top of the warehouse, toward the roll-up door side. The searchlight was now sweeping back and forth over the front parking lot, its intense white glare bouncing off every surface except for the back side of the building where they now crept out to take a better look. The police ground vehicles had pulled around the corner, apparently drawn to the front by radio reports from the chopper. The red and blue strobe of their overheads still reflected off the brush and mesquite, but headlights and spotlights were concentrating on the roll-up door side of the lot. Farther away, a cacophony of receding sirens indicated some of the cars were pursuing the black Range Rover or possibly one of the vehicles that had been parked inside the warehouse. Either way, it seemed the chase was concentrated on the Rendón brothers and Millstone and his cronies due to their fleeing in motor vehicles, a poor choice when pitted against a helicopter with a spotlight. For whatever reason, the activity was gone from this side of the building for the moment, and Carlton waved Reynaldo forward as he sprinted across the lot.

At the edge of the parking lot, everything changed instantly. Gone was the smooth blacktop asphalt of the well-tended lot. Just over a bordering concrete curb they were instantly swallowed up by South Texas' vastness, with its spiny vegetation and accompanying thorns of various lengths and angles. Still blind from the light show, Carlton tried to pick a line through the brush, but in the fading twilight it was difficult to dodge the patches of prickly pear and keep any kind of straight line. After several minutes of weaving through the maze of cactus, he turned to see they had only progressed fifty yards or so away from the warehouse, as evidenced by the still-hovering chopper.

Reynaldo was breathing raggedly as he stumbled up to a waiting Carlton, who was not faring too well himself after a few minutes of running. "I'm not in shape for this," he gasped. "How much farther do we have to run?"

Carlton was leaned over, hands on his knees, and took a few deep breaths before he could answer. "I don't know. How far is San Antonio?"

"Shit!" was the extent of Reynaldo's response to the disheartening news.

Carlton straightened up, but kept sucking in deep breaths. "Let's go. We've got to get a long way from here before they go in to clear the warehouse. When they don't find us, they'll come looking." He had barely finished speaking when he turned and jogged away.

Reynaldo looked questioningly after him, but didn't have the breath to shout an inquiry. He concentrated on taking deep, even breaths and following Carlton through the brush, which, luckily, was beginning to thin out. Another few minutes went by, and the sparser vegetation had enabled the pair to cover several hundred yards. The activity behind them was still loud, but diminishing with each step. Carlton was heartened by their progress, but the adrenaline rush was dying and he slowed considerably. Behind him, Reynaldo was tiring too, but he knew he had to keep pushing and take advantage of Carlton's slowdown while he could.

Within another hundred yards, both men had slowed to a fast walk, then a moderate pace more suited to brisk walking through a shopping mall. Ahead of him, Reynaldo could see Carlton's back in the faint light and could tell the escape was now punishing his bad knee. He had a pronounced limp and had slowed even more. He pushed himself to catch up, wondering how long either of them could keep this up. He knew from talking with Tino that Carlton kept in good physical shape with an ongoing regimen of exercise, at least up until the gunshot wound to his knee. Since then, exercise probably had been limited to physical therapy sessions—and doing the occasional horizontal bop with the pretty DEA agent, according to Tino.

The memory of Tino's telling of the gossip brought a brief smile to his face and respite from the pain in his legs and lungs. For a few seconds, he relived the funny moment with his lifelong friend before his tired brain reminded him that memories were all that remained of Faustino Perez. A flash of the gory scene in the passenger seat of his pickup caused him to wince as a flood of remorse, disgust, and sorrow swept over him. He forced the feelings aside and concentrated on trying to run and breathe smoothly, something he'd never managed even as a schoolboy trying out for the track team. A few yards ahead of him, Carlton continued to push, but it was clear that neither of them was going to last much longer at this pace. Between Carlton's injury and his own sedentary lifestyle, cross-country running wasn't their strong suit.

"Carlton!" he called out as he closed the gap to a few feet. "Take a break, Buddy! You're killing me back here, and I know your knee needs a rest."

Carlton pulled up and stepped aside to let Reynaldo come up beside him in the narrow corridor between an inhospitable patch of catclaw brush and something else, something equally thorny. He turned to check progress and was pleased to see they had covered a good distance from the warehouse, maybe a half-mile. He leaned over and took deep breaths with his hands on his knees again. Massaging the injured right one, he could feel the tenderness and swelling assaulting the damaged joint, though not as bad as while running or walking. It felt as bad as it had right after the first surgery, and he knew he wasn't doing the right thing for long-term recovery by pounding the hard ground, escape crisis or not. "Okay, I know we've got to slow down. We can't keep up this pace. I don't think my PT gal would approve of this anyway."

Reynaldo was overjoyed at the break and took deep breaths until he could talk. "Your PT girl? What about your *DEA* girl?" he managed to gasp with a grin, trying to put some humor, or at least normalcy, in their dire situation.

"Don't think she'd approve either, but for a different reason. That's probably her riding shotgun in that chopper. And I mean '*shotgun*' in the literal sense."

"*Really?* What makes you think that?"

"I texted her from that storeroom while you were busy chatting with your new friends. I asked her to ping my phone and rescue us from the Rendón brothers and Millstone's bunch. It only took about ten minutes before I heard all hell break loose, so they might have been tracking us already, or at least had some idea of where we were."

Reynaldo shook his head. "Never thought I'd be glad to hear police coming, but it was going to be bad for us if the Rendón boys hadn't hauled ass out of there. Not sure about you, but I had about five minutes to live."

"Yep. And Millstone's not a fan, either, him or those thugs with him. You think they're some of the *Bayito* warehouse enforcers?"

"I'd say so. But they might have their own troubles with the *Golfos* after what I told Israel and Gilberto about their recent activities. Cartel guys have nasty ways to handle insider theft so it makes a lasting impression."

"Good. Couldn't happen to a better bunch of thieves."

"What now?" Reynaldo asked, already knowing the grim answer. His breathing was now easing back to normal though he could still feel his heart thumping wildly inside his chest and he dreaded moving out again.

"We have to keep moving, no other choice. I turned my phone off as soon as I heard the commotion, but they'll know we're in the area and start searching as soon as they're done with those guys."

"How do we know which direction? We can't just stumble around out here with no water or food."

"We have to, Reynaldo," Carlton persisted. "But as to the direction, we turned left off of Mines Road, so we have to keep angling back toward our right, going north, and we should cross it, then keep going into the ranchland out there. Maybe we can catch a ride and put some distance between us and them, get far enough away to call Paula to come get us."

"Okay, but let's take it slow, okay? And how do you know which way north is?"

Carlton smiled in the gathering darkness at the question. Even though he was a savvy drug lord, a kingpin with power and influence in his and Tino's sphere of operations, Reynaldo Gomez was not an outdoor person. Moreover, he was nervous at the prospect of being out here in the wilderness at night, notwithstanding the pursuers. Carlton figured he probably had not served in the military where basic map reading and field operations training taught all soldiers, down to the most junior of infantry grunts, to tell directions and move through unknown territory with some degree of proficiency. Even without a map, Carlton had noticed the setting sun's position relative to the warehouse and calculated they had been moving to the northwest from it. His internal compass told him to bear right to intercept Mines Road, which ran northwest to southeast, roughly parallel to the Rio Grande.

Like Reynaldo had done earlier, he decided to inject something besides danger and tragedy into their predicament. "We just have to follow the North Star, Polaris" he intoned solemnly.

"How do you know which one it is?" Reynaldo asked, swiveling his head around, clearly disoriented. "I don't want to wander around out here until we die from exposure."

"Damned if I know, Reynaldo. They all look alike to me."

Reynaldo looked at him with genuine worry on his face and gave his fallback response for troubling news. *"Shit!"*

As predicted, Mines Road was just ahead, and they watched carefully for traffic in both direction before dashing across. The grassy right-of-way ended at a barbed-wire fence less than thirty feet ahead, entailing a confrontation with tight strands and sharp barbs that didn't want to part for trespassers. A few nervous minutes later, they found the other side of the road was a continuation of the brush-covered terrain, with less light being reflected into the sky from transport and storage facilities. Most of the commercial enterprises lay on the south side of Mines Road and, even if it entailed being on someone's private property, it seemed a good idea to push ahead through ranchland instead of crossing parking lots that might have night shifts, security guards, or CCTV coverage.

At Carlton's insistence, the pair walked through the night, making good time through less-brushy areas and struggling to keep moving when the thicker vegetation blocked their intended path. Luckily, the night wasn't very cold, so the effort kept them reasonably warm while they were moving, and rest periods ended when both became too cold to sit still any longer.

The eastern sky was lightening when Reynaldo called for another rest, the third in the past hour or so. Rest periods were becoming more frequent, and they still hadn't run across any other roads. Fatigue was setting in on both of them, and lack of food and water would become a real problem when their energy level dropped due to adrenaline depletion. The good news was the lack of any sign of pursuit. Except for the sporadic howling contests between coyote packs, they could be the only living things on the planet, or this part of it, anyway, which pleased both of them.

But Reynaldo was still not convinced. "Are you sure we're going the right direction?" he asked for the third time.

Regretting his earlier pricking with his friend, Carlton moved to calm him. "Yes. There has to be a road or two for access between the ranches out here and the city of Laredo, and I don't have to know every bend in them to know that we will eventually run into one by going north," he said, pointing ahead of them. "That way."

"And you know this is north *how?*" The concern in Reynaldo's voice increased with every inquiry about their path of travel.

Carlton stopped and turned to his right. "Because the sun is going to come up over there, in the east. Just like it has for six billion years or so, Reynaldo," he added in exasperation. "So that's north," he said pointing ninety degrees from the brightening sky. "And forty-five degrees more is northwest. We don't have to be exact to run into another ranch road somewhere ahead that runs into Mines Road and on to Laredo. Bear with me, Reynaldo."

Reynaldo's response was positive, but guarded, so Carlton was relieved a half hour later when a break in the brush revealed a glimpse of paved road ahead, proving him right. Reynaldo waited while he climbed clumsily over a barbed-wire fence, then walked across the right-of way to the edge of the pavement. Looking left and right he saw its general direction of travel appeared much as he had predicted. "This looks like one that eventually runs back into Mines Road to the right, and there's nowhere else a paved road would go out here, except to get to town from a ranch.

"We've got to walk out here in the right-of-way to hitch a ride, because I don't want to get caught in anybody's pasture. We've been lucky through the night, but daytime is another story."

He backtracked to help Reynaldo through the fence. Both of them were stiff and sore, and it took effort on both their parts to accomplish the task. They plopped down in a bare spot near the fence to rest before tackling the road section, glad to be free of the thorny brush which seemed to have attacked Reynaldo with a vengeance. He sat massaging his legs and cursing the numerous gouges and scratches on his hands. Carlton's knee had long since ceased to ache, moving instead to a vaguely throbbing numbness, which at least enabled him to keep moving. As to the longer term effect of such punishment, he didn't know, but figured it wasn't good.

Reynaldo was dog-tired, but his feet weren't raw and blistered as he had feared, a testament to the expensive hand-made cowboy boots he wore. It would take all his effort, but he could still stagger on, a fact he made known to Carlton with assurance and a touch of pride. "My hands feel like pin cushions and I'm plenty tired, but I can keep moving for a little while. What's our plan from here?"

Picking up on his companion's new-found confidence, Carlton grinned at him. "You've come through this well, Reynaldo. Better than I thought either one of us could. Walking all night through a thorn patch isn't for old men, you know.

"I think we need to rest a bit, then continue on this road and try to catch a ride to get farther from Laredo, or even back into town where we can get among a bunch of people while waiting for Paula. Doesn't matter where, but we've got to have a story for our driver."

Reynaldo cocked his head to one side, straining to hear something in the cold silence of breaking dawn. "Better come up with one pretty soon then, because here comes a possible ride," he said, gesturing to his right.

The vehicle, an older green Ford Excursion, still had its lights on in the brightening morning. As it neared the pair, it looked as though the only occupant was the driver, an older man in a cowboy hat. Good news and bad, Carlton thought: Good, because a single older man appearing to be a rancher might be old enough to remember when picking up a pair of hitchhikers was okay; bad, because he was a single older man who might not trust anyone, middle-aged hitchhikers or not. He and Reynaldo stood side by side and stuck out their thumbs in traditional hitchhiker style. Both felt like a couple of idiots.

The Excursion slowed down, and Carlton could see the driver squinting through the windshield, assessing the unlikely sight of two mature men, not poorly dressed, but bedraggled and tired-looking, trying to bum a ride out here in the middle of nowhere as the sun rose. As it approached, the driver kept the same speed and Carlton dropped his hand. As it passed them by, Reynaldo followed suit, and both turned to start walking northwest on the road, away from Laredo. At that second, the driver, apparently watching them in his mirror, made his decision. The Excursion braked hard and pulled over to the side about thirty feet beyond the stunned pair.

"This is incredible," Carlton mouthed softly to himself as he started to jog toward the vehicle, Reynaldo right behind him. Carlton almost smiled when he heard his companion take in a big breath and exhale it in exhaustion, relief, or a prayer of thanks—maybe all three. Something was finally going right.

"What's our story?" Reynaldo asked quietly when they slowed, just a few feet from the big SUV idling at the roadside.

"I'm going to try something entirely new, something that's been in short supply lately."

"Huh? What's that?"

"The truth."

CHAPTER 30

"Good morning, Sir. Thanks for stopping." Carlton used the handhold to hoist himself into the passenger seat and reached to pull his right leg onto the seat without making the knee tendons take the strain. Behind him, he heard Reynaldo stifle a groan as he hauled his tired body into the comfortable right-hand rear seat of the monstrous SUV. Both reached for seat belts and dutifully clicked them.

"Mornin'," came a gruff response. "Y'all running from the law or somebody worse?"

Carlton was taken aback by the sudden question—not just its content, but its immediacy—and he could almost feel Reynaldo's similar shock behind him. He turned to look at the man, try to get a feel for his odd question before responding. After all, it could be his standard opening line, a joke maybe, especially given his and Reynaldo's appearance, which was in contrast to their age and mannerisms. Or he might be a retired lawman, attuned to the look of someone on the run and prone to using straight-forward interrogation tactics. The tone of his question didn't give a hint; it was delivered with the same inflection he might have used to say "where y'all headed?" No accusatory or suspicious tone, just a simple question.

He appeared to be in his late seventies, tall and rangy rather than thin. His face was weathered, with piercing blue eyes and iron gray hair that still maintained a curly texture despite the thinning that comes with age. Both hands, still on the steering wheel, showed signs of years of hard work, but the nails were clean to the point of being professionally manicured. His clothes were simple enough—jeans and a snap-button, western-style shirt—but looked more expensive than the items from a local department store. More likely mail-order or a specialty western-wear shop, he thought.

Enough wardrobe critique, Carlton, time to answer the man's question.

Sticking to what he'd said to Reynaldo, he replied, "Somebody worse, I'm afraid. We've run afoul of some dangerous people, and we've been on the move all night, trying to get away."

"Where'd y'all run onto these dangerous people?"

"It started in Mexico, yesterday afternoon."

The man nodded as if that explained it all, or at least a lot. Five seconds went by before he blind-sided the pair with his next question. "It have anything to do with drugs?"

Carlton heard Reynaldo's sharp intake of breath, but gritted his teeth and maintained his vow. "Yessir, it did. Those kind of people are worse than the law, a lot more dangerous."

"Well, if you got mixed up with them, you must have something to do with drugs, too."

It was a statement, not a question, and Carlton was wondering how to respond when Reynaldo spoke up from behind him. "Sir, *I'm* the one who got involved with the drug guys. My friend here tried to get me to leave this thing alone, but I ignored his advice. And because of that, my lifelong friend was killed, and the two of us have been on the run most of last night to avoid having the same thing happen to us. Believe me when I say I learned a valuable lesson."

The mysterious man went silent for a few seconds, then lifted his foot from the brake and coasted away. Carlton had been holding his breath, and he exhaled quietly, hoping the quasi-truth had addressed the man's questions satisfactorily and that they could get a ride to someplace farther away from Laredo than here—wherever "here" was. The respite from interrogation was short-lived.

"They still on your trail, those dangerous people?"

"That's hard to say," Carlton replied. "We pushed on through most of the night to put some distance between us and them, and we haven't seen a sign of them on our tail. But they have plenty of resources and manpower, so we're not going to feel safe until we get back to San Antonio."

"Well, you're only about twelve or fifteen miles from the outskirts of Laredo, so you've got a ways to go."

"The going was pretty tough in places, so I knew we didn't cover a lot of miles. And we've got to go back to the east to catch IH thirty-five."

Taking his cue, Reynaldo leaned forward in his seat. "Sir, I'd be glad to pay you whatever you think's fair to get us back to San Antonio. Tell me how much you'd charge, and I'll show you every dollar in my wallet. If we can get together on a price, we'd certainly appreciate the ride."

The man was shaking his head before Reynaldo finished his spiel. "Don't want to go to San Antone, I came out here to do some shooting, and that's what I intend to do."

At the mention of "shooting," Carlton felt a spasm of foreboding flow through his body. The reminder of yesterday's battle and its sickening results were still with him, barely restrained from dominating his entire being, and he wondered if Reynaldo might be on the verge of a meltdown. Neither of them was a stranger to gunfire or violence, but the events of the past fifteen hours—combined with exhaustion, fear, and worry over their predicament—lent a disturbing tone to the odd-acting man's firm declaration. Under different circumstances, it would have been time for a conference between the pair to assess how the man's intentions might be related to…anything. But sitting here in the man's vehicle, it was time to hope the old man was exactly as he appeared—a hard-ass Texan who wanted to send a few rounds downrange and see if he could still shoot. Maybe when he finished taking a few shots, he'd reconsider taking them farther away from here, at least where they could safely use his phone to call Paula.

Reynaldo's next remark told Carlton he'd handled the man's remark better than he had. "We're in a seller's market, Sir," he persisted. "Tell me your price for a ride to San Antonio."

"Nope. Hell, son, I've *got* money; it's shooting practice I'm short on!" The statement was delivered with something more than confidence, yet not even bordering on arrogance. It bespoke an attitude of one who had not always been able to dictate how he passed his time, but today, he was beyond that stage of his life.

Carlton had been agreeing with Reynaldo's thinking all along, but now he thought it was time to change gears before the mercurial man pulled over and told them to get out. "Where do you shoot?" he asked. "You have a place out here?"

The man slowed down and pointed to a cattle guard about fifty feet ahead, on the right. Beyond it, a gravel road led between scrub brush and

257

mesquite a short way before disappearing from view. "This is my place here. I have about three hundred acres, and I come out and shoot when I get time. And today I've got time," he added, looking in his rear-view mirror and driving home the point he'd made to Reynaldo.

He drove across the cattle guard and followed the gravel road for over a mile before taking a left on a narrower, less-defined road, nothing more than a pasture road, which led up a gradual rise for several hundred yards before petering out at the crest of what passes for a hill in South Texas. During the drive from the cattle guard, he'd not said a word. Neither had his passengers, but with Carlton sitting sidewise in the front passenger seat, he and Reynaldo had exchanged a few nervous glances.

When the man spoke again, it was as if the previous conversation had not occurred. "Sit tight, I'm going to set up some targets. Then we'll go up there and I'll shoot back this way.

"When I'm done, I'll think about taking y'all up the road a piece."

He opened the driver's door and went around back to open the rear hatch. Carlton turned farther in his seat to watch. Catching Reynaldo's perplexed gaze, he shrugged. Reynaldo did likewise. As instructed, both of them sat tight.

Pulling out a metal framework apparatus, he strode a few yards to the left of his vehicle and planted the barbed legs of the framework in the hard ground, pushing both sides home with his feet, then rocking it to test its stability. Apparently satisfied, he returned to the SUV. Back at the rear hatch, he pulled out another target frame, this one much larger, and rested it on the lowered tailgate in order to get a better purchase before moving it. Reynaldo opened his door and went back to help. He took one side of the frame so it could be tilted out to the ground, then walked with the man to a spot some twenty feet beyond the smaller target frame. When the frame was facing the direction he wanted, the man motioned for him to set the framework down. He pushed down on the barbed leg while Reynaldo did likewise with the other side. Not a word was spoken.

Mystery Man stepped back a few feet to survey his work, then turned to his left and stared at some point in the distance, apparently the location from where he intended to shoot. A few seconds went by before the man called out to Carlton. "Say, open the console and bring me those targets, would you? And get those binoculars out, you'll need those."

Carlton complied and limped over to hand him the package of paper targets, simple eight-by-ten sheets of coarse paper with concentric rings surrounding a bulls-eye about two inches in diameter. Both watched while the man clamped a target in each available section of both frames, a total of twelve targets. Then he stepped back to study the results before turning again to the distant spot.

At that point Reynaldo took the opportunity to clear up part of the peculiar scene taking place. He stepped forward and extended his hand. "My name is Reynaldo Gomez, and my companion is Carlton Westerfield. We always like to know a man who takes his shooting practice seriously."

If the man was surprised by the offbeat introduction, he didn't show it. He shook Reynaldo's hand and turned to shake Carlton's before saying anything. "Bonham's my name, Herbert Bonham." He let the name sit there, not adding a word of enlightenment, or anything that sounded apropos to the strange situation.

Carlton tried to think of a way to segue into an actual conversation with the taciturn man. "Watching you set up targets makes me agree with Reynaldo; you must take your shooting seriously. And if you're looking at that next hill as a spot to shoot from, you're a *really* serious shooter. I think I know why I need binoculars."

The result was a smile, the first sign of any emotion he'd shown in the fifteen or so minutes since they'd first laid eyes on one another. It lasted a second or two before disappearing, replaced by a terse command: "Hop in, let's go see how seriously I can shoot."

Bonham steered the Excursion off the rise, down into a small valley, then up the adjacent hill. Driving slowly, he glanced in his mirror a couple of times, possibly gauging the distance to the receding targets. Two or three minutes later, he was still driving away, ascending the next hill, down a slight ravine, then back up another rise. Carlton tried to watch him in his peripheral vision, but couldn't tell if he was still watching the targets, now an impossible distance behind them.

A Stinger missile won't reach those targets!

Another minute went by as the SUV crawled slowly to the crest of the hill, where Bonham turned sharply left and braked to a stop near a large patch of prickly pear cactus which was half as high as the vehicle's door. "This should be good," he announced, exiting the vehicle again and going to the back end. He returned with a canvas gun case which he laid on the hood and unzipped. The rifle he extracted wasn't familiar to Carlton, nor was the scope; however, it didn't take a gun expert to know it was a quality combination of equipment. He leaned forward in his seat to get a better look and wondered if he and Reynaldo would have fared better waiting for the next car before sticking out their thumbs. Glancing back at Reynaldo, it was clear he was having the same thoughts.

Bonham was examining the rifle, not paying any attention to his passengers, so it surprised Carlton when he spoke as though reading his mind. "It's a Three hundred Weatherby Mag. The scope's a Swarovski. Shoots flat, over three thousand feet per second, and the recoil's about as hard as a German mother-in-law."

Carlton grinned at the quirky explanation and took it as an invitation to get a closer look, so he got out and joined Bonham at the front of the vehicle. Reynaldo was close behind and leaned around to scrutinize the weapon. "Very nice, Mr. Bonham. How far away are those targets?"

"Oh, about seven or eight hundred yards, I'd guess. Won't know until I scope it."

Reynaldo looked at Carlton with arched eyebrows. Carlton just shrugged. He knew next to nothing about high-powered hunting rifles and less about long-range shooting. The weapons they'd gathered at the flea market and smuggled into Mexico were specifically for combat fire-fight situations, usually no more than two hundred yards. During his military stint, optics were not commonly used for that application, just the adjustable iron sights. Seven hundred yards sounded like an impossible distance to toss a tiny projectile with accuracy, something usually encountered by a military sniper, not an infantryman.

"You'll want these," Bonham said, handing over two cellophane packages of disposable ear plugs. "I've only got one set of real ear protection, so you'd best put those in and stand back a ways. And don't drop those glasses, they're Swarovskis, cost a damn fortune."

From the gun case he pulled a set of padded ear muffs and put them on before climbing back in the driver's seat and running down the window. He rummaged around under the seat for a minute and came up with a sandbag, which he placed on the door ledge, then propped the rifle's fore stock on it. He followed with a series of adjustments and movements before opening the bolt and inserting a single cartridge.

Carlton and Reynaldo inserted the cheap ear plugs and retreated to well beyond the opposite side of the vehicle. They watched as Bonham closed the bolt and sighted his target—or so they presumed, since they couldn't see what he was aiming for from their vantage point. A few more agonizing seconds passed while Carlton wondered what was taking so long. It was a relief to be a little farther away from Laredo and relatively safe for the moment, but it would be better to be rolling down the road than standing here watching a shooter follow some ritual known only to him. He pushed the ear plugs deeper into his ears and waited for what would probably be a loud report, given the appearance of the weapon. But when the sound came, he and Reynaldo were more surprised than they would have been by a gunshot.

"Say, do those guys chasing y'all drive a big maroon SUV, maybe an Explorer or a Lincoln Navigator?" Herbert Bonham had turned in his seat to face them, his thumb cocked over his left shoulder and a look of inquiry on his face.

Both men jerked their heads toward where Bonham was pointing, in the general direction they'd come from after placing the targets. For a few seconds, they were stunned into inaction by the news. How could Millstone track them so quickly, so efficiently, out here in the wilderness? Reynaldo pointed to Carlton's pocket, and he grabbed his phone to make sure it was turned off. It was dead, as he knew it was, since he'd checked a couple of times since the warehouse escape.

They went around the car to the driver's window and looked past the next hill toward the target area. Winding slowly around the crest of the hill was the same car Millstone and the enforcers had parked in the warehouse, a dark maroon Lincoln Navigator, an older model. As they watched, it crept up to the target frames and slowed even more. Both front doors opened before it had come to a complete halt.

Carlton raised the binoculars and adjusted the focus. As before, barrel-chested Millstone emerged from the passenger side, and the driver looked like one of the men who had shoved them around at the warehouse. A back door opened, and two more men got out to join Millstone. The other back door swung open, but no one got out.

Carlton watched through the binoculars as the four men stood looking at the targets, apparently discussing their presence or significance in hunting down the pair of men who were now watching them from several hundred yards away. A few more seconds of observation changed that theory; from the turned bodies now standing still in a wide semi-circle, it was clear they were relieving themselves in the direction of the target frames.

Watching the men through his rifle scope, the activity was not lost on Bonham. "Sons of bitches pissing on my targets! Y'all were right, those guys aren't very nice. And they're not only dangerous, they're living dangerously."

Carlton and Reynaldo had both turned at the sound of his voice and saw him pull the rifle to his shoulder and move his head closer to the big scope's eyepiece. Reynaldo's sharp intake of breath told Carlton he was about to say something to stop him from firing, and he reached to quieten him. Reynaldo turned to him, wide-eyed, nearly in a state of panic at what Bonham was about to do. When he opened his mouth, Carlton shook his head and raised a forefinger to his lips to convey his silent message, that whatever Bonham was about to do, he wasn't likely to kill anyone for taking a leak on his targets, which would draw lawmen like flies at a picnic.

But what if he did? Even if he and Reynaldo were apprehended later, whatever investigation followed would include ballistic analysis, and neither could be connected to a long-range rifle. If a bullet from this scene was traced to anyone, it would be the crusty old guy now peering into a scope.

Or if he just terrorized the bunch who had killed Tino, then kidnapped him and Reynaldo, it had to result in something better than running a losing race through the semi-desert scrub brush of South Texas. He and Reynaldo were exhausted. They had no food or water, they were lost, out of luck, and out of time. Nothing could change Tino's death, but this odd-acting character might change the way things were going for the deceased's tired friends. Besides, something about the menacing-looking rifle and scope, manned by an eccentric old guy who didn't like people pissing on his property, gave Carlton a sense of *good riddance, it couldn't happen to a more deserving bunch.*

The report from the muzzle was deafening this close, even with the earplugs. Shocked by the noise and Bonham's impulsive act, both jerked their heads in the direction of the targets. While Carlton was raising the binoculars, Reynaldo was squinting unsuccessfully to see the results. For over a second, nothing changed. Then, a puff of dust flew up from the lower front of the Navigator, and the entire car slumped forward. When the sound of the rifle's bolt opening diverted their attention, neither saw the reaction of the men, which was another second in occurring. Because the sound of the gunshot traveled much slower than the bullet itself, the tire was destroyed almost three seconds before the men would have heard it.

By the time they looked back toward the Navigator, the target area was a scene of pandemonium. The tiny figures of men scurrying around, obviously not knowing where the attack was coming from, was comedy at its best for Carlton, especially given the victims of Bonham's revenge. The second shot hit the rear tire, and the car squatted down with the same puff of dust as before. With the shot still resonating in their ears, Bonham jacked the empty out and slammed the bolt home on another round. The third shot didn't have an immediate visual effect, but a few seconds later, the cloud of steam from the grill told Carlton the radiator was history—as was their pursuers' transportation.

He turned to Reynaldo and gave him the news gleefully, but Reynaldo gave him a blank, wide-eyed look and pointed to his ears: he couldn't hear a word being said. Carlton handed over the binoculars and pointed to the scene. After a minute of finagling with the focus adjustment, a smile played over Reynaldo's face, the first in many hours. A tiny victory over their tormentors to be sure, but the one-upmanship of the gesture was significant. Everyone present at this scene knew the three shots could have punctured three pissing intruders as easily as tires—and nothing indicated the shooting was yet finished, as evidenced by the scrambling men who were pushing and shoving each other, vying for space to squat against the ruined SUV, unsure of where the assault had come from and terrified of what lay in store.

Reynaldo lowered the glasses. Both turned to look at Herbert Bonham still sitting in the driver's seat, gazing toward the targets with a look of satisfaction on his face. The rifle rested on the sandbag with the bolt open, while a fine wisp of smoke curled from both the chamber and the business end of the barrel. Carlton was flabbergasted, unable to think of anything to say, but Reynaldo came to the rescue with an appropriately humble remark.

"Mr. Bonham, you are a hell of a marksman. Remind me never to take a leak on your target frames."

CHAPTER 31

Bonham started the Ford while Carlton and Reynaldo got in and buckled up. He pulled away briskly, turning in their original direction of travel. Evidently he knew another way out of the pasture, one that didn't lead back past the target area. Carlton wondered if the men hunkered down by the wounded Navigator heard the engine start or could see or hear the Excursion as it pulled away from the cactus patch, out of their sight over the crest of the hill. Given the past few minutes, they had to be wondering what was next. Was the attack over, or would it resume from a different place? No matter—with their transportation disabled, they now faced what he and Reynaldo had endured for the past twelve hours or so: walk out or call someone to come get them. Their predicament delighted Carlton. Either way, Millstone and his group would be exposed and vulnerable to the law enforcement people who had chased them the previous night—and would be really agitated for losing them.

Advancing that line of thought, Carlton thought the police raid must have concentrated on taking the Rendón brothers, or Millstone and his cronies had been adept at sneaking through the dragnet in their old SUV. Knowing that law enforcement types didn't like to accept defeat, he figured their chances at avoiding capture were reduced in the bright light of day, out here in a brush-choked pasture. He turned in his seat to see Reynaldo with a smirk on his tired face, obviously entertaining the same thoughts as he was.

But their current respite from pursuit, plus a much-needed rest, were temporary luxuries, not salvation. Within a couple of minutes Carlton's mind started going over the inconsistencies of their seemingly good fortune. Why had Bonham stopped for them when his destination lay only a quarter mile up the road? His intentions to take some target practice had been made clear; he hadn't even considered deviating from his plan, not for any amount of money. Could the old man simply have been wanting some company on his early-morning jaunt and changed his mind, made up the story of going for target practice? "Wanting company" didn't seem likely, given the paucity of conversation he'd offered. What he had initiated had been an interrogation, so maybe he was an old lawman, forever curious about strange individuals and occurrences out here in his part of the world.

Then there was the timing of Millstone and company's arrival and Bonham's casual and specific alert to his hitchhiking passengers. He had known the make of the vehicle, not that common among older people who usually only knew their own—"a maroon SUV, maybe an Explorer or a Lincoln Navigator" was pretty spot-on for a seven-hundred yard observation, big scope or not. Again, his methods pointed to a law enforcement background, as did his verbal condemnation of the illegal drug business. In holding that attitude, why hadn't he ejected them from his vehicle when he reached the turnoff to his property? Or the second he saw the vehicle following them? That would have been the time to tell him and Reynaldo to shove off, whether or not he had initially wanted some company. Instead, he had helped their cause immensely by disabling their pursuers' vehicle and leaving them stranded. Why? Now able to sit and think things through, nothing made sense, not a single part of it.

Carlton tried to observe Bonham in his peripheral vision, but he couldn't discern anything helpful to unraveling his suspicions. The old man simply drove through the pasture, keeping to the faint road and not bothering to look left or right. Clearly, he knew where he was headed, and Carlton wished he were so well-informed. But right now, approaching mid-morning, the past several hours were taking their toll. The throbbing in his knee had slackened a bit, and he felt so drowsy his vision was blurred. It was all he could do to keep from leaning over against the window and falling asleep.

He forced himself alert and turned to look at Reynaldo, who was in the same shape: bleary-eyed, blinking, and shrugging his shoulders to stay awake, but it was a losing battle. He turned back to Bonham, determined to further his understanding of this, the most horrific, tumultuous, and baffling twenty-four hour period of his life, because it was looking like the rest of his life might depend on what he could learn.

"Mr. Bonham, where are we headed?" he asked casually, as though it didn't really matter.

"Thought we'd go out of here the back way, and I can catch eighty-three up to forty-four. Taking a right on forty-four will get us into Encinal in less than an hour. I've got to drop y'all there, I'm going on to Freer, then Corpus. But y'all can get a ride on thirty-five or call somebody to come get you."

Carlton racked his tired brain to follow the path he had described. U. S. Highway 83 went north to Uvalde, and State Highway 44 went back toward the east, intersecting IH 35 at Encinal, the little settlement where he'd met Tino and his shot-up crew over a year earlier. Except for the stark reminder that Encinal would generate—dead friends, body bags, and several funerals—the travel plan was great. He and Reynaldo could get something to eat and drink, call Paula, and hang out long enough for her to pick them up without worrying about Millstone or his buddies, at least for a while. After that, it was going to be another miserable period of days or weeks living with the aftermath of the massacre in *Nuevo Bayito* and on a side street in Laredo. It looked like he and Reynaldo might yet survive this, the mother of all boondoggles. Incredibly, they might be the only ones on the survival list. He dreaded learning the final tally.

A brief flash of the savage murder they'd witnessed near the Laredo bus station was the last conscious thought he had before falling asleep in the front seat of Herbert Bonham's green Ford Excursion.

"Time to wake up, boys."

The voice came from somewhere far away, and Carlton struggled to look around for its source. Looking around was hard to do through closed eyelids, a detail his foggy brain sorted through the second time he heard something. This time, it was the word "Encinal" that drew his attention enough to force his eyes open. Ahead of them to the right lay the small town of no more than a dozen streets laid out in checkerboard pattern. Just ahead was Interstate 35, and a truck stop/convenience store dominated the intersection of State Highway 44 and the interstate.

"I'm heading on to Freer, so I'll let you boys out here at the truck stop," Bonham informed his passengers as he pulled onto the parking lot.

"This is perfect, Mr. Bonham," Carlton said. "Why don't you pull up to the pump, and we'll fill your gas tank."

"Not necessary. I'm at over half a tank."

Reynaldo leaned over the console. "Mr. Bonham, no amount of money could repay you for getting those guys off our tails, but I wish you'd let us do *something* for you and for the trouble we caused with your shooting practice."

"Hell, there wasn't any trouble with the shooting practice. I put all three rounds right where I wanted to, didn't I?"

That got a laugh from his departing passengers. Both stepped out and took turns leaning in the passenger door to shake hands, Carlton first. When Reynaldo gripped his hand, he said, "Mr. Bonham, we really appreciate your help. If those guys had caught up to us, we wouldn't have lived through it. Your skill with a rifle is incredible. Thank you for using it to help us."

Bonham waved off the gratitude. "Y'all might want to think about helping yourself, you and your buddy. You need to steer clear of that drug business, because there won't always be somebody around that can save your bacon with a little shooting demonstration.

"Besides, that shooting was fair, but not incredible. For that, you'd need to see my boy shoot."

"*What?* Your son can outshoot you?"

The man laughed aloud, the first time he'd done so. "I can shoot alright, but I can't hold a patch to him."

CHAPTER 32

Bonham pulled away without another word, turning right onto State Highway 44, toward Corpus Christi. Carlton and Reynaldo exchanged tired grins at the odd man's behavior and walked across the concrete expanse to the convenience store where they bought water and snacks, the first sustenance either had had since the previous morning before leaving Reynaldo's ranch. They left the busy store and walked to the parking area to eat while they considered their next move. Carlton pulled out his phone and powered it up as they walked.

"I still don't know how Millstone and his guys tracked us while this thing was turned off," Carlton said, frowning at the screen as it came to life. "Maybe I should have left the battery out."

"Maybe you should have listened to me in the first place."

The voice, a familiar one to Carlton, came from behind him. He and Reynaldo whirled simultaneously at the remark, looking like a pair of dancers performing an intricate joint pirouette.

The window on the plain brown sedan was down, its engine idling quietly. In the noisy parking lot, DEA Agent Heather Colson had managed to maneuver the car behind them, using the surrounding activity to mask her approach. She sat behind the wheel, her face drawn and tired…and angry. "If you could ever get anything into your thick skull, you'd find out you're not the smartest guy on the block. Other people know more than you do about a lot of things, and you're—"

"He *did* listen to you. But I didn't listen to *him*." The interruption came from Reynaldo, who had eased from beside Carlton to a position directly in front of the driver's lowered window. "And what took place was entirely my fault, not his, so I'm the one with the thick skull.

"By the way, my name is Reynaldo Gomez, and you must be Heather— excuse me, *Agent* Colson."

She nodded and made a thin attempt to smile, but the emotion wasn't there. Apparently, the long night hadn't gone much better for her. "I figured. You don't match the description we have of Faustino Perez. By the way, where is that missing member of your group—The Three Musketeers, is it?"

Beside him, Carlton opened his mouth to intervene, expecting Reynaldo to react badly to the agent's untimely comment, but to his credit, Reynaldo maintained his poise in the face of her ridicule. "I'm afraid we're down to two," he replied calmly.

The look on her face told Carlton that her knowledge of Reynaldo's and Tino's background had dawned on her, making her snide remark sound more callous than she had intended, whether or not she was speaking to a suspected drug trafficker. Too late to change now, she looked away and said nothing for a minute. Carlton took the opportunity to change the subject. "So what happens now?"

When she turned back to face them, she was back in control, the brief embarrassment gone. "Interesting that you picked now to ask, Carlton." She gestured between them with a flip of her left hand.

Carlton turned and was startled to see three men only a few feet away. Again, the noise of the parking lot had covered the approach of Stan Ikos, Agent in Charge, and two other agents. They could have been standing there for the last two or three minutes; now they stood abreast, gazing warily at Carlton and Reynaldo and waiting for Agent Colson to continue answering Carlton's question.

"These gentlemen will be escorting you, Mr. Gomez," she informed him, "and Mr. Westerfield gets to ride with me."

Without a word, Ikos stepped forward and gripped Gomez' left arm, then turned him around while another agent moved in front of him and began reciting the Miranda warning. The third agent produced a set of handcuffs and started to secure Reynaldo's wrists behind him until Ikos shook his head and motioned for him to be cuffed with his hands in front. When the cuffs were clicked into place, the Miranda guy gave the prisoner a thorough pat-down search, followed by a quick head shake to his boss. "Clean," he murmured, barely audible in the noise, followed by a hand motion as though summoning a taxi.

Right on cue, a black Suburban pulled up, and the two junior agents gripped Reynaldo on each arm for the short walk to the back door. Ikos watched as one agent placed a hand on Reynaldo's head and guided him into the back seat, then climbed in behind him. The other one went around while Ikos climbed into the front passenger seat and nodded to the driver. The Suburban glided away silently.

Evidently, they wanted the ride to San Antonio to be uneventful, but comfortable, Carlton thought, before realizing that he may have seen Reynaldo Gomez for the last time. He sighed and walked around the undercover car, where he had to wait while Heather unlocked the passenger door. When he sat down, he again used his hand to assist the right leg into the car, then leaned back to wait for the stab of pain to subside. During the ride with Herbert Bonham, it had stiffened, so any bending of the joint was met with a painful reminder.

Seeing his discomfort, Heather used the opportunity to launch another verbal attack on him. "Looks like you pay as much attention to your physical therapist as you do to me. Stumbling cross-country through sage brush and cactus at night isn't part of your rehab program."

"Not likely. Didn't have much choice, though. It was looking pretty bleak where we were. We appreciated your quick response, by the way, even if today isn't looking too good."

"Glad to help. We quit getting help from our contacts when Miller decided to change teams. You were right to turn your phone back on and make contact. That provides a stronger signal than ongoing time updates, and one that can be pinged by using triangulation of cell towers. Easier than tracking Miller's gadgetry."

Carlton ignored the technology lesson portion of her response. "Wait a minute—who's Miller?"

"Oh, you know him as Millstone, Clive Millstone, but his name is really Cletus Miller. At least that's one of his names, the one he uses when he's working for us."

"Cletus Miller, Clive Millstone. Same initials, same guy, different names to confuse background searches," Carlton observed aloud, but more to himself than the federal agent. He recalled his conversation with Reynaldo regarding this subject, citing the difficulty of getting a full background report on a professional who knows how to retain his or her anonymity. Small wonder that he had gotten back no information—which he had mistakenly seen as a good sign—on the British gun runner/mercenary. No doubt that Gustavo Mendoza, his ill-fated accomplice, had been operating under a similar guise.

Carlton fell silent for a few minutes as Heather made her way out of the crowded parking lot, back onto I-35 and headed north. He was mentally and physically exhausted, completely drained of any ability to sift through the myriad of information—and *mis*information—to figure out all the reasons the endeavor had taken such a hapless and fatal turn. He leaned his head against the headrest and tried to sleep.

For about five minutes, his mind was racing with a replay of the past twenty-four hours, which now seemed to encompass about three weeks' worth of activity, most of it bad, some of it horrendous. Every image that flashed through his consciousness was bloody and disastrous. The mental slide show ended with their near-comedic apprehension in a truck stop parking lot—a pair of middle-aged men picked up by law enforcement as easily as a couple of middle-school kids being nabbed by an old-style truant officer. If not for the end result, it would have made him laugh.

He shook his head in disgust at the absurdity, not only of that scene, but the past several weeks' hectic activity and preparation which had led up to the disaster in a Mexican drug warehouse. If he had noticed Heather watching him in her peripheral vision, he might have guessed from her smug grin that she knew exactly why he was disgusted.

"Everyone involved down there is going to die, Carlton. Don't be one of them."

He had chosen to ignore her warning, even after trying vainly to get Reynaldo and Tino to heed it. Staying for the firefight had been a monumental mistake, to be sure, but what would have been the outcome had he not gone to Mexico and made the effort to scuttle the plan? Any better? *Worse?* Not much chance of that, he thought grimly, just as Hypnos shoved him into an uneasy slumber that lasted for the next two hours. When Heather killed the engine in Carlton's apartment parking lot, the change of sound awakened him…sort of.

"Okay, Sleepyhead, wake up. This is your stop."

He opened his eyes, saw where they were, and struggled to come fully awake. The familiar surroundings made the past days seem even more surreal, like leading two different existences and debating which one was real and which was not. Overall, he preferred this one, though his sleep-deprived brain was slow in engaging. He turned to look at Heather with bleary eyes. "Sorry I'm such poor company on a road trip."

"That's alright. What makes you think I wanted to talk to you anyway?" She put the car in Park and turned off the key. Then she turned to glare at him, but it lasted only a few seconds before morphing into a grin, albeit a wicked one. "Westerfield, you are such a pain in the ass. Why didn't you listen to me? Did you think I just made that up? I passed along information to you that could have gotten me fired—or worse. And what did you do with it? *Ignored it!*

"This is what I do for a living—keep up with bad guys!'" She finished her tirade with a raised voice that left no doubt about her sincerity, nor her confidence in her ability to perform the job well.

Carlton raised his hands in surrender. "I know that. I took your warning seriously, but Perez and Gomez didn't. Or rather, they were talked out of taking it seriously by Millstone—or Miller as you know him. He just dismissed the warning, saying it was common to receive warnings prior to an armed engagement, and that most of them proved false."

She stared at him incredulously. "*You went down there just to deliver my warning?* Why didn't you call or send a message? Or use a damn carrier pigeon, for crying out loud!"

He explained the part-time communication blackout and his reservations about delivering a message that might be intercepted by the wrong party, possibly revealing what Reynaldo and Tino had planned. "So I rode down there, thinking I had a better chance of getting the whole thing called off if I went in person. That seemed better than risking an information leak which would get them set up for a massacre—which is what happened anyway, thanks to your sleazebag Miller, who plays all sides."

"Well, abandoning the attack plan beforehand would have been better than what took place," she observed, ignoring the reference to Millstone.

Carlton shook his head. "That's just it, those two guys wouldn't have called it off, certainly not with Millstone/Miller bending their ears, telling them that pre-battle warnings were often misinformation.

"Heather, he *wanted* the attack to go forward, because he wanted the massacre set up. That's apparently what someone in Mexico paid him for—either the *Golfos* or the Mexican drug force, their version of the DEA."

Heather was quiet for a moment, thinking about what he'd said. "Miller has a reputation as a loose cannon. And he's certainly not above dipping into the funds on both sides. But that's why his type of guy is called a *mercenary*."

"He's a sick, sadistic, turncoat bastard is what he is, so don't sugar-coat it with a term that simply means he works for money! We *all* do that."

"I take it your attitude toward him has to do with Faustino Perez being listed as MIA at this time?"

He stared at her for a minute, putting together the time frame of events and realizing she had received some statistics regarding the *Nuevo Bayito* warehouse battle, but perhaps knew little of events between it and the Laredo trucking warehouse bust. "You really don't know about Tino Perez?"

She shook her head. "I saw the look on Gomez' face, so I know he's either missing, presumed dead, or dead. Which is it?"

"Clive Millstone, aka Cletus Miller, shot him in the face with a forty-five caliber pistol from about two feet away, after Tino made a remark about returning their overnight bags and the middle of the street in Laredo being a bad place to stop and chat. He told him to take his poofter accent and get lost. Nothing more serious than a junior high schooler smarting off.

"Actually, that wasn't like Tino at all. He usually kept his cool in verbal confrontations, but he'd had a belly full earlier that day, and he chose to retaliate the only way he could under the circumstances. He made a smart remark, and it cost him his life.

"Miller had no reason to do that. He and his guys had us cornered, and we had no weapons, nothing that was going to endanger him. He just wanted to kill somebody, Heather. That's the caliber of person your illustrious DEA does business with, the same point I made to you the first time we met at Gaido's in Galveston!"

She stared at him for a full minute, digesting the news, before responding. "I'm sorry for the loss of your friend, even if I don't agree with his chosen field of employment. And I wish I hadn't said that to Gomez, because I know they go back to childhood. Even if both of them chose to take up criminal enterprises to make a living, it's not my place to gouge someone's personal feelings. It's my place to put them out of business and in prison.

"But as to Cletus Miller, *all* law enforcement agencies do business with unsavory characters—present company excluded, of course. He's a prime example of the scum we have to work *with*, in addition to the scum we try to prosecute. I'm really not surprised he was working both sides of the street, possibly three sides: the DEA, the Mexican drug interdiction force, and the cartel."

"So he was he working for the DEA to begin with, then jumped ship?"

"Sounds like it. This started out as a joint operation between the DEA and Mexican Ministerial Federal Police. Unlike previous Mexican agencies, we've been able to work pretty well with PFM. They wanted help with an operation to bring down the *Golfo* cartel—or at least reign them in a bit—and the DEA agreed. To begin the operation, a program of intelligence sharing was deemed to be the best starting point before planning an interdiction operation.

"When intel sharing got serious, one of the big importers near the Border was described as 'a big player from North Texas'. That turned out to be your bud, the handsome one who got a separate ride into town today with cute little bracelets on his wrists." She delivered the last part with another smirk.

Carlton ignored her verbal jab. "So Tino and Reynaldo picked the worst time in history for trying to pick a fight with the *Golfos*, even if their intentions included helping out the home-boy laborers who were getting kicked around by the warehouse enforcers."

"If that was their intention, they could have picked a better way to help them. As it turned out, it got a lot of them killed, if we can believe what's been reported to us. And we don't have any reason to doubt them. The PFM spokesman put the figure at thirty-four dead, no survivors found. That's a one-hundred percent kill rate."

Carlton was quiet for a moment, reliving the guided tour through the warehouse led by an arrogant Clive Millstone. In a few minutes' time, they had seen bodies heaped upon bodies and on the floor, so thirty-four dead didn't seem an unreasonable number.

He wondered how much Heather knew, or could disclose, about Millstone/Miller's role in the joint operation between the U. S. and Mexico. "So how did Miller fit into this? Is he a contract player who simply names a price and performs the job?"

"Essentially, yes. He's worked for the DEA in the past, so he had a track record with us, a good one, in fact, due to some work he did in Afghanistan. He uncovered a smuggling ring operating on a U. S. military facility. It was a major bust, a big victory."

"So the DEA keeps him around, even if he is a psycho maniac with no civilized boundaries, no loyalties."

Heather shifted uncomfortably in her seat. "He doesn't get paid to observe civilized boundaries, Carlton. He gets paid for results.

"I'd say the reason he killed Perez was to collect a bounty from the *Golfos*. Who knows what went on between them in past years, something Perez didn't tell you about. Or they may have been doing a favor for another party he pissed off. Anyway, they don't offer a different amount of money for an adversary on a 'dead versus alive' basis; they just want proof that the undesirable party is really dead. And a dead target is usually easier to keep control of, you have to agree."

Carlton nodded at her explanation. It made sense from an operational standpoint; therefore, Tino would probably have been executed at some point anyway—for absolutely *no* provocation. Tino's verbal insult had simply provided a timely excuse for Millstone to make things tidier and illustrate to his other prisoners what non-cooperation would get them. It had worked, because he and Reynaldo had been shocked into submission for the trip to the warehouse, to be sure. The harsh, brutal professionalism employed by Millstone/Miller didn't make the sight of Tino's death any easier, but it further stirred Carlton's curiosity about the Brit turncoat. "So where does this guy Miller call home base?" he asked.

"I don't know, and if I did, I couldn't tell you. And I *wouldn't* tell you, because I know what you're thinking."

"*Really?* The DEA employs mind readers now, as well as assassins?"

"You know perfectly well what I mean, Carlton. You've got revenge on your mind, and—"

"Not against the trigger man," he said sharply, regretting that his feelings were so easily deciphered. "But I am curious to know who in the *Golfo* organization ordered him hit—and why. Perez didn't deal with the *Golfos*, so what was the reason? It's bound to have cost them some money—Miller's type doesn't work for free—so why?"

"Generally, that would have to come from the top, or very near, so it has to be Carlos Benavides or maybe the Rendón brothers, Gilberto or Israel."

The mention of Gilberto and Israel gave him the perfect opportunity to steer the conversation to safer ground. "Speaking of the Rendóns, did they get caught? When they heard the chopper, they took off like cockroaches. Miller and his helpers did too, and they were successful at getting away, but tell me about the Rendón brothers."

"They made it about a mile before the chopper sat down in front of their vehicle, blocked them until our agents got there. Pretty easy, actually. No shots fired, probably because they were thinking they would be turned over to Mexican authorities and not be extradited back to the U. S. for prosecution.

"But all that was worked out previously between the two countries' justice departments. If they had been turned over to Mexican authorities, they might have gotten as far as a holding cell, but might have conveniently escaped within a few hours. As agreed, if they were apprehended on U. S. soil, Mexico will let them be held here to stand trial without filing to have them extradited to Mexico."

"So they were the priority over Miller and those thugs he had with him," Carlton concluded. "Besides, they're probably faster cockroaches than the Rendón boys."

Heather's silence at his smart remark told him he was missing something. He waited a beat, trying figure out why she'd neither confirmed the raid's priority target nor denied it. It took about ten seconds for it to dawn on him. "Something tells me that Miller didn't have much to fear about being picked up by your strike team," he said, watching for her reaction.

"I wouldn't know about that," she answered smoothly. "Those decisions are above my pay grade.

"But Stan Ikos may have wanted to use Miller to keep up with you, especially after he did such a good job of tracking Perez and Gomez from the beginning. So he suggested the use of a tracker in your phone."

Confused, Carlton put up a hand to stop her. "Wait a minute! *A tracker in my phone?*" He reached for his burner and started inspecting it. It looked like his, but he changed often and couldn't be sure. If true, his bag and phone being left in Tino's pickup, while theirs' were taken, was starting to make sense now. "What's Ikos got against me, the guy who's responsible for ridding his territory of Brujido Ramos?"

Heather grinned at him. "Patting ourselves on the back a bit, are we?"

"Nope. *You're* the one who told me that Ikos knows I was a lot more connected to the Ramos takedown than anyone thought, so I'm just sticking to his theory, not mine.

"But back to the subject at hand: Miller did seem to have a particular dislike for me, called me the 'hot shit Yank shooter' or something like that, in a tone of voice that didn't imply admiration. I thought it was because of Reynaldo or Tino jerking his chain about me, but now you're telling me Ikos made me another of Miller's targets?"

Heather gave an exasperated sigh. "He may have wanted Miller to be able to keep up with you, since he figured Gomez and Perez would have you near them. That enabled us to keep up with those two at the same time.

"And *you*—being a documented CI—meant that he didn't have to obtain a warrant to have your phone tracked or bugged, because you're technically a contract employee. *Just like Cletus Miller is,*" she added forcefully, getting a quick glare from Carlton.

"So Ikos turns me into his Judas goat in order to keep up with Perez and Gomez, while saving him from some paperwork."

Heather shrugged nonchalantly. "Something like that."

"That figures. Taxpayers getting their money's worth again." Carlton thought for a moment about the arrangement Heather had just outlined. "But what if I hadn't gone down to deliver the warning in person?"

She shrugged again, a trait that was starting to irritate Carlton. "While Perez and Gomez were in Mexico, it didn't matter. Different rules about phone tapping and tracking down there.

"But Miller, bending the rules a bit as usual, had all that covered from the time those two met with him at the *La Posada* Hotel in Laredo, the time Gomez made his second payment and met Miller's helper, a guy named Gustavo Mendoza. It was early in the month, maybe the seventh or eighth.

"I heard about the contact arrangement; it was pretty smooth tradecraft. A couple posing as British tourists served as the cutouts. Miller stopped at their table and made the handoff right under the noses of Perez and Gomez. They were standing there, five feet away, being identified by the very people who were going to keep up with them.

"The couple put a tracker on Gomez' vehicle when they came back to eat dinner and drop off Miller and Mendoza at the hotel. Then they followed them to Gomez' ranch in Sabinal, but they couldn't get close enough to learn anything. So they backtracked to *Santa Monica* and spent a day or two there getting information on the town residents. Easy enough to do if you approach the local Catholic Church secretary, because she knows everything about everyone, and isn't shy about telling it."

"The church secretary dimed the town residents?" he asked incredulously.

"Not on purpose, I'm sure. They probably just asked some innocent-sounding questions about the town, what people did, where they worked, and she told them. Nothing sinister on the secretary's part."

"I guess the Lord really *does* work in mysterious ways."

The revelation stunned Carlton. All along, Millstone/Miller and Mendoza had been harping on security during the training sessions, right along with Tino and Reynaldo. As he had just told Heather, security was the reason for his trip to Mexico to deliver the warning in person.

Now he learns that the traitor Millstone had been the enabler, if not the direct source of the information leak. That way, he didn't even have to expose himself by giving the attack info over to the DEA, the Mexican authorities, or the *Golfos'* enforcers; instead, he had seen to it that the intel was passed along efficiently by a couple posing as British tourists! Meanwhile, he was collecting pay from all parties: Reynaldo, the DEA, the *Golfos*, and the Mexican PFM.

Nice work if you can get it, he thought, putting the old jazz standard's title to use and apologizing to the Gershwin brothers, who penned the lovely song.

Carlton leaned back in the seat and looked at Special Agent Colson. She looked exhausted; clearly, she was one of those people for whom lack of sleep showed on her face. Her head was back against the headrest and her eyes nearly closed, so it seemed she was about to make up for his non-communicative trip home with a short snooze of her own. In any event, she wasn't making a move to leave, so he stretched, sighed, and followed her lead, head back.

Even with the earlier nap, he was still exhausted. The past few days of travel, poor sleep, worry, and tension had taken their toll, not counting the experiences of a bloody gun battle, being kidnapped, witnessing the violent death of a friend, and a tough, all-night trek through a patch of thorns without food or water. And now, having all the failures of those past few days explained and highlighted as orchestrated events in a DEA sting operation made it worse. The entire tragedy could have been avoided if only…

He forced that useless thought aside and returned to last night's hard trek through the Webb County scrub brush. The long walk might have been a mere inconvenience for a young man doing a military exercise, but it had completely demolished his and Reynaldo's reserves by the time Herbert Bonham picked them up. Odd as that meeting had been, it was the highlight of this entire debacle, and recalling it led to another line of thought. He reached over and touched Heather's arm.

She jerked awake and gave him much the same look he'd had when she'd awakened him a half hour before. Shaking her head, she yawned and looked at her watch. "Damn! I've got to get to the office."

"Forget the office. Ikos has all the help he needs."

She shook her head. "No, I was only going to deliver you home, then go to the office and work on the after-action report. He knows I'm here and—"

"You're getting information for the report by interviewing your CI," he said, interrupting her with a logical excuse for her boss. "Besides, I want to know one more thing: does Mr. Bonham work for y'all?"

She sighed and rubbed her eyes. "You're just full of questions, aren't you? Mr. Bonham owns some property near there, and yes, he agreed to do that little job for us as a favor.

"Coming out of Laredo, you were bound to hit that road where he picked you up. We had him wait until you and Gomez got there, then he just drove up and offered you the ride."

Even though Mr. Bonham's odd questions were no longer a mystery, Carlton was shaking off her explanation before she finished. "That's not all there was to it, though. He knew we would be along, but did he know Millstone and his guys were following us?"

"Yes, we told him. We were tracking the same device Miller was, then passing your location on to him. Oh, that reminds me: give me that burner phone in your pocket, it's government property."

Carlton fished the phone from his pocket and handed it over, glad to be rid of the tainted device. Heather looked it over, then put it in her purse before continuing. "Ikos thought he might have to slow Miller down a bit, so he instructed Bonham to take care of it if the chance arose. Otherwise, we'd have to drive down and baby sit you three—make that *two*—ourselves."

"Mr. Bonham took care of it very nicely, thank you. He put Millstone's ride out of commission from several hundred yards away."

"Then delivered you and Gomez right into our waiting arms," she finished for him with a smug look of satisfaction.

Annoyed by her attitude, Carlton couldn't resist a final comment on the matter, puerile as it was. "Helluva shooter, that Bonham guy. I wish I could have convinced him to sight in on Millstone's head instead of his tires. Would have saved someone else the trouble."

"I think that's been tried. Ikos said Miller's dodged some bullets before. He seems to lead a charmed life. I guess that's why Stan was already talking about using him again."

"Good for him," was all Carlton could say, reaching for the door handle before spouting off something clever, something he'd regret later. He eased out of the car, then leaned down to look at Agent Colson before closing the door. "Thank you for the ride. And thank you for the warning, heeded or not."

She gave him a brief smile. "So what are you going to do now?"

"Get some sleep."

Santa Monica, Coahuila, Mexico. The town's center, the Zócalo, where most social events of small-town Mexico occur.

The square in the middle of town was the focus of all activity this evening, as it had been for the past two days and nights. A crowd numbering several hundred souls, representing the extended families of the slain workers stood talking, gossiping, praying, and weeping in the gathering darkness. Every report that had arrived had been worse than the one preceding, and the latest figures of dead townspeople was thirty-one, with a couple still unaccounted for. It seemed that every able-bodied man in the community had been involved in a fierce gun battle with "unknown persons;" however, it was no secret that the little town depended heavily upon work created by the movement of illegal drugs trafficked through the area. Therefore, it was assumed the slaughter was connected to the cartel bosses, the hated enforcers about whom the workers had often talked bitterly, if quietly. Or possibly it was the work of the government officials tasked with halting drug trafficking, the PFM, the Policía Federal Ministerial. There were even rumors circulating that the massacre had been a joint effort by both groups, with the hapless workers caught in the middle and slaughtered like so many chickens.

Throughout the past forty-eight hours, local police had escorted or driven family members, mostly women and children, to the city morgue in Nuevo Bayito where identification of the mangled bodies was a gruesome and anguishing task, carried out in the only manner possible, given the circumstances found at the bloody death scene: In addition to being horribly mangled by vicious bullet wounds, it seemed none of the dead carried any identification.

Therefore, the bodies were lain out side by side on the floor (not enough tables to accommodate this number of bodies) and covered with sheets. The doors to the already-occupied refrigerator vaults were opened to keep the area a bit cooler. Upon entering the holding room, family members were led to the beginning of the que and shown the first victim's face. Watching the reactions as they progressed down the line, even hardened police officers and experienced morgue employees were moved to tears when the correct victim was uncovered, due to the frightened faces that disintegrated into harsh screams of anguish when a husband, father, or brother was found to be among the dead.

One by one, the bloody remains were identified and paperwork begun to claim the bodies. For most of the survivors, the expense of burial was an overwhelming one, and the Church was being petitioned to provide some relief for the beleaguered families. The Church had, in turn, petitioned the Nuevo Laredo Dioceses for assistance in monetary matters and a legal ruling for expanding the Nuestra Madre de Merced Cemetery. Clearly, the departed would soon outnumber the remaining inhabitants of tiny Santa Monica.

The talk in the crowd on this sad night varied from discussions of future plans and possibilities—which ranged from bleak to non-existent—to remembrances and prayers for the departed loved ones—which ranged from reverent to pure anguish. Throughout the crowd was a pervasive mood of disbelief, of complete and utter incomprehension that a good and loving God could forsake the entire community as He apparently had done, thus bringing forth the obvious question: Why?

PART IV

CHAPTER 33

Carlton twisted in his seat and looked around the crowded church, trying, without success, to spot Reynaldo. According to Paula, he had been released only a few hours before, and she was going to pick him up—hopefully in time for the memorial service about to begin. From his seat in the front row, it was difficult to see much without getting up and facing the crowd, so he stayed seated and hoped Reynaldo would be escorted to the front where several seats still remained, reserved for those closest to Tino. From surveying the crowd earlier, he now wondered who among the hundreds of people milling through the church and its parking lot were *not* close to Tino, or at least claimed to be.

A murmuring stir in the crowd caused him to turn his head again. This time, Tino's sister Marta was being led up the aisle by ushers, one on either side. She walked tentatively and looked as though the events of the past few days had aged her by ten years. As she approached the front row, Carlton stood, followed by the rest, mostly men, all close friends of Faustino Perez. One by one, the men approached and offered condolences.

When Carlton's turn came, he extended his arms and pulled her short body to his for an awkward hug. "Marta, words fail me right now," he said quietly as he leaned down to her ear. "I wish I had been able to do something to stop this, to prevent Tino's death."

"Oh, Carlton, I know you would have! Faustino depended on you so much, I know, and he thought you could do everything. But *El Señor* has decided differently, *y tenemos que creer Sus decisiones siempre son los mejor.*"

Carlton, struggling to follow the softly spoken mixture of English and Spanish, nodded politely at her pious belief that God decided what was best, then stepped aside for the next mourner in line. Noticing Paula coming up the aisle alone, he wondered about Reynaldo and stepped around the others to escort her to a seat in the second row, as she had earlier insisted would be appropriate in light of her little-recognized kinship of half-sister, compared to Marta's well-known relationship to Tino Perez, *El Patrón* of the community.

After seating her, he leaned down to whisper, "You weren't able to get Reynaldo?"

"Yes, he'll be along in a few minutes. I let him out at the back of the parking lot to keep this bunch from having something else to gossip about."

"That's good thinking. They'll have enough to yap about for the next two years without giving them fresh subject matter."

When the greetings were complete, everyone waited for the front row to sit down, a process that was interrupted by another stir from the back of the packed church. A few minutes passed before the standing congregation parted to let Reynaldo Gomez through. Carlton spotted him as he emerged from the crowd, looking somewhat harried from his ordeal, but dressed immaculately. Apparently, Paula had been able to arrange for toiletries and a suit to be taken to the county lockup prior to his release. Carlton smiled inwardly, knowing he would have been horrified to allow this group to see him as he had looked after their overnight trek and a four-day stay in jail.

Stopping to receive handshakes from numerous men and hugs from two women, it took several more minutes for him to make his way forward. When he reached the front row, Carlton remained standing and extended his hand, then gestured to the seat next to his. Noticing the look of relief on Reynaldo's face upon escaping the gauntlet, he was glad his own connection to Tino and the resulting brush with fame in the community was minor. He and Reynaldo took their seats and remained facing forward as the murmurs died down, but feeling the curious stares of hundreds of mourners behind them. The front row dignitaries were now in place, and the ceremony began a few minutes later.

Beginning with a seemingly endless prayer, the ordeal lasted over two hours. Carlton didn't understand the ceremony protocol with its multitude of kneelings and risings prompted by some phrase from the priest, but he followed Reynaldo's lead, leaving no one the wiser. By the end of the religious portion, he was mentally exhausted and dreading the next phase, a series of eulogies to be delivered by individuals chosen by Marta for their relationship to her brother. When his turn came, he rose and stepped to the podium, straightening his tie as he went. He turned to the audience, adjusted the microphone height and began to speak:

"Tino Perez was my friend, although we had a rough beginning. We met under unusual circumstances, thrown together by events beyond our control. As you may or may not know, certain authorities demanded that we work together, and neither Tino nor I were in a position to decline. That was the beginning of a most unusual friendship, one that I will cherish for the rest of my life.

"In the first few weeks, I worked at the market with a young man named Mauricio. We became friends, and he told me things about Tino that I didn't know, things about what he did for his community—*this* community—how he felt a responsibility for everyone's welfare and made sure everyone was treated equally and fairly. That seemed at odds with what I had thought about Tino, but it proved to be correct as I observed what was going on around me."

He paused for a moment and scanned the crowd, looking for the reaction he was hopeful those words would elicit. He wasn't disappointed; nods of affirmation were scattered throughout the crowd, so he pushed ahead.

"In my dealings with Tino, I had lots of opportunities to hear him criticize the people who were involved in things that took place, situations where he would have been better off to let things take their course and not interfere. Or, he could have taken a stance to set the wrongdoer straight. But Tino didn't waste time placing blame on someone else, even when that would have been easy to do. Instead, he just wanted to fix the problem and make sure everyone was okay in the end, that they had a job, had a way to support their family. His first concern was always for the people of the community, *his* people. In other words, *you*. Each and every one of you has surely been influenced and affected by Tino's actions, whether it was a job, settlement of a dispute, or an extension of credit, some accommodation that only he could supply, or even money he didn't expect to get back."

Again he stopped and checked the audience for reactions. Besides the expected approval and agreement, he was surprised to see a mood of rapt attention. Initially, he attributed it to their wondering about his status as an outsider, both in ethnicity and culture. He figured the crowd was simply curious to hear what this gringo had to say about one of them, especially one as important as Faustino Perez. But studying their expressions closely, he realized that his ethnicity and relatively brief tenure weren't that important. Apparently, his actions in supporting Tino—even if they didn't know the exact nature of that support—had given him a measure of credibility with this bunch.

While he was aware that his star had risen after rescuing Paula's daughter, he only now realized the story may have spread beyond the group involved in Tino's trafficking operations. Most of the people sitting near the front were top community business and social leaders, not the hands-on, drug business guys. No, those guys were sitting farther back, doubtless wondering what would happen to their jobs with Tino gone and probably hoping Reynaldo Gomez and Carlton Westerfield would be their salvation. *If they knew what I learned in the past week, they'd all get up and walk out*, he thought grimly before pressing forward and finishing his talk with an expression of sorrow for Marta, Paula, Reynaldo, and Tino's estranged wife, Carlotta (oddly absent) and himself, as well as the entire community. Of the entire speech, he thought the last part was pretty good, and he hoped the crowd focused on it instead of the earlier, glossy praise.

As he walked to his seat, he noticed looks of appreciation, almost admiration, from several well-dressed mourners near the front. He wondered if the looks would have been the same had they known the exact circumstances surrounding the community leader who was being fondly eulogized and Carlton Westerfield's support of those circumstances. *Not likely*, he thought. *Tino was a great asset to his community in many ways, but he was involved in an illegal, tawdry, ugly business, and it cost him his life. Reynaldo and I escaped the same fate by sheer luck.*

Reynaldo took the podium next, and did a much better job, regaling the crowd with tales from their childhood and adventures as young men. Watching his delivery, Carlton noticed a few times when he became emotional and realized Reynaldo's personal loss was much greater than perhaps anyone present, save Marta.

Raul Vega followed with stories of his early days after arriving from Cuba, how Tino had befriended him and his wife, Caterina. Vega credited Tino Perez with salvaging the life of an immigrant revolutionary exiled from his home country by Castro's regime. A few times, he slipped into Spanish and related what must have been funny events, judging from the crowd's laughter. Carlton was surprised at his animated nature and the ease with which he spoke—in both languages—in front of so many people.

Watching the wiry old man, he thought about their brief meeting two days ago at the flea market, when he'd first heard about the escape of Vega and five of the attacking force, including David Avila and Ramón Espinoza, plus three *Santa Monica* men. Hearing the story, he'd figured it had been a miracle they had escaped, but Raul's dry telling made it sound like an ordinary event.

It probably was an ordinary event in Cuba, during the revolution.

Two other men, community leaders Carlton didn't know, followed with much longer and more elaborate speeches, and the crowd became restless near the end. When the marathon ceremony was over, it took another hour to extract himself from the crowd. He was surprised, even pleased, with the expressions of thanks for his brief eulogy, even though he thought it had sounded canned and rehearsed to his ears, much like the presentation of a gold watch at someone's retirement party by a boss who'd not known the retiring employee.

In truth, he had barely rehearsed the short talk; instead, he'd mentally gone over the basic facts surrounding his introduction to Tino and his own personal take on the *patrón's* attitude toward his community, the sanitized part, developed over the weeks and months he'd worked for him. A few obligatory phrases thrown together, leaving out recognition of the departed's intellect and humorous side, his penchant for paying what he owed, his achievements outside the confines of this section of town and its heavily Hispanic culture—most notably, his perfect diction while speaking English, devoid of accent, something Carlton had admired from their first encounter.

Thinking about it now, he wished he had done a more thorough job of eulogizing his friend, but this close-knit community revered Faustino Perez mainly for providing jobs, wealth, and security—some of which stemmed indirectly from drug trafficking. Even with the juicy rumors surrounding

Tino's death—and there were many—Carlton figured most of the crowd either ignored his role as crime boss, denied it, or weren't aware of it. In fact, many of the mourners may have wondered if this Anglo really had any connection to *El Patrón*.

If they only knew.

Right now, Carlton didn't care about their wonderings. He'd miss his friendship with Tino, but it was clearly time to change his life, move on to something akin to normalcy and leave drug trafficking to someone else. With those thoughts in his mind, he unlocked the Cadillac, got in, and started the engine. When he put the car in gear, he heard a tapping on the passenger window and turned to see Reynaldo pointing at the door lock. He hit the unlock button and waited for him to get in.

"Am I glad to be done with that!" he muttered, closing the door and buckling his seat belt. "Look, I'm sorry to barge in, but can we take a drive, go get something to eat? Paula's going to Marta's and there will be a bunch of people there, probably half this crowd."

Carlton grinned at his dire prediction, probably an accurate one. "Sure we can. You're right, so I don't want to be in my apartment either. Too close to Ground Zero. Where to?"

"Hell, I don't care. Somewhere we don't usually go. You know any place—"

"Let's go to Ernesto's," Carlton interrupted. "Of all days, we deserve a change of pace."

The pair spent the next two hours over a fine meal at Carlton's favorite restaurant, sitting at a duce table on an elevated floor section of the secluded upscale establishment. After eating, they ordered after-dinner drinks and sat back to catch up. Though there had been brief communications through Paula, neither had felt comfortable about Carlton visiting the lockup. It was the first time they'd met privately since being picked up by the DEA in Encinal five days ago.

"First, tell me how you got out. Paula was researching defense attorneys when she got word you'd be released today."

"They decided they really didn't have anything to hold me on," Reynaldo explained. "Even with all the digging around in Wichita Falls, they couldn't find any product, and my storage and street crews went underground, just like we had always planned. It wasn't going to be easy to get me indicted.

"What did they do with you? Haul you in for questioning with a rubber hose?"

Carlton grinned at the question. "Worse than that. Heather drove me home, then talked to me outside my apartment for about an hour. She wasn't very sweet about it." He proceeded to relate everything about the joint DEA/PFM operation, the use of rogue contractors like Cletus Miller, aka Clive Millstone, the tracking device implanted in a look-alike burner phone, and Herbert Bonham's role as taxi driver and curbing Millstone's pursuit.

When he recounted Heather's take on the brutal assassination of Tino, Reynaldo's face darkened, and he interrupted for the first time. "That sounds right," he conceded, anger rising in his voice. "If he could collect from the Rendóns or old man Benavides without having to deliver him alive, it would make sense to kill him and avoid having to guard him. With three of us to control, he just wanted to make his job easier."

"True, but he had all those goons from the warehouse. They didn't have any problem pushing us around. How many were with him, six or seven?"

"My eyes weren't working too well, but that's about right."

Carlton forced himself to think about the scene near the bus station. The gory scene and its immediate aftermath prompted a fresh round of revulsion, along with a reminder that the brutal killing had served another purpose, one he'd thought about earlier. "Even with enough help to guard all of us, it made sense to drive home his point about not trying anything cute. I was so shocked, I couldn't have walked away if I'd had the chance."

"For sure, neither could I. And it's something I've had four days to think about. Every time I close my eyes, I see it again."

Both men went quiet for a minute, savoring their drinks; thankful for their survival; relieved to be done with the day's sad activities; missing their friend…and wishing the other would change the subject.

Carlton obliged by venturing into his earlier thoughts. "I've got to do something else, Reynaldo. I'm too old to do this anymore, and I don't want to, anyway. I'm sick of the drug business.

"I'm sure you've figured out that I haven't made a living by performing acts of kindness. But my previous occupation had protection, a built-in barrier against outside influences. I worked strictly alone, for one guy. I made sure I didn't have any connection to the job at hand, I did it quickly, and I got paid the minute it was done.

"Being a solo practitioner, I never had to worry about connections or relationships tripping me up. The guy who extended the contracts made good money, so there was no reason to be set up by him, no matter what happened with the target. If I performed, he saw it in the morning newspaper and cashed me out, same day. If not, I didn't get paid—simple as that." He spread his hands to demonstrate the simplicity of the matter.

Reynaldo had been listening quietly, nodding at a couple of points made during Carlton's concise recitation of his former job's perks. Sensing the opportunity, he leaned forward in his chair and spoke quietly. "I realize this is probably a poor time to bring this up, but since you've expressed a dislike for drug trafficking *and* recounted your past occupation with glowing terms—both within two minutes—I can't resist asking: would you take on one more job like you did for Big Mo?"

At the mention of his former contract man, the obese pawnbroker who out-sourced jobs on a percentage basis, Carlton was taken aback. Big Mo had been dead for almost three years, long before Reynaldo Gomez had come to San Antonio at the behest of his friend Tino. The surprise must have shown in his face, and he waited for Reynaldo to explain how he knew about Randall (Big Mo) Morris, although he knew the answer.

With a grin, Reynaldo confirmed his curiosity. "Of course, Tino told me about your days as a button man for some fat gangster named Morris, Big Mo. And Paula knew about it, too. She said the two of you went back to a job involving him, but she didn't provide any details."

Carlton returned the grin with one of his own and a shake of his head. "Like most women, Paula can be a bit short on details. *Unlike* most women, Paula is great at doing it and getting away with it.

"Anyway, to answer your question, I'm going to take a pass. In spite of it being a better fit for me than smuggling narcotics, I'm done with that life too. I'm too old—"

"You haven't even heard the job description," Reynaldo interrupted, dismissing the question of age with a wave of his hand. "Or the price."

Carlton had to laugh. "You sound like Big Mo did when he offered me the job to take out Tino. By the way, that led to my meeting Paula. One of the details she left out."

Reynaldo leaned back in his chair and looked at him quizzically, but didn't say anything.

"It's a long, complicated story, Reynaldo," Carlton said. "You'll have to get Paula to explain it to you, because I'm not sure I ever knew the whole truth behind it."

Reynaldo drew a deep breath, then exhaled loudly. "A quarter million dollars."

For the second time in the conversation, Carlton was surprised. During his tenure of performing contracts for Big Mo, most jobs paid five to twenty thousand dollars, with an occasional hit for thirty grand, Carlton's part. Two hundred fifty thousand dollars was an enormous sum to apply a few ounces of pressure on a trigger—depending on the target, of course.

As if reading his mind, Reynaldo waited a beat to give the information Carlton wanted to hear, regardless of whether or not he took the job. He leaned toward him again to ensure privacy. "Clive Millstone."

For a change, Carlton wasn't surprised. Obviously, he'd had the thought himself, several times in fact, when the murder scene intruded on his consciousness...the sweating, pig-like face of the British mercenary spitting out words in an over-done accent, the raised gun, the blast, and its sickening result. Now, he was being offered a large sum of money to perform a job very similar to what he had done many times for far less reward.

This job had one element that he had steadfastly avoided during his past life, though: he had a definite connection to the target. Although obscure and brief, several people knew of his contact with—and hatred for—Clive Millstone/Cletus Miller, most notably several federal law enforcement agents. One of them—one he'd slept with—had seen through his weak attempt to locate the target. If Millstone/Miller turned up dead, it wouldn't take Sherlock Holmes to deduce a likely killer. Or would it? The Brit mercenary had plenty of enemies, no question about that. Heather Colson had mentioned that he had "dodged some bullets before," so there would be other possible suspects.

Plus, Carlton's methodology left little for investigators to go on. Discrete research for a time and location, a cold, untraceable weapon, quick in-and-out execution, and no fanfare threats during the job all added to the difficulty of solving the murder. Also, as in his former life, this target wasn't likely to elicit a huge manhunt response. Law enforcement people were constrained by time and funds, so a dirt bag like Millstone would have the same status as the many low-life characters who'd gotten on Big Mo's list in past years: Go through the motions, fill out the required paperwork, and move on to a better citizen's problems. It wasn't likely that a civil rights group would march on City Hall waving placards that read: "*Justice for sleazy gun runners!*"

Carlton's quick evaluation of the job offer took a couple of minutes. Meanwhile, Reynaldo sat back and sipped his drink, patiently waiting for a decision and, hopefully, a positive response. He'd had several conversations with Tino regarding Westerfield's career with Big Mo, and Paula had told of her terrifying experience at the ransom pay-off site during her kidnapping ordeal. Blindfolded at the time, she had been thrust into a car with four men and taken to a car wash for the exchange. Seconds after hearing Carlton's voice, she heard four or five gunshots and was pulled from the car by Carlton—kidnapping over, no ransom paid, victim safe… while her four abductors lay on the concrete.

From those accounts, he had a good idea of Carlton's capabilities, and he'd deduced from the stories that something unique happened when the quiet, middle-aged man raised a handgun toward a target. Apparently, he had a knack for turning off outside interference and a natural instinct for shooting accurately without traditional aiming, skills Reynaldo had heard of several times, but observed only once.

Second-hand information from parties he knew and trusted was fine, but the best example of Carlton's work product had occurred a few days earlier in the *Bayito* warehouse when Reynaldo had witnessed three armed men being taken out with four or five quick shots. Then, he watched as Westerfield swung the big auto-pistol smoothly from one target to the next, successive rounds slamming into the men, dropping them like flies in a bug zapper. Too bad he didn't take one more shot and drop Clive

Millstone too, he thought. Would have saved us a lot of trouble, saved Tino's life, and saved—

His musings were interrupted by his companion seated across the table. "Where is he?"

CHAPTER 34

The weather turned colder as February progressed, and Carlton spent time at the flea market helping Marta get a handle on the business, at least the parts he had gleaned from watching Tino interact with the vendors. She proved to be adept at picking it up, and her mood improved with the activity. For his part, Carlton was surprised at the friendly reaction from the vendors; apparently, he had become well-liked among them during his months of delivering goods to their stalls. It made the introduction of Marta as their new landlord and inventory supplier a more comfortable transaction than he'd expected.

Raul and Caterina Vega stepped in to help with the other business entities, which was beneficial since they could switch to Spanish with Marta and the operators when the need arose. As with the flea market vendors, all readily accepted Marta in her new role. Within a few days, things seemed to be running at a normal pace in the community, though moods remained subdued.

Reynaldo and Marta had several long, private meetings in Tino's office, which Carlton figured had to do with the trafficking operation. Though he'd recently learned from Reynaldo that Tino had bequeathed all the regular business enterprises to Marta, with a sizeable share of profits to be distributed to his wife and children in Mexico and a nice stipend to Paula, he'd never gotten any indication that Marta was aware of the *illegal* business, so it was likely to be an eye-opener for her. To Carlton, Reynaldo Gomez seemed the likely candidate to run the trafficking operation, if it survived the turmoil. Or maybe Tino and Reynaldo had come up with something between them during the war with Brujido Ramos. Carlton didn't know and wasn't about to ask.

Aside from the lengthy meetings with Marta, Reynaldo divided his time between researching Clive Millstone's whereabouts, running his Wichita Falls construction company by phone, and teaming up with Tino's crew to learn the details of the trafficking operation, which was currently at a standstill. The street vendors operated at a much-reduced capacity, aware that no new product was scheduled to arrive, but everyone in that end of Tino's empire seemed content to let Reynaldo Gomez take over and find his way to do things.

Respecting Carlton's declaration that he didn't want any more of the contraband smuggling business, their encounters only involved Millstone strategy sessions over meals, during which Reynaldo revealed his own considerable clout in the crime world. He had contacts in Mexico, specifically in *Nuevo Laredo*, who could help in locating the hangouts of Clive Millstone, aka Cletus Miller. No matter what name he went by, the loud-mouthed Brit wouldn't be able to blend in easily, and within days, Reynaldo told Carlton he'd gotten a report that Tino's murderer was currently staying somewhere in the border city. That was encouraging news. Carlton had been concerned that the globe-trotting mercenary might have fled to parts unknown, but it seemed his traitorous little arrangement with the *Golfos* had led to a more permanent relationship, perhaps one headquartered in Northern Mexico.

A week after Tino's memorial service, the pair met at the flea market and retired to Tino's office to talk. Like Carlton, Reynaldo was pleased that their quarry had chosen to stay in *Nuevo Laredo*, an area where he already had the necessary contacts to observe and report the target's movements.

"I have four people working this for me," he said. "Three men and a woman. They're not geared to be at the sharp end of any action, but they are very good at tailing and observing, exactly what we need for this.

"They made a few subtle inquiries, got a lead immediately, and it seems our target is hanging around just across the border. This morning, I got a vaguely worded text from the woman, who said a guy matching Millstone's description and accent is living at the Colon Plaza Hotel."

"That's good news," Carlton said, "even if the hit has to happen over there. But they're going to have to pin down a schedule, a set regimen of his, some place where he can be predicted with some accuracy. I can't wander around very long without being made by him or his cohorts."

"He's coming across from time to time, they're certain of that. But he's slippery, and they've lost him a couple of times at the border crossing. One minute, he's in line at the bridge, then he's disappeared, no trace."

"Maybe he's doubling back, not coming over at all? Or checking for tails and spotted them?"

"I don't think he would feel the need to do that. Remember, he's got to be feeling pretty cocky right now. He engineered and pulled off the massacre at the warehouse, he locked us up, but stuck us with a tracking device, he killed Faustino Perez and collected money for it, he killed his partner Gustavo Mendoza, and he got paid by the DEA *and* the *Golfos*," Reynaldo listed the ugly facts, ticking them off with his fingers.

"Then maybe he's worried about us gunning for him. Or, he's just slippery by nature."

"Well, a slime ball he is, so he is definitely slippery. But more likely, he's meeting somebody over here that he doesn't want old man Benavides finding out about, hence, the elusive tradecraft."

Carlton nodded. "That makes sense, the devious bastard. He may be cozying up to the enforcer guys he had strong-arming us, trying to figure another way to screw the *Golfos* out of product or money."

"Could be. Or maybe he's meeting with the other side, which wouldn't please the *Golfos*. Didn't you say the DEA likes his work well enough to hire him for another job?"

"That's what Heather indicated. She says Ikos was already planning to use him, doesn't hold it against him that he double and triple dips on money and double-crosses every employer."

"Unbelievable. I guess independent contractors can do that, but regular agents would be handing over their badge and gun on the way to max lockup for that kind of action."

The pair went silent for a few minutes, mulling over options, possibilities regarding Millstone's mysterious movements. Carlton thought of another avenue. "Maybe we need a lure, something to draw him in. Put out word for a high-paying job that would appeal to his greed."

Reynaldo thought over the suggestion. "I like the idea of a lure so we can get a handle on his movements, find out where and when he could be hit. But I had in mind something even better than a lucrative job," he added with a sly grin, reminding Carlton of their absent friend.

Carlton returned the grin. "What, the most effective lure in the history of mankind?" Carlton guessed, knowing he was right.

"Yes. And Paula said she'd do it."

Carlton stared at him in amazement. *"Paula? Are you serious?* Reynaldo, Clive Millstone is a professional murderer! And—"

"So are you."

That stopped Carlton in mid-sentence—not the interruption, but the veracity of the statement. Reynaldo's follow-up provided proof. "Carlton, you're one of the most perceptive men I've met, but I think Paula was able to fool you about a few things, just as she did me.

"But to put your mind at ease, I did try to talk her out of it for the same reasons you're thinking: Millstone's a professional killer; plus, he's got a mean, sadistic streak that knows no limits. He's operated in circumstances where all human norms are ignored. Also, he's way ahead of her—and us—in terms of surveillance and clandestine activities. I talked to her at length, and she understands all those things. But she assures me she wants to avenge Tino's death, and she can do it by setting him up."

Carlton thought it over for almost a minute while Reynaldo waited patiently. Finally, he took a breath and shook his head, not in disagreement, but submission. "I guess you're right. Paula is a terrific actress and one of the most charming women I've known. And the obvious plus is her appearance, though it's not politically correct to suggest that women need to have that going for them."

"Right, but we're men and we know better," Reynaldo said, his dead-pan delivery deteriorating at the end, prompting both to snicker like school boys. "Seriously, she can dazzle any man with a few years on him, so that sleazy clod won't stand a snowball's chance in hell!"

Carlton smiled inwardly, agreeing. He knew the feeling all too well.

Two weeks later, on Wednesday, the three sat in a booth in the Jim's restaurant at Broadway and Loop 410, finishing breakfast and talking quietly. After being led to this booth by restaurant staff, Paula had asked to be moved to another one, so the waitress rarely returned to serve the picky trio. There were no interruptions, and no one gazed zombie-like at hand-held electronic devices. At this gathering, like the two previous ones—at different restaurants—no one even carried a cell phone, nor was there a phone in their cars.

Carlton's recent realization that electronic surveillance had advanced far beyond his knowledge had prompted the precautionary measures. The look-alike burner phone/tracking device planted by Millstone had taught him a valuable lesson regarding privacy, and he, Reynaldo, and Paula were employing every possible countermeasure tactic to ensure their planning went unmonitored, even if their efforts were over-the-top.

Reynaldo updated the group with the latest intel he'd gotten from his sources in *Nuevo Laredo*, which confirmed Clive Millstone was staying at the Colon Plaza, but crossing over to the U. S. side almost every day. Unfortunately, he'd still proven to be elusive in his movements and his destination was never determined. "But my guys think he's meeting someone close to the bridge, probably at *La Posada*, because they always lose him in that vicinity, and we know he likes the place. One time, he went into the San Augustín Cathedral and didn't come out, so he must have slipped out the back."

"I'd be willing to bet he didn't get stuck in the confessional booth," Carlton said sarcastically. "He doesn't seem the penitent type."

Reynaldo agreed. "I'm surprised the church didn't collapse when he walked in. Anyway, the next day, he simply vanished into that plaza in front of the church. It's just a small park, but with a lot of people around, a guy like him can shake anyone but the very best tails—and my contacts aren't pros, not by any stretch. They're doing this as a favor to me—a well-paid one, though—and I told them not to get made, no matter what, even if they lose him.

"As to the enforcers, my men went by the *Bayito* warehouse several times, and it was still shut down, surrounded by police tape and flowers. On the third or fourth day, three men were outside, pointing to various parts of the building like they were assessing damage or something. From the descriptions, two of them had to be Jese Felan and Gordo Carillo, the two top enforcers, according to what all of the laborers told us while training at the ranch. The third guy didn't match, but he's got to be another of those thugs.

303

"So, Paula and I agreed that *La Posada* would be a good place to start. And early in the game, she would be able to use hotel phones to call me, not have to use her cell and replace it so much." He turned to Paula. "This was only your second trip, but it sounded like you might have spotted him at *La Posada*, right?"

She nodded vigorously. "I went down on Monday evening and checked in. Got up early on Tuesday, and I didn't spot anyone at breakfast or anywhere on the hotel grounds. I went to lunch with a friend on the east side, out by the airport. We did a little shopping, then I went back to the hotel for a nap.

"That afternoon, I went across to shop at the old mall on the main street leading from *Puente Uno*, but it's all changed a lot, so I came back to the hotel before going next door to the Streets of Laredo Mall.

"I didn't stay long, and when I walked toward the pool in the west wing, I saw our guy, I'm sure of it. He was heavy, had a ruddy complexion like he was sunburned, and was talking with two Hispanic men in a little patio just outside the kitchen. I couldn't get close enough to hear his accent, but it looked like a really intense discussion about something."

"Did he see you, look at you, make eye contact or anything?" Carlton asked.

She shook her head. "No. I mean, I don't think so. They were too involved in their conversation. I kept walking, went straight to my room." She hesitated before continuing in a husky voice. "I stayed there…" Her voice trailed off, and she looked away, visibly upset. Both men leaned in toward her, Reynaldo touching her shoulder. Suddenly she looked ready to cry.

Carlton glanced around and spoke softly. "Paula, I'm sorry. I guess I'm just too anxious for success. I didn't mean to sound like I was grilling you. I just know that any man looking at you isn't likely to look away very soon."

The comment got a weak smile. "I'll take that as a compliment," she said, digging in her purse for a tissue. "But when I saw him and was pretty sure it was…*him*, I almost lost it, thinking about what he did to Tino.

"I just kept my head down and went to my room. I locked and dead-bolted the door, called Reynaldo, then went to bed and left first thing this morning. In fact, I drove straight here. I haven't even been home."

Reynaldo leaned in closer and stroked her arm. "Look, I'm sorry you had to experience that. And I'm sorry you're having to do this, but I can't imagine how else we—Carlton and I—can get close to the guy. He'd spot us in a minute. And if those guys he's meeting with are the same enforcers, they'd be able to ID us too."

She drew a deep breath and exhaled, which seemed to calm her. "I know. And I'm okay with doing it, I told you that. In fact, I *want* to do it, since it's all I can do for Tino now."

She paused, then took another breath before continuing. "Tino and I weren't always close through the years. We got crossways a couple of times." She turned to face Carlton. "But when he thought I'd been killed in the car bomb, I realized he really cared about me."

Carlton nodded. "Yes, he did. He was devastated when he called me. And he was plenty happy when we found out we were mistaken. So was I."

She smiled at the memory. "And now, I can do something about his death. I've been disappointed, not being able to spot the guy, even though we were pretty sure he's been staying in Laredo or *Nuevo Laredo*. So seeing him yesterday made me feel better about this...but seeing him was also hard—and scary. Does that make sense?"

"Of course," Carlton answered. "I can't speak for Reynaldo, but I've never been as scared in my life as I was facing him."

Reynaldo nodded in agreement. "And I've been worried about you doing this, knowing what I told you about...that day. I expected it to be frightening, but maybe I shouldn't have given you the details—"

She shook her head, interrupting him. "It's okay, Reynaldo, I promise. Just tell me what we do next."

"If you're up to it, go back down there and check into the Posada. If he shows up again, you'll have to play it as you see fit. I mean, I'm not sure how you, uh...go about..."

"You mean go about hitting on him?" she asked, grinning at Reynaldo's sudden embarrassment.

"Well, yes," he mumbled. "I guess that's it."

Carlton laughed at his friends' awkward exchange. "Paula, believe me, Reynaldo and I both know it won't be hard for you to get a man's attention!" Then he turned serious. "But you'll have to play it right for this guy to buy in. He's smart and crafty. He's not a suave, handsome dude by any measure, but he's smart and hard to outwit. He'll be suspicious of a woman who looks like you paying attention to him. It's going to take some finesse, some kind of opening to look natural."

"Commenting on his accent might provide a believable opening," Reynaldo suggested. "He's never lost his British accent, and it varies, depending on his mood. Not many British-sounding men hang out in Laredo, Texas."

"Okay, I can see that working. But I'll have to get close enough to overhear him and make the approach seem natural."

"And the first contact needs to be brief. I mean, not *too* brief, but—" Reynaldo was clearly having trouble coaching his girlfriend on snagging another man.

His discomfort made Paula's eyes dance with merriment. "I know. I know just the thing: brief, but *promising*, right?"

Reynaldo looked helplessly at Carlton, who repeated the phrase Reynaldo had used two weeks earlier. "Nope, not a snowball's chance in hell."

CHAPTER 35

"Welcome back to *Hotel La Posada*, Ms. Hendricks. We have you booked for a small suite for three days. Would something in the West Wing be satisfactory?"

"Thank you, yes. Is there one available near The Tack Room?"

"I think so. Give me a moment, please." The reception clerk turned to his computer screen and began scrolling and clicking.

Paula looked around the lobby area, now becoming too-familiar territory to her on this, the fifth time she'd checked in as many weeks. Nice as it was, she wondered how some people could spend their entire lives moving from one luxury hotel to another. Maybe they have different reasons to do it, she thought. Something besides waiting for a murderer to show up so I can get him to take me to dinner and get murdered himself.

She abandoned the maudlin thoughts and concentrated on the layout, wondering if there were any places she had failed to see in previous trips, anywhere Millstone might be meeting with the men Reynaldo's watchers had spotted. Only last week, they had reported seeing the trio again, leaving the hotel's underground parking lot. Paula had been staying there at the time, but didn't see the target or his companions. The continued failure was becoming more frustrating by the day.

To the right and beyond the reception counter, a pair of doors led to the pool deck and the main guest room building, the older part of the hotel. Taking a right turn from the pool deck, a broad tiled walkway led to the West Wing, a separate set of guest rooms preferred by experienced guests for its proximity to the exclusive dinner restaurant, plus some degree of seclusion from the bustle of the lobby and nearby coffee shop. Plus, the West Wing pool included a swim-up bar, making it less attractive to those guests with children and a hang-out beyond posted hours for the adults-only crowd. The experienced hotel staff had learned how to recognize new guests' preferences and the best fit for accommodations the minute they walked in, while returning guests sometimes specified a room they had previously occupied. It was that kind of hotel—not the newest or fanciest…just the best, in the minds of its moneyed clientele.

Within minutes, she had her key and, declining help with her single bag, headed through the main lobby to the Zaragoza Grill for a snack before going to her suite. Trying hard to quell her nervousness, she had decided on the drive down to make use of every minute, trying for maximum exposure to the public parts of the hotel, especially areas where a clandestine meeting might be held. After her second trip and the harrowing experience of laying eyes on the target for the first time, she had become determined to overcome her anxiety and do whatever was necessary to draw Tino's killer within range of Carlton Westerfield. But so far…nothing.

When she had finished her coffee and pie, she opted to leave by a rear door which led to the small, secluded patio adjacent to the West Wing breezeway, the place where she had spotted Millstone three weeks ago. In more recent stays, she had noticed a few people using the area for small private meetings, most of which looked like lovers' rendezvous. On this day, however, no one was in the vine-covered spot, and she felt a twinge of disappointment before reminding herself she had only just arrived. Besides, just because the near-hidden patio would be the perfect spot for another assignation among the likes of gun runners and drug traffickers, it was unrealistic to hope for success this soon. She'd check this spot several times a day.

So far, there had been no set pattern to Millstone's movements or any information regarding the purpose of his forays into the U. S. Her single sighting remained the bright spot for the three of them, if one could call a hasty retreat to her room and fleeing for home the next morning a bright spot. Going over this in her mind renewed her determination to focus on the end result and put aside her fear of this monster who had entered her life by killing her brother in cold blood. Although she had known about Tino's involvement in the most statistically dangerous crime enterprise of all, Reynaldo's disclosure of the details of his death haunted her and made her desperate to give Carlton an opportunity to exact revenge for a murder that served no cause whatsoever beyond convenience to the killer in collecting his fee.

Paula spent the rest of the day migrating between both pool decks and the small lobby shopping area. Since it was still early spring in South Texas, she was dressed casually in an outfit suitable for outdoor reading in a deck chair, but still accentuated her curves. By late evening, she had given up on spotting Millstone, but she had renewed faith in her ability to draw attention to herself due to the three men (one was impossibly young) she'd politely fended off.

The next morning, she left the hotel after breakfast and walked the entire area around the hotel, starting at the San Augustine Plaza directly across from the hotel entrance. The tiny park served as the center for social activity in the immediate area of the city, much as did the *zócalo*, or town square, in most small Mexican towns, where it might be referred to as simply *el centro*. And like its Mexican counterparts, the plaza was filled with vendors of everything from candy to key chains, T-shirts to tacos, in spite of city ordinances regulating street commerce. She made the block slowly, pausing to check activity around her, and even monitoring pedestrian traffic in and out of the hotel entrance when her vantage point allowed. She bought some crackers and sat at one of the benches for a while, doling out treats to pigeons and sparrows until she realized she was breaking another city ordinance by doing so. She shook her head and sighed, wondering if she was cut out for clandestine surveillance.

From there, she wandered across the street to San Augustine Cathedral, where she went in and lit a candle for Tino and deposited extra money in the jar, foregoing saying a prayer for the time being. It was the first time in memory she had entered a church without praying. Exiting to the front steps, she chastised herself for the failure, but justified her action by admitting the prayer would have likely only asked God for help in locating her much-despised quarry.

From the Cathedral, the next logical stop was the Republic of the Rio Grande Museum, located next to the hotel's east wall. She strolled quickly among the artifacts and scanned the descriptions and histories in order to kill time, knowing she wouldn't remember a single exhibit when she left. In less than thirty minutes, she left the museum and turned left, back to the hotel. She checked her watch as she stepped inside the lobby and looked to the Zaragoza Grill entrance on her right. *Just eleven forty-five; that's barely the hour for lunch, and only if one wanted an early one.*

She spent the afternoon on the hotel grounds, lounging at one pool, then the other, reading until her eyes watered. By four o'clock, she was going stir-crazy, frustrated with the lack of action over an entire day. Thinking through her movements, she suddenly realized her clumsy surveillance might be exposing her to any watchers Millstone or his cohorts might have in place to check before meeting. If so, would they automatically make her for a lure, like something in a spy novel? Or just a hooker, trolling for well-heeled trade? The ultimate irony—being made before she could make her quarry, solely by her unusual and amateurish methods! Realizing she was over-analyzing into irrational territory, she closed the book and went to her room.

At six o'clock, she strode through the hotel lobby, dressed to kill, and asked the doorman to summon a taxi. Standing on the sidewalk, she drew appreciative looks from a pair of older businessmen headed into the Zaragoza, even though they were accompanied by two women who looked to be their wives. Then, three Hispanic men pulled up in a BMW sedan and exited, handing the key to a valet attendant. As they walked by her, one of them slowed and looked her over closely before stepping up his pace to join his companions heading toward the Tack Room. Right reaction, wrong guys, she thought. But it beat the fruitless trolling she'd been doing all day.

By six thirty, she was on the other side of the border, ordering dinner at *Restaurante Tomatillos*, an Italian place on the *Avenida Reforma*. The fantastic meal entertained her for two hours and relieved the tension caused by the futile day, but she finally had to call it quits and return to the Posada. A late evening line at the bridge, plus over-zealous scrutiny of her passport (and her legs) made the crossing process longer than she wanted, and it was closing in on ten o'clock when she paid the taxi driver and crossed the sidewalk. Near the front entrance, she slowed her pace to wait for the doorman, having learned the Posada staff preferred to adhere to tradition, especially where women were concerned.

At this time of night, the doorman was doubling as luggage handler. He was helping an older couple unload their luggage from the trunk of a vintage Cadillac, so Paula stepped up to open the door herself when a Hispanic man she recognized as one of the three she had seen earlier reached in front of her for the door. "Please allow me, *Señorita*."

Flustered by his quick move and suave manner, she managed to say, "Thank you" and ascend the two steps to the open door. As she stepped in, the man followed her inside and moved to her right. In her peripheral vision, she saw the man wave to someone who was emerging from the Zaragoza Grill. The movement automatically caused her to glance in the direction of whomever he was greeting, and she felt her heart stop cold.

A big, barrel-chested man with a florid face and meaty arms had nodded to the gracious door opener and was crossing the lobby, coming straight at them. For the second time, she was looking at Clive Millstone from a distance, but at his present course, they would be face-to-face in about five seconds. Her interrupted heartbeat commenced and was now hammering in her chest. She pulled in a deep breath and concentrated on maintaining her composure, knowing it might be the most difficult—and dangerous—acting job of her life.

"Well, Jese, seems you have followed a lovely lady into this hovel of an establishment!" he bellowed, clearly speaking through alcohol-soaked vocal chords. "Might I say I'm delighted he did, by the way, such a sight she is!" he added, leering at her.

Paula met his stare with a polite gaze of confusion, not difficult under the circumstances. As he drew nearer, she forced a smile, albeit a rather frigid one, before turning in the direction of the reception desk.

Undeterred, the big man moved in front of her, stepping into her line of vision. From her side, she sensed disapproval from the other man, now identified as Jese. She heard him clear his throat and saw a small jerk of his head intended to motion Millstone away from her and, presumably, on to wherever they were to have met before an excess of liquor and boldness prompted him to intercept the attractive woman coming in the door.

"Come on now, pretty bird that you are! I haven't been seeing the likes of you in a while, being stuck down here in the land of darker skin. And by what name are you called then, luv?"

She turned back toward him with a questioning look, as though only now realizing he was addressing her. Nervous as she was, she could barely suppress laughing at herself, at the acting job that must look like something from a 1940s movie. She tried to remember the adjective used to describe actresses of that time and finally came up with "sultry." The term sounded ridiculous to her; in fact, she nearly laughed, but stifled it into a smirk.

Even though unintended, it got the right response from the drunken Millstone. "Come on then, I'm Clive Millstone, so tell Clive your name, would ya?"

Paula could feel the presence of Jese behind her, along with his displeasure at this sordid, semi-public turn of events. He had moved closer behind her, and she could almost feel his simmering anger. She struggled to come up with something that would defuse the spectacle while keeping one man at bay and the other interested. Trying to play both sides of the street was difficult, but she came up with a response she hoped would work. "My name is Paula. And if I heard correctly, yours is Clive. But the only reason I caught it was to listen to your accent—which would sound better if you were sober." She moved forward and pushed her way past the obnoxious man and headed toward the door leading to the original guest rooms, not wanting to reveal she was staying in the more remote West Wing.

Behind her, she heard Jese's hissing voice berating him, then Millstone's braying call out to her retreating backside. "I'll be sober tomorrow at breakfast, then luv!"

She forced herself to stop abruptly and turn around. "And so will I. Good night, Clive." She turned again and stalked out to the pool area, then turned right toward her room. It took all her willpower to keep from running. Once in her suite, she locked and dead-bolted the door, took off her shoes and plopped across the bed, exhausted. After a while, she looked at her watch and remembered she had to call Reynaldo and report, keeping to the bare facts in order to minimize their time on the phone.

Millstone's experience in his field of expertise, plus possible access to sophisticated tracking equipment had caused Carlton to be adamant about keeping calls short and removing batteries after talking due to his own recent experience with DEA gadgetry "Probably overkill," he'd said, "But why take any chances? Millstone may be a sleaze bag, but he's a smart one."

Turning on her new burner phone, unused until then, she punched in Reynaldo's new number and reported the encounter excitedly, keeping to the events in concise, chronological order. Less than two minutes in the telling, she paused before asking for instructions on her next move.

"Paula, you've done a great job!" Reynaldo said, excitement evident in his voice. *"It sounds like you responded perfectly, not too much, not too little.*

"I think the next thing to do is show up in the breakfast area—that's still in the Zaragoza Grill, right?"

"Yes. There's a buffet table set up for breakfast, and they even open the bar for Bloody Marys, except on Sundays."

"Well, you deserve one. Obviously, if he shows, you'll have to play it by ear. Hopefully, he'll be sober—and alone," he added. *"The one he called Jese has to be Jese Felan, one of the enforcers, a bad guy himself and not as likely to stumble over a woman as that drunken ass Millstone. He might not be as easily fooled. In fact, the first thing he'll do after learning your name is to bribe the desk clerk for all the information they have on you."*

That part worried her. *"You think so? What if they find out I'm—"*

"There's nothing to find out, Paula, not in the short term. You used the driver's license with the Houston address to check in, right? So that's the information they'll get from the desk clerk, an apartment address that doesn't exist anymore, because it burned down last year. It's a dead end that would take days to verify through real estate archives, even if Felan has sources in Houston.

"Remember, we checked everything we could think of to expose a connection between you and Tino, me, or Carlton. Even most of the people here don't know you're Tino's half-sister. Besides, who would they ask? No one in the community would answer questions from an outsider, not after the last few weeks.

"But you're right to be concerned. Carlton and I talked about it this afternoon, and he worried that it was happening quickly, but that leaves less time for extensive research, even if Felan or any of the enforcers have sources here in San Antonio.

"So set something up and call me. Use another burner, not the one in your hand. Carlton and I will be on our way first thing in the morning.

"Okay, that's three minutes. End the call and take the battery out of your phone."

The conversation ended abruptly, without pleasantries, and Paula went to bed and tried, unsuccessfully, to sleep. One hundred fifty miles away, Reynaldo had the same problem, so he called Carlton with the news. Carlton had nearly been asleep, but the call put him in wide-awake mode, the first time he could recall being anxious about killing someone. Realizing the futility of lying in bed, he turned on the television and surfed old movies.

An hour later, he tried to sleep, still without success. Staring at the ceiling, he attributed it to the special nature of this upcoming job, the one he kept grilling himself about with details of every possibility he might encounter. However, he'd always been meticulous in his planning, so that wasn't keeping him awake. He knew only a single factor that made this one different from any other he'd done, except for his very first, years ago, when he'd killed a crooked insurance peddler who had scammed his mother with a worthless policy.

This time, just as that time decades ago, he was going to enjoy pulling the trigger.

CHAPTER 36

Paula arrived in the Zaragoza Grill a little after eight o'clock. Passing on the popular buffet, she chose instead to order something light from the menu. Almost an hour later, she was finishing the leisurely breakfast, and hadn't seen Millstone or Felan. Neither had she seen the other two men who had been with Felan the previous evening, when the trio had pulled up in the Beemer. Thinking they could be observing her, she knew she had to act naturally, not wait around, despite last night's vague allusion to witnessing each other's sobriety at breakfast.

She went back to her room to retrieve her book, planning to take advantage of the morning sun, which was only now making its appearance above the adobe walls and onto the main pool deck. On the way to the pool, she detoured through the vine-covered trellises forming a tunnel that passed near the small patio. From the corner of her eye, she spotted four men at one of the two tables and forced herself to look straight ahead, angling away from them and toward the tiled pathway to the pool. Her breathing quickened, along with her pulse. It was them, she knew it, sitting at the same table they'd used before. She almost wished they wouldn't see her, just let her pass by so she could read her book and—

"There's the lovely bird who's sober as an Old Bailey judge!"

Millstone's voice had lost its grating alcoholic slur, but the volume was still there. Without altering her pace, she looked around as though unsure of where the voice had come from, studiously avoiding the table and its occupants. Seeing no one, she continued walking, seemingly without another thought as to the source of the voice.

"Over here, luv! In the shade of the sweet-smelling vines, we are."

The voice was too loud to ignore, and she paused to turn her head in his direction. A look of mild surprise appeared on her face, but without anything that could be construed as a smile. Calling on every ounce of courage she had, she pivoted around and shaded her eyes against the pale sunlight filtering through the vine foliage. Playing it for all she could, she feigned non-recognition for almost five seconds, then allowed a tiny smirk to appear on her countenance before acknowledging his presence.

"Oh. Um…the British man with the drunken accent, right?" she intoned without a hint of interest. "Or is it the drunken man with the British accent?"

The catty remark would have been poorly received had the subject of the barb been less brazen than the oafish mercenary, and likely would have resulted in an embarrassed retreat or an angry retort. Instead, Millstone laughed heartily and slapped his hand on the table, rocking it enough to splash coffee from each of the four cups sitting on it. His three companions all scrambled clumsily to avoid being scalded and grabbed for napkins to absorb the mess.

Ignoring his ill-timed faux pas, Millstone stood and motioned for Paula to approach their table. "Come on over, luv, and witness Clive at his soberest moment."

Paula hesitated and took a look at her watch before giving an "oh, okay" shrug and heading toward the shade of the patio. As she drew near, the helpful one from last night, Jese, rose and pulled a chair from the adjacent table. He, along with Clive, remained standing while she sat, but the others barely acknowledged her arrival. The look on their faces indicated this interruption was not welcome.

"I can only stay a minute," she began.

"Nonsense, luv! A bit of brekkie will do you good."

"I've already eaten. And I have somewhere to be, very soon."

"And where might that be? How could you need to be elsewhere than with Clive and these fine lads, eh?"

She hoisted the carry-all bag she had substituted for a purse. "I'm going to do some shopping today, then relax while I finish my book. It's what I came here for."

"What about a bit of tea tonight?"

Paula looked at him, confused. "Tea? At night? I don't think so."

Millstone laughed. "Sorry, luv. I meant dinner. *Tea's* what it's called in the north country of Her Majesty's Kingdom, but it's just dinner in London. And here in Laredo, I suppose."

"No wonder a British accent sounds cool, because the words make no sense at all," she replied through gritted teeth, wishing she were anywhere but sitting here with four murderous men, making idle chit-chat and trying to set one of them up to be killed.

His offer of dinner was, on the surface, too good to be true. She had dreaded the prospect of enduring several meetings—*dates, for God's sake?*—with this slime ball, which would certainly entail fending off his meaty hands and listening to his loud, grating voice. Now it seemed all she had to do was demur a bit, put him off until she could contact Reynaldo and Carlton for further instructions. Meanwhile, she had to do something with the clod staring at her with bloodshot eyes from across the table—

"Ah, but they'll make sense when you let ol' Clive explain things to ya, luv," he promised lewdly. "So how about it? Din-din at eight?"

On impulse, she rose abruptly from the table. "I've got to go. And I've already made plans for tonight," she said sharply, turning to leave. Before she reached the edge of the patio, she turned back. "But I may change them."

Heading toward the pool, she again fought the impulse to break into a sprint. Behind her, she could hear the men already resuming their conversation, but speaking too quietly to be overheard and in tones that indicated a serious subject. It was as though the comical scene a few seconds ago had already been forgotten—or that the entire encounter at the table had been orchestrated. The thought increased her fear, but she forced herself to maintain her pace to the pool deck.

The short walk calmed her, and she arranged a deck chair so her back would be to the brightening sun. Pulling out her book, she sat down to read, but the print on the open pages didn't register. Instead, she started going over her options for getting Millstone in the right spot to be killed.

First, there was the matter of which side of the border would be best. It was a topic the trio had barely touched on in their planning, assuming the operation would evolve for a while and options would become clearer. She tried to recall what had been brought up in one of those earlier meetings, the things Carlton had brought up for consideration.

Both cities had good local police forces, which made quick response time a factor. Due to its proximity to the States, *Nuevo Laredo* had access to resources from its wealthier sister city, and cooperation between local law enforcement agencies was better than any other similar setup in the world, if frequent news articles were to be believed. In addition to the threat of apprehension at the scene, a big drawback to doing the job across the border was obvious: coming back through the heavily controlled international border crossing. Since the troubles began, tourist crossings were down to a trickle, and if a witness saw an Anglo at the scene, an all-out alert would be implemented instantly. Getting back across had to be quick, before that occurred, since the few Americans coming back would be screened vigorously. Reynaldo had waved aside the concern by reminding them of his ranch and his greater influence in that remote rural area. They could go there and venture back through another crossing days or weeks later, he'd said.

Second, Carlton had strongly suggested that the murder take place in a parking lot or garage. Whether arriving or leaving, it made no difference, but inside a restaurant sounded too much like some Mafia movie where the mobster pulls a piece in front of a crowd of diners and wait staff ("also known as witnesses") he'd reminded them. Neither Reynaldo nor Paula could disagree with his reasoning on that point.

Third, she had to inform them beforehand how many would be in the party. Would Millstone/Miller take along one or more of his thugs to dinner? If he were thinking along the lines of a first dinner turning romantic (*God forbid!*) probably not; however, the crafty soldier of fortune-turned-murderer might want to keep somebody around to guarantee his safety, if only because of his sketchy, three-timing reputation in the world of crime.

Paula took a deep breath and looked at her watch. Almost ten, and she had to call Reynaldo soon. If they left San Antonio this morning, they would be approaching Laredo very soon. She packed up her book and took the long way around to the West Wing.

"Hi. I just ran into the four of them, sitting at the same little patio as a few weeks ago and talking about something really serious. It seems like that's their regular little hangout.

"Oh, by the way, he's going by Clive Millstone, not Miller."

"Alright, it's good to know that. Hopefully, it means he's not doing some deal with the DEA right now, since Cletus Miller is what they know him by.

"And the other three guys are Hispanic, right?"

"Yes. Jese and two others. I got the impression those two don't speak English, and that slob didn't introduce them. They sat there and didn't say a word."

"Okay, where does it stand right now?"

"He asked me to go to dinner at eight tonight. I made excuses about tonight, but left it open as to what I might do later. I said I might change my plans."

"Have you scouted any restaurants that might work? On either side?"

"Last night I went across to Restaurante Tomatillos on Avenida Reforma. It's Italian, a nice, upscale place with parking in back and on one side. From my taxi, I didn't see any valet guys, so I think it's self-park."

"That sounds good. We'll go across and check it out, then text you with our take on it."

"Okay. Meanwhile, I'll try to avoid that disgusting creep and let him wonder about tonight."

"Do that. We'll be in touch."

Reynaldo turned to Carlton. "Did you hear all of that?"

"Yes. And it sounds good—almost too good. This thing is moving a lot faster than I thought it would, Reynaldo, and that still has me worried."

"I agree that it's happening pretty fast, but what can we do? Cancel because it looks too good?

"Following what we learned about his movements and meetings with those guys on this side, we laid out a basic plan of using Paula as bait to draw him in. It's taken four—no, *five*—trips, but *La Posada*'s not that big, so they ran into each other, just like we wanted, right?

"And we have no reason to think they could connect Paula to us, not without spending a lot more time checking her out." He looked over at Carlton to see how he reacted to the short—but accurate—description of what had taken place in a relatively short time period.

Carlton didn't respond for a minute. When he spoke, his tone was measured, almost doubtful. "So it would seem. It's just hard to imagine somebody as experienced as Millstone hanging out where he's just survived a huge shootout, murdered a man on a public street, and double-crossed several people. I'm just wondering what we might be missing."

"I'm with you on that. But remember, we agreed that he's got to be feeling confident, since everything you just mentioned has gone his way."

Carlton nodded in agreement. "That's true. I guess I'm just a lot more cautious than he is. I'd be ten thousand miles away from January's action."

"Which is why Clive Millstone won't celebrate as many birthdays as you," Reynaldo replied, grinning at his friend.

"Unless his birthday is today, he won't celebrate another one."

Reynaldo was relieved by the remark. He knew Carlton to be extremely cautious, even overly so, and his remark indicated he'd come to terms with the fast-evolving plot to rid the world of Clive Millstone. From his point of view, Reynaldo couldn't see how things could go any better, regardless of how long Paula stalked the target or how more time and planning would improve their chances of success.

Two hours later, they were finishing lunch at *Restaurante Tomatillos*. Neither was a big Italian food connoisseur, but the fare tasted good and the layout of the place lent itself to privacy. Although Carlton wanted the play to occur outside, the multi-level floors and individual booths created a sense of seclusion which would, hopefully, put Millstone at ease as the night played out. On the negative side, its seclusion put Paula in a lonely, vulnerable position while inside.

The pair walked outside and turned left toward the parking area, which extended along the side of the building and wrapped around to the back. Carlton didn't see any cameras on this side of the building. The only one they'd noticed was directly above the entrance and facing down, which would catch everyone coming in and going out, but wouldn't cover this lot. Climbing into Reynaldo's Lexus, they cruised around to the back portion and agreed it would be the perfect place for Paula to park her Mustang. Or, if conditions forced the issue, whatever Millstone drove. The best scenario, they agreed, would be for Paula to arrive separately, thus ensuring that Millstone walk her to *her* car, which Carlton would readily recognize without having to be there to spot Millstone's arrival or mode of transport.

Without hanging around longer than necessary, the pair left the restaurant and headed back across the river. During the drive, they discussed location aspects of the job, covering the what-ifs that are always present and contingency measures for every possible problem they could think of regarding the *Tomatillo*. By the time they reached their hotel on the interstate, both felt comfortable with the setup, but each wished privately that Paula were there to join in, to hear what they thought and give her take on it. She was, after all, the most important component in the plan to kill Clive Millstone. Reynaldo spent some time pecking out a detailed text for her to study, along with instructions for her to call him with a response—using another new phone, of course.

Paula left the parking garage just after noon and drove to a small seafood place on the east side, in hopes that leaving the hotel would clear her mind, while avoiding a premature meeting with Millstone. After eating, she remained seated and read the text from Reynaldo, then jotted down responses and questions in order to speed up the phone call she would make from her car. Perusing the text, it seemed the *Tomatillo* had struck Carlton as a good place to do the job, but when she'd finished reading, she wondered about coming up with an alternative due to Reynaldo's—or was it Carlton's?—inquiry about the speed with which the plan was coming together.

Thinking back on the ransom exchange for her daughter, she remembered Tino telling her that Carlton had chosen several places before narrowing it to two, then down to the final one after researching all of them over a few days. At one point, Tino had let it slip that he had even called on the female DEA agent for advice, the one who had ended up in the garage shootout with Brujido Ramos.

In almost three years of observing Carlton Westerfield, Paula had learned that careful planning and lots of options were his best operational assets, and it made her wonder if he and Reynaldo were in full agreement with her single suggestion—or were they crediting her with a better eye for a location than she deserved? And should she be watching for any sign that Millstone's cohorts were on to something hinky about an attractive woman spending even a minute talking to the likes of the loutish mercenary? Especially Jese, who seemed to be miles ahead of the others in manners and sophistication—could he see through the insincerity of her subtle flirting, thin as it was?

The questions bothered her and raised doubts about her ability to carry out the plan. She took several deep breaths and reminded herself of the reason for the extreme measures the three of them were taking and the reward which lay at the conclusion. To that end, she began thinking about how to approach Millstone and accept his invitation, plus a backup idea for the rest of the operation, much as Reynaldo and Carlton had done after examining the restaurant. The mental process calmed her down, and she went to her car to make the call.

Using her notes, the trio managed to iron out the details of matters that had arisen in a few minutes, and Paula was informing the others of her planned approach to make the engagement happen. They agreed to a fall-back communication if something went wrong and the job needed to be delayed or cancelled. No one mentioned the speed and ease with which the plan had coalesced, and within a half hour she was back in her room making preparations for a dinner engagement she hadn't yet agreed to.

CHAPTER 37

Paula went back to the Posada and retrieved her book, then settled into a chair at the main pool deck. It was after 2:00 p.m., and she had no idea if Millstone was still around, or if her vague suggestion about changing her mind would entice him to find her. If not, she would contact Reynaldo and convey the cancellation for tonight and try something different the next time she ran into the target. For the moment, though, it was early, and she felt the hint she'd dangled before him was enough to keep him interested.

As she began reading, she found herself enjoying the story's opening, replacing the irritation and doubt she'd experienced earlier. By the end of the first chapter, the pleasant read was making her feel better about the entire day. She took it as a good sign, one that raised her confidence in the evening's outcome. Three chapters later, she was hooked on the tale, but felt herself getting sleepy. After having to read the same page twice, she gave up and leaned back to catch a few winks in the warming spring afternoon. After last night's fitful slumber, this was heaven...just a few minutes, and...

"Well, as I live and breathe, there she is!"

Millstone's voice shook her from what had turned into a real nap. She opened her eyes slowly to see his face peering down at her from scant feet away. Beside her chair, the book lay open on the tile, its pages fluttering in the breeze. Knowing she needed to be on full alert at this opportunity, she nevertheless stretched languidly and reached down for her book with only a glance in his direction. She hoped the discomfort she felt didn't show on her face or in her actions. Playing her lack of interest card to the fullest, she waited for him to speak again. It didn't take long.

"Tell me you changed your mind, then, about dinner tonight, luv. Surely you can't read and shop without fuel for the fire, can ya?"

"Don't plan to. I'm going to *Restaurante Tomatillo* tonight."

Millstone made a face. "*Italian?* Be a good sport, luv, and let Clive take you somewhere with better nosh—"

"Might be hard to find fish 'n chips in *Nuevo Laredo*. Besides, I like Italian food."

He emitted loud sigh, more like a groan. "Well, more's the pity, I guess. But would ya like some company with your bloody wop din-din?"

She gazed at him appraisingly, hoping she wasn't overdoing it—and that she would never, *ever* have to do this again. "I wouldn't mind a companion—one that can mind his manners, that is."

"Splendid! And you've got my scout's honor on the manners. You'll ride with me, then? A tad before eight, say?"

Paula shook her head. "No, I'll take my car."

He looked hopeful. "Then you'll give me a lift?"

"No, I like to go everywhere by myself. That way, if I see a better prospect, I won't have to stop and let you out."

That got a belly laugh, which put Paula's lunch in danger of exiting her own belly. "Lovely! I'll be there with bells on, luv."

"Fine, but make sure you're sober. If I wanted to listen to a drunk Englishman, I'd pick a good BBC re-run filmed in a bar—make that a *tavern*."

"Now, Clive's not a tosser, luv, and he won't be bladdered tonight, Queen's honor on that one."

Sensing the end of the uncomfortable face-to-face, she allowed a smile to make its way to her face. "Fine. Until eight, then."

Without another word, she flipped through the book to find her place and started reading, wishing her heart would quit hammering in her chest so the words weren't so blurred. Apparently, Millstone had the good sense to leave on a winning hand, as evidenced by his immediate exit, whistling as he walked toward the door that led to the registration desk. Sitting in the deck chair, Paula took deep breaths and felt her pulse returning to normal, but she couldn't expel the revulsion she felt. And worse, she'd just made an appointment to sit across a cozy table from the slob, which was still hours away. The only bright spot was knowing how the evening would end.

CHAPTER 38

After hearing from Paula, Reynaldo and Carlton waited a couple of hours before crossing over and driving to the outskirts of *Nuevo Laredo* via the Old *Monterrey* Highway. It took two phone calls, but they located one half of Reynaldo's contacts, a couple, and went to pick up a weapon. Carlton wasn't enthused by the method, but the middle-aged pair seemed level-headed; there were no questions about the quiet gringo, no comments regarding the past few weeks of trailing Millstone, and no questions regarding the gun's use. Less curiosity showed good tradecraft in itself, because the less they knew, the less they would be able to convey to another party, no matter the circumstances. Besides, being Mexican citizens and suppliers of a deadly weapon in Mexico, they were at greater risk than Carlton, especially if the gun could be traced back to them.

Back in the car, Carlton donned gloves and checked out the piece. As he had requested, it was another Colt .45 auto pistol, almost identical to the one he'd lost to Millstone, who had then used it to kill Tino. He racked the slide a few times, ejecting all the rounds before releasing the magazine and disassembling it to check its spring and ramp. He wiped each bullet carefully and reloaded the magazine, then checked the bore and trigger action before slapping it home in the grip.

Reynaldo probed some, asking about the similarity to the murder weapon, but Carlton denied that being the reason for his request. "Nope. Same reason I asked y'all to get me one before we got to *Nuevo Bayito*. It's just a fine weapon, with good balance, reliability, and stopping power. An automatic spits brass everywhere, but it doesn't matter this time. If forensics matches it to another job, I know it wasn't Carlton who did it, and this piece goes away minutes after I'm done with it.

"And wherever they're finding these things over here, there must be a good supply. Maybe the Mexican Army bought a bunch from the U. S. military when they went to the nine millimeter Beretta."

"Long as it does the job," Reynaldo commented, his sparseness of words revealing a bit of nervousness.

"Oh, it will do just fine.

"And if tonight doesn't play out, it would be nice to get it back to your contacts for safekeeping, until we can get re-scheduled."

"Shouldn't be a problem. I've paid them for it, and if I don't ever show up again, they're three grand better off, plus they have the gun back."

Done with the weapon examination, Carlton looked over at his companion. "But I'm going to do all I can to finish tonight; there's not going to be a rain check for Millstone. Paula sounded like she's got that creep right where we want him, so he'll walk her to the car. Depending on how she plays him in the parking lot, when she's in and shuts her door is when he'll lean down to close the deal."

"Lights out for the asshole Brit gun runner." Reynaldo's voice was quiet, but grim.

"Yep. I only wish he could see it coming and know what it's for."

"But you don't operate that way."

"No, that's for the movies. Long, dramatic speeches, threats regarding what's about to happen—good for suspense, bad if something goes wrong while the shooter is pontificating about righteousness and justice served."

Reynaldo nodded, He'd had the discussion with Carlton earlier, tip-toeing around the subject of what to expect, and Carlton had simply said, "I walk up and kill him. Just like every job I've ever done."

His tone of voice left no room for further discussion, and Reynaldo dropped it.

Paula checked her watch for the fourth time in ten minutes. It was just past seven, twilight at this time of year at twenty-seven point five degrees north of the equator. She avoided the elevator and headed down the inside stairs for the parking garage where she'd self-parked earlier in the day, taking care to hide the Mustang as best she could. No sense in running into Millstone or his buddies and having another awkward conversation. All she wanted was to get to dinner, ply the creep with a smile or two and let him follow her to her car like a lost puppy. Again, she took deep breaths and worked hard to control her nervousness, reminding herself that Carlton Westerfield—her *former* lover—was enormously skilled at his craft and was being paid a lot of money by her *current* lover to do this job. All she had to do was give Millstone a tiny hint that he might join the que to make the evening successful. The catty thought made her smile, the only time she had felt so inclined in the past twenty-four hours.

A half hour later, she was stuck in traffic on *Avenida Reforma*, but even at the slow crawl, she pulled into the *Tomatillo* main parking lot well before her eight o'clock reservation and pressed "send" on the text message she had prepared. She pulled around the building to the rear parking lot and looked for a spot that fit Carlton's descriptive request: away from the building itself, close to a dumpster or a wall if possible, and be able to pull away without first backing up. Obviously, it would be ideal to back into a spot against the privacy wall, which ran the length of restaurant and the secondary lot. At first pass, nothing seemed exactly right, so she turned around and idled back toward the primary lot. Seeing a car's backup lights on, she braked and was rewarded by seeing the car leaving a space adjacent to the dumpster. She pulled forward and backed into the spot, leaving adequate room behind her car for Carlton to wait unseen. From that point on, Carlton had assured her, she needed only to suffer through a meal with Millstone and make sure he remained sufficiently interested to walk her to the car.

"There you are!" Clive was bellowing from the bar as she walked in. She flashed a smile as he approached, but turned quickly to follow a hostess to her table, leaving Millstone to follow in her wake. Once seated, she reminded herself to act civil enough to make it through the meal without giving the target any reason to be upset, or worse, suspicious that the evening's activities were a trap. She decided the best tack might be to express an interest in his meetings with Felan and the other two men, since their presence at *La Posada* was the only common ground they shared.

"What are your friends doing tonight?" she asked casually. "Did they need a break from all those negotiations you've been going through?"

"Ay, likely so. I drive a hard bargain, if I may say so myself, so they may be licking their wounds, trying to forget what the day's cost them."

"So, are you an investor or something?"

"A *something*, luv. Let's leave it at that for Clive's back story, eh?

"But you—now, what's a lovely creature like yourself doing so far away from San Antonio?"

Paula froze at the mention of her home town. All the information she'd given at reception was tied to the non-existent address in Houston, and they'd never spoken of where she was from. She sensed a test, but played it for a mistake on his part. "Wrong city. I live in Houston."

Millstone raised his eyebrows in surprise. "Could'a sworn you hailed from the Alamo place. Now why did I get that impression?"

"I have no idea. But I know I'm ready to order." She looked around for their waiter, but none was in sight.

His next remark pointed out her error, made in the tension of the moment. "Why luv, we've not even ordered a drink, now have we? A bloody waiter will be 'round shortly, I'm certain of it."

Paula smiled, putting some effort into it. "Of course. Well, you go ahead, but I'm having wine with my meal, so I'm not drinking anything else tonight. That's my rule when I eat Italian."

The explanation seemed to satisfy him, and he flagged down a passing waiter. Three quick drinks later, the Brit was, as he put it, "getting into his cups a bit" and Paula gently reminded him of their earlier agreement about sobriety. In reply, Millstone downed the last of his double Crown Royal and smacked his glass down on the table with more force than intended, drawing a look from another table. Luckily, they had ordered their meal, so Paula gritted her teeth and told herself the evening was progressing toward its conclusion—if too slowly.

When the food arrived, Millstone dug in with what might be described politely as gusto, while reality would label his table manners as abysmally inadequate. Paula picked at her own plate, nervousness threatening to render her stomach unable to do its job. She sipped her wine, tentatively at first, then decided to let the magical grape help her make it through the ordeal. By the end of her second glass, the night was looking marginally better, good enough to let her finish most of her shrimp and pasta dish. Meanwhile, Clive had long finished shoveling down some veal Milanese dish swimming in a red sauce and was starting on another mixed drink.

Having drunk beer with his meal, Clive was getting well-oiled before he'd finished the fourth whiskey, and the alcohol loosened his tongue regarding what had seemed a mysterious secret earlier. "I *am* sort of an investor, ya know. I invest in all sorts of things, things you wouldn't believe."

The phrasing left Paula no choice but to ask. "Like what?"

"Oh, mostly I invest time in people. I do that by training them to use weapons, all kinds of weapons."

Fully informed on the mercenary's background, Paula knew she had to play this innocently, lest he be laying a trap to uncover her knowledge. "So you're in the military? What, the British Army?"

"No, hardly that lot of losers," he laughed harshly. "I work free-lance. In fact, I've just completed a little training course down here for some other free-lancers and a big government agency."

Paula didn't like where the conversation was going, nor did she like the change in his tone. The overblown British act was more subdued now, his voice lower, quieter, and menacing. Clearly, the tipsy, going-on-drunk was an act, she was certain of it. He was glaring at her now, and Paula felt the accusation coming before he said it.

"You know exactly what I do for a bloody living, luv, now don't ya?"

"I'm afraid you've lost me, Clive. I have no idea what you're talking about." The words sounded right, like the perfectly innocent response to the sudden change in the man's demeanor. She briefly considered that the change was due to the man's intolerance for alcohol. Maybe he was one of those functioning drunks who became surly after a few drinks. But she could tell she was on thin ice here, and decided to call it a night and hope the timing worked out. If Carlton were already in place the plan would work, even if Millstone was, as he appeared, suspicious and angry.

"I think I've had enough company for one night, Clive. And you seem to have lost your cute British accent. So if you'd just walk me to my car, I'll be leaving."

Millstone grinned wickedly. "Without paying the bloody tab, then?"

Paula realized she'd made another mistake. Posing as an independent woman, accustomed to providing for herself, she shouldn't have forgotten the check. She decided to play it out, even if it threw the plan out of time. She reached into her purse and extracted two fifty-dollar bills. "Here, this will cover mine, and you don't need to walk me to the car." She laid the bills down and rose from her seat.

The ruse seemed to work, sort of. He looked from the money to her face and smiled, if without mirth. When he spoke, his tone was measured. "Now luv, don't get your undies all bunched up. Clive's just a tad bladdered here, so let me pay the bloody tab and walk you to your car."

The tone of voice was less menacing, and Paula again wondered if alcohol was the culprit, or if he had a serious mental disorder that caused the mercurial changes—or perhaps some combination of triggers that produced lethal results, such as the wrong word at the wrong time. From Reynaldo's description of Tino's murder, that seemed likely. The story had seemed horrific enough when Reynaldo was telling her, his emotions barely in check. But now, two feet from the dangerous man, an experienced killer who was obviously unstable, she was more frightened than she'd ever been in her life. She swallowed hard and forced her breathing to remain slow and to stand, calmly looking at him, though she wanted to turn and run until her lungs gave out.

She made a decision to play it out as boldly as she could. "My *undies* are just fine, thank you." She delivered the quasi-suggestive line with a hint of a smile.

Millstone smiled back and rose, pulling his wallet and extracting a hundred-dollar bill. He laid it on the table and motioned toward the way they had entered. "That should cover whatever these bloody beaners charge for wop food here, plus a tip for less than stellar service."

Paula walked ahead, feeling him behind her; without having to face him, she calmed down and concentrated on what she could say or do to keep the play going for a few more minutes, when it would all be over. The front door was opened by the hostess, who smiled and wished them a good evening and speedy return to *Restaurante Tomatillo*.

Not in this lifetime, I hope, she thought, her heart rate ramping up as they stepped into the parking lot. Turning the corner to get to the back lot, she felt Millstone slackening his pace, so she risked a slight turn of her head to see what was happening. It wasn't good. He was motioning with his right hand to someone as yet unseen, but had to be in one of the parked cars. Then he stepped forward quickly and reached for her purse. Feeling her last card being taken, Paula lurched back, but the big man was too fast. He snatched the strap so hard she was pulled off balance and had to reach out to keep from falling. Her hand fell against his arm, and she jerked it back as though burned.

"Let's just take a looky-see in the handbag, luv. Don't want any surprises there, do we?" He quickly rifled through the bag and came out with the small revolver she had placed inside after solidifying the evening's plan with Carlton and Reynaldo. "Well, expecting trouble were we, luv? Surely not from ol' Clive, was it? Now let's just move on quietly to your little car, luv, and see what else you might have tucked away before we take a little ride in it."

A movement behind him caused Paula to look over his shoulder, into the glare of light from the side of the building. Three men, just silhouettes in her view, were approaching. As they neared, she saw it was Jese Felan and the other two. They fanned out to form a semi-circle before her, and she immediately shifted from fear to outright panic. Her only hope was to get to her car, now less than fifty feet away, and hope Carlton was in place. Even then, everything would depend on his skill against four men.

Oddly, her thoughts went to the last time he had faced such odds, months before at the car wash kidnapping exchange. They had survived then, leaving four dead hoodlums lying on the concrete. But Carlton had pointed out their weakness, inexperience, and bravado as having been the deciding factor in that confrontation. The four men before her now were surely armed, a lot more experienced and, most importantly, alert to the possibility of danger.

She turned and headed for the Mustang, aware that the walk might be the last she'd ever take.

CHAPTER 39

Reynaldo slowed to a stop and let Carlton out for what might be a long wait. While the Lexus cruised around and searched for a nearby parking spot, Carlton looked around for anyone who might be guarding the lot against car break-ins. Several cars down, two couples were walking to their car, and he played his credibility card. Pulling the key fob from his pocket, he pressed and held the trunk release button. The Mustang's trunk lock thunked loudly, and he silently thanked Reynaldo for remembering to bring Paula's spare key with him.

It was one of many details the trio had discussed in past weeks, a tiny part that might never have come into play. But tonight, in the upscale restaurant lot, it gave undeniable credibility to the man who was walking over to the Mustang convertible. To any observer, he had every right to open the trunk and stand behind it. He spent a few minutes looking around the area surreptitiously...before closing it and squatting to the pavement unseen, with the Colt auto pistol within easy reach of his gloved hands.

Only twenty minutes elapsed before his knee was complaining, so he turned around and sat on the pavement. Several customers, all in groups, had come and gone during the vigil behind the car. To his right, the big green trash receptacle negated any problem from that side, but he had to squirm around between the smelly garbage container and the left wheel of the car when the right-side adjacent car's owner and three companions came out to leave. As soon as they pulled away, another waiting car moved into its place. Carlton waited until the occupants emerged, talking loudly, and headed into the restaurant for a night of pleasant dining before he scooted back into position behind the Mustang. They would likely be well over an hour, maybe two, so he could relax a bit and wait for Paula and Millstone to approach. By the half hour mark, his butt was numb and he idly wondered if he was simply too old to do any kind of work at this stage of life, regardless of the pay.

As the wait approached an hour, he changed positions, stretching and extending his legs and twisting his torso, moving every muscle in his body to keep circulation and flexibility at peak levels. After five minutes of the excruciating maneuvers, he paused to listen. Hearing nothing at first, he resumed the exercise, but stopped when he heard the unmistakable sound of approaching footsteps. Unfortunately, there were too many to signal the approach of Paula and Millstone, and it was too early for them anyway. This sounded like a larger group, mostly men by the stride, coming directly toward the Mustang at a fair clip.

Risking a look, he lay down and peered around the driver's side of the car, staying beneath the level of the rear bumper. What he saw made him flinch, the involuntary shiver of fear starting in his stomach and rising through his entire body. He could see the outline of Paula's body walking toward him and Millstone's bulky form beside and slightly behind her. That would have appeared to be normal for a gentleman escorting his date to her car. But the other three men fanned out behind the couple weren't supposed to be there. He couldn't imagine a more unwelcome sight.

As the five people drew nearer, Carlton saw the trailing men looked to be among the enforcers who had grabbed him and Reynaldo at the scene of Tino's murder, then herded them into vehicles and forced them to the warehouse. The lucky escape from that situation wasn't going to repeat itself this time; from their stances, these men looked wary and alert. Obviously, Paula had been made, her identity uncovered, and the plan compromised beyond repair. He withdrew from his vantage point and squatted uncomfortably behind the car while straining to hear the conversation heating up ten feet away. The pain in his knee prompted the ridiculous thought that he should have brought a stool.

"It cost a damn king's ransom, that's for sure, but I managed to find out about you, luv," Millstone was saying, his loud voice again laced with a clipped British accent.

"You wasted your money, then. If you were so curious, you could have just asked me," Paula answered curtly. "Not that my background should be any of your business," she added.

"My business is staying informed, luv. And I gathered from my learned sources that you're lovely self is indeed connected to one Reynaldo Gomez, a bloke who's not on my list of favorite mates at the moment. In fact, when I get him drawn down here to fetch you, I'll kill the bastard, just like I killed his partner! Just so I won't have to worry about him in the future," he added sarcastically.

Paula had been thinking desperately while he ranted and played the only card, feeble as it was, she could come up with. "He's not on my boyfriend's favorites list either, and it's *him* you need to worry about. He's a lot more dangerous than Reynaldo, especially if your snooping around lets him find out about my private Houston address."

The revelation set Millstone back, even if slightly. A brief look of confusion crossed his face, evident even in the bad light. "Ah, and who might that lucky lad be, luv? A Houston oil man with tons of money and bodyguards to track down your lovers? Think that makes him dangerous to me and my lads here, do ya?"

From the rapid-fire questions, it seemed Millstone was revealing that his source hadn't been as knowledgeable as he'd bragged. She forged ahead, knowing that prolonging the parking lot verbal standoff was the only thing separating her from being abducted and rendered helpless—or worse. "No. He's just a guy, a *Yank*, you'd say. I think you called him the 'hot shit Yank shooter,' or something like that. Your stupid British slang vocabulary makes it hard to recall the exact term."

As soon as the last words left her mouth, she wished she had left them out of her reply. Reynaldo had told her of Tino's last words, a similar smart-mouth comment that had gotten him killed. This might not have been the best time to test Millstone's trigger for violence, she thought vaguely. However, seeing the change before her, she thought she might be onto something useful. The mercenary's head twitched— only slightly, but a definite tell that the identity of her "boyfriend" had shaken, or at least surprised him.

Behind the Mustang, Carlton heard the exchange clearly. He marveled at Paula's ability to think on her feet, to say something, *anything*, that might rattle her oppressor enough to tilt the advantage. And with her accurate recounting of Millstone's label for Carlton Westerfield, he knew she'd played her final card. Whatever slight advantage it produced, now was the time to take it. No one was coming or going from the parking lot at the moment. The wariness of Jese Felan and his cohorts would be waning somewhat, a natural occurence given the passage of several minutes of listening to back-and-forth banter between the pair, most of it not well understood by the other two and perhaps not even by Jese.

He took a deep breath and stood while bringing the Colt's front sight to the left-hand silhouette and squeezing the trigger, then swinging it smoothly from left to right in the same motion, the targets barely more than a Mustang's length away. By the time he had become fully upright, the pistol had spoken twice, and Jese Felan's two guys were slammed back before reaching for their weapons. The third shot came simultaneously, but not from Carlton's weapon. Not being as accurately fired, the smaller bullet fired by Reynaldo caught the lead enforcer of the *Nuevo Bayito* warehouse in the ribcage, spinning him around and into Millstone's back.

The big man reacted well, regaining his balance quickly and thrusting his right arm out to grab Paula's wrist, then jerking her toward him. He pulled her to his front side and backed into the Mustang's front fender, using her as a shield against what he had instantly determined was a two-pronged attack, one assailant in front, the other at a ninety-degree angle to his right. As he squeezed Paula against him, he could feel her gasp for breath, so he loosened his grip enough to prevent her passing out. A limp body in front of him was a lesser shield than one that could stand upright.

With his left forearm pinned securely against her neck, he kept the revolver low by his side to prevent its being a target for either of the two guns he now faced. Only three or four seconds passed before he made his only possible move. He raised the gun to Paula's head, placing it behind her right ear where it would be plainly seen by the gunmen threatening him from two positions. Behind him, he could hear the labored, gurgling breathing of Jese Felan. From the sound of it, he wasn't going to be any help. In fact, he wasn't long for the game.

Millstone had to force the issue, and quickly, before the parking lot turned into a circus. Already, five or six people had emerged from the restaurant and were peering into the lot, trying to see what had happened without getting too close. In *Nuevo Laredo*, as in all major cities in Mexico, gunfire was not uncommon, and interfering with it might prove fatal. The gawkers were probably only concerned that their cars would have bullet holes revealed by the morning light. However, restaurant personnel would soon call the police and, notwithstanding stories of ignored call-outs, there was no point in taking the chance.

"Don't do the foolish thing, Yank! As you can see, I've got your lovely in a good position to get shot by someone, and whether it's me or one of you makes no difference to me! So toss the guns, there's good lads, and I'll be on my way. All of us need to be moving along, I'm sure you'll agree, so get to it."

Reynaldo chose the moment to approach from Millstone's right, his pistol held in front as he walked slowly but steadily toward the Mustang. "Let her go, Millstone. This will get you killed, I promise you."

The hollow threat did nothing, as Carlton had figured. Millstone's sneer was plain to see, even in the bad light. "Your lot isn't going to kill me, Reynaldo, not a chance of it! So toss the little barker over here at my feet and tell your Yank friend to do the same before his lovely bird catches a round in her pretty head."

Carlton hated to enter the conversation, but there was no other choice. Against every instinct, every bit of common sense and past experience, he spoke. "You're right Millstone, I'm not going to kill you." He paused to let him wonder what the caveat was, feeling like a bad actor in a worse film.

Surprised at hearing Carlton speak, the mercenary turned his attention away from Reynaldo. Paula, unable to do otherwise, twisted with him as he squinted in Carlton's direction. Her lower body shifted slightly, leaving Carlton all the room he needed—he hoped. Dropping the Colt's muzzle a few degrees, he squeezed off a round, which caught Clive Millstone squarely in his exposed right kneecap.

The big man's scream was blood-curdling, something non-human, as though it had come from a machine designed to infuse horror into anyone within hearing distance. His right arm flew out, slinging the revolver halfway to the building where it clattered on the pavement without discharging, indicating the mercenary had wisely held it to Paula's head in uncocked position to prevent his hostage from losing her value by mishap. Feeling Millstone's arm loosened at her throat, she slid from his midsection and sprinted away while he shrieked and leaned heavily to his right, quickly exceeding the tipping point and falling over. Before he hit the ground, Carlton altered the muzzle slightly and placed a round in his other knee. In his turned posture, the bullet entered the side of the joint, obliterating the entire hinge mechanism and exploding the patella. The ensuing scream was other-worldly, but it lasted only a few seconds before Clive Millstone, aka Cletus Miller, went into shock and lost consciousness, tumbling clumsily onto the body of the late Jese Felan.

With no time left to stick around, Carlton reached for Paula's wrist and tugged her in Reynaldo's direction, trying to avoid stepping in the spreading puddle of blood in front of her car. Not seeing the Lexus immediately he nearly panicked, but a revved-up engine and glaring headlights coming straight at them told him that Reynaldo had been thinking ahead of the action curve, quickly ruling out the possibility of Paula leaving in her car. They were all leaving the scene with Reynaldo, and the Mustang would be handled later.

Carlton grabbed the door handle before the Lexus screeched to a stop and jerked it open. Paula didn't waste any time, either. She bailed into the passenger seat and slammed the door while Carlton got in the back. From the final shot into Millstone's remaining knee, only nine seconds had elapsed when the Lexus shot out into *Avenida Reforma* and headed south, away from the border crossing point. Less than a block from the restaurant, Reynaldo slowed down and blended in with the nighttime traffic, just another car on the heavily traveled thoroughfare.

"Good thinking, Reynaldo!" Carlton said excitedly, uncharacteristically clapping his driving friend's shoulder. "I was hoping you'd see Paula's car was blocked in, and we didn't have time to drag bodies around."

Reynaldo was still breathing rapidly, his eyes shifting back and forth between mirrors and the street ahead. "It seemed better to leave it parked there, instead of running over the guy's legs. That's always a sign of someone leaving in too big a hurry to be innocent."

The nonsensical remark, combined with an extreme adrenaline overload and disbelief at still being alive, caused a round of nervous laughter from all of them. For Paula, the mixed emotion was too much, and her laugh was interrupted by a choking sob. Carlton reached over the seat to touch her shoulder. "You okay?"

"Yes! Yes, I'm just—I don't know, overwhelmed. I thought I was dead, I thought we all might be.

"I had no idea he had gotten those guys to the restaurant ahead of time. Oh my God, when I saw them…" her voice trailed off as the tears of fright came in a flood.

To her left, Reynaldo, still visibly shaken, reached for her hand. "You did a great job, Paula. I don't know how you kept your cool, but you did it. Your quick thinking did it."

"It was a remarkable performance on your part," Carlton agreed. "I couldn't believe you kept coming up with things to say to keep him talking. That gave us the edge, the only chance we had at getting out of that alive."

Having received praise from both men, Paula turned in her seat to address them. "I'm glad I was able to do it. Scared as I was, I don't know how I kept thinking of things to say."

"I do," Carlton answered. "It's genetic, Paula. It's exactly what Tino would have done. He'd be proud of you."

The declaration was accurate and timely. For the next few minutes, unlike the previous hour or so, silence reigned and no one said anything.

By the time they neared the edge of the city, the weapons had been tossed into a sewage reservoir, along with rubber gloves. Turning onto the narrow street where Reynaldo's contacts lived, he laid out a plan to recover Paula's car, the weak link in their quick departure. "Carlos and Betina can go for your car and bring it back here. He's got a shop out back, so he can just store it there as long as it takes. After a while, if he asks around, and it's still too hot, he can just chop it and sell it."

"I hate to lose my Mustang. I really like that car."

Reynaldo smiled at her. "I'll see to it that you get a satisfactory replacement. But it needs to be moved tonight, in case the police decide to run all the license plates."

After a brief visit with the Mendez couple, Reynaldo drove them away from the city, going west toward his ranch, over two hundred miles away.

Less than an hour into the trip, they reached *Santa Monica*, very dark at this time of night. As they drove slowly through the village, past *el centro* and the church, *Nuestra Madre de Merced*, Reynaldo began relating the sad story of the town's bold young men to Paula—their desire to hold good jobs and raise their families, while being able to hold their heads high. He told of his and Tino's plan to help them escape the cruel treatment of the *Golfo* enforcers, Jese Felan among them, while securing a better position for himself in the cartel's business structure. He talked quietly and included every aspect of a dire situation that had presented itself as an attractive opportunity to him and Tino. Although Paula had known the basics, she was hearing the details for the first time, and Reynaldo's quiet monologue seemed therapeutic to both of them, judging by the absence of the night's earlier tension.

The town receded behind them, and Reynaldo fell silent for a few miles before he continued with the story, a recap as it turned out. "It seemed a workable plan, a good one. Tino and I thought we could do something for the people of this little wide spot in the road, the place we came from. It seemed like a way to repay the town for our success, give something back and gain something while doing it.

"Now I can see that was stupid to think I could use them to take on the *Golfo* cartel, especially after learning it might be a trap. And worse, it was pure *idiocy* from the beginning to think I could lead them to something better. I only succeeded in leading them to their graves."

In the seat behind him, Carlton listened without comment. He knew the entire story all too well, every bloody minute of it. He had re-played it many times in past weeks: the bold, idealistic enterprise, the irony of being warned of its folly, but ignoring it, the brutal truth of the deception, and its final cost in human suffering. Hearing Reynaldo tell Paula the bare, unvarnished truth, Carlton found himself admiring his friend's ability to admit his mistakes. He only regretted that he had been unable to prevent them.

CHAPTER 40

"Agent Colson, please come in here!" Special Agent in Charge Stan Ikos called out without bothering to use the intercom.

Less than ten seconds later, Heather Colson stuck her head in the door. "You bellowed?"

Frowning at her impertinence, he motioned her in. "And shut the door, please, then sit down and take a look at this." He handed her an envelope with a neat, hand-written address that began "ATTN: STAN IKOS, SAIC," followed by the mailing address for the San Antonio DEA office below it, though not in all caps. The envelope, lacking a return address, had been slit open and was now empty of whatever it had held.

Heather took a quick look, then looked inquiringly at her boss. "So what was in it?"

"First, is that Westerfield's writing?"

She looked again, trying to think of a clever way to answer without endangering her job. Nothing came to mind. "I don't know. I'm not familiar with his handwriting. Or his printing skills."

"You going to tell me what he sent you? If it really is from Westerfield, that is?"

Ikos reached to the side of his cluttered desk and picked up a folded newspaper story which looked to comprise a couple of partial pages, stapled together. The bright colors foretold of a dramatic scene, even without looking at the headlines or the story, which was in Spanish, in large print. "You tell me if this sounds like your boy."

She reached for the paper and turned it to see the main photograph below huge, bold headlines which read "*TRES HOMBRES ASESINADOS!*" The photograph showed three bodies, Hispanic men by their appearance,

341

lying haphazardly in what appeared to be a parking lot. Blood had spread from each of the bodies across the pavement in rivulets which had coalesced into one giant puddle, apparently due to the slope and drainage characteristics of the lot.

She turned to the second page where a smaller photo depicted a big man, an Anglo, being loaded onto a stretcher. Like the first page, blood was abundant on the pavement and the stretcher; additionally, unexplained by the photo, both lower legs of the victim were drenched in blood. Never having become accustomed to Mexican newspapers' use of gore in their photo opportunities, she frowned and handed the paper back across the desk.

Ikos didn't reach for it. "Look closely at the guy on the stretcher. Then look at the bottom of the page."

She reluctantly withdrew the proffered paper and followed her boss' terse instructions. Her eyes widened as she realized the man on the stretcher looked a lot like a file photo she had seen during several meetings regarding the recent joint operation with Mexico's drug interdiction force, the PFM. His name was Cletus Miller, but he had operated on a contract basis for the DEA under the name of Clive Millstone. Dreading what she was about to see, she looked at the bottom of the page where the same neat printing job had been affixed, delivering a cold message:

LOOKS LIKE YOUR BOY MILLER DIDN'T
DODGE VERY WELL THIS TIME—WONDER
HOW CHARMED HIS LIFE WILL BE NOW.

With a rush of recall that she hoped wasn't evident on her face, she went over her words to Carlton the day she'd driven him back to San Antonio and filled in the gaps of his knowledge about the joint operation. Trying to dissuade Carlton from doing anything (else) foolish, she had said something flippant like *"Miller's dodged some bullets before. He seems to lead a charmed life."* She had first heard the words from the man seated across the desk from her, during one of many meetings about the operation. Now, she could only hope he didn't remember saying them or the exact circumstances surrounding their utterance—like the names of everyone who had been in attendance.

Forcing herself to remain focused, she looked up and met the AIC's stare with a level gaze of her own. It was plain to see he was waiting for her take on the printed message, so she looked down at the message again, then back to the man on the stretcher, feigning interest in the mystery. "I don't know, but the last time I talked to Carlton Westerfield, he was sick of the drug business and sick of being my CI. So I don't think he would have anything to do with this."

Ikos sighed and reached for the newspaper clippings. "Westerfield's a real smartass, so I can see him sending such a message. But how would he happen to see this in a Mexican newspaper?

"Anyway, I talked it over with our go-to guy down there at the *Nuevo Laredo* P.D. He got to the scene before they tagged and bagged them and helped their CSI crew document victims' positions and entry wounds. All except one was made by a large-caliber, probably a forty-four Magnum or a forty-five. One vic caught a smaller round, maybe a thirty-eight, from the side and was still breathing when they arrived, but died before the ambulance got there.

"After drawing the scene layout, they put the main shooters twelve to eighteen feet away, near a trash bin, and the thirty-eight guy off to the side. He said the hit had to be made by a two, maybe three professionals, not one old geezer."

Agent Colson kept her expression neutral, her response professional and monotone. "I'd have to agree with that assessment, Boss. What about the guy on the stretcher? What's his name, Miller?"

"Yeah, Cletus Miller. He lost a lot of blood and hasn't regained consciousness. They think he's circling the drain, but if he survives, it'll be a long time before he's able to talk, if ever. And he'll never walk again."

EPILOGUE

Reynaldo leaned forward in the beach chair and watched Paula walking toward him, a drink in each hand. This stretch of beach, cordoned off by the hotel, was downright peaceful in late evening, but farther north, closer to town, die-hard crowds of young people would just be getting wound up for a long night. It was mid-April, and Port Aransas activity had slowed considerably from the frenzy of spring break in March and, while not the most glamorous of sea-side destinations, it was a convenient spot for a few days away from the city.

Paula handed him both drinks and pulled her chair closer before spreading a towel over it and taking a seat. She reached for her drink and tipped the plastic cup toward his. "Here's to a perfect day away from that mess in San Antonio. *Salud.*"

He touched the rim of her cup with his and tasted his drink before replying. "*Salud.* It's beginning to get better, though. I convinced Marta to hire Costello's accounting firm to set up separate books on each of the business enterprises. She's following all the activity—"

"May I join y'all?" Carlton's approach had been stealthy on the soft sand.

Both turned look at him and Reynaldo gestured to a vacant beach chair to their right. "Sure, pull that chair over here. You just get here?"

Carlton complied, arranging the chair on the other side of Paula's, canted so he could more or less face both of them. "About a half hour ago. I've spent some time putting all my stuff away, just like I live in that room. I'm going to be here a few days, and I didn't want to live out of a suitcase."

"I hope you put everything away nicely and left room for Heather's stuff," Paula said in a tone that indicated she didn't care whether he had or hadn't. But when Carlton looked at her, she flashed a smile that said she was joking. As usual, neither man present could tell.

"She won't be here until tomorrow. And she can just throw my stuff to one side," he countered, returning a smile that said he didn't care, so long as she came and stayed in the same room.

Paula's smile disappeared and Reynaldo moved to change the subject. "You get moved into your new apartment? In Castle Hills, right?"

"Yes, got it all set up. Nice, but I kind of miss my little place at Marta's By the way, how is she?"

"She's handling everything better than I thought she would, especially after I disbanded the trafficking business."

Carlton looked at him in surprise. "You disbanded it? Just dropped it like a hot rock, huh?"

"I had a meeting with all of Tino's crew—what was left of it, anyway, some individually, and a few in small groups. Hell, it took me almost a week. I made sure everyone was okay for short-term cash, fronted some rent and car payment money and set them up with jobs in Marta's businesses. Everyone was happy, especially Marta."

"I take it she wasn't disappointed to see that facet of the empire go away."

"Nope. And neither was I. Actually, I'm doing the same with my operation. My crew can either take jobs in my construction business or collect unemployment. I don't care which."

Surprised again, Carlton raised his eyebrows. "So we're all done with that industry, all of us." It wasn't posed as a question, just a tone of confirmation, as though making sure he'd heard right.

"Yes, it's over." He let the finality sink in for a few seconds before turning his head to look directly at Carlton. "What about you? What are you going to do?"

"Not sure. But it will be quiet, slow, and completely legal. And something where I deal only with the things I want to, when I want to."

Reynaldo laughed. "Nothing like the drug trafficking business, then."

"Exactly."

"A good choice, Carlton. I'm going to take the same path. I make enough money in the construction business to live quite well. Plus, I'll have time to go to either of my ranches and haul cows back and forth and let the USDA supplement me for bad years of hay crops."

Carlton laughed at the well-known irony that enabled amateur ranchers to get tax money for unsuccessful operations, just like the big professional farming conglomerates on which the nation depended for food. Both men fell silent for a moment, thinking about the drastic change each had just described.

When Reynaldo spoke again, he succeeded in surprising his friend once more. "You know, Tino and I weren't really cut out for that business, not from the beginning. We both had other things going, things that made money, legal enterprises where we could skim enough to live comfortably without paying Uncle Sam every spare dime in the cash register.

"But as things got more profitable, it occurred to us to invest in another industry, something different, and the smuggling gig had available openings and huge market potential. Since the drug trade has a lot of profit in the form of cash—which had to be washed through our existing businesses—they flourished, too. So it was a self-generating cycle of trade."

"But y'all weren't really cut out for the drug smuggling business?" Carlton asked, going back to Reynaldo's opening sentence and wondering what explanation he was going to hear. He had assumed all along that the pair of childhood friends were proficient and well-positioned in the mid-level tier of drug distribution—not giant cartels, but very successful in their regional markets.

"No. In spite of the money we made, we lacked the essential elements that we saw a few weeks ago—the insatiable greed, the lying, double-crossing personalities, and the capacity for violence—all beyond anything we could match. It took over forty lives, including Tino's, and the destruction of an entire town for me to see that."

"So it wasn't worth it, even with all the money you two made through the years." Carlton persisted, again making a statement out of a question to which he knew the answer.

"Not even close. I'd give every dime for Tino to be sitting here with us..." his voice faltered and trailed off.

Hearing the emotion in his voice and seeing Paula lay her hand on his prompted Carlton to look away, out at the rolling surf, to avoid embarrassing his friend. A minute passed before Reynaldo resumed speaking, and he was over the lapse in control, his voice again strong and business-like. "I have your money for the Millstone job, all in bills from different sources and denominations. When are you going to pick it up?"

Carlton shook his head firmly. "I didn't earn it, Reynaldo. I didn't fulfill the contract, remember?"

"No, you did better than the contract agreement called for, much better. Taking out Felan and the other two enforcers has law enforcement looking at Carlos Benavides for the job, since they figure he caught on to their little side agreement with Millstone. Just another lesson in loyalty administered by the *Golfos*, and that means there's no blowback on us for the job. So take the money, Carlton."

Carlton started to shake his head again, then recalled something. He stopped and looked at Reynaldo. "Remember when we got out of that trailer after working in the dark for an hour? When we all agreed to donate to something for the vision-impaired of this world?"

Reynaldo laughed at the memory, one of his last of Tino, when he had made the bold proclamation under dire circumstances. It had broken the tension of the moment, even if temporarily. "Sure! That was typical Tino Perez, wasn't it? Making a promise to do something, then goading us to pitch in."

Carlton smiled at accurate reminder of their friend's favorite tactic. "Yes, and I remember his exact words to get us interested: 'If I get out of here alive, I'm going to donate some money for eyesight research and help for blind people.'"

The quote took Reynaldo by surprise, but he nodded emphatically. "That's right, I remember. That's exactly how he put it."

The two men looked at each other, the same thought lying unsaid between them: Tino *didn't* get out of it alive. But they did.

Carlton started to speak, but the emotion of the moment made him stop and clear his throat. He took a breath and started over. "Then do it, Reynaldo. Do it in a way that gets Tino's name associated with something worthwhile, whether it's here or in Mexico. Maybe even in *Santa Monica*. He'd like that. And so would I."

Reynaldo, too, was overcome briefly, but he blinked rapidly a few times and managed a smile. "That makes three of us, then."

Printed in the United States
By Bookmasters